NEW MITZVAH STORIES
for the Whole Family

ALSO AVAILABLE FROM RECLAIMING JUDAISM PRESS

Mitzvah Stories: Seeds for Inspiration and Learning

Seeking and Soaring: Jewish Approaches
to Spiritual Guidance and Development

Reclaiming Bar/Bat Mitzvah as a Spiritual Rite of Passage

Illuminated Letters: Invisible Threads of Connection

Mitzvah Cards: One Mitzvah Leads to Another

AVAILABLE THROUGH
www.ReclaimingJudaism.org
and all major booksellers

New Mitzvah Stories for the Whole Family

EDITED BY GOLDIE MILGRAM AND ELLEN FRANKEL

WITH ARTHUR KURZWEIL, BATYA PODOS, PENINNAH SCHRAM,
MINDY SHAPIRO, DANNY SIEGEL, AND SHOSHANA SILBERMAN

Anne Andrew
Noa Baum
Janet Berenson
Randi Ya'el Chaikind
Mitchell Chefitz
Rachel Coles
Gerald Fierst
Rinah Rachel Galper
Yehudit Goldfarb
Dan Gordon
Leslie Gorin
Daniel T. Grossman
Jill Hammer
Nancy Handwerger
Alide Huyser-Frijda
Barbara Solomon Josselsohn
Jennifer Voigt Kaplan
Melissa Klein
Geri Kolesar
Arthur Kurzweil
Alex Lazarus-Klein
Janet Madden
Cindy Rivka Marshall

Goldie Milgram
Lynnie Mirvis
Seth F. Oppenheimer
Marden David Paru
Gail Pasternack
Geela Rayzel Raphael
Jack Riemer
Barbara Rush
Cassandra Sagan
Peninnah Schram
Rebecca Schram-Zafrany
Sandor Schuman
Cherie Karo Schwartz
Howard Schwartz
Danny Siegel
Donna Jacobs Sife
Shoshana Silberman
Anna Sher Simon
Devorah Spilman
Susan Stone
Marc Young
Jennifer Rudick Zunikoff

Reclaiming Judaism Press

New Mitzvah Stories for the Whole Family

Copyright © 2015 Reclaiming Judaism Press and Reclaiming Judaism

All rights reserved. Other than by contributing authors, no part of this book may be reproduced or reprinted in any form or by any means electronic or mechanical, including photocopying, recording, or by any information storage and retrieval system without written permission from the publisher to be obtained by e-mail from rebgoldie@gmail.com. Reclaiming Judaism Press books and resources may also be purchased in bulk at a discount for educational, business, or sales promotional use

Reclaiming Judaism Press: http://www.reclaimingjudaism.org

Publisher's Cataloging-in-Publication data

> New mitzvah stories for the whole family / edited by Goldie Milgram and Ellen Frankel.
> p. cm.
> ISBN-13: 978-1508989950
> ISBN-10: 1508989958
> "With Arthur Kurzweil , Batya Podos , Peninnah Schram , Mindy Shapiro , Danny Siegel , and Shoshana Silberman."
> Includes bibliographical references and index.

1. Short stories, Jewish. 2. Judaism—Fiction. 3. Jews—Fiction. 4. Jewish way of life—Fiction. 5. Families—Fiction. 6. Conduct of life—Fiction. I. Milgram, Goldie, 1955-. 2. Frankel, Ellen. I. Title.

PN6120.95 .J6 M58 2014
808.83/1088924

10 9 8 7 6 5 4 3 2 1

Cover image: Copyright 2014 Susan Leopold
Cover & Interior design: Taylor Rozek

Manufactured in the United States of America

Published by Reclaiming Judaism Press
17 Rodman Oval, New Rochelle, NY 10805
Tel: 914-500-5696 http://www.ReclaimingJudaism.org

"...The wise: cling to them,
and drink thirstily of their words."
Pirkei Avot 1:4

This volume is dedicated in honor of
Danny Siegel

Please Note

1. "Whoever reports a saying in the name of its originator (*b'shem omro*) brings deliverance to the world."—Talmud, *Megillah* 15a

    Accordingly kindly follow the practice of citing this volume and a story's author as your source, when retelling or reshaping any of these tales.

2. Several letters in Hebrew, Yiddish, and Aramaic have a guttural sound, akin to clearing your throat: khhhhhh. In this volume these are primarily transliterated with the letters ch.

Table of Contents

Foreword   11
    by Arthur Kurzweil

An Interview with Danny Siegel   13
    by Goldie Milgram

Introduction   19

  1. The Radiance of the Lights   21
      by Anne Andrew

  2. My Grandmother's Gefilte Fish   29
      by Noa Baum

  3. The Lesson of a Lost Phone   37
      by Janet Berenson

  4. Seraphina's Heart   45
      by Randi Ya'el Chaikind

  5. When the Torahs Stopped Singing   53
      by Mitchell Chefitz

  6. The Prisoner   61
      by Rachel Coles

  7. The Baal Shem Tov and the Werewolf   69
      by Gerald Fierst

  8. A Little Torah Scroll   75
      by Rinah Rachel Galper

  9. Yosef Loved to Walk in the Woods   83
      by Yehudit Goldfarb

10. The Choice   89
      by Dan Gordon and Donna Jacobs Sife

11. The King Comes to Rottingham   95
      by Leslie Gorin

12. What Is, Is: A Midrash   101
      by Daniel T. Grossman

13. The Phoenix on Noah's Ark   105
    by Jill Hammer

14. Teeg, The Tiger   111
    by Nancy Handwerger

15. The Surprise of the Butterfly Aurelia   117
    by Alide Huyser-Frijda

16. The Stranger at the Passover Table   125
    by Barbara Solomon Josselsohn

17. Dimes for David   133
    by Jennifer Voigt Kaplan

18. The Secret Ingredient   137
    by Alex Lazarus-Klein

19. Treasure from Grandpa   143
    by Melissa Klein

20. Where's Derek Ericks?   153
    by Geri Kolesar

21. Adira's Pocketbook   157
    by Janet Madden

22. Painting   161
    by Cindy Marshall

23. The Mime's Rosh Hashanah   167
    by Goldie Milgram

24. Finding Peace   177
    by Lynnie Mirvis

25. Two Candles for Maria   183
    by Seth F. Oppenheimer

26. A Minor "Profit" in the Land of Israel   195
    by Marden David Paru

27. Asmodai in Portland   199
    by Gail Pasternack

28. The Magic Soup   207
    by Geela Rayzel Raphael

29. The Story of the Magic Apple   217
    by Jack Riemer

30. The Reward for a Good Deed　221
　　by Barbara Rush

31. Each Bird Must Carry Her Own Light　227
　　by Cassandra Sagan

32. Bringing Joy to Others　237
　　by Peninnah Schram

33. Tzedakah in the Market　249
　　by Rebecca Schram-Zafrany

34. Three Wishes　255
　　by Sandor Schuman

35. Here's to Healing!　259
　　by Cherie Karo Schwartz

36. Saving Lives BIG TIME　265
　　by Danny Siegel

37. The Wall　271
　　by Shoshana Silberman

38. Bending The Laws of Physics　277
　　by Anna Sher Simon

39. Lost In God's Hand　287
　　by Devorah Spilman

40. Heavenly Soup　293
　　by Susan Stone

41. The Wine of Paradise　297
　　by Marc Young

42. Binah and the Broken Pieces　307
　　by Jennifer Rudick Zunikoff

43. Finishing The Tale　313
　　by Howard Schwartz

Mitzvah List　317

Acknowledgments　321

Recommended Reading　323

Index　327

Foreword
by Arthur Kurzweil

New Mitzvah Stories for the Whole Family is dedicated in honor of Danny Siegel because Danny is a role model to all who care about mitzvah-centered living. To this day Danny keeps up the pace of the never-ending mitzvah-centered world tour he began fifty years ago.

Danny's sage influence extends into many aspects of contemporary Jewish life. Many synagogues throughout the world use prayer books in which Danny's poems appear as prayers, sometimes with attribution, too often without. As a poet Danny echoes the timeless yearnings of the Prophets. His poems have literally become a part of the liturgy for many of us.

The curriculum in our synagogue schools includes more wisdom from the Sages than it did a generation ago, the "gutsy Torah" from the Talmud as Danny calls it. This is in large part due to Danny's passionate crusade, going from educator's conferences to youth movement conventions, from rabbinical conferences to countless congregations, insisting on a rediscovery of our sacred sources. In fact, it was Danny who introduced me to Talmud, forever changing the course of my life.

The very way in which the institution of the Bar and Bat Mitzvah is celebrated has changed—in large measure due to Danny Siegel's singlehanded efforts. And yet, most young people today, including most of their teachers, don't even remember the way it was before Danny Siegel arrived on the scene.

A generation ago, synagogues primarily required *b'nei mitzvah* students to memorize prayers and to participate in rote ritual. Today, the majority of synagogues in the United States require, as part of their core curriculum, the active participation of each young person in acts of social responsibility and *tzedakah* (deeds of giving and caring) that connect them directly with what it means to come of age in a Jewish community. It was Danny Siegel who put these issues on the contemporary Jewish map and campaigned for them for decades with extraordinary dedication, enthusiasm, and intelligence. Today, their absence is unthinkable.

Danny Siegel is not a rabbi; he is a rabbi's rabbi—an advisor and guide to many clergy, youth, educational, and philanthropic leaders. Danny is a steadfast trailblazer leading us ever deeper into performing and caring about *mitzvot*. He is the one person I know since the legendary days of the '60's who *never* sold out. He makes his own schedule and is his own boss. He has published his own books and curricula, and established his own charitable foundation. He sets his own priorities, and never lets go of his highest visions.

Danny Siegel is a living example of a person so influential and nourishing that his presence on earth has brought about a merging, a kind of holy unification. His words and ideas have become a true part of us. We are all a part of Danny's legacy.

An Interview with Danny Siegel
by Goldie Milgram

Interviewing Danny Siegel is first and foremost a plunge into an overflowing river of ways to help and heal our world—tikkun olam.

When I had the Ziv Tzedakah Fund we distributed more that $13,000,000 to worthy individuals and projects. When I can repair something simply, with a few dollars or a check, I do so immediately, quietly, and privately. Primarily though, my teaching to students, parents, and educators is to encourage you to talk about the good works you do. Share what you are doing, be an inspiring example in order to encourage wider and ever more effective involvement. My personal approach is to do the advance legwork quietly, to begin by figuring out a simple approach to a given need or problem. I go on to test it out, and if it works out well, reveal it as an example, and if the need is great enough, I open the project up for wider support.

And then there are the 15,000 USY Israel Pilgrimage participants who went on mitzvah missions with you all over Israel. Danny, I understand you still lead these to this very day.

This is my 38th year as the *tzedakah* resource person for USY Israel Pilgrimage. Along the way I began to encourage *b'nei mitzvah* projects, and to create Israel experiences to reveal examples in action. Initiatives I discovered among our participants and on the ground are as diverse as taking blind people bowling, collecting food for the pets of homeless people living in shelters, teaching ice skating to a child who couldn't walk. I recall that one participant was the assistant coach for a cheerleading team of autistic and intellectually limited girls. I have also been able to introduce youth to someone who takes in infants with Down syndrome and raises them, to the founder of therapeutic horseback riding in Israel, and then there are those setting up social services in Sderot in Israel where playgrounds have to be 15 seconds from a shelter.....*Danny starts telling me their names.*

Whoa Danny! This is supposed to be about you.

Well, I didn't invent the idea of Bar and Bat Mitzvah mitzvah projects. I first heard about it from Rabbi Bernard King in California, may his memory be for a blessing. From there I had the idea to focus on identifying what I call "Mitzvah Heroes." The idea being that if have your Masters in Physics you would want to go study with J. Robert Oppenheimer, or get your PhD with Rabbi David Weiss Halivni in Talmud, or study Tanach with Moshe Greenberg, of blessed memory...so for mitzvahs we also need to go study with those who are doing them. For example, Av Shalom Beni, Israel's pre-eminent animal-assisted therapist; Moshe Cot, at Lev Ramot, of Jerusalem used to have a printing business and gave it up to create an organization that feeds tons of families who live with food insecurity in Ramot Jerusalem...there's Sid Mandelbaum who started Rock and Wrap It Up—the largest rescuer of edible food all over America; John Beltzer's program, Songs of Love, where he has written more than 20,000 individual songs for youth with life-threatening diseases; and Ruth Messinger's American Jewish World Service that sends volunteer service teams worldwide.

Danny's mitzvah heroes just keep coming until he hands me a book with some of his memories of driving the Atid-United Synagogue Bookmobile on 136 stops around the United States. I remember when he used to come to our town; we would run out to the orange and green vehicle filled with books carrying the light of Torah. But it was most of all Danny's very presence that would enlighten and empower each of us, creating a generation of teachers, activists, and seekers of the very Source and sources of the spirituality emanating from this remarkable man.

Perhaps you have encountered Soulstoned, *Danny's early book of poetry that breathed spirituality into the trauma-deadened prayer services of the post-Holocaust Judaism experienced by so many of us. Danny's poetry taught us to roll up our shirtsleeves, sit down at the table and talk about our lives with God. The very idea of being given permission to do so blew so many minds.*

Or, maybe you were in Israel with Danny on his famous Shabbos walks and hikes up mountains.

Every year I walk from Emek R'faim all the way to Hadassah Ein Karem. In 1948 my mother was the first Jew from Arlington, Virginia, to go to Israel. It was for the opening of the Hadassah hospital there. I think my inspiration for this walk also came from Emil Fackenheim, who is said to have done this into his seventies. I take people for early *Shabbos* walks in Jerusalem at 5:45 a.m. It's a magical time, and then we go to shul (synagogue).

Danny was deeply influenced by his family. He tells me:

My mother was a kind of *tzaddeket* of what was called the Arlington-Fairfax Jewish Center. She was one of these people of generosity and integrity who had great wisdom. My brother, who was two years older than me, and I learned kindness because of our sister, who had cerebral palsy. My grandpa came to America in 1908, and my dad was born about nine months later. My paternal grandfather was from a little bit north of Warsaw, and my grandmother came from a *shtetl* about ten miles further. On my mom's side, her mother came from near Minsk, and her father was born in America in 1892. They had dry goods stores. Ours was a straight Conservative home. We often hosted bunches of USYers on *Shabbat*.

My mother knew that I learned differently and discovered a new experimental high school where I went in Washington, DC. It was for dropouts and creative kids. My father was a physician, a general practitioner. I used to go on house calls with him. In 1946 he was able to buy a house with an acre and a quarter of land. I recall my mom's rose bushes and fruit trees and a big brick fireplace for cookouts. My mother had three great heroes: Henrietta Szold, Golda Meir, and Eleanor Roosevelt.

Danny, who were your heroes growing up?

Mickey Mantle, the Lone Ranger—and Mom. I was thirty when I started doing the *tzedakah* work. Then my heroes were Myriam Mendlow, founder of Lifeline to the Old, Irena Gaster, one of the real pioneers working with learning disabled people in Israel, and Hadassah Levi who worked with those with Down syndrome. There was also Yaakov Maimon, who before there were *ulpanim* for learning Hebrew would say: "You go into that house and teach them Hebrew," and Phyllis Heimowitz and her daughter Tamar who founded an organization to provide emotional support for girlfriends and fiancées of fallen soldiers serving in the Israel Defense Forces.

Danny, who has impacted your Jewish identity?

In Arlington, Virginia, my rabbi Noah Golinkin. I studied my first page of Talmud with him; and certain teachers—Mrs. Rachel Reinitz, and Mr. Harold Schlaffer, our Hebrew High School director, a grad student. He made it wonderful and he found us such good teachers.

And later? I see you have a B.S. in Comparative Literature from Columbia University and a Masters in Hebrew Literature from the Jewish Theological Seminary and that you received the Covenant Award for Exceptional Jewish Educators.

I studied at JTS for seven and a half years, starting as an undergraduate. For me the late Yochanan Muffs was a very profound teacher. He was all over the place, all over and outside the blackboard with constantly brilliant insights. Several years ago I was walking out of a restaurant in Jerusalem and he walks in with his wife and full-time attendant. I walked right back in and sat down with him. He was very responsive, and I told him I wish I would have known back then that he was the kind of teacher that I wanted to be. And I became teary-eyed, because my ADD was only diagnosed ten years ago and prevented me for many years from thinking sequentially and logically. When I was finally liberated into living more free-associatively, and given respect for how I was meant to think and be, my life came together in new and amazing ways.

I heard you teach at CAJE.* It was such a beautiful session. You suggested that God wrote Torah down in stone for Moses because, as we know, Moses was slow of speech. Perhaps this kindness showed that Moses might have also had learning issues. So, I'm wondering how was your ADD discovered?

I read Samantha Abeel's book *Reach for the Moon*; she wrote it as a teenager. She has what is known as dyscalculia. I reached out to her and in half an hour she taught me more about how my brain works, my learning problems, and my poetry than any one had ever done before. We used to bring her to CAJE and she would help teachers to understand either themselves or one of their students right then and there. No matter how many people say, "Danny, you're doing great *tzedakah*"...or

---

* *Coalition for the Advancement of Jewish Education, now called NewCAJE*

"Danny, I really love your poetry," that didn't necessarily help me understand and like myself. That comes from a deeper understanding that has been such a blessing these past ten years.

Danny, long ago you began publishing your own books. They are in almost every Jewish library and so many of our homes. Danny, where are you going? ...Wow, that's a vast stack of books that you are placing into my bag. Yes, I see, all are written by you and some with the help of your dear friend of blessed memory, Allan Gould. Is there one that particularly stands out for you now?

That's so hard to say, because they are in such different areas. *Soulstoned* for poetry because it got me started, *Where Heaven and Earth Touch* because it has the largest collection of sacred text that I have put together, *Healing: Readings and Meditations* because I think it is most useful. *Who, Me? Yes, You!* because it would be the most successful in getting people engaged in *tikkun olam*.

Any closing words?

Absolutely. Life is mitzvahs—it is what we are here for.

Introduction

In this second volume of the Mitzvah Stories series at Reclaiming Judaism Press, we continue to pursue our goal of forging an inclusive genre of Jewish stories, respectful of the divine nature within the full spectrum of Judaism, gender, life, and peoples. This is a juried volume of original and adapted Jewish tales as well as contemporary true stories. *New Mitzvah Stories for the Whole Family* is part of the Reclaiming Judaism Mitzvah-Centered Life Initiative—programs and books that take to heart the mitzvah of *k'vod ha-briyot*—honoring all that lives for how it has been created. We hope you will be able to find yourself reflected, challenged, and uplifted in these pages.

Mitzvah-centered, rather than self-centered, living is the goal of a meaningful Jewish life. A mitzvah is a category of behavior to engage in, or refrain from, in order to increase goodness in the world. In the third century, Rav Simlai declared that there are 613 mitzvahs (*mitzvot*), and in the thirteenth century, Rambam (Maimonides), affirmed this tally. In the nineteenth century, the Chofetz Chayim (Rabbi Yisroel Meir Kagan), pointed out that since sacrificing animals as a form of prayer is no longer practiced, there are really only 271 mitzvot that apply in our times. 194 of the mitzvot are good things "to do", i.e. *mitzvot assei*. 77 are good things "*not* to do", *mitzvot lo ta'aseh*. To date, at least 114 *mitzvot* are part of the *Mitzvah Stories* series! These are listed on pages 317-319.

This volume's study guide is based on the emerging principles and methods of Jewish spiritual education. Questions, additional sacred stories, texts, and projects are provided. The parent organization of Reclaiming Judaism Press, P'nai Yachadut-Reclaiming Judaism, also offers distance learning in Jewish experiential and spiritual education, including Maggid-Educator ordination. For further information and to submit your own mitzvah stories for future volumes please visit: www.ReclaimingJudaism.org.

    Rabbi Goldie Milgram
    Editor-in-Chief
    Reclaiming Judaism Press

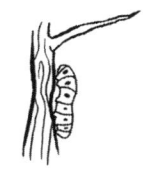

Chapter 1
The Radiance of the Lights
by Anne Andrew

The puzzled Ruler stared at the twelve flame-shaped glass bulbs arranged in a row on a mahogany shelf in her book-lined study. Although their golden glow had once filled the whole room with radiant light, now only one shone brightly. The others were so dim they barely cast a shadow.

The Ruler couldn't understand it. The lights had been in her family ever since her grandfather, a wise and much loved teacher, had received them from an elderly rabbi under mysterious circumstances. Each light, she had been told, represented one school district. As long as the students in that district were inspired, the light for that district would burn brightly. But if the children failed to learn what was important to learn, or if the teachers were not wise enough, the light would dim.

How was it possible, thought the Ruler, that eleven of the lights were now dimming? After all, the Ruler valued education so highly that she spent more money to hire the best mathematicians, scientists, philosophers, and poets to teach in her schools than she spent on all the rest of her departments combined. Why then were eleven of the districts failing to educate their students? And what was the secret of the one successful district? She had to find out what had gone right there and wrong everywhere else.

The Ruler sighed as she devised her plan. She'd have to consult her Chief of Staff, of course, and for that she would have to brace herself. That man was so prim and proper that he would undoubtedly dress up in an expensive suit and tie, polished shoes, and a starched white shirt. And he would stiffly bow when he entered the room and stand at attention, and, of course, expect the Ruler to behave in the same way, dressed in her best suit, even on a hot day. How the Ruler disliked such formality! How she wished that she could just relax, wear comfortable clothes, eat fries with her fingers, and joke around with a good friend from time to time. Instead, her position as Ruler kept her remote and rather lonely. But what choice did she have? She needed her Chief of Staff, so, after putting on her formal attire, the Ruler sent for him.

The Chief of Staff came at a run to serve his Ruler, asking what he could do for her. The Ruler explained about her grandfather's lights, explaining that she was worried about the declining state of education in much of the country. They must discover why students were not learning what was most important to learn, and discover the secret of the one bright spot in the district furthest from the Ruler's Residence. She told the Chief of Staff about her plan.

"You must travel to one of the districts where the lights have dimmed. Find a student there and ask him how he spends his time. Then go to the furthermost district, where the light shines brightly. Find a student there and ask her how she spends her time."

The Chief of Staff bowed deeply (as expected), thanked the Ruler for giving him such an important mission, and left to carry it out. He traveled north to the first town outside the capital city. There he came across several students kicking a ball around during recess. He called one of them over and asked him his name.

"I'm Jonathan," he replied. "Who are you?"

"I work at the Ruler's Residence. I'm the Chief of Staff. The Ruler would like to know how you spend your time, Jonathan. Please tell me."

"Well," replied Jonathan, "I work very hard at school all day because I want to be a doctor. Then I spend time visiting the Home for the Aged, and in the evening I practice my clarinet."

Thanking Jonathan for sharing his impressive schedule, the Chief of Staff traveled onwards to a town located in the district represented by the brightly burning light. There he found a group of students sitting together in conversation in the schoolyard. He overheard them discussing the Torah verse that their teacher had shared with them that day. They sounded delighted with this new treasure and were eager to share their opinions. One of the girls noticed the Chief of Staff standing nearby and asked if he would like to join them.

"I'm Miriam," she said introducing herself. "Can I help you?"

The Chief of Staff explained that he was from the Ruler's Residence on a mission to find out how the students spent their time. Would she please tell him how she spent her time?

"Well," said Miriam, "I work hard at school all day because I want to be a doctor. I visit the Home for the Aged in the afternoon, and in the evening I practice my clarinet."

The Chief of Staff thanked Miriam for helping him with his task, and set off to make his report to the Ruler.

As soon as the Chief of Staff returned, the Ruler called a meeting to hear about the students. The Chief of Staff was just as puzzled as the Ruler by the similarities in Jonathan's and Miriam's schedules. Their behavior didn't begin to explain the difference in the radiance of the lights. The Ruler scratched her head, rubbed her chin, and eventually called her wisest advisor, her Rabbi.

The Rabbi came as soon as she had finished her afternoon hospital visits. With careful attention, she listened as the Ruler and her Chief of Staff told her about the problem indicated by the lights and of their failed attempt to find out what had gone wrong with the schools in all but one district.

"Ah," said the Rabbi, "you must ask a different question. Go back and find Jonathan and Miriam. Ask them why they spend their time as they do. Then you will have a vital clue to the puzzle of the dimming of the lights."

The Ruler told the Chief of Staff to do as the Rabbi suggested. Bowing low and thanking the Ruler and the Rabbi for giving him such an important mission, he set off again on his journey to find Jonathan and Miriam.

The Chief of Staff found Jonathan shooting hoops with his friends at recess. He called Jonathan over and asked him, "Why do you study hard in school, visit the Home for the Aged, and play clarinet?"

"My father is a famous surgeon," answered Jonathan, "and I feel pressured to follow in his footsteps. If I can get high enough grades to be accepted into medical school, I'll be able to become a plastic surgeon, attract famous clients, and make a lot of money. Then my parents will be proud of me."

Jonathan continued, "I pay a quick trip after school to the Home for the Aged so that I can get the volunteer hours I need in order to graduate. And I play the clarinet because it looks good on my resume. I need a good-looking resume to get into medical school."

Thanking Jonathan for his honest reply, the Chief of Staff continued on his journey to find Miriam. He found her in the school cafeteria, helping younger students sort leftovers from their lunch into compost and recycling bins. She smiled and waved when she noticed the Chief of Staff approaching.

"Miriam," he asked, "why do you spend your time working hard at school, visiting elders in the Home for the Aged, and playing your clarinet?"

"Well," said Miriam, "I try to do well in school because I want to become a plastic surgeon. I have heard about a country where there is an unusual number of babies born with cleft palates. If I have the right skills, I'll be able to operate and help them live normal lives, free from the social isolation they would otherwise face. I visit the Home for the Aged in order to learn from the woman in charge of the volunteers. She is an expert in the art of Gentle Human Touch, something I want to master.

"I've learned to play the clarinet so that I can entertain the elders at the home and the children in the hospital, or maybe one day give a concert to raise funds for the cleft palate operations. It's a *mitzvah* skill that I have always wanted to have."

The Chief of Staff decided to take the initiative and ask Miriam a further question.

"Miriam," he began, "who inspired you to want to help others as much as you do?"

"We have a very special Torah teacher in this district," she explained. "He travels from town to town, teaching verses of Torah that inspire us to fix the world, to give *tzedakah* and perform acts of lovingkindness. He finds people who demonstrate unusual kindness to others, helps them to do their work by giving them money or whatever supplies they need, and brings students to meet them so that we can learn to be kind, too."

"Where can I find this fine teacher?" asked the Chief of Staff excitedly.

"It's lunch time, so there's a very good chance he'll be at the Shwarma Café across the street. His name is Danny."

Miriam pointed towards the café, and the Chief of Staff set off to find this splendid Torah-teaching sage.

When he got to the Shwarma Café, the Chief of Staff sat in the corner where he could observe the group of men enjoying their meal at a table in the middle of the room. He asked the waitress if she knew which one was Danny. She explained that he was the one with the beard, wearing the blue Hawaiian shirt. The Chief of Staff's jaw dropped. This man was not like any sage he had ever seen before. He was eating fries with his fingers from his friend's plate, and laughing raucously at a joke that had just been shared. Disappointed, the Chief of Staff finished his lunch quickly, getting indigestion in his haste to leave the café and return to the Ruler to make his report.

Back at the Residence, the Ruler was waiting anxiously to hear from her Chief of Staff and to gain a clue to the mystery of the lights. As soon as the man returned, she called a meeting. The Chief of Staff, stiffly dressed as usual in his formal fineness, the Ruler uncomfortable in her suit, and the Rabbi wearing her best *kippah*, met in the Ruler's study. The Chief of Staff reported on what he had discovered about why Jonathan and Miriam spent their time the way they did.

The Rabbi nodded and smiled, knowing that her question had indeed revealed an important difference in what was inspiring these two students, a clue that explained the difference in the radiance of the lights. The Ruler scratched her head and rubbed her chin, but before she said anything, the Chief of Staff cleared his throat, puffed out his chest and said, "Your Excellency, I took it upon myself to ask a further question of Miriam. I asked her if someone had inspired her to be so kind. She told me of a remarkable Torah teacher who travels from town to town in that district. He teaches verses that emphasize kindness, giving to others, and fixing the world. He finds remarkable people who do good things, supports them in their work, and has them teach students the best ways to be kind, too."

"Well done!" said the Ruler. "I must meet this sage! Bring him to me at once!"

The Chief of Staff nervously shifted his weight from one foot to the other, looked at the Ruler, then down at his feet.

"He is not a typical sage, Your Excellency," he began. "You see, he might not wear a suit and tie to meet with you. Perhaps he'll even wear a Hawaiian shirt and shorts. And he might eat food from your plate with his fingers. He may even tell a joke on a solemn occasion! I am not sure that he is fit for the Ruler's Residence."

The Ruler threw back her head, gave a laugh that was so deep it seemed to come from her toes, and demanded that no time be wasted in bringing this wonderful man to the Ruler's Residence. The Chief of Staff was hastily dispatched to find the teacher and to bring him to meet the Ruler. And he did.

Danny arrived at the Ruler's Residence, carrying a shoulder bag with Torah texts and samples from *mitzvah* projects protruding from its ruptured seams. He shook the Ruler's hand, and then, with a few questions, quickly established that he knew five of the Ruler's own teachers from elementary school and also shared the Ruler's love of sushi. After requesting that the Ruler consider one particular verse of Torah for later discussion, Danny spotted a sofa, headed straight for it, put his feet up, and promptly fell asleep.

The Ruler knew immediately that Danny held the answer to the radiance of the lights. And so, the very next day, the Ruler appointed Danny as Secretary of Education for the whole country. And the Ruler also knew that she had finally found the friend she had always wanted. When she was with Danny, she could discuss Torah over French fries, dispense with wearing a formal suit to meetings, and always find an appreciative audience for her jokes.

Over time, all the other lights grew brighter. When other rulers and leaders asked the Ruler how this had been achieved, she proudly pointed to the new curriculum that her Secretary of Education had introduced. In addition to mathematics, science, and Torah, the students were now also learning dignity-restoration, dream-weaving, world-fixing, hope-giving, soul-repairing, and numerous *mitzvah* skills. Parents were happy that their children were growing up to be *menschen*, even if they did not all aspire to become doctors.

Within five years all the lights were back to full strength, and the citizens were happier than ever. Even the Chief of Staff relaxed a little and tried wearing a Hawaiian shirt instead of a suit once in awhile. In celebration of the lights regaining their radiance, the Ruler held a banquet. Danny sat in the place of honor at the Ruler's right side. Only the Ruler noticed and smiled as Danny reached over to help himself to fries from the Ruler's plate.

Provenance: The idea for this story came from Danny Siegel's list titled "Hyphenated Terms That Help Define Tikkun-Olam-Type People." Included in this list are: life-saver; dignity-restorer; dream-weaver; soul-repairer; creator-of-radiance and many more.

Anne Andrew is the co-founder of Clear Purpose Consulting. She is an education consultant to the Jewish Federation of Greater Vancouver and long served as the principal of Temple Sholom Religious School. Originally from Leeds, England, she holds a Bachelor of Science from The University of Edinburgh, and Masters in Science and Doctorate of Philosophy, focused on Isotope Geology, from The University of British Columbia. Recipient of the Paula Lenga Jewish Family Services Award, Anne is exploring prevention of bullying, addictions, and suicides through rigorous teaching of specific healthy attitudes in elementary schools. She lives with her husband in Vancouver, Canada. www.clearpurposeconsulting.com

Study Guide: Questions, Sources, and Projects for Reflection, Discussion, and Action

1. How many ways of increasing goodness, i.e., *mitzvot*, can you find in this story? (Note: The Mitzvah List can be found on page 317 of this book.) How many additional *mitzvot* can you also relate to this story?

2. How might your talents better bring joy for living for yourself and others?

3. In what condition are the "lights" where you live and learn?

4. What makes Danny so effective? Do you know anyone like him?

Sacred Story and Text Connections

1. [Rabbi Yochanan ben Zakkai] said to his students: "Go out and see which is a good path for a person to attach to." Rabbi Eliezer said, "*Ayin tovah*—a good eye (being happy and not envious of the good fortune of others)." Rabbi Yehoshua said, "*Chaver tov*—a good friend." Rabbi Yossi said, "*Shachen tov*—a good neighbor." Rabbi Shimon said, "One who foresees the outcome (of one's own actions)." Rabbi Elazar said, "*Lev tov*—a good heart." He said, "I prefer the words of Rabbi Elazar, for included in his words are your words."
—Pirkei Avot—Ethics of the Ancestors, chapter 2, Mishnah 13

2. There are four types of those who sit before the sages: A sponge, a funnel, a strainer, and a sieve. The sponge absorbs everything. The funnel lets in at one end and lets out at the other. The strainer lets out the wine and retains the sediment. The sieve lets out the powdery stuff and retains the good flour.
—Pirkei Avot 5:12—Ethics of the Ancestors, chapter 4, Mishnah 15

    a. How do these texts connect to our mitzvah story?

    b. What type of learner are you?

    c. Create lists of people that you know, each of whom fit the four types of people (some may even fit more than one type). If you were creating a Jewish teaching in honor or memory of someone, which of the people on your list might be a good mentor for content, or for practicing your way of presenting that teaching? (Your teaching could be in the form of a play, a dance, a ballad, a poem, a collage, or...?)

d. What are four other qualities that could also be good pathways for a human life?

Project: Create an event or program at your school or camp to honor inspiring educators. Create your own criteria for a good educator; involve all possible students in the process of reflection. Can you find a way to honor every teacher for something authentic and worthy? What response do you have to this idea? What, do you imagine, are the effects on a person who is being honored?

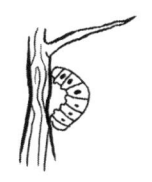

Chapter 2
My Grandmother's Gefilte Fish
by Noa Baum

Some grandmothers are really good at telling stories. Mine wasn't, but she made the BEST gefilte fish in the WORLD!*

I was born and raised in Jerusalem. My maternal grandmother, Mina, my *Savta* (grandmother in Hebrew), came from Poland and settled in Tel Aviv. Although my *Savta* Mina lived in Israel for more than fifty years, she never had the time or means to learn the new language, so her Hebrew was mainly a mixture of Yiddish sprinkled with German and Polish. Perhaps that was the reason she never *told* stories, but let me tell you, my *Savta* made the BEST gefilte fish in the WORLD!

OH! I loved my grandmother's gefilte fish! It melted in your mouth like butter and was so sweet! She made gefilte fish only twice a year: on Rosh Hashanah and Pesach (because it was such a time-consuming, difficult task, long before food processors were invented).

The secret to good gefilte fish, my *Savta* always said, is…the fish.

"The fish has to be fresh."

Not just supermarket-wrapped-in-cellophane-fresh. We're talking FRESH, as in still swimming.

In order to get the best, largest fish, you must go to the market very early, at least three, four or even five days before the holiday. Otherwise you're left with the scrawny ones, and it's more work to clean several small fish than one large one.

***

So, days before the holiday, my *Savta* Mina is up before the sun, and since I'm with her on all school vacations and holidays, I am up with her! We walk the five long blocks of King George Street in Tel Aviv to the market: *Shuk Ha'Carmel*. Down the main market street and then turn to a sloping side street where the asphalt is glistening black, water runs along the gutters on both sides, and the air has that unmistakable stench of…fish. This is Fish Street with stalls and shops on both sides solely devoted to all manner of kosher fish.

My *Savta* goes to Yuda'le.

---

* Gefilte fish are traditional eastern European minced whitefish patties.

"He has the best!" she says, and as she exchanges morning greetings with him, I go to the back of the store where along the entire back wall stands a gigantic, dark water tank. I press my face against the glass until my nose is completely smooshed flat, and I stare. Soon, big, wide-eyed carp appear from the black murky waters, pass by staring at me with that amazed-glazed look, and disappear back into the darkness. A moment later—there they are again! Materializing out of nowhere, appearing and disappearing again and again. It's magic!

My *Savta* points to one and says:

"*Dieze, de groisse*. That big one," in Yiddish.

Yuda'le takes a net and fishes out "that big one." The fish flip-flops hysterically, desperately trying to jump back into the water, and just when it looks like it will hit the ceiling, Yuda'le quickly puts it in a large plastic bag, dumps in fresh water, ties a knot at the top, and hands it to my grandmother.

And that's how we walk back home—me and my *Savta* and the fish dancing like crazy between us in a large plastic bag. When we arrive, she goes straight to the green tiled bathroom, fills the bathtub with water, and dumps that fish in. That's where it will live for three, four, sometimes five days, because you see, the fish has to be FRESH!

I loved that bathroom with that fish! It never ceased to fascinate me. I would spend hours there, my chin on my arms, leaning on the rim of the bathtub, staring at that fish going back and forth, back and forth in its trapped world. I loved staring very hard, without blinking, until the walls of the bathroom dissolved, everything around me becoming blurry green and….there I was on the back of *my* Magic Carp! There I was, the Queen of the Seven Seas diving into bottomless oceans conquering the world with *my* Magic Carp!!

There I was, making up stories for hours on end in my blurry green world…

But every story comes to an end. Mine was always the same: a Yiddish-speaking giant with a flowered apron pulled out the plug…the water was sucked away, the ocean was gone, and my magic fish was whisked away to the kitchen…

This was the part I really hated. From the kitchen comes the loud WHACK, and I know that I will never ever see *my* Magic Carp again. I closed my eyes and vowed:

"I will never, never, NEVER eat gefilte fish again!"

This vow usually lasted about…two hours. Because, my *Savta* made the BEST gefilte fish in the WORLD! It melted in your mouth like butter, and it was so sweet!

Without the Magic Carp swimming in the tub, life in the bathroom is very boring, so I inch my way across the hall and peer into the kitchen. There is my *Savta* cleaning the fish. With a large knife she scrapes off those sticky, stubborn scales, and then she slits open the fish's belly, scooping out with both hands all the bloody, gooey, slippery insides. You would think that she'd just dump that into the garbage, but no! Not my *Savta*!

She stands there carefully examining all that gory mess in her hands.

I say: "*Ichsa*! (Hebrew for yuck!!!) *Savta*, what are you doing??!!"

"Ach, you never know," she says, "could be like that...nu, what's his name, that Yankl."

"Yankl? What Yankl?"

"Nu! The one from the story."

My face lights up. I love stories!

"Story? What story?"

"Eh! Who remembers? It's a *maiyse* (a story)!"

And with that, she dumps the fish's insides into the garbage, wipes her bloody hands on her apron, and with a wistful voice says:

"Ach! But he had *mazel* (luck)!!!"

And that was it! That's how my grandmother told stories...

***

I never learned how to make gefilte fish like my grandmother. But I became a storyteller and found the story about "that Yankl":

Yankl lived in a small *shtetl* (village) in Poland, and he was famous! Why was he famous, you ask? I'll tell you. He was famous because he was so poor that his family was always hungry, and his children walked barefoot in the coldest days of winter. But no matter how difficult the days, every Friday Yankl always bought the biggest fish in the market to celebrate the Sabbath. The merchants in the market thought he was mad.

"Yankl!" they said, "with the money you're spending on one fish, you could feed your family all week long!"

To which Yankl smiled his big, warm smile and said: "Ah! You may be right, my friends, but you tell me: what is the point of living all week long if you cannot receive the Sabbath with joy and generosity like a Queen?"

So that was Yankl! His family hungry all week long, but for the Sabbath, the Queen, there was always a joyous celebration at his home, to which he would invite every poor and hungry beggar to join them for the Sabbath feast.

Not far from that *shtetl* lived the landowner, the *porets*, Lord Filtz. He owned land, barns full of grains, stables full of horses, and a large mansion full of beautiful things. He was a very wealthy man but quick-tempered and closed-fisted. If anyone in need came to his door, if anyone dared ask for some charity, or even a little loan, his answer was always the same: "Ahmmm....NO!" And he'd slam the door.

Oh, there was not a stingier man in the entire country than that *porets*!

One night Lord Filtz had a very disturbing dream: A large hole appeared in his dream, opening up in the middle of the earth, and coins of gold and silver were being sucked into it. In his dream he heard a terrible, hissing voice:

"Someone will inherit you before you die!"

"AAHHH!!!" he woke up screaming and covered with sweat. This was his worst nightmare, to lose his precious possessions!

"Someone inherit *me* before I die!!" he cried. "Someone will put *their* filthy hands on *my* possessions? Not as long as I breathe!"

Determined not to let the dream come true, he set about to protect his possessions. He ordered new fences around his estate, new guards to patrol his property night and day, and new locks on all the cupboards, drawers, and chests in his house. That night he went to bed content, thinking: "Now my possessions are safe. No one can touch them!"

But the minute he closed his eyes, a rather disturbing thought occurred to him:

"What if while I'm lying here snug in my bed, someone is lurking out there in the dark, trying to break into my barns? Conspiring to rob me like in that horrible dream?"

In panic he ran through the house, out the door to the barns.

But all he found there were his guards. Everything was locked. Nothing was touched.

He returned to his bed.

But a minute later, another disturbing thought seeped in:

"What if while I was out running to the barns, someone sneaked in here? Someone could be lurking in the dark inside this very house, trying to put his hands on my crystal cups, my porcelain dishes, my silver and gold! Oh, my precious things!"

Trembling, he jumped out of bed and ran all over the house, lighting the lamps, checking the cupboards, opening drawers, lifting carpets, pulling bricks from the walls (to check his secret hiding places). But all was well. Nothing was touched. He blew out all the lamps, locked and closed everything, and returned to bed.

But not for long. The minute he closed his eyes he thought: "What if while I was checking the house, someone was out there, trying to break into my barns?"

Once again he jumped out of bed and ran to the barns, but on the way he worried:

"My crystal cups, my porcelain dishes, my silver and gold!" So he turned back and ran to the house. But when he got there, he panicked: "What about the barns?"

All night long he ran back and forth, checking on his possessions, and in the morning, he was exhausted! It went on like this for two more nights before he realized he couldn't go on living like this.

"I must find a way to keep things under control," he said to himself. "There must be a way to keep everything in one place where I can keep an eye on it."

And then he had an idea: "I will sell and invest!"

He sold everything—the barns, the horses, the silver and gold, the crystal cups, and porcelain dishes. Then he went to the capital city, and with all the money, bought one enormous diamond, the likes of which had never been seen before. He had a special pouch made for this diamond, and he clutched it in his hands.

"Ah! Now I can keep my fortune with me at all times," he cried, his heart filled with joy.

Now he was a happy man! Everywhere he went—the pouch was with him, safely clutched in his hands. When he ate and drank, the pouch was clutched in his hands. When he slept, the pouch was clutched in his hands. He never un-clutched his hands.

One day, in the beginning of autumn, he was walking (since he had sold his horses and carriage) from one end of town back home and had to cross the old wooden bridge that connected both parts of town over the river. Now, I know you may find this next part hard to believe, but this is the way the story is told: Just when he came to the middle of that bridge, a wind began to blow! But not just a soft autumn breeze. It was a full force gale wind! Dark clouds covered the face of the sun. The water in the river turned gray, and the wind whipped up fierce waves that rose and hit that bridge.

Lord Filtz tried to go back, but couldn't. He tried to go forward, but couldn't!

The old wooden bridge creaked and groaned, rocking violently from side to side. The wind grew stronger and wilder. He had to hold on to the rails with both hands or he would fall into the raging river! "Aahhh!" he screamed, as the pouch flew from his grasp. In horror, he watched it disappear in the stormy waters below.

That afternoon Yankl and his wife Leah were in the market. One of the merchants came running up to him and said:

"Yankl, a friend of mine caught a fish so big no one wants to buy it. You're his last hope. Please come take a look at it!"

Yankl took one look at that fish and said:

"Now that's a fish fit to receive the Sabbath Queen!"

"But Yankl!" whispered his wife at his side, "it's too expensive! And so big! Who will finish such a fish?"

"Leah'le", he said, "there are enough hungry people in the world to help us finish the fish!"

"But Yankl...!" she pleaded.

But Yankl had already paid for the fish and was walking through the market inviting every poor and hungry beggar to join them for the Sabbath feast.

What could she do? He was crazy, but he was still her husband.

So with tears in her eyes, she put on her flowered apron and began the tedious task of cleaning that fish. With a big knife, she scraped off all those sticky, stubborn scales, and then she slit open the fish's belly. With both hands, she scooped out…the biggest diamond she never dreamed could exist! The jewel filled the entire house with dazzling light.

When Yankl saw that, he smiled his big smile and said, "You see, Leah'le! God does not forget those who receive the Sabbath like a Queen with joy and generosity!

Indeed, it was a joyous celebration at Yankl's house that night! All the beggars rejoiced in his good fortune. After the Sabbath, he sold the diamond, and with the money—why Yankl and his family lived in prosperity and happiness for the rest of their days.

May we all be blessed with such good *mazel*!

Provenance: My beloved *Savta* Mina passed away two months before my daughter was born in 1991. Creating this story helped me mourn her loss. I began to light candles soon after that to honor the *Shabbat* and her memory. Telling this story helps me stay connected to her. What I love best about this story is that every time I tell it, someone comes up to tell me *their* story: how there was a carp in their bathtub, how *their* grandmother made the BEST gefilte fish in the world…

The "Yankl" story is my adaptation of a famous story from the Talmud about Joseph, the Keeper of the Sabbath. My grandmother never told stories, but referred to them as "the one with the *mazel*" and the characters were always named Schlemiel or Yankl. So I kept Yankl.

Noa Baum, born and raised in Jerusalem, lives in the Washington, D.C. area. Noa was an actress with the Jerusalem Khan Theater, and received an MA in Educational Theater from NYU. She is a winner of a Parents' Choice Recommended Award, a 2014 Storytelling World Award and numerous Individual Artist Awards from The Maryland State Arts Council and The National Storytelling Network. She has presented at the World Bank, the Mayo Clinic, The Kennedy Center, United States Department of Defense, and universities and communities worldwide.

Study Guide: Questions, Sources, and Projects for Reflection, Discussion, and Action

1. Which *mitzvot* are illustrated by this story? Which additional *mitzvot* can you also relate to this story?

2. Is there a storyteller in your family or community?

3. What brings happiness to Yankl?

4. What are obstacles to happiness for Lord Filtz?

5. What feelings come up for you when recalling holidays or *Shabbat* with your family? What special foods bring to mind the flavor of memorable Jewish experiences?

6. What feelings and attitudes toward a person come up when you realize someone is a miser, or perhaps sometimes is cruel to others? What was your reaction to the miser's losing his diamond?

7. What do you take from this chapter for your own life?

Sacred Story and Text Connections

1. "*Lo tisna et achicha bi-l'vavecha*—Do not despise your fellow human in your heart"—Leviticus, *Vayikra* 19:17

2. There were once some thieves in the neighborhood of Rabbi Meir who caused him a great deal of trouble. Rabbi Meir prayed for them to die. His wife Beruriah said to him: "How do you discern this [that such a prayer should be permitted]?! For [while we know in Psalms, *Tehillim* 104:35 it says], 'Sinners will cease from the earth, and the wicked will be no more' which, [just look at the end of the verse] really means when sins cease sinners will be no more. Rather pray for them that they should transform their ways (*teshuvah*), and [that is how] there will be no more sinners." He did pray for them, and they did change their ways—*Talmud, Berachot* 10a

3. A story of Reb Levi Yitzchak of Berdichev comes to us where he observes a Jew eating on Yom Kippur. He asks the person if he knows it is a holiday when eating is not permitted. The person replies: "Yes, I am aware of this." So Reb Levi looks up to the heavens and calls out: "Master of the Universe! How great are your children; even those who eat on Yom Kippur will not lie."

4. On the one hand there is the phrase: "When your enemy falls, do not rejoice" —Proverbs, *Mishlei* 24:17 and on the other hand Proverbs, *Mishlei* 11:10 relates: "When the wicked perish, there is joy."

    a. Based on the four texts cited above, discuss what path to take in relating to the people in your life who are like Lord Fitz. What are healthy or reasonable approaches? How might you best relate to someone who is not generous and who has a major loss like Lord Fitz?

    b. What connection does fasting have to this story? For those with comfortable lives, what is lost by not accepting the experience of hunger on a fast day?

    c. Using the vignette that features the person who does not fast on Yom Kippur, is the rebbe being sarcastic or does he believe in the Jewish principle of finding something to love or respect in everyone?

    d. Try strengthening your ways in one of the *mitzvot* in this vignette. Keep notes on how each mitzvah integrated into your life impacts upon your relationships. Discuss what you do, feel, learn, and aspire to after you experience things with those at home, with a teacher, with a mentor, or in class.

Project: If you can, obtain a fish (or another food) far larger than what is needed to feed just your family, and find a way to share the extra with those in need. How does it feel to help others in this way? What might hold a person back from generosity when they do have some resources?

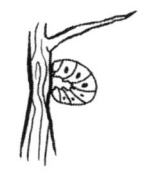

Chapter 3
The Lesson of a Lost Phone
by Janet Berenson

"Can I borrow your phone, please? Mine's been stolen—again!—and my parents are going to kill me! I'm such an idiot! I left my bag on the wall at lunchtime and when I came back, the phone was gone. Now I have to tell them, and I know exactly what they'll say: 'How can you be so irresponsible—losing your phone for the second time? Didn't you learn anything the last time?' I'm going to be grounded for a month, I just know it, and I'll never get another phone."

Rachel's distressed face made Deborah smile sympathetically at her friend. She knew exactly what Rachel was feeling—it had happened to her just three months earlier, and she remembered the sick feeling in her stomach as she had prepared to tell her parents what had occurred. Deborah had been given her phone as a bat mitzvah present—of course, it had to be an iPhone with a pearlescent pink case! And of course, she had waved it around deliberately everywhere she went, just to make sure all her friends—and even the nerds she didn't like—would see it. So when, just three weeks later, it had disappeared from her bag during lunch, she had been overwhelmed by anger, fear, and distress. It had taken all her courage to admit to her parents what had happened.

As Deborah passed Rachel her new cellphone, another iPhone as it happened, her smile broadened.

"You'll have to text them. I don't have any minutes left, and my Dad said if I go over, he'll make me pay the excess from my allowance. Anyway, it'll be easier if you don't have to talk to them. It'll give you time to think up a good story."

Rachel accepted the phone gratefully, but her eyes widened as she heard her friend's suggestion that she lie to her Mom about how it had happened. She had already been thinking frantically about how she was going to explain her own carelessness. The last time it had happened really wasn't her fault, but her parents were so furious that they wouldn't listen to her explanation. Rachel had lent her cell to Alex, whose battery was dead, so he could call to tell his Mom that he'd be late getting home. They were standing by the bus stop, and a gang of guys from another school had cycled past, grabbed the phone out of Alex's hand, and ridden off. They'd shouted and chased after them, but the thieves had quickly disappeared around the corner and were gone.

Alex was so sweet, he'd even offered to go with her to the police station to report the theft. The police took all the details but offered no sympathy or hope of recovering the phone.

"It's an epidemic, young lady. You're lucky you and your friend weren't hurt. Just be more careful in the future and don't tempt people by showing off your smartphone."

Rachel came out of her reverie and turned back to Deborah.

"No," she nodded emphatically. "I can't lie to them. My parents have always trusted me, and anyway if I lie, they'll find out eventually and be so disappointed in me. But it's not just that. My Mom worked extra shifts at the hospital to earn the money for that phone. It's been really hard since Dad lost his job, and I just couldn't do that to them."

Deborah's cheeks reddened, as she suddenly felt ashamed of what she had suggested.

"I'm sorry, Rachel. You're right. It's so easy to take things for granted. My parents have been really strict with me since they split up, and I guess I've just gotten used to trying to find ways to avoid confrontations with them. I can't stand it when they're angry at me, 'cause it feels like they're taking their resentment of each other out on me. Sometimes I feel like a ping pong ball being batted back and forth across the table."

A tear squeezed out of her eye and rolled down her nose. She tried to ignore it, but Rachel reached into her bag and pulled out a Kleenex, which she passed to her friend.

"Here, wipe your nose. It's okay. It must be really hard trying to please both your parents when they're in different places. I thought my life was tough, with Dad out of work, but I guess yours is just as hard. You know, it makes me wonder if everyone might have some really difficult challenge going on that nobody else knows about?"

The two girls were silent for a moment. Then Deborah nodded with understanding.

"I think you may be right. My Mom told me yesterday that Sam's brother was diagnosed with leukemia and might die. I don't know what I'd do if that happened in our family! It's beyond awful. Mom said she's going to Mrs. Becker at school to see if she'll support setting up a bone marrow testing drive for parents. We're too young to be allowed to do it, though I think I'd be too scared."

"But if we could save someone's life just by giving some of our own bone marrow, that would be awesome! Remember when Rabbi Green taught us about *pikuach nefesh*—that saving a life is the highest Jewish value, and if you save one life it's like saving the whole world?"

"Yes, I do remember, Raych. It was the day that Ruth told us about her grandmother, who had survived the *Shoah* by being taken on the Kindertransport train. She was just two years younger than us when she had to leave her family behind in Czechoslovakia and get on a train to Holland and then to England. Rabbi Green showed us the film about Sir Nicholas Winton, who organized the Kindertransport and saved almost 700 Czech Jewish children from certain death. It was so sad, when Ruth told us that her grandmother never saw her parents or her grandparents again."

"You know, Debs, if we could save someone's life, then maybe our parents wouldn't get so worked up over stuff like losing our cellphones."

"Right! Rachel, there's Alex. Let's ask him and Ruth to come over to my house and see if we can come up with something we can do together. Maybe we can get the whole class to join in with us."

Deborah reached out and held her friend's arm.

"Listen, Rachel. I'll come back with you to your house so we can tell your Mom together about the phone and our project. Maybe she won't be so upset when she hears what losing your phone has led to."

Much to Rachel's surprise, her parents didn't shout or punish her for losing her phone. After listening calmly to her explanation, they simply asked her what she intended to do about it. Rachel suggested forgoing her weekly allowance until she had covered the cost of replacing the phone. Her parents agreed that she would only have to pay the insurance deductible fee, but that she'd also have to manage without a phone until that payment was made. Then Rachel explained how she hoped to turn the incident into something worthwhile and asked if she could go to Deborah's on Sunday. After a brief glance at each other, her parents nodded.

***

That Sunday afternoon, Rachel, Ruth, and Alex gathered at Deborah's home. Alex carried a pizza, juggling it to keep from burning his hands. Ruth had a bag of corn chips and some salsa, and Rachel had baked some brownies. Deborah opened the door with great excitement.

"Come on in. Mom has made lemonade and a plate of veggies for us and given us the dining room, so we can spread out and work on the project."

Three hours later the empty pizza box and chips bag were stuffed into the small waste basket in the corner of the room, and the four young people were sprawled in their chairs with satisfied grins, like four Cheshire Cats escaped from *Alice in Wonderland*.

From the start, Alex had spontaneously taken on the role of organizer.

"It's so simple that it may actually work. Debs, can you type up the notes and email them to us all so we can present it to Mrs. Becker at school tomorrow? If she agrees, we'll set up a Facebook page and get everyone involved."

After much discussing and rejecting dozens of ideas, the group settled on a simple project, which they decided anyone could participate in. They knew it would only succeed if it was something that both teens and adults could do with little effort, however, it also had to be something that people believed would make a difference, or they wouldn't continue supporting the project. They chose the Hunger Site, a worldwide internet-based campaign to raise food to feed hungry people suffering in the poorest parts of the world.

Everyone would be invited to join the campaign to feed the world by signing up for the school's project. Each day, they would simply have to go to www.thehungersite.com and click once on the yellow tab. Sponsors would provide an agreed amount of food for each click, and the organization ensured that the food would be distributed to those who needed it. Then, every Friday participants would log onto the school's project page and record how many times they had visited the Hunger Site. Alex would lead the team whose task would be to calculate how much food was being provided each week through the school's participation.

"Let's see what your mother thinks of our idea, Debs," Alex proposed. "She can be our research subject."

Deborah's mother walked into the room with a phone in her hand, a serious expression on her face.

"Rachel, it's your Dad. He has something important to tell you."

Rachel took the phone and whispered anxiously into it.

"Dad? What's wrong?"

"Nothing's wrong, Sweetpea. I've got some good news for you. We've just had a call from the police station to tell us that someone handed in your cellphone. Can you believe it? A woman found it when she was walking her dog and sat down to rest. It was wedged between a bench and the wall by your school. It turns out that it wasn't stolen after all. It probably fell out of your bag and got stuck behind the bench."

That day, the four friends grew closer than ever. Deborah turned to her phone, selected a song and put it on loudspeaker, and they all listened to the words of *Save a Life* by Debbie Friedman, of blessed memory:

> ....In the garden, voices singing.
>
> Wipe your eyes now, no more fears.
>
> Take my hand, we'll build the world together.
>
> Save a life and you will save the world....

Janet Berenson is a writer, poet, and professional Jewish educator living in Hatfield and teaching independently in the UK, after many years working for the British Reform movement and the Leo Baeck College. She is the author of *Kabbalah Decoder* and anticipates a 2014 release for her new volume of poems *Riding the Rainbow*. Janet holds a BA and MA from the University of Pennsylvania, and a teaching certificate in Jewish education from Gratz College. Janet teaches Jewish ethics to teens and Kabbalah and Jewish meditation to adults, and offers workshops and training in the UK, Europe, and the United States.

Study Guide: Questions, Sources, and Projects for Reflection, Discussion, and Action

1. Which *mitzvot* are illustrated by this story? Which additional *mitzvot* can you also relate to this story?

2. What are the mitzvah-centered actions and tensions in this story?

3. The loss of the phone became an opportunity, resulting in potential benefit to many hungry people. Can you think of other examples of how a loss can turn into a mitzvah opportunity?

4. Look closely at the dialogue. How do the parents make it safe to be truthful with them? Can this be true for your family?

5. How do cellphones affect your quality of life? From the point of view of the condition of your spirit, what changes in cellphone use might benefit your life, friends, and family?

Sacred Story and Text Connections

1. Rabbi Zalman Schachter-Shalomi told of how there was a *Shabbos* Box in his childhood home. Those arriving home after school or work on Friday would take off their watches, and then remove wallets and coins from their pockets and put them into the box until after *Shabbat*.

Project: Make a *Shabbos* Box to hold cellphones, watches and money from wallets and purses, and try this approach to opening up space for more time and togetherness. If it feels like too much all at once, try starting with just one item.

   a. What are the losses and gains of this practice to you and your family?

   b. How might this practice connect to the mitzvah of honoring your parents, or help create a closer relationship?

   c. How might this practice help affect your relationship to the demands of school and/or work?

2. The *Tamchui* (donations and food for the local soup kitchen) is [collected] each day, and the [funds for the poor] every Sabbath evening.—Maimonides, *Mishna Torah, Hilchot Mattanot l'Evyonim, 9:3*

Project: Do you and your family regularly send support for the poor and hungry? Why? Why not? How often? Convene a family discussion on how to take this mitzvah seriously in a new and better way in your home and at school. Take responsibility for making sure the plan is implemented and that this practice doesn't subside as a mitzvah in your life.

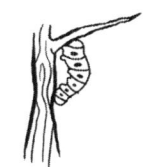

Chapter 4
Seraphina's Heart
by Randi Ya'el Chaikind

"Sera! C'mon now, get it in gear, or you'll miss your bus again!" Seraphina's mother yelled through the bathroom door, while applying mascara and drinking her morning coffee. "I will not drive you! I can't. I have a meeting with the firm's architect. Now get a move on it, young lady!"

"Fine, I'm going!"

Seraphina looped the scratchy wool scarf around her neck. As she buttoned her winter coat, her mother snuck up from behind and kissed her cheek with a dramatic "mmmwaa" sound.

"Mom, did you leave lipstick on me? Ew!"

Seraphina pulled away, rubbing her face. Her mother sighed and put her hands on her hips.

"Don't forget to stop at Mrs. Simon's house after school. Wait there until I get home, 'kay?"

Seraphina hoisted her purple backpack around her shoulders, and rolled her eyes. "Yes, yes, yes, Mom," she said while staring up at the ceiling, "I've been going there for two years. I think I've got the drill by now."

She stopped at the front door and looked back at her mother. "Umm, so, have a good day. 'kay?" She quickly ran and hugged her mother, as best she could, all bundled up in thick clothing. Her mother kissed the top of her head, and Seraphina stepped onto the snowy front porch. Another ordinary January day.

Crunching through the snow in her boots, Seraphina walked to the end of their road and waited for the bus. The sun's heat beamed through a crack in the overcast sky. She stood in the ray of sunshine and pretended it was summertime. Turning her face up to the sky, she closed her eyes and suddenly, there she was, sitting on the beach on a hot, sunny day. It worked! The daydream warmed Seraphina up and distracted her until she heard the bus driver grind gears, slowing down.

Quickly, Seraphina lost all her happy thoughts as the bus doors creaked open before her. She swallowed hard, and then climbed aboard the bus. Seraphina heard her heartbeat drumming in her ears as she looked down the aisle, praying that her best friend was sitting near the front of the bus. There! Shun-Li smiled brightly and waved from her seat just a few rows behind the grumpy bus driver, old Mrs. Francie. Seraphina slid into the seat and slouched, hoping she was really as invisible as she felt.

"Mooooose! Hey, fat girl!"

Seraphina knew Cindy's voice, familiar as a sister's. An evil sister, like in Cinderella. She felt something hit the back of her head, and pretended nothing happened. Shun-Li held her hand, and Seraphina willed herself not to cry. She wouldn't let them win. Not ever.

Suddenly Seraphina felt a sharp pain in her neck. She cried out in distress, and pulled her shoulders up to her ears. Turning around she saw Cindy had traded seats with the boy behind them. A smile curled her mouth, but her eyes were cold. Cindy raised her eyebrows in mock surprise and gasped, "Wha-what? Are you okay... moosey? Fat got your tongue?"

Several other girls giggled and pointed at Seraphina. She rubbed her neck, and faced forward again, feeling nervous, feeling her face turn red. How far would Cindy go with this torture? Her chest heaved in fear, and she lost the battle to hold back her tears. Shun-Li stood up. Seraphina tried to stop her, telling her to shush.

Shun-Li shouted at Cindy, "Cut it out, you stupid girls!"

Her thick black hair flared in the air as she spun around to sit down again.

"Cut it out! Stop it!"

Cindy mimicked Shun-Li in a high-pitched voice, entertaining her minions once again. Seraphina worried that Cindy would turn her abuse on her best friend, but was silent.

The bus finally arrived at school. Seraphina waited for Cindy to get off first. She didn't want to expose herself by walking in front of Cindy. Like a feral animal, Cindy waited for her prey, but she held back. A group of teachers waited at the curb, greeting the students when they all got off the bus. Seraphina felt safe, for now.

For months Cindy haunted Seraphina, sometimes even getting off at Seraphina's bus stop with some of the other girls, several stops after their own homes. "Mooooose girl, giant moose girl, fatter than a caboose girl!"

Though it was a short walk to Mrs. Simon's, Seraphina bolted from the bus to her neighbor's house. She pulled open the door with a swift yank, and slammed it shut, her breath ragged. Every taunt that Cindy hurled at Seraphina left a mark, like a flaming arrow hitting a bull's-eye.

Seraphina kind-of-on-purpose missed the bus many more times that school year. She preferred to risk the wrath of her mother rather than endure the shame of being called fat.

Shun-Li got mad at her one day. When they were washing their hands in the bathroom, she asked, "Why don't you fight back, Sera? Why do you let her get away with hurting you?"

"I can't, I mean, just because she's being a jerk doesn't mean I have to." Seraphina looked at Shun-Li in the mirror, and then hung her head. "Besides, well, she's right. I'm fat. I'm ugly. I'm a loser. My dad doesn't even call me anymore."

Seraphina started to cry. Shun-Li didn't know what to do. So she just put her arm around her friend and said nothing.

A few weeks later, Seraphina went home with Shun-Li after school. Seraphina knew that Shun-Li was adopted. She had told Seraphina that her parents had flown to China only a few weeks after she was born and had brought Shun-Li back home with them. But what Seraphina hadn't known was that Shun-Li's parents were Jewish, and so was Shun-Li! Seraphina was Jewish, too, but she didn't really know anything about it. Though she had a Jewish grandma from Poland, who made the best chicken soup in the world, Seraphina had celebrated Christmas and eaten chocolate Easter bunnies her whole life. It had always felt funny to celebrate these holidays, knowing she was Jewish, but she didn't have an idea what that even meant.

When Shun-Li's Mom dropped Seraphina off at her house later that afternoon, she invited Seraphina and her mother over for *Shabbat* dinner.

A few days later, the two drove over to Shun-Li's house. Seraphina was impressed by the beautiful table, set with fancy china and gleaming silverware. Shun-Li's mother lit candles, then the whole family sang a prayer to give thanks for the delicious challah bread. Seraphina even sipped some red wine for the first time.

After dinner, it was story time. Shun-Li and Seraphina curled up on the couch while Shun-Li's father told a story about what he said was one of the most important Jewish laws: *la-shon ha-rah*. When a person says mean things to another person, he explained, that's *la-shon ha-rah*.

"Some people call it 'gossip.' But it literally means, 'the evil tongue,' because of the harm it can do."

Shun-Li's father now bent down, lifted up a small, flat board lying by his feet, and handed it to his wife. She held it firmly on top of a pile of newspapers lying on the coffee table. Then he handed a hammer and nails to Seraphina's mother.

"Take the hammer and pound one of these nails into the wood," he instructed her. When she had driven in the nail with a few hard whacks, he said, "Good. Now do a few more, please." She pounded three more nails into the soft wood.

When she was done, Shun-Li's father turned to face everyone. He wasn't smiling when he said, "This is what happens every time you say something mean to another person, or they say something mean to you. Oy! It's like we hammer nails into each other's hearts."

Shun-Li's father took a deep breath, and continued, "Now Seraphina, you're a great girl." Seraphina looked up at him, and cocked her head to the side.

He cleared his throat dramatically. "Pardon me. I meant to say, 'young lady'!"

Seraphina and Shun-Li giggled. Shun-Li's father looked at Seraphina's mother and winked.

"Of course! You are being raised by a *mensch* of a mom! But," he considered Seraphina with a raised eyebrow, "has there ever been a time when you've said something, without even knowing it, that's hurt someone else's feelings?"

Shun-Li pushed Seraphina off the couch playfully. Seraphina grimaced when she hit the floor and shot her best friend a withering look. "Ow! I mean, sure, I guess. Why?"

"Well, what's one of the most common things we say if we've said something that may have caused an 'Ouch!'"

"Um, dunno." Seraphina sat back on the couch and crossed her arms over her chest. "Um, sorry?"

Shun-Li's father pulled a nail out of the wood. "This is what happens when you say you're sorry. You pull the nail out."

They all gathered around the coffee table now, intrigued. "Say it again, anyone," Shun-Li's father asked.

"I'm sorry!" yelled Shun-Li. He pulled another nail out of the wood.

"Saying you're sorry helps, but what is left after you pull the nail out of the wood?"

Seraphina looked closely. "A hole. There's still a hole, even though you say you're sorry."

"Right, so even though we can be sorry for the words we say, once we speak them, we must be careful not to leave holes in each other's hearts. 'Sorry' only goes so far."

Seraphina's mother spoke up. "So, we're human. We say things we regret sometimes. How do you fill the hole after you apologize to someone?" Her voice sounded tight and far away to Seraphina.

Shun-Li's parents nodded their heads and shrugged their shoulders. "May we live so long as to find the answer!" Seraphina's father said optimistically.

"May we practice thinking before speaking!" said Shun-Li's mother.

Before long, summer vacation started, and Seraphina spent her days happily at the lake with Shun-Li. One day, she noticed a moving van down the street from her house. Seraphina walked over to meet her new neighbors. With horror, she saw Cindy carrying a box from the truck.

Seraphina quickly ducked behind a tree, and then peeked around it to watch Cindy and her family. Just the very sight of Cindy raised the hairs on the back of Seraphina's neck, and her fists pumped open and shut. She looked left and right, waiting for the right moment to catch Cindy off guard when her parents were inside the house. Seraphina's heart raced as she plotted a payback plan for all those times Cindy had teased her, bullied her, and shamed her.

Thoughts raged inside her head. She imagined walking over to Cindy and calmly saying, "This is for all the times you called me Moose!" and then punching Cindy hard in the stomach. She pictured running at Cindy like a warrior, screaming at the top of her lungs, "Oouuuucccchhhh!" before pulling Cindy by the hair and flinging her into the dirt. Seraphina wanted to watch Cindy sob and shake with fear before her. She wanted Cindy to understand what it felt like to break into a million pieces and disappear when the wind blew.

Yet Seraphina was afraid. She had never felt so much anger and bitterness before, and it scared her. She slid down to the grass and sat with her back against the tree. "One," she breathed in. "Two," she breathed out, just like Mrs. Simon had taught her the day she had run home from the bus. She counted to ten, then to fifteen, to make sure her anger had subsided.

Seraphina turned to watch Cindy and bit her lip as her anger flared all over again. It was no use! She was a walking wound, like that piece of wood, with lots of nails sticking out of her, and Cindy had done the hammering. Seraphina felt hopeless. Tears of frustration filled her eyes. To make matters worse, if she moved from behind the tree, Cindy would surely see her crying. *My life is a huge nightmare*, thought Seraphina.

As she leaned against the tree, a shaft of sunlight broke through the leaves, beaming soft summertime warmth directly on her face. Seraphina remembered the cold winter days, and how she could warm herself with just one shaft of sunlight. She sat enjoying the familiar strength of the sun's glow, wondering what to do, when suddenly she felt the snap of inspiration inside her. She stood up and stepped out from behind the tree. Her knees were shaking as she walked with purpose towards Cindy.

"Hey, Cindy."

Seraphina dug her fingernail into her palm to stay focused and resist the urge to run.

Cindy was rummaging through a box and held up a Barbie doll. "Oh, hey, Seraphina! Do you live around here, too?"

Seraphina was astonished. How could Cindy not remember taunting her down the entire length of this very street? Seraphina pushed herself to speak. She was so anxious that her words came out in a flood. "Cin, Cindy, you, you were just horrible to me this whole year, and, ah, well…" Seraphina's voice steadied, and she said with conviction, "You nailed holes in my heart!"

A few steps away, Cindy's mother put down her box and walked up behind her daughter.

"What's going on here, Cindy? Are you going to introduce me to your new friend?"

Cindy looked at her toes for a long time, but Seraphina's eyes never left Cindy's face. Cindy finally looked up at Seraphina and said quietly, "Mom, this is Seraphina.

Seraphina…" She hesitated, then looked down at her feet again and swallowed hard. "Seraphina…I…uh, I'm…sorry."

Seraphina froze, filled with mixed feelings and confusion. How do you fill the holes left behind after someone apologizes? Immediately, Seraphina knew the answer. She lifted her face to the sky, and imagined the warm, yellow sunshine flooding her body, filling the holes in her heart.

After what felt like an eternity, Seraphina opened her eyes and saw Cindy and her mother staring at her. She smiled brightly at them, straightened her shoulders, and said, "Welcome to the neighborhood!"

Then Seraphina skipped home, bursting with good news. She couldn't wait to call Shun-Li.

Randi Ya'el Chaikind is a professional coach, author, and facilitator, and is active in Jewish leadership in Santa Fe, New Mexico. Passionate about the healing powers of personal narrative, particularly through rites of passage, she is publishing a book of Omer poetry and finishing her memoir, *Jewish Shaman Storyteller*. After a long career in healthcare communications, among her many publications are *Scientific American Presents: Great Extinctions of the Past; Scientific American Presents: Weather, And How It Works*; and *Worm World*. Randi Ya'el holds a Master of Public Health in Environmental and Occupational Health from the University of Medicine and Dentistry of NJ-Rutgers University. www.JewishShamanStoryteller.com

Study Guide: Questions, Sources, and Projects for Reflection, Discussion, and Action

1. Which *mitzvot* are illustrated by this story? Which additional *mitzvot* can you also relate to this story?

2. With which character(s) do you identify?

3. How does a person refrain from holding a grudge?

4. How does a person refrain from taking revenge?

5. What are the holes (wounds) referred to in this story?

6. What wounds do you have that need healing?

7. What steps are taken in the story that help healing begin?

Sacred Story and Text Connections

1. There was once a person named Tal who spoke badly about everyone in town, creating false tales and generating rumors. The people of the town became very upset. The rabbi met with Tal, saying: "I've heard you've been spreading untruths and gossiping. I'd like you to take this pillow I'm giving you and go up to the roof, cut off one corner of the pillow and give it a good shake so that all of the feathers fly out of the pillow. Then return and tell me what happened." Confused but obedient, Tal did so, thinking: "I can barely wait to tell people the crazy thing the rabbi asked me to do!" Upon reporting back to the rabbi, Tal was told, "Good. Now go and gather the feathers back into the pillow." "What!! Rabbi, I can't do that. They flew in all directions and would be impossible to retrieve." The rabbi replied, "Yes, and that's how it is with words; once you have spoken them, you can't gather them back."
   —Eastern European Jewish folktale in the oral tradition. A Hasidic version has been attributed to the Chofetz Chayim.

2. One who shames another in public; it is as if that person shed blood.—*Babylonian Talmud, Baba Mezia 58b*

3. *Lo tikom v'lo titor et b'nai amecha*—You shall not take revenge or bear a grudge against your fellow human.—Leviticus, *Vayikra* 19:18

4. The Ramban writes that as the verse above continues with, "*Hochei'ach tochi'ach et amitecha*—Surely you are to rebuke your neighbor," the meaning is that if we feel someone has wronged us, we should make sure to tell that person how we feel.

5. When I was young I admired clever people; now that I am older I admire kind people.—Rabbi Abraham Joshua Heschel

   a. How do these quotes relate to our story? Do you agree with them?

   b. What are ineffective and effective ways to tell someone they are wronging us, or others?

Project: Is there someone in your past or current life with a hurt caused by you that you have left unhealed? Reach out with an apology. Don't say why you acted as you did, just indicate that what you did was wrong and that you are sorry, and hope never to repeat such wounding of another person. Even if you don't get a call or email back, you will have planted the holy seed of healing. How do you feel after doing this? Or even upon thinking about doing it?

Project: As a family or class, find a prominent person in the news who has made a deeply hurtful or untrue statement regarding an ethnic or immigrant group. Compose messages reproving this individual, fine-tune them together, and then either email them or deliver them in person, if feasible.

Chapter 5
When the Torahs Stopped Singing
by Mitchell Chefitz

You would think a morning *minyan* (quorum) of fifty or sixty would meet in the chapel. The chapel was sized well for fifty or sixty, but the *minyan* chose to meet in the sanctuary. Much too large, the sanctuary. Six hundred might fit there, under the dome, beneath the chandeliers. But the *minyan* chose the sanctuary, close in by the steps leading up to the *bimah* and the *aron kodesh* (ark), sparkling in the morning light.

The acoustics were better in the sanctuary, they said. The atmosphere was better. They sang better. The chapel muffled their sound.

This was a *minyan* gifted with singers. As good as his church choir, Ernie thought.

Ernie was a simple man, simple from birth. He cared for the sanctuary. In turn, the congregation cared for him.

When the *minyan* sang, Ernie mopped the tile floor outside the main doors. The tile floor was mopped clean every day, every day, while he listened to the minyan sing. When the singing stopped, when the people scattered, Ernie tended to his other daily chores, replacing books, collecting papers, so the sanctuary would be clean and ready for the minyan the following morning.

Over the years, membership in the congregation declined. The fifty or sixty became forty or fifty. The forty or fifty became thirty or forty. The thirty or forty became fewer and fewer, till there were not many more than ten.

And, then there were nine.

The nine asked the rabbi of that day: if we open the ark, can we count one of the Torah scrolls to make a ten? They could. So, they sang through the service.

Beyond the sanctuary doors, Ernie mopped the tiles.

The nine became eight. Could we count two Torah scrolls? They did. But when the eight became seven…

The trustees downsized the staff, but they cared for Ernie. Ernie remained to care for the sanctuary.

Rabbi Dave became the caretaker for the remnant of the congregation.

Aging, aging, so many years.

***

Rabbi Dave looked up from his learning to see Ernie at the door. "Yes, Ernie, what do you need?"

"Nothing, Rabbi. Nothing. But I thought you should know…"

"Know what, Ernie? What should I know?"

"You should know the Torahs have stopped singing."

"Stopped singing? The Torahs have stopped singing?"

"Yes, Rabbi. They've stopped."

"What do you mean, they've stopped?"

"Well, each morning during *minyan* time, all these years, I mop the tile floor outside the sanctuary doors. I hear the singing. After the *minyan* stopped, the Torah scrolls kept singing. They sing. I mop. I listen. But two days ago, the Torah scrolls did not sing. And, yesterday, they did not sing. I thought, today they would sing, but they didn't. So, I thought you should know."

"Thank you, Ernie. Will you show me where you mop? Will you show me where you listen?"

Ernie led the rabbi the back way up the steps to the foyer before the sanctuary doors. The tile floor glistened.

"I mop here," Ernie said. He nodded toward the closed doors. "Through there, the Torahs sing. But now they've stopped singing."

Rabbi Dave unbolted the doors. He and Ernie walked down the center aisle, under the dome, the chandeliers suspended to either side. Up the six stairs to the *bimah*, then another three to the holy ark. He opened the doors. The lights came on, illuminating two racks of Torah scrolls, four above, four below, and two small ones, each tucked into a corner, left and right.

"Tell me," Rabbi Dave said. "How large was the *minyan* when you first came to work here?"

"Fifty, sixty," Ernie said. "Then thirty, forty. Then ten. And, then…"

Rabbi Dave continued, "I understand. When there were nine, they would count a Torah scroll as one of the *minyan*. Then, there were eight…Then, seven…And finally, there weren't any people left, just the ten scrolls."

Ernie and Rabbi Dave stood together contemplating the Torahs, each bright in its silver breastplate and sparkling crown.

"Help me," Rabbi Dave said.

They took down the scrolls one by one. The rabbi opened and examined each. All were fine, complete, kosher for use, all but the small one tucked into the right corner of the ark. When they removed her, they saw a hole in the corner of the cabinet.

"A critter came through there," Ernie said.

"Let's see what the critter might have done."

Rabbi Dave opened the scroll to inspect the damage. The scroll was no longer kosher, not suitable for use.

"So there are only nine," Ernie said. "Without ten, they cannot sing."

***

Rabbi Dave wrapped the damaged scroll in a *tallit* and carried her to his study.

He considered the decay of the congregation, a *minyan* of fifty to sixty, diminishing to ten. Then, to less than ten.

He imagined what it must have been like to hear the ten Torah scrolls singing, then not singing when one of them was no longer able to join the chorus.

He called the president of the congregation, went out to lunch, began to sketch a plan. Then he called the treasurer. One by one, he coached and coaxed the leadership of the congregation, so when the trustees assembled, he presented more than a plan. He presented an opportunity to reverse the decay within the congregation.

They would restore the damaged scroll.

"It's a singing Torah," the rabbi said.

"A nice story," said the trustees, "but we can't be public with that. Restoring the scroll will be enough. Our members will take care of it."

But the story went private, from one person to another. Word of the *Singing Torah in Need of Repair* spread through the community. A great multitude wanted to participate, donating funds and hands to the task.

For eighteen dollars a person restored a letter, his or her hand guided by the hand of the scribe upon the parchment. Restoring even a single letter counted as fulfillment of the *mitzvah* to write a Torah in one's lifetime. For a hundred and eighty dollars, a verse. For special passages, more. Still more for a weekly portion. A new mantle, a new breastplate, a new crown.

The restoration was chronicled in the press over a period of months. The *Singing Torah* (all knew it as such) was complete and ready for rededication.

***

On the assigned *Shabbat* morning the community gathered and filled the sanctuary, standing room only, though all were standing when the *Singing Torah* was raised, then settled on the table to be read.

At the conclusion of the service the sanctuary pulsed with dancing. The *Singing Torah* passed across raised fingertips under the overarching dome. A resounding chorus thundered. The chandeliers swung in rhythm.

At last the *Singing Torah* rested in the hands of Rabbi Dave.

"She doesn't go back in the ark," he said. "It's not for the Torah scrolls to make a *minyan*. That's our responsibility. As for this joy we have experienced here in the sanctuary, the joy can go home with us. The *Singing Torah* can travel from home to home. Gather your family and friends to celebrate."

That's what they did.

Those who repaired the *Singing Torah* submitted a request for a particular week, came to the synagogue to carry the Torah home. So, home after home knew such a celebration.

***

The Sunday morning after that Saturday of rededication, there were nine Torah scrolls in the ark and twenty to thirty in the *minyan*. It was a singing *minyan*, a gloriously singing *minyan*.

Ernie mopped the tiles outside the entry doors and listened to singing as good as any he heard in his church.

The next month the twenty to thirty became forty to fifty.

The *Singing Torah* moved from home to home. Months passed before she found her way back to the synagogue for a few days, waiting for the next family to come to take her home. She rested in a chair in Rabbi Dave's study.

One late afternoon, Rabbi Dave called for Ernie. Rabbi Dave cradled the *Singing Torah*. Ernie led him the back way up the steps to the foyer before the sanctuary doors. The tile floor glistened.

They walked down the center aisle under the dome. They climbed the steps.

"Just once," Rabbi Dave said. "We'll try this just once."

They opened the ark and tucked the *Singing Torah* into the corner where Ernie had repaired the hole the critter had made.

They stepped back. The Torah scrolls glistened, ten in number.

Rabbi Dave closed the ark.

"Ah, I had my hopes," he said, not so terribly disappointed.

"They can't sing," Ernie said.

"Why not?"

"Because you are here to do the singing."

Without another word, they turned and walked back toward the front doors, under the dome, the chandeliers attentive above.

Ernie closed the doors. He put his ear to the wood and summoned Rabbi Dave to do the same.

"Listen," Ernie said, smiling.

Together, they listened.

Mitchell Chefitz is a widely published author. His books include *The Curse of Blessings*, translated into German, Korean and Mandarin; a best-selling novel, *The Seventh Telling*; and a digital novella, *White Fire*. Mitch served first as rabbi and then scholar-in-residence at Temple Israel of Greater Miami. He was the director of the Havurah of South Florida and a chair of the National Havurah Committee. He studied at M.I.T., Berkeley, and the Hebrew Union College. Mitch served as a line officer in the U.S. Navy, with service aboard destroyers in the waters off Vietnam, and also in the Mediterranean during the Six Day War. www.MitchellChefitz.com

Study Guide: Questions, Sources, and Projects for Reflection, Discussion, and Action

1. Which *mitzvot* are illustrated by this story? Which additional *mitzvot* can you also relate to this story?

2. Can a Torah really sing? What does this mean?

3. Why is the Torah sent from home to home, rather than living in the synagogue?

4. Does a song need words to be a prayer?

5. Ernie says that we are here to do the singing. What does he mean?

6. Ask a rabbi, cantor, *maggid*, or teacher to see an open Torah, with its beautiful calligraphy, and ask for any help recognizing letters, words, and sections. What feelings and questions arise for you?

7. Are there people you know whose voices are not being heard? Can you help them "sing?"

Sacred Story and Text Connections

1. "Now write for yourselves this song [Torah], and teach it to the Israelites, put it in their mouths, so that it will be a witness for Me within the Children of Israel."—Deuteronomy, *Devarim* 31:19

    Are there aspects of Torah and the *mitzvot* that sing within you as you walk in your day?

2. There was a couple that owned a local bakery, and as they were walking home in one direction, many bricklayers were also walking home, coming from the opposite direction. The couple greeted one of the bricklayers, saying, "Good evening," and "How was your day?" "Terrible," replied the laborer. "The bricks are so heavy, and because the deadline draws near, the supervisor just doesn't let up." They greeted the next person similarly, "Good evening. How was your day?" He answered with shining eyes: "I had a wonderful day. We are building the most beautiful temple, and the deadline for completion is drawing near. I do believe we will make it on time!"

a. Using the two views of work in this story, how do you think Ernie viewed his work and relationship to his job?

b. Would sharing this tale with people possibly help them reflect upon their relationship to their own work? How does it affect your view of the work you do, or might do, some day?

3. There was a professor who made the last question on the final exam: "What is the name of the janitor here at school?" A student's hand went up towards the end of the hour of the class exam. "Yes?" "Will we be graded on the last question?" "Absolutely," replied the professor.

   a. Why was this question on the final exam? Was it a fair or unfair question? Was it an important or irrelevant question? Can you think of professions and exams where this question might be particularly well-placed?

   b. The word for "work" in Hebrew is *avodah*, service. Is work different from being of service? Should it be? Have you ever been treated as less than valuable in work or service you've done? Have you ever treated someone else with less than honor because they are "hired help?" What was that like for you? For them? In retrospect, what might you have done to affect your situation?

   c. Of the people whom you come in contact with daily, whose names don't you know? What aspects of Torah sing to you as guidance for better ways of relating to those who serve where you study, live and work?

4. *Avodah l'ma'an hechalutz, hechalutz l'ma'an avodah...zum galli...*
   Work exists for the pioneer, and the pioneer exists for work...*zum galli...*
   Ha-shalom le'ma'an ha-amim, ha-amim l'ma'an ha-shalom
   Peace exists for the sake of all nations; all nations exist for the sake of peace.
   —Traditional folk song relating to the formation of the State of Israel to which later generations added the second verse for peace.

   a. What does it mean to believe in peace? Does this transform the meaning of work of the pioneers? Would you interpret the word *avodah* in this song as work or service? Why does it say *ha-shalom*, the peace, instead of just peace?

b. When you interpret the words of Torah and tradition by turning them into action, this is considered to be a form of holy work or service. This is why one who lives a mitzvah-centered life is said to be an *eved Adonai*, a "servant of God." How could this idea be expressed in contemporary wording? Try crafting a mission statement for being Jewish. Might this *avodah* and *eved Adonai* fit in?

5. A person walked into a salon and was dismayed by the unhealthy appearance of the hairdresser assigned to her. Turning to walk away, the customer paused as the hairdresser called out, "Wait! Be assured I will give you a great haircut." She returned and sat in the salon chair. At the end of the haircut the hairdresser turned the chair so the customer could see the results in the mirror. Rising, the customer exclaimed with a face wreathed in smiles as she strutted to the register in a little dance of happiness: "My, my! You've gone and changed my way of walking!"—Adapted from Barry Bub, *Communications Skills that Heal: Towards a New Professionalism for Medicine*, Radcliffe Medical Press, 2005

   a. Are you aware of your own body language in relationship to others?

   b. How might a small gesture, kind word, or reaction affect someone else's day?

Project: Select a story or Jewish practice from the Torah to write and illustrate, and use it to create a little scroll to present. Discuss with someone who is lonely or has been almost invisible to you. If you know the trope (musical phrases), consider chanting it for, or with, this person. After writing in your scroll, another possibility would be to collectively turn the story or mitzvah into a ballad or other art form.

Project: Involve the members of your school, camp, or study group in creating and carrying out a way of honoring those who are not usually publicly recognized by institutions. *Hakarat hatov*, "recognizing the good," often translated as gratitude, is a mitzvah, too.

Chapter 6
The Prisoner
by Rachel Coles

Monday began for Becca the way it always did, as Mommy patted her bedcovers for the umpteenth time to wake her up for school.

"Becca, Honey, it's time to get up."

"Noooo! I'm sick. Can't I stay home?"

Mommy felt her forehead with the back of her hand.

"No fever. You're fine. Time to get up," Mommy insisted.

"But you didn't use a thermometer! How do you know I don't have a fever?"

"I don't need one. You're cool."

"But—"

"Becca, no games this morning! I have an early meeting. I don't have time for kvetching right now."

"What's kvetching?"

"Becca!"

"Okay, okay." Becca sulked for a second, then slid off the bed.

Her mother twisted her lips, clearly peeved by Becca's sluggish speed.

"I guess you don't want snuggle time..."

"I want snuggle time!" Becca hollered as she stomped down the stairs to the living room and held out her arms.

Mommy sat down on the couch and pulled Becca into her lap. Becca rested her head on Mommy's shoulder. Mommy kissed her head and put her arms around Becca.

"You're almost seven, Becca. You're getting so big! Soon you'll be too big for snuggle time."

"No!" Becca protested, burrowing deeper into Mommy's lap, her arms wrapped around Mommy's neck.

Mommy laughed, and they sat quietly for another few minutes as they did before every school day.

After Becca got dressed in her uniform, Mommy came back to the table carrying two plates of eggs and toast, and then went back for Becca's chocolate milk.

But as they sat and ate, Becca noticed that Mommy was very quiet. Usually, Mommy asked her questions, like what she would be doing today at school. But this morning, she didn't. She was unusually quiet in the car on the way to school, too.

"Are you okay, Mommy?"

"Yes, Sweetie, why?"

"You always talk to the radio when we go to school."

Mommy laughed. It was a comforting sound, and Becca was glad that whatever funny thing she had said had made Mommy happy. "I'm just thinking."

"About what?"

But they were already at the car line for school drop-off. Mommy didn't answer her question, just kissed Becca and sent her off to the school entrance.

***

When she picked Becca up at the end of the day, Mommy had gotten more stern-looking. Now Becca was worried.

"What's wrong, Mommy?"

Mommy shook her head. "Nothing, Sweetie, just thinking."

"You were thinking when you took me to school. You think a lot."

Mommy chuckled, and her face lightened.

"Are you mad at me?"

"No, of course not! Nothing like that. It's not about you."

"Well who is it about?"

"It's complicated."

"How come grown-ups always say 'it's complicated'? That's grown-up talk for being mad and not talking." Becca scowled. "What is your mad-face for then?"

Mommy slowed to a stop behind another car and turned around to face Becca for a second, patted her hand and turned back around. The car started moving again.

"I'm mad at myself."

"Why?"

"I assumed bad things about someone because they were different, and because someone told me bad things about them."

"But didn't you always say that it's okay for people to be different, and that you shouldn't think bad things about someone just because someone else says bad things about them?"

"Yes." Mommy said quietly.

"So why don't you go say sorry?"

"It's not that simple, Honey."

"Why not?"

Mommy didn't say anything for a few minutes as houses and trees flashed by on the way to their house. Then she parked in the driveway and turned around. She took Becca's hand.

"You know what, Honey? You're right. Why not?"

After they entered the house, instead of pulling out ingredients to make dinner, as Mommy always did before Daddy got home from work, she pulled out a piece of paper and a pen. Then she got Becca's colored markers out of the art bin.

"Would you help me write a letter? Would you help me find the right words?"

"Of course, Mommy! Are we writing 'sorry'?"

"Yes."

"To who?"

Mommy frowned and pulled out her laptop. She went to the Internet and pulled up a picture of a man, a scary picture. Becca peered at it. The man wasn't scary like a monster. He was scary the way that *Zeity* Mayer had been scary when he was in the wheelchair after he'd had a "heart tack". His breathing had been raspy, and he had had trouble talking. She hadn't known at the time why he scared her like that. Then she realized that it was because she was afraid he would break if she hugged him too hard. And maybe she had been a little afraid she would get sick, too. But he had smiled at her and reached into his pocket and given her a tiny rock with a ribbed oval pressed into it.

"Do you still want to be a fossil hunter, Rivka?" he'd asked.

She had gasped and grabbed the rock. It was a 'trilobite', and it looked just like the pictures in her favorite book.

"A real live fossil! Thank you, *Zeity*!"

He had laughed despite his wheezing. And he no longer seemed as scary. He was still her same, old *Zeity*.

This man in the picture even looked a little like *Zeity*, but thinner, terribly thin. He had bulging eyes and a tube in his mouth.

"Who is he? Why did you think he was bad? Is he sick?"

Mommy rubbed her hands over her face, and now Becca knew she was really upset, the kind of upset she got when she saw bad things happen on television. The kind of bad things Mommy and Daddy couldn't fix. It seemed to Becca that grown-ups should be able to fix anything. But they talked about those very bad things to each other sometimes, things like war, people shooting other people. Sometimes that scared her too, until she imagined herself like Spiderman fighting bad people, except dressed pretty.

Mommy finally answered, "He's a prisoner. He's in a place called Guantanamo Bay. And he's not eating because he's angry that he's been there so long. His name is Hamzid Salah."

"What did he do? Isn't prison where the police put bad people?"

Mommy shook her head. "Usually, but he might not have done anything."

"Then why is he in prison?"

"Because our government was afraid of him, afraid he did something, or maybe afraid he would do something in the future."

Becca felt a stab of guilt when she thought of how afraid she had been of *Zeity* because of how he looked. "What were they afraid he did? How come they put him in jail for something he didn't do yet?" Becca chewed on her finger.

"They were afraid he was a terrorist, or worked with terrorists, the people who blow up buildings and hurt people."

Becca's eyes got wide. "Did he blow people up?"

"No. I don't think so." Mommy put her finger on the screen. "I've never heard the prisoners tell their stories before. He told a reporter what happened to him. Can you read it?"

Reading was not Becca's favorite subject in school. She frowned at the print, not understanding some of the long words. She struggled over the first few sentences for another minute before looking at Mommy in frustration.

Mommy explained the rest of the article to her. "This man went to a country called Yemen to find work in order to send money home. He didn't know that the man he went to for a job was suspected of terrorism. Then he was arrested and sent here to prison."

Becca gulped in indignation. "So he didn't do anything at all? That's not fair!"

A flash of anger made the back of Becca's throat burn as she remembered last Thursday when McKenzie had threatened to tell the teacher that Becca had copied her math answers—unless Becca let her play with her fossil at recess. Becca hadn't let her because McKenzie never gave stuff back. So McKenzie had gone ahead and lied, telling the teacher that Becca had copied from McKenzie! The teacher had believed McKenzie's lie, so Becca had had to pull a card, and now she had to wear her stupid uniform on Friday when the good kids all got to wear t-shirts and jeans. She had stewed in anger all the way home. She was still mad. Being punished for something she hadn't done, and then having no one believe her had made Becca feel horrible. It was the worst feeling ever.

But this was worse. This man was in permanent time-out because of someone else telling lies about him, or because no one would believe his side of things.

Becca looked up from the screen to see Mommy watching her.

"No, Becca," Mommy said. "It isn't fair. That's why I was mad. And sad."

Becca looked at the man's picture again. This prisoner was someone else's Daddy. One of the things she had been able to read was how old his kids were. He had been in prison so long that his kids were mostly grown-ups now. She thought about how she would feel if anyone took her Daddy away. She couldn't imagine such a terrible thing. Every time Daddy went on a business trip, she would hover by Mommy's cellphone asking when he was going to call and say goodnight. And she was always relieved when he came home. He always laughed at her when she refused to let go of him for the first hour he was back.

And she thought of *Zeity* again. "Didn't *Zeity* come from here from 'Hungry'?"

"*Zeity*'s father did, your great-grandfather, yes, from Hun-ga-ry."

"Didn't you say he came here for work to send back money?"

Mommy nodded. "And then he helped his family escape here during the Second World War."

"Just like him?" Becca pointed at the picture. "He went to send stuff back to his family."

Mommy nodded again, her eyes sparkling. But she coughed and pointed to the sheet of paper and the colored markers. "So what would you tell him if you wanted to make him feel better?"

Becca thought for a minute, and then started writing. Her letter started with: "We believe you."

A few weeks later, Mommy called Becca downstairs from her room where she was drawing on her art board. There was a letter spread out on the table. Mommy beckoned her daughter closer and showed her the letter. It was typed and serious-looking.

"This is from Mr. Salah's lawyer. The man we wrote to a few weeks ago. It says that since Mr. Salah can't send you a letter right now, he wanted to pass a message along. Mr. Salah wanted to say 'thank you' for your letter. It meant a lot to him. He keeps it in his room and looks at it, and it makes him feel better. He said he wished you could meet his youngest daughter, Abal. She's older now, but when she was your age, she was very artistic and wrote like you do."

Becca remembered the letter. She'd taken a lot of care to use a different color for every letter, and drawn curly designs all around the edge. She wondered what his daughter looked like.

"Do you think they'll let him go home soon?"

Mommy took her hand. "I hope so. And I'm sure Abal does, too."

Provenance: I got the idea for this story from the news articles I'd been reading about Guantanamo Bay and the controversy around holding people without due process. It is very concerning to me that a nation which values human rights so strongly, as part of the founding dictates of our society, can so easily overlook the rights of people, citizens or otherwise, because of our fear of their background, nation of origin, or religious beliefs. Some of the prisoners of this prison may be connected with terrorists. But it seems as if many are not. Many of them, as their stories come out, indicate that they were simply unlucky, victims of circumstance that led to them being suspected based on Homeland Security profiling, not on real evidence. I wanted to write this story to bring people back to the fact that there are real humans in the midst of all this, real humans, many of whom are not that different from us. We have gotten so wrapped up in fear in this country in the past few years, that I am afraid that we are sacrificing our own national values of justice, and ultimately our compassion and empathy for other human beings.

Rachel Coles lives in Denver, Colorado, with her husband and daughter. Author of the young adult fiction volume *Pazuzu's Girl*, she received a Master of Arts degree in Medical Anthropology from Arizona State University; her love of mythology often shows up in her fiction. Rachel is from an Ashkenazi Jewish family, with a background in Semitic and Middle Eastern folklore. She works in public health emergency preparedness and response, assisting with the coordination of disaster response and recovery. She and her family make and wear costumes from their favorite shows, comics, and novels, to attend ComiCon, the comic book and fantasy convention. www.RachelColes.wordpress.com

Study Guide: Questions, Sources, and Projects for Reflection, Discussion, and Action

1. Which *mitzvot* are illustrated by this story? Which additional *mitzvot* can you also relate to this story?

2. Do Becca and her mother have a good relationship? What aspects of the story give you answers to this question?

3. When you are emotionally feeling down about something, does it help to be told to "cheer up?" What helps in this story?

4. Share a time when someone didn't believe you and you were telling the truth.

5. Why are immigrants often distrusted and blamed for things that happen?

6. What does it take to see people for who they are, rather than for what they look like?

7. Is it ethical to show kindness to a person who has done evil or worked with those who do evil?

8. Even if the prisoner turns out to be unquestionably guilty, is it a mitzvah to write a compassionate letter to him?

9. What other situations do you know of where people can become painfully isolated?

Sacred Story and Text Connections

1. Reb Aryeh Levin was known as the "*Tzaddik* of Jerusalem" and the "Father of the Prisoners". Many Jewish men and women, who fought in the underground against the British occupiers of Palestine, were captured and imprisoned. Their hope was to establish the State of Israel as a renewed Jewish homeland and haven for those fleeing the war in Europe. Some were sentenced to hang, and asked Reb Aryeh to be with them in their last moments. Until his death in 1969 he made a special point of being with prisoners on *Shabbat*.—Peninnah Schram

2. The Lubavitcher Rebbe encouraged reaching out to Jewish prisoners, for example, making sure they have a joyous Purim and can do the mitzvah of giving gifts to the poor. He emphasized that it is important to tell prisoners that they are, in many ways, not that different from those who walk around freely. [Summarized from *Sichos Kodesh,* 1977, volume 1, page 552]

3. Rabbi Yonatan Eybeschutz taught that you can pray for an evil Jew to recover [from an illness]—*Ye'arot Devash* page 15. Whereas, Rav Aviner cites Rabbi Mordecai Tzion saying that "…it is preferable, however to take the middle path and pray for [such a person] to engage in *teshuvah*."

    a. Is it an anti-mitzvah to show caring to an imprisoned person? What if that person is not Jewish? Or is a convicted criminal? Or an outright enemy? Or an unconvicted criminal, or unproven enemy? How do you take guidance from these texts?

    b. What difference might letters make to those in prison? How about in the case of a Jewish family writing to a Muslim?

Project: Ask your rabbi, or a local rabbi, if there is an imprisoned person (or the prisoner's family) which your class, family, or camp could help in some way.

Project: Is there someone in the circle of your life who is isolated, or has chosen to be? Make contact, listen actively more than you talk. Write about what happens, and discuss your experience with someone you trust.

Chapter 7
The Baal Shem Tov and the Werewolf
by Gerald Fierst

When Eliezer lay dying, he called his young son, Israel, to him.

"My child, the Evil One surrounds the world with darkness, dark clouds that stop our prayers. He is in our flesh and in our dreams. But so long as you remember the sacred name of God, he cannot inhabit you. You are safe."

After Eliezer died, kindly Jews took the young Israel and sent him to school. But the boy could not stay with his head bowed down, sitting and reading. Instead, his eyes would lift up out of the window and over the fields to the line of trees where the forest began. The wind would sing to him—and when the teacher's back was turned, he would run...run...run...out, out, out, into the open air, flying on the breeze, out into the trees, until the teacher would chase him, catch him, and bring him back to his desk.

One day, Israel heard the call of earth and sky, and ran away, but now the teacher said, "Let him go."

And so it was that the boy lived by himself in the wild places, sleeping in mossy hollows, eating berries. He learned the language of the beasts and birds, and became the friend of all living things. Sometimes he would stand in silence and listen to the stillness, and then he could hear the earth singing a sweet song, praising God who made us all.

Now the time came when Israel returned to the world of humankind. He was ten years old. He took the job of collecting the children to take them to school, knocking on their doors and bidding them come.

Then he would lead them through the grass, picking the flowers for garlands that they would weave into their hair. Singing and dancing, they would march through the forest, taking pine boughs as banners, which they waved above their heads, until they came to an open meadow where they would stand quietly in a circle. There, in the silence, they could hear the singing of the earth, praising God who did make all. And their hearts gave forth prayers, which shot like arrows to the heavenly throne.

Hearing these beautiful chords, the Messiah rose up on one elbow and wondered, "Is it time then? Is it time to return to the world?"

And Satan, the Evil One, saw about to happen that which was not yet supposed to be. Then he went before God and said, "Let me strive against these children who would stop my evil designs."

And God said, "Strive."

So Satan went down to the surface of the world. He tried to enlist the insects, beasts, and birds in his terrible design, but none of them would turn against the boy Israel, who loved and was loved so well.

It happened that near the village where the children lived, there was a woodsman who had been cursed with a terrible curse. This creature had been born without a soul. At night, when the moon shone bright, the woodsman would fall upon his hands and knees. Hair would grow all over him. His nose and teeth would grow long, and his ears would come to a point. He would run on all fours and howl like a wolf. At dawn, the creature would fall under a bush, exhausted, and return to the shape of a man.

Here, Satan found him asleep. The Evil One reached into the poor woodsman's chest and plucked out his heart. Then, Satan took his own heart of evil and placed it in the body of the woodsman.

The next day, when Israel led the children into the fields, as they came to the line of trees, the monster appeared. The heart of evil had made him grow to a terrible size. All the children fainted or ran away.

When their parents heard what had happened, they refused to let the children go again with the boy Israel.

But Israel said to them, "It was only a wolf who ran from the trees. The creature is gone. Trust me."

And he spoke with such purity that on the next day the parents again gave him their children.

In the morning, Israel collected the children and led them into the fields.

"Do not fear," he said to them. "Whatever happens, remember the name of God and stand fast."

And so it was, as they reached the edge of the forest, that the monster appeared. Immense, shoulders stretching from horizon to horizon, smoke and fire coming from its mouth and nose, creating dark clouds which blotted out the sun. The children shook with fright, but they did not run.

And Israel marched forth toward the beast, not stopping until he had entered into the very being of the monster, until he reached the heart of evil. Then Israel reached forth and took that black heart, filled with all the envy and cruelty of the world, and placed it in his hand.

When it lay in the boy's palm, the heart quivered like a bird with a broken wing. Poor wounded beast that it was, Israel felt its pain and understood that all the darkness of that heart came from fear and self-loathing.

Israel pitied that heart and took it and laid it upon the earth, which opened wide. And the heart fell deep, deep into the forgiving world. Then Israel led the children to school.

The fate of the boy Israel was to go out into the world where he became a great teacher called the Baal Shem Tov. The children, without him, stopped going into the forest. They became again like their parents, serious with eyes turned down into their work.

Ah, but we have heard the story and know the mystery that waits for all to see when our eyes rise up to field and tree and sky. Let us go then, let us go to where the flowers blow in the wind that rushes past the trees. Let us stand in the midst of the forest where the earth heals all pain. Let our hearts sing songs of joy, and let us stand silently while the world in sweetness praises God who made us all.

Provenance: A traditional Hassidic story of the Baal Shem Tov, also available on the recording by Gerald Fierst, *Tikun Olam: Stories to Heal the World*.

Gerald Fierst is a performer, writer, and teacher. He has appeared throughout the US, in Europe, and in Asia, telling stories and leading workshops in writing and performance, as well as at NewCAJE, Limmud conferences, and the National Havurah Institute. Gerald is a recipient of the JustStories Fellowship for his work in the field of Jewish, Muslim, and Christian identity in 21st Century America. Author of *The Heart of the Wedding*, he has released four recordings, including *Tikun Olam: Stories to Heal the World* for which he is a Parents Choice Silver Honoree, and *Jewish Tales of Magic and Mysticism*. www.GeraldFierst.com

Study Guide: Questions, Sources, and Projects for Reflection, Discussion, and Action

1. Which *mitzvot* are illustrated by this story? Which additional *mitzvot* can you also relate to this story?

2. Young Israel's spirit comes alive in nature. What lifts your spirits?

3. What can you learn about God in nature?

4. What does Israel learn from his contact with the heart of the wounded beast?

5. What are the qualities of a great teacher that are illustrated by this story?

6. What do you think the monster really was?

7. Why wasn't Israel afraid of the monster?

8. Why does God allow the story's evil character to "strive" with the children who had awakened the messiah's attention?

9. What disguises evil in our world today?

10. What do you do when you are afraid?

Sacred Story and Text Connections

1. Israel's father stresses the importance of remembering God's name. In Judaism there are at least 105 names for calling upon, or "knowing" God. Reflect on the names of God that follow, then circle and discuss the names to which you connect. Learn one to help you fulfill the mitzvah of calling out to God. Here are several:

   Ozi—My Strength; *Rachamana*—Compassionate One; *Shechinah*—Indwelling Presence; *Ma'ayan Raz*—Font of Mystery; *Tzuri*—My Rock; *Rofeh Kol Bassar*—Healer of All Flesh; *Matir Asurim*—Freer of Those Who Are Bound; *Ribono shel Olam*—Master of the Universe; *Shalom*—Peace; *Ehyeh Asher Eyheh*—I Am Becoming What I am Becoming (God as the Infinite Potential for Change); *El Ro'i*—God Who Sees Me; *Adonai*—My Lord; *Seter Li*—My Hiding Place; *HaMakom*—The Place; *Ein Sof*—Infinite, Without End; and many more.

2. In Hebrew the root *adon* can also mean Threshold. *Melech* is not only king, but also the "governing principle(s) of creation" (see *Shaarei Orah* by Gikatilla). *Olam* is world or eternity. Consider how this might help with finding a contemporary translation for the traditional opening for Jewish blessings: *Baruch atah* (blessed are you) *Adonai eloheynu* [Our God] *melech ha-olam*.

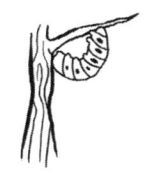

Chapter 8
A Little Torah Scroll
by Rinah Rachel Galper

Chava was in full and final preparation to become a bat mitzvah: a daughter of the commandments and a woman in Jewish tradition. All of her years spent in Sunday school and synagogue, learning Torah, *tefillah* (prayer), Jewish history, and Hebrew had brought her to this moment. Chava knew she was as ready as she could be. Yet she felt strangely unsettled in a way she could not quite explain. Her parents told her it was just nerves. But Chava knew that what she was feeling was more than nervousness; something just wasn't right.

A few days earlier, Rabbi Raachel Jurovics had given a *d'var*, a sermon, on *Parashat Yitro* in which she told the whole congregation about the 613th mitzvah:

"This mitzvah requires us all to write a Torah scroll at least once in our lifetimes. Most of us take this to mean that we must write at least a letter on actual parchment. While this is true, we are really being asked to create Torah each and every day of our lives. So what have you inscribed on your hearts today?" she asked in a playful yet earnest tone.

The room fell silent—except for Chava.

"How can I create Torah when it's already written?" she asked. "Won't God be upset?"

All this time, Chava had thought Torah was just what you had to study each week, along with stories she'd learned since she was a small child. She was ashamed to admit that she wasn't sure she believed in or even liked the God she read about and didn't find the stories all that interesting either. After all, there were very few women in Torah, and Chava didn't think she had much in common with the ones who were mentioned.

"Maybe," Rabbi Raachel gently suggested, "you just haven't found your Torah yet. Perhaps your Torah is waiting inside the letters, white spaces, and stories. After all, people just like you have been making new meaning and stories from Torah for thousands of years. Ask God; I am sure She will help you."

An audible gasp rippled across the room. God could be a *She*? Chava had never heard this before.

By Sunday morning, Chava's brain was ready to burst. She went to school and asked Mrs. Bernstein about making her own Torah. Mrs. Bernstein gave her a puzzled look.

"I guess the Rabbi and I see God and Torah a bit differently," she replied. "But maybe Honi Ha-Ma'agel can help you. After all, he helped our people when they were in trouble many years ago."

After snack, Chava begged Mrs. Bernstein to tell Honi's story. "Honi Ha-Ma'agel," she said, "was a sage known by the ancient Israelites to be a miracle worker. In a time of drought, the people asked him to pray for rain. Honi drew a circle around himself and refused to move until God brought rain to the parched land. Impressed with Honi's *chutzpah*, or courage, God brought the rain. But the people complained that it wasn't enough to quench the thirsty land. Honi then prayed for more rain, and God brought such torrents that the land flooded. The third time, the people asked for a moderate rain—not too little, not too much. Honi prayed again, and God listened, bringing a gentle, persistent rain that continued for weeks. The people grew afraid. They asked Honi to pray for the rain to stop. 'I never pray to God to stop a good thing,' he told the people. Instead, he prayed to God to never give the people too much or too little of a good thing, because clearly they couldn't handle either one."

"So," Mrs. Bernstein concluded, "maybe when you need help from God you must draw a circle around yourself like Honi did and wait for an answer. Just be careful what you ask for."

Chava went home and told her parents about drawing circles and making her own Torah. "Sunday school sure has changed since we were kids," they mused. "We were taught that Torah was Torah. You live by it, and that's that. But maybe it is more open for interpretation these days. Perhaps you should just be patient and let your Torah come to you."

Chava's parents had not given her the answers she needed. Her bat mitzvah was fast approaching, and although she didn't dare tell her parents, Chava had decided that if she couldn't find or make her own Torah, then she shouldn't become a bat mitzvah. Wasting no time, she called the spirit of Honi and drew a circle with sidewalk chalk around her bed. She prayed to God for help in finding her own Torah. Heeding her father's advice, Chava waited patiently. But no answers came, at least none she could recognize. Chava was getting worried.

"Maybe God is too busy," she thought. "Or worse, maybe She's not really here."

Refusing to think the worst, Chava wrote a letter, put it in a stamped envelope with God's four-letter name in the address box, and placed it in the mailbox. Then she watched with anticipation as the postwoman picked it up. Here's what the letter said:

Dear God,

Rabbi Raachel told us in synagogue that we were all little Torah scrolls and that we need to write our own Torah because it is the 613th mitzvah. She said we have to find out what is really important and inscribe it on our hearts so we can live it. She told me You would help, but You haven't answered me and I am running out of time. So I'm drawing a circle of chalk around myself in the backyard, and I'm staying in it until You talk to me like you did with Honi. I have food, water, wet wipes, a toothbrush, candles, a journal, a blanket, and a portable potty. I am prepared to wait.

Please show up soon,

Chava

    It wasn't long before everyone in the congregation found out that Chava was camped out in her backyard like a modern day Honi. Her parents were a bit worried. Mrs. Bernstein felt responsible. Chava's friends laughed and thought she'd lost her marbles. The neighbors peeked out their windows and drove by her house extra slow. Finally, the rabbi came to give her a *bracha* (blessing). Three days passed.
    At 12 midnight on *Shabbat*, Chava heard a Voice. It was clear and unmistakable.
    "So you are looking for your Torah?" the Voice asked. Frozen to the spot, Chava nodded. "Chava," the Voice said, "Your Torah is in your name. Your ancestor, Chava, was *em kol chai*—the mother of all life. Like Chava, Torah is a mother, always giving birth. Just remember, Torah is more about asking your questions and drawing your chalk circles than getting answers. Becoming bat mitzvah doesn't mean you have to have everything figured out. Just be yourself and share your bold and beautiful *neshama* (soul)."
    "Whoa," Chava said, "Thanks for the Torah. Can I keep it?"
    "You helped make it," said the Voice. "It's yours."
    Suddenly, a calm settled over Chava. She left her food and water as a thanksgiving offering, stepped out of her chalk circle with a smile, and went back into the house to practice her *parasha*. She was ready.

Rinah Rachel Galper is an ordained *Kohenet* (Jewish priestess), *Maggid* (Jewish storyteller and spiritual support), and a licensed celebrant performing Jewishly rooted life cycle rituals in Durham, North Carolina where she currently resides. Dedicated to honoring and transmitting women's wisdom, she is the founder of Mamash, an intergenerational women's collaborative. Rinah also works as a special education teacher and an arts educator, offering creative and healing programs to adults and children. www.RinahRising.com

Study Guide: Questions, Sources, and Projects for Reflection, Discussion, and Action

1. Which *mitzvot* are illustrated by this story? Which additional *mitzvot* can you also relate to this story?

2. What does it mean to create Torah each and every day of our lives?

3. While Hebrew is limited to male and female forms, need God have a gender? Could people possibly experience God as without gender or with their own gender? Try this thought experiment: Imagine God as male and express gratitude for something in your life. Now do the same imagining God as female. And now do so with your own gender orientation, if it is neither of those. And, lastly, do so without assigning a gender. Is one of these approaches more effective for you? Judaism gives you the choice, for as we learn in Genesis, *Bereishit*, we are all created, *b'tzelem elohim*, in God's image.

4. Have you ever despaired and called out to God for guidance? Has a message ever come back to you? In what form did it come? A sound? A sight? An incident?

5. Chava wanted a meaningful bat mitzvah. What would you want to change about *b'nei mitzvah* in your region that would add meaning and spirituality for you and your family?

6. Why did the rabbi give Chava a blessing instead of answering her question?

7. There are many Honi stories. What is the moral of this one?

8. Why are questions usually more important than answers?

Sacred Story and Text Connections

1. [Yehuda ben Teima] said: Five years old for Torah. Ten for *Mishnah*. Thirteen for *mitzvot*. Fifteen for Talmud. Eighteen for marriage. Twenty for work. Thirty for power. Forty for discernment. Fifty for advising....—*Ethics of the Ancestors, Pirkei Avot,* 5:24

This text is the evidence for the word "mitzvah" in the ritual of bar and bat mitzvah. The concept of bar or bat mitzvah isn't actually mentioned in the Torah. The first evidence of a ritual is for a parent to say a blessing when it's clear their child is able to self-monitor living a knowledgeable, mitzvah-centered life. The ritual's focus has changed greatly over the years, to the point where the young person comes up to the Torah for an *aliyah* and to teach Torah.

How many *mitzvot* do you know and practice? How does studying a wide range of *mitzvot* help you, too, to become a living "Torah scroll?"

2. PARENTS: Research by John Allan and Pat Dyck found that adolescent rites of passage like bar/bat mitzvah can be very valuable and "Clearly demonstrate the ability and readiness of young people even at this early age (12-13) to absorb 'mature' concepts… such new coping skills (a) awareness and understanding of the process of transition, (b) learning about fear and how to overcome it, c) devising and passing their own tests [Ed. "setting the 'bar'"], and d) communicating their thoughts and feelings to their parents. We hoped…[to] help strengthen the new emerging self-concept."

Learning to chant Torah, to lead services, and to give a Torah teaching (*drash*, or *d'var* Torah) is an approach to *b'nei mitzvah* that began when parents started to turn their children's Jewish education over to rabbis and cantors. The original *b'nei mitzvah* focused on knowing how to be Jewish every minute of the day. Many communities are now involving parents and students in gradually shifting the process to focus more on life skills and values. What would you like to see included?

Note: *Reclaiming Bar/Bat Mitzvah as a Spiritual Rite of Passage* by Rabbi Goldie Milgram (Reclaiming Judaism Press) and *Putting God on the Guest List* by Rabbi Jeffrey Salkin each offer differing, unique approaches to help you find ideas.

3. The Jewish mystics did not hesitate to use feminine God language and imagery for their experience of God as present in every aspect of life and creation:

"She so pervades this lower world…that if you search in deed, thought and speculation, you will find Shechinah, for there is no beginning and no end to her." *Sefer Tashaq,* Rabbi Joseph *(*13th century*)*

What is your gender orientation? That of members of your family? Of friends and neighbors?

Project: The high priest in the temple wore a hammered gold piece on his forehead that read "*Kodesh l'Adonai*—Holy to God." Perhaps it was a mirror, where all present could get to see that message with their images reflected in the shiny gold.

Make such a *Kodesh* sign and paste it onto a mirror at home or in school—so everyone can experience this message as true about themselves in connection with their own reflection.

Project: Hold a Honi's Circle Day. First, have a storytelling day where each person receives a different Honi story and practices telling it well, with the help of a partner of community (*maggid*, storyteller/guide). Have a "tellathon" at an open mike.

Next, ask everyone to think of a question about life for which they really would love an answer. Now go to a beach, or a parking lot, or into nature, and have each person make a circle of sand or chalk or yarn. Write your question in the circle and stand in it firmly for five minutes. Does some form of response arise within or come from beyond you? Sound a bell when time is up, and ask all to step out of their circles and to reflect on what has changed for them. Those who want to keep their questions private can erase them; others can leave them for a silent walk to harvest meaning for living from the questions of others, and to consider what has shifted for themselves during this activity.

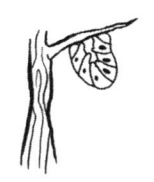

Chapter 9
Yosef Loved to Walk in the Woods
by Yehudit Goldfarb

Yosef loved to walk in the woods alone, especially early in the morning, even before the sun came over the horizon and lit up the small clearings in the woods. He was seven years old, the eldest child of an elderly couple who lived sparingly but comfortably.

One December day, when it had already begun to get cold but before the first snowfall, Yosef wasn't able to take his usual early morning walk because his mother needed him to help at home to prepare for Hanukkah guests who were coming to stay for several days. But his duties were over before the sun had set, so he decided to go to the woods for just a little while. He had a specific tree he liked to visit and sit under to sort out any problems he had in his life.

That day, when he approached the tree, he found an elderly man with a long, white beard and a dark brown woolen cap sitting in the very spot where he liked to sit. He hesitated at the edge of the clearing, undecided about whether to enter into what now felt like the old man's space. The old man, who had been poring over a very large book, sensed his presence and raised his head. He stared straight at Yosef with large, clear blue eyes that seemed to penetrate deep within his soul.

Yosef shivered, but he didn't feel afraid. The man's eyes had a kindly look. Deciding that he would approach the old man, he gathered the courage to say, *Shalom*. The man didn't respond in words, but he motioned him to come closer. Yosef stepped into the clearing. As he did, he felt a change come over him. His feet felt bigger, his legs longer; he found it difficult to walk upright. It felt as if some outside force was making his back curve and was forcing his hands toward the grass below. He noticed his hands were changing; they were becoming paws with long nails. Coarse hair was growing on their backs and pushing his shirt out from his arms. He was turning into a bear, a large brown bear.

He wanted to pinch himself to see if he was dreaming, but that was impossible with his new paws. He tried to calm himself: "I am just imagining this. This isn't really happening to me. It is impossible." He wanted to ask the man: "Who are you?" But when he raised his newly furry head, he saw that the space under the tree was empty. He was alone in the clearing in the woods. The sun had sunk below the tops of the trees. And he was a bear!

He moved slowly but gracefully in his new body. He realized his new fur protected him from the cold, and he couldn't help but utter to himself *Baruch Ha-Shem* (Thank God!).

Needless to say, Yosef didn't return to his elderly parents. How could he, now that he had been transformed into a bear? He knew they would be suffering a great deal because of his disappearance. He tried to think of a way to let them know that he was still alive, that they shouldn't lose hope of seeing him again. All he could think of was to visit the garden of his old house every week before *Shabbat* and move something around from where it had been. He knew his mother would notice the changes, and he hoped that if she saw that there was a change from week to week, at the same time each week, she would recognize that someone or something was trying to send her a message. But he didn't want to frighten her, should she happen to see a brown bear coming out of the woods and entering her garden. His concern for her kept him from carrying out his plan. He contented himself with watching the house from the woods every Friday afternoon until he could see the light of the *Shabbat* candles glowing in the window.

This pattern went on for many years. Yosef became a full-grown bear. He learned to find food and places to sleep, and he thanked God that he had at least been transformed into a strong animal with good survival skills and that he hadn't lost his sense of identity as Yosef. He had been an avid reader even at the age of seven and decided during that very first week that he would observe each *Shabbat* by resting all day and telling himself stories that he had read when he was still a boy. He tried to keep himself from thinking about the future, or speculating on whether the transformation would last forever, or if there was a way to become a person again.

He lived as much as he could in the present and appreciated each gift of food and drink that kept him alive. He remained alone. Once or twice when he saw other bears in the woods, he walked the other way, making it clear to them that he didn't want to socialize. He also remembered to say the *Shema* (prayer) upon waking in the morning and going to sleep at night. He did not feel the instinct to hibernate, which meant that he had to work very hard in winter to find enough food.

One Friday afternoon, after Yosef had watched the light of the *Shabbat* candles in the window of his parents' home for an unusually long time, he walked back into the woods along the same path he had taken as a seven-year-old boy. And there, under his favorite tree, sat an elderly man with a long, white beard and a dark brown woolen cap. He was holding a very large book, and like that day so many years before, Yosef hesitated at the edge of the clearing. He realized that this strange man might have the power to transform him back into a human, and he felt a fear deep in his belly. What would it mean to be a person again? Would he be able to live with humans and be accepted after so many years living the life of a bear? Did he want to live with humans again?

The old man sensed his presence, raised his clear, bright blue eyes and stared at him. Yosef felt a great change come over him, and he fell to the ground in a profound sleep.

When he woke up it was night, *Shabbat*, in fact. It didn't take him long to realize that he no longer had bear fur growing from his skin. He had indeed turned back into a person, a young adult who was wrapped in a heavy bearskin pelt. The old man with the clear, bright blue eyes was leaning over him, singing to him softly in a language he didn't recognize but which caused beautiful images to appear in his mind's eye: flowers of many colors and shapes, mountains with vibrantly green trees and glistening streams, lakes with all kinds of animals and birds moving along their edges and reflected on their smooth surfaces, and many other visions that soothed his spirit and felt like gentle guiding lights to accompany him in his transition back into the human world. Then images of humans began to appear, starting with those of his family and friends as they looked when he had last seen them. When the singing finally stopped, Yosef's heart was awake with a desire to reconnect with the human world.

The old man helped Yosef stand up and walked with him in silence to the edge of the woods. With slow deliberate steps Yosef walked through his mother's garden and around the house to the front door. As he approached, tears welled up in his eyes when he saw two small lights shining through the glass box containing his family *Hanukkiah* (menorah). He paused to breathe deeply, letting the Hanukkah lights open his heart in yearning to see his parents whom he had hidden from for so many years. Then gently but firmly he knocked on the large wooden door of his family home.

Provenance: This story comes from a work-in-progress, *Tree of Life Tales: A Collection of Stories for Chanukah*, and is designed to be read on the Second Night to illustrate the Kabbalistic *sefirah* (aspect of divine energy) of *Gevurah*—strength or restraint. The original version of this story was written in response to a prompt in my Tzfat writing group in December 2007 during Chanukkah.

Yehudit Goldfarb is a writer, teacher, photographer, spiritual guide, healer, and founder of *Otiyot Hayyot*-Hebrew Letter Movements. She lives with her husband in Tzfat, Israel, where she co-directs the Bayt Maor HaLev Center for Movement, Healing and Language Arts. Yehudit holds a doctorate in English from the University of Victoria, *smicha* from Rabbi Zalman Schachter-Shalomi as *Morataynu,* "Our Teacher," and has also been honored as an *Eishet Chazon, "Woman of Vision,"* by the women of Jewish Renewal. Yehudit co-founded the Aquarian Minyan of Berkeley, California, and long served as Associate Editor of *Agada*, an illustrated literary journal.
www.YehuditGoldfarb.blogspot.com

Study Guide: Questions, Sources, and Projects for Reflection, Discussion, and Action

1. Which *mitzvot* are illustrated by this story? Which additional *mitzvot* can you also relate to this story?

2. Do you have a special place where you go to be alone, feel your feelings, and sort out problems?

3. What were the practices that sustained Yosef during his time as a bear?

4. Do you know anyone who stopped talking to family, or a family member, for years? Or even disappeared, like Yosef? What do you imagine it was like for them? For their parents? What might bring family members back together in such situations?

5. The old man sings to Yosef and many images arise for him. Do songs affect you, too, even without understanding the words? Does your soul experience delightful or meaningful colors or images when hearing music? Try doing this in synagogue at different services during the high holidays. Did you know that there are different modes of sound for the melodies depending upon the time of day? How does each affect your spirit differently? What tone and movements might you create for morning, afternoon, and evening? For a happy, harvest holiday or a serious, contemplative holy day? Why, then, do we have music instead of just saying prayers?

6. In the provenance section, the author tells us that she wrote this for the second night of Hanukkah and associates it with the quality "*gevurah*—strength or restraint." What connection do you make between this quality and the events in the story? Who showed restraint? Yosef? His parents? The old man?

7. What stage of life might becoming a bear symbolize? And who or what might the old man symbolize?

8. Though Yosef's outer form changed drastically from boy to bear, his core identity and values remained the same. Are you able to remain true to good values under challenging circumstances?

Sacred Story and Text Connections

1. The child of a certain rabbi used to wander in the woods. At first his father let him wander, but over time he became concerned. The woods were dangerous. The father did not know what lurked there. He decided to discuss the matter with his child. One day he took him aside and said, "You know, I have noticed that each day you walk into the woods. I wonder, why do you go there?" The boy said to his father, "I go there to find God." "That is a very good thing," the father replied gently. "I am glad you are searching for God. But, my child, don't you know that God is the same everywhere?" "Yes," the boy answered, "but I'm not."—David J. Wolpe, *Teaching Your Children About God*, HarperPerennial, 1994, page 44, quoted in *Howard Cohen*, "Guiding Spirituality in Nature" in *Seeking and Soaring: Jewish Approaches to Spiritual Guidance and Development*, Reclaiming Judaism Press, 2014.

2. Rabbis Jane Litman and Marcia Prager entered the student lounge at rabbinical school after a study session, saying they'd found a new way to express something difficult. "When people ask if I believe in God, I say, 'No.' Then I surprise them by saying 'Actually, I experience God.'"—Goldie Milgram, *Meaning & Mitzvah: Daily Practices for Reclaiming Judaism through Prayer, God, Torah, Hebrew Mitzvot and Peoplehood*. Woodstock, VT: Jewish Lights, 2005.

Project: Are the texts above helpful for considering your own relationship to the divine? Find out if there is a *mashpia* in your community, a professional trained in Jewish guidance and development, and ask for time to explore these texts and questions in depth. Also, explore other questions such as: When do you have a sense of the divine? Is God more of an idea to you, or an experience? How can these types of experiences help to enrich and inform your journey in life?

Chapter 10
The Choice
by Dan Gordon and Donna Jacobs Sife

It had been twenty years since Donna's last trip to Jerusalem. Her primary mission, the one thing she *had* to accomplish before leaving the Holy Land, was to find the perfect *tallit* for her son Jacob's bar mitzvah. A *tallit*, the garment to wrap around her son's thirteen-year-old shoulders, is the fabric that would welcome him into Jewish manhood. Nothing less than perfect would do.

She found many that were less than perfect. Oh, they were beautiful, but Donna wanted the one *tallit* that spoke to her, the one that would be a symbol of how Judaism had enriched her life and how she hoped it would enrich Jacob's. When she found it, she would know.

Finally, when her days in Israel were coming to an end, she saw it in a shop window. It was everything she had dreamed of. A big, bold, colorful *tallit* decorated with a huge rainbow. The Torah portion Jacob was to read on his bar mitzvah was about Noah and the flood. What could be more perfect than to wrap yourself in God's promise while reading His covenant, the Hebrew vow that the world would always be safe from destruction? There was no question...she had to have it.

Of course, such a perfect *tallit* did not come without a price. Though it was certainly more expensive than Donna had planned for, she did not hesitate for a moment. She bought it quickly, the decision made for her by being in the presence of such a splendid work of art.

When she returned home to Sydney, Australia, she couldn't wait to give out all the gifts she had bought in Israel for her children. T-shirts, hats, candy, books and jewelry all came tumbling out of her bag. She saved the best for last.

"Jacob, wait till you see this," she said. "I know you're going to love it."

She pulled the *tallit* out of the bag, held it up for him to see, and wrapped it around him with a hug.

"Ohh, Jacob, what a perfect *mensch* you are, what a man!" she said. "I can't wait to hear you reading the Torah for all our friends and family wearing that *tallit*. You look perfect!"

When Donna heard Jacob's mumbled "thanks, Mum," she thought about how much the *tallit* embodied her relationship with Judaism, a religion as bold and beautiful and colorful as the cloth wrapped around her son's shoulders. Together they carefully folded the *tallit* and put it in the closet, and Donna thanked God for the joy of belonging to such a tradition.

A few days before his bar mitzvah, Donna said, "Jacob, let me see how you look in your bar mitzvah clothes."

Jacob changed into his black dress slacks, green silk shirt, and classy, thin black tie.

"Oh, what a fine, handsome young man," she said as she kissed him. "Now, let's get the whole picture. Go ahead...let's put on your *tallit*."

Jacob went to the closet and brought out the *tallit*. Once again, Donna hugged the *tallit* around her son's shoulders.

"What a *mensch*!...What a man you are!...I'm so proud of you..."

"Uh, Mum..."

"I can't wait for everyone to see you. They'll be just as proud..."

"MUM!"

Donna stopped *kvelling* (beaming with pride) for a moment to listen.

"Mum," Jacob said softly. "I don't know how to say this but...I hate this *tallit*."

"*How could you possibly hate such a wonderful, beautiful tallit?*"

...is what Donna didn't say...

"*But I spent so much money to find you the absolute perfect tallit!*"

...is what she didn't say...

"*I'm sure you'll grow to love it as much as I do.*"

...is what she didn't say...

"Then we must change it."

..is what she did say...

Then the three of them—Donna, Jacob, and the *tallit*—went to their local synagogue, where Jacob picked out a new *tallit*. This one was small, plain and understated, with a simple, traditional stripe. They made an even exchange with the *shul's* gift shop, leaving the big, colorful, expensive Israeli *tallit* to be sold to someone else while they took home the small, plain, inexpensive *tallit* that Jacob had chosen.

On the day of Jacob's bar mitzvah, a crowd of friends and family prayed together as Jacob read from the Torah about Noah, the rainbow, and God's promise to humanity. As Donna watched and listened to her son, she thought again about her relationship with Judaism, the big, bold, colorful tradition she had come to embrace. She looked up at her son and realized that his relationship was different. Jacob's connection to Judaism was more like his *tallit*: tentative, quiet, simple, and understated.

Donna closed her eyes and listened to her son read from the Torah. She did not hold back her tears while thanking God for giving each of them a choice.

Dan ("Dante") Gordon is professional storyteller and the rabbi of Temple Beth Torah, Humble, Texas. He is the National Rabbinic Advisor to March of Remembrance, an organization of churches who collaborate to honor the Holocaust. Dan has offered stories throughout the United States, Israel, Australia, and Argentina, including to groups of Christians interested in Judaism, mentally challenged adults, and prison inmates. His published stories appear in *What's Jewish About the National Pastime* and *Mitzvah Stories, Seeds for Inspiration and Learning*. www.RabbiDanGordon.com

Donna Jacobs Sife is a teacher, storyteller, and writer. She has taught on Jewish story and Bible in the Melton Adult Education Program, lectured in Sacred Story and interpretation at Universities of Sydney and Western Sydney and Hebrew University, New York's 92nd St Y and Jewish Museum and Limmud UK. A well-known peace and social activist, Donna co-founded Jewish Voices for Peace and Justice and regularly presents workshops on conflict resolution and peace studies. She is currently also School Programs Director at Together for Humanity, a multi-faith anti-prejudice educational organization. www.DonnaJacobsSife.com

Study Guide: Questions, Sources, and Projects for Reflection, Discussion, and Action

1. Which *mitzvot* are illustrated by this story? Which additional *mitzvot* can you also relate to this story?

2. Sometimes what parents want for their children is not what children want for themselves. Was there a time when you, as a parent, experienced this? Was there a time when you, as a child, did? How did you feel about each other at that moment? What is the best way to treat the other person when something like that happens?

3. What is your personal relationship to Judaism? How does it differ from that of other people you know? Do you think people should be more alike in their relationship to their faith and traditions, or do you think it is more important to be an individual in your relationship to your faith?

4. It took courage for Jacob to tell his mother how he really felt about her gift of the *tallit*. How do you say difficult things to someone you love?

5. Jacob's mother really listened to her son when he said he hated that particular *tallit*. Can you think of a time when your parent or another adult in your life really listened to you? How did it make you feel? Have you been able to really listen to your parents or other adults?

Project: Create a design for your own *tallit*. What are the symbols of Judaism you would want to put on it? How will the design let people know about your relationship to Judaism?

Sacred Story and Text Connections

1. "Speak to the children of Israel, and tell them to make fringes on the corners of their garments, for all generations. It is a fringe for you to see as a reminder of all of the *mitzvot*, so that you will do them, and not [just] follow a thought or vision [towards a choice of action]."—Numbers, *Bamidbar*, 15:38-9

    Do you appreciate guidelines and guidance? Is a physical reminder effective? What other physical reminders are prominent in Judaism?

2. Said Rabbi Shimon bar Yochai: When a person rises in the morning and puts on *tefillin* and *tzitzit*...the *Shechinah*—the Divine Presence, dwells upon this person and proclaims: "You are My servant, Israel, in whom I will be glorified!"—*Zohar Chadash, Terumah* 41d

    a. These high expectations of shining a good light on God's name by following the *mitzvot* are wrapped up in the mitzvah of wearing a *tallit*. Do your actions reflect well on your family? On Judaism? In the sense of the text, do you "serve?" Is serving simply helping others, or can it include expressing gratitude, such as offering blessings at meals, when a child is born, upon seeing the first tree of the year in bloom, and more?

    b. Contemplate being sheltered by what Jewish tradition calls the "wings of the *Shechinah*"—a loving, compassionate Divine presence—while under a *tallit*. What happens for you?

    c. How might expressing the prayer of your heart along with morning prayers under a *tallit* at home change your day?

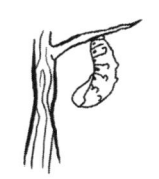

Chapter 11
The King Comes to Rottingham
by Leslie Gorin

Eli the errand boy dashed through the village of Rottingham, clutching a scroll. He had to get it to the mayor, and fast. The future of Rottingham depended on it.

"Good day, Master Goodman!" called Eli as he whizzed down the street.

"Take a hike, Schnitzelshorts!" Master Goodman scowled in reply.

"Excuse me, Madam Sachs!" Eli shouted as he rushed through the marketplace.

"Watch it, Gerbiltushie!" Madam Sachs shouted back.

Everywhere Eli went, Rottinghammers were rotten. They lied, cheated, and played mean tricks on each other. And no one wanted to do business with them. After all, who would buy clothes from a tailor who sewed pants bottoms closed so people couldn't get their legs through them? Or babka bread from a baker who slipped pickles into it for a laugh?

Eli knew that the mayor feared for Rottingham's future. With no one to do business with, the town would go hungry for want of work. And then Rottingham would be in a pickle more sour than the baker's babkas. But the scroll Eli carried could change everything.

Eli sprinted down the last stretch to City Hall. Out of breath, he burst into the mayor's office.

"Sir!" he said. "A message from the king!"

The mayor grabbed the scroll and read it aloud. "The king is coming to visit! He is touring the kingdom and wants to see Rottingham. He wants to reward towns that please him with gifts from the royal treasury!"

Eli and the mayor beamed with excitement. As the mayor read on, though, his smile faded.

"What is it, sir?" asked Eli.

"To get a true picture of Rottingham, His Highness is coming in disguise. He wants to be sure that his subjects don't change just because they know their king is watching. Eli, you know what this means, don't you? It means that the king will see Rottingham in all its rottenness, and we will be lost." The mayor shook his head in despair. "There's nothing to do but tell the people the truth," he said at last. "And heaven help us when the king sees how rotten Rottingham really is."

The day after the mayor announced the king's plan to visit in disguise, business in Rottingham began as usual. Villagers snarled and shoved each other. In the market, the baker got ready to push a cheesecake in a customer's face for complaining about his pickled babkas. Before he did, though, he spotted a stranger in the crowd. And then a funny thing happened.

Glancing at the stranger, the baker lowered his cheesecake, smiled sweetly, and offered to sell it for half price.

As another visitor went by, a villager stepped on her foot. "Hey, watch it, Toad Toes!" the Rottinghammer yelled. "Your stinky feet are—" She stopped short, eyeing the man. "Your stinky feet are…are…the prettiest stinky feet I've ever seen!" And she stepped aside to let the stranger pass.

Because no one could guess which newcomer might be the king, everyone who spotted a stranger suddenly became the nicest person Rottingham had ever seen. "Please!" and "Thank you!" and "Pardon me!" echoed through the village like a glorious symphony. What's more, the villagers found they enjoyed the change so much that they began acting kindly toward people they already knew.

Watching from the balcony, Eli and the mayor cheered.

"What luck has come to Rottingham!" the mayor crowed. "Surely the king's gifts will rain down like jewels from heaven!"

He slapped Eli on the back, grinning. Eli grinned back.

But now it was Eli's smile that faded.

"Sir," he stammered, "I-I-I have another message to deliver."

"Yes, Eli? Where is it?"

"I'm afraid this message isn't in writing. It's from me. The scroll I brought you… well, I wrote it."

"What?" shouted the mayor. "It wasn't from the king?"

"No, sir." Eli shook with fear.

"You'd best explain this, Eli, before I have you thrown in jail!"

"Well, sir," said Eli, "I, too, feared for Rottingham's future. And I wanted to do something about it. But who would listen to a lowly errand boy? If the villagers had a reason to behave, though, I thought there might be hope."

"So you made the whole thing up?"

Eli nodded. His eyes welled with tears.

The mayor stared silently for a moment.

"Eli," he said, "I have only one thing to say."

Eli lowered his head, trembling. Then the mayor threw back his head with a laugh so large it thundered through the town. He leaned down and put his hand on Eli's shoulder.

"Take this scroll to Nastyton, the next town over," he said, "and give it to the mayor. Tell him," he said with a wink, "it's from the king."

Provenance: I adapted this story from a commentary on a tale included in *Solomon and the Ant*, a collection of Jewish folk tales retold by Sheldon Oberman, with an introduction and commentary by Peninnah Schram. Many cultures have stories of important people coming to town, which causes the townspeople's behavior to change for the better. Many variants occur throughout oral traditions.

Leslie Gorin's works for children are published or forthcoming in *Highlights for Children, Hopscotch, Stories for Children, Home Education Magazine*, and on National Public Radio. She is a graduate of Wesleyan University with a degree in educational psychology. Leslie later attended film school at California Institute of the Arts as a Disney Fellow, which led to a career as an animator and storyboard artist. She has taught elementary school on the Navajo Indian Reservation, received a Highlights Foundation grant, and developed a basic animation and graphic design program in Kuala Lumpur, Malaysia, during her year as a Luce Scholar. www.LeslieGorin.com

Study Guide: Questions, Sources, and Projects for Reflection, Discussion, and Action

1. Which *mitzvot* are illustrated by this story? Which additional *mitzvot* can you also relate to this story?

2. Eli told the Mayor of Rottingham that the town would be rewarded with riches if the King liked what he saw when he visited. What were the real riches Eli meant?

3. How do our behaviors affect others? If we are mean to someone, how do they respond? What are some things you can do to change that behavior?

4. Sometimes people need help being nicer to each other, like thinking the King might be watching. Who or what does the king symbolize in this story?

5. Can actions change thoughts and behavior? What mitzvah might you take on regularly that might change your thinking and/or behavior?

6. It is often said that what bothers us most in others is to be found in some measure in ourselves, often in our shadow, i.e., outside of awareness—unless we look carefully and honestly at ourselves. Is that your experience? How might this affect our relationship to others?

Project: Create a draft of a scroll like the one Eli had in the story—out of paper, and perhaps later create it out needlework or a collage tapestry. Write down the ways you wish people would behave in your environment, then hang up this list at home.

Sacred Story and Text Connections

1. Love your neighbor as you would best love yourself.—Leviticus, *Vayikra*, 19:18

2. Ezekiel was standing on the River Chebar looking down at the water. And the seven heavens were open to him and he saw the Glory of the Holy One. The matter is like the following story: A man entered a barbershop and [the barber] cut his hair. He gave him a mirror and he looked in it. As he was looking in it, the king passed by. He saw the king and his retinue by the doorway. The hairdresser said to him: "Turn around and see the king." He [The person having his hair cut] said to him: "I have already looked in the mirror."
—*Re'uyot Yehezkel*

Texts often use words as a code to show us something that is difficult to express directly. It helps to know that Ezekiel was in Babylon with those Israelites who survived the Babylonian invasion, but who were then sent into exile in Babylon. So, there was much hair cut.

    a. What was Ezekiel really seeing reflected in the water? What effect did it have on his spirit? Who was the barber?

    b. Spend time gazing at the surface, flow, and depths of a living body of water—river, lake, or sea. What can be learned about the divine nature of life from doing so? This ancient practice comes from the *Merkavah* (Chariot) mystics who wondered what all of the metaphors in the biblical story of Ezekiel's chariot might mean.

3. Rav Elai said in the name of Rav Elazar ben Shamua: "It is permitted to modify in the interest of peace"…Rabbi Natan says, "It is a mitzvah to tell a lie for the sake of peace." At the yeshiva of Rabbi Yishmael it was taught: "Peace is great, for even God lied for its sake."

This is one of the six times that the mitzvah of refraining from lying does not always apply.

1. for the sake of fulfilling a mitzvah;
2. for the sake of peace;
3. for the sake of marital harmony; 4. for the sake of humility;
5. for the sake of modesty regarding the private matters between a couple;
…and 6. to protect oneself and others from harm.

To learn when God, Abraham, and Isaac lied in different stories in the Torah, see Talmud, *Yevamot* 65b.

    a. Eli lies to the Mayor for a good reason. When is it okay to lie? Is it ever okay?

    b. Two *mitzvot* are in conflict in this story. Decide which and then have a family debate: Which is more important?

Project: Monitor the truth levels in your life. Do you respect yourself after looking at the data? What might you hope to do differently in the future?

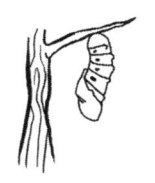

Chapter 12
What Is, Is: A Midrash
by Daniel T. Grossman

The time was long ago, in the distant past of humanity. The Garden of Eden was closed to humans, but life continued on the farms and in the cities. One day, three humans left their homes and travelled to the Place of Gathering to speak to the One who had created them. The three had never met, and they sat for a long time before anyone moved or made a sound.

The first traveler had eyes but could not see. He was an old man, and he had walked from a distant city for almost a month. With a gnarled wooden staff he walked, step after step, calling out and listening whenever directions were given. The second traveler had ears but could not hear. She was a young woman and she rode up from her farm on a gray horse. She felt the horse's strength beneath her as her eyes scanned the road ahead. The third, a small child, had feet but could not walk. He was brought in a carriage that left as soon as it arrived. The child felt abandoned both by the guardian, who had pushed the carriage, and by God. They had all come to ask the Creator: Why?

After nearly a full day had passed, and the sun was about to set, the blind man spoke.

"Creator of all things, why am I blind? Why can I not see the sunrise or a flower bloom? The people of my city speak constantly of all the things I cannot see. And so I ask You, Creator, why?"

The deaf woman could not hear the old man's questions, but watched his lips as he spoke, and she understood. She began to speak and sign, "Why can't I hear the rooster's crow or the Torah's chant or my mother's hello? I have been told of things I cannot hear. I, too, ask You, Creator, why?"

The child shouted, "I cannot run freely or ascend the steps of the Temple or walk in the sunset with my brothers. Why?"

The Creator answered, "What is, is."

Speaking all together as one voice, the three persisted, "Are we being punished?"

"No, never," said Creator. "What is, is."

"Are we being challenged so that we may find strength elsewhere, in other ways?"

"No, never. What is, is," said Creator.

"Do we exist to show by example that people must work as one?"

"No, never. What is, is," replied Creator.

"The Creator does not care for any of us," the man said to the others. The woman nodded in agreement, but the child only drew lines in the dirt without speaking.

"This is ALL You will say to us?" the woman spoke and signed. Her gestures were sharp, and her lips and eyes were drawn tight in a grimace. "We shouldn't have come. I was so naive. Tell me this, Creator. Are You so very callous with all Your creations or only with us?"

And then the Creator spoke softly, "My children, I did not create you as a punishment, or a challenge, or to teach a lesson. You were created, like all Creation, to exist. Yes, there are things to be learned in all Creation. But My children, do you presume to know the work of My hands or My eyes or My ears? You believe I work in one way for one reason. You assume I shaped you, folded you around some mold, some norm, some reason. And so you ask, why did You create like this…? Why not like that?

"For seven days I shaped the clay of the earth and curved the breath of the air. But my greatest sanctification was just to exist, to be. On the *Shabbat*, I ask you just to exist, to be. For I am all. I am everything, each possibility and its opposite at once. When you look at all existence and say: 'And it is very good,' then your first questions will be answered. New questions will arise, and new stories will be told. Until that time you will continue to ask the question: 'Why?' over and over and over."

The three travelers stood before the roads that had brought them to the Place of Gathering. Each body was filled with questions swimming bright and frantic like a thousand fish in a cool narrow river. And again, they stood and they sat at the Place of Gathering wondering, not "Why?" but "How?" and "With whom?" and "Where next?"

As the blind man leaned against his staff, the grimace of "Why" faded from his face, and in its place, wonder. The woman's fingers flickered lightly, as new questions rose up to her fingertips. And the child, now in the midst of the company of questions, no longer abandoned, grew curious to explore and to play.

One by one, when each was ready, the travelers began to journey once again, for what is, is.

Daniel T. Grossman is an author, educator, and performer. He serves as rabbi of Adath Israel Congregation, and lives with his family in Lawrenceville, New Jersey. His focus is Jewish special needs within a normative congregation. Dan co-wrote and participated in the video *Someone Is Listening*, the story of a young deaf Jew and his search for fulfillment. Dan and his wife perform *Siman Tov*, an educational entertainment program which uses sign language, mime, music, and storytelling to bring audiences closer to the world of the Jewish deaf. His story "The Taxi," is published in *Mitzvah Stories: Seeds for Inspiration and Learning*.

Study Guide: Questions, Sources, and Projects for Reflection, Discussion, and Action

1. Which *mitzvot* are illustrated by this story? Which additional *mitzvot* can you also relate to this story?

2. Does the story ever explain why people are born blind or with other physical challenges?

3. Expressing bitterness and anger towards God is permitted in Judaism. Why might that be?

Sacred Story and Text Connections

1. Tell your child on that day, it is because of what God did for me when I left Egypt.—Exodus, *Shemot* 13:8

   It is a mitzvah to tell the story of our origins. Why is it made so important as to be a mitzvah?

2. "For I settled the children of Israel in *Sukkot*." —Leviticus, *Vayikra* 23:43
   "They were clouds of glory," said Rabbi Eliezar [ben Hyrcanus].
   Rabbi Akiva said: "Real *sukkahs* (harvest booths—*sukkot*)..."
   —Talmud, *Sukkah* 37b

3. "The school of Rabbi Ishmael taught: 'My word is like a fire....and like a hammer shattering rock.'—Jeremiah 23:29 As a hammer creates innumerable sparks, so does a single text yield many meanings."—*Midrash Sanhedrin* 34

   Rabbi Eliezar and Rabbi Akiva take different positions on the meaning of text #2. Is it always fine for some people to take things literally and others figuratively?

Project: Grieving a loss is necessary and healthy, so long as we don't remain stuck in this condition. The story suggests that a time comes to shift from asking, "Why?" towards asking, "How [can I move forward]?" "With whom?" and "Where next?" Write a paragraph about an important loss of your own; answer these three questions. See if some helpful feelings and/or awareness emerge.

Chapter 13
The Phoenix on Noah's Ark
by Jill Hammer

The phoenix had been sunning herself on a desert rock when she felt something within her and knew she needed to fly east. She flew and flew, not knowing what she was looking for. Then she saw the half-built boat, and seven people working on it. She didn't understand why there was a boat, since the ocean was miles away.

Somehow, she felt drawn to land nearby. When she did, she saw dozens of other animals gathered around, waiting. There were giraffes and foxes, frogs and chickadees. Nearby were big piles of grain, vegetables, and fruits, and boxes filled with all kinds of things. The phoenix grumbled. She liked to be alone, and this was a big crowd.

A man was opening the door of the ark. The phoenix noticed something strange: there were two of all of the other kinds of animals, sometimes even more than two, but the phoenix was all alone, and no other phoenix came.

That was fine with her. One phoenix was enough. She fluffed up her golden feathers so that all the other animals could see them. She amused herself by chasing the peacocks and making them squawk, but then it began to drizzle, and it was time, though she didn't know for what.

The animals began to board the ark. The phoenix felt pulled to join them, though the ark looked dark inside, and not big enough for all the beasts that were creeping or galloping or darting inside. A woman waved to the phoenix and showed her a spot on the ark. The spot was much too small—she was cramped between the flamingoes and the hippos! And she wasn't close enough to the one window. Tiny insects and lizards were curling up near her feet.

The phoenix looked down. One of the animals near her feet was changing colors. It was a little lizard, and every time it would pass an animal, it would become the color of that animal.

"What are you?" she asked, annoyed that someone was standing in her spot.

"I am a chameleon," the little lizard said.

"Are there two of you?" the phoenix asked.

"I don't know. I haven't seen another creature like me," said the chameleon.

"What is going to happen now?" the phoenix wanted to know.

The chameleon tried to answer, but there was a loud, banging noise. Noah closed the door and latched it. The phoenix heard the patter of a heavy rain on the roof of the ark. Alarmed, she let out a squawk. As the ark began to rise and shake, the lions roared and the wolves howled.

"When do we eat?" the nearby ravens croaked.

During the days and nights of rain, Noah and his family ran everywhere feeding animals. The phoenix and the chameleon watched as the humans served hundreds of meals. The bear needed honeycombs, which Naamah had stored in wax and piled on shelves. The koala needed eucalyptus leaves, so Japheth's wife Adata opened the precious wooden box that contained the leaves she had saved. Shem piled up the bundles of grass he had stacked for the horses, goats, and cows. Japheth brought packets of bamboo shoots for the pandas and leafy branches for the elephants. And Ham had a sack of brightly colored flowers for the bees and the Galapagos tortoises. The chameleon, overwhelmed by all the sounds and colors, fell asleep against the phoenix, and turned gold to match her feathers.

The phoenix listened to what Noah and his family were saying to one another. She could understand human speech and even speak it, since she was a phoenix, a magical creature. She found out about the great waters that God had said would flood the whole earth—and that the humans and animals on the ark would be saved so that they could begin again.

The phoenix was confused. Why her? And why did she not see any other phoenix on the ark?

Meanwhile, Noah opened clay jars and took out salted meat for the lions, owls, and ferrets, and salted fish for the polar bears, penguins, and kingfishers. Ham's wife Neela fed the spiders and insects, and opened a bag of dirt for the earthworms. Every animal ate something different, and every animal ate at a different time. The rabbits, deer, skunks, and wombats would only eat at dawn and evening. The wolves and porcupines ate at night. Monkeys and squirrels ate during the day. The humans were completely exhausted. The phoenix saw them dozing over pails of grain or catching a snooze on the grass-pile. Noah in particular had baggy eyes and seemed to have a perpetual cold.

The phoenix, who usually only ate pomegranates, watched everyone else eat. She began to start feeling hungry herself. She opened her mouth to demand a meal. But then she saw that the little chameleon had curled up, and he wasn't gold anymore. He was very pale, and when the phoenix tried to wake him, she couldn't.

"Noah," she called. "I think my friend the chameleon may be sick."

Noah was surprised that she had spoken. He came over to where the phoenix stood on her golden talons, looking down at the chameleon.

"Let me see your friend," he said. He picked up the chameleon, but the little lizard did not wake up.

Noah's wife Naamah came over. "What does he eat?" she asked.

"I don't know," the phoenix said.

She was sorry she hadn't asked him while he was awake. She had only been thinking of her own comfort. Now she noticed again that she was hungry, but she didn't want to say anything. Noah and Naamah seemed so tired.

For hours, Noah's family held pieces of food near the chameleon's nose—meat, figs, caterpillars, and cheese—but he did not stir. Finally, Naamah insisted the humans all eat something. She went to the food stores, bought back a pomegranate, and cut it into sections for the family to eat. As she was cutting, a tiny worm fell out of the pomegranate.

"Oh, no," Naamah exclaimed. "The fruit is spoiled."

But the little chameleon sniffed, turned over, woke up, and snapped up the little worm.

"That was delicious," the phoenix heard him mutter. The chameleon drifted back to sleep, and his color turned gold again against her feathers.

The phoenix was so relieved she forgot to ask for a piece of pomegranate herself.

"Sleep well, friend," she whispered. She thanked Noah and Naamah for finding the chameleon some food.

Then Noah looked closely at the phoenix. "I don't think you have had anything to eat this whole time," he said to her. "Aren't you hungry?"

The phoenix burst into tears. "I am hungry," she admitted, "but you and your family looked so exhausted, I didn't want to say anything."

Noah patted the phoenix's beak while she sniffled. "Listen, phoenix," Noah said. "You have been kind and thoughtful to us. May God be kind and thoughtful to you. May you live a life that lasts thousands of years."

Then Naamah gave the phoenix some pomegranate seeds, and Noah went to bring her a bowl of oatmeal.

Eventually the chameleon woke up and wanted to play games. The phoenix met the flamingoes and the hippos and liked them. She even started to help feed the chicks and cubs on board by grabbing fruit in her talons and dropping it in the right mouths. Time on the ark was often boring, but the phoenix found herself so busy that she did not even feel jealous when Noah picked the raven and the dove to look for land.

After many, many days, the rain stopped. The ark gently touched down on a rocky mountain. The animals stepped out carefully onto the muddy ground. Above them, a rainbow spread across the sky.

As the little chameleon left the ark, another chameleon, who had been hiding against the wall of the ark and was completely brown, slithered out and left with him. The phoenix waved goodbye, and the chameleons invited her to come visit sometime.

The phoenix was still the only phoenix, but she was happy. She had once been a bird who kept to herself, and now she had many friends. She flew in circles around the ark, bathing her golden feathers in the sun.

Noah and Naamah called the phoenix to fly down.

"Phoenix," Noah said, "you are generous and a good friend. God has granted my prayer concerning you. You will live for a thousand years. At the end of a thousand years, return to this spot, and you will find a fire burning. Dive into the fire, and you will be reborn as a young phoenix."

Naamah smiled. "I have planted a pomegranate tree here near the ark, and it too will live for thousands of years. When you are reborn, eat from this tree, and your strength will return."

Now the phoenix knew why there was only one of her—she would live again and again throughout history. She promised Noah and Naamah that she would be a messenger to all the generations, reminding them to sustain all living things, and would care even for the smallest of animals. She soared off into the sky, and flew through the rainbow, looking for her next adventure.

Provenance: According to Jewish tradition, it is a mitzvah to be kind to animals. Many Torah laws, including the law that one may not take a calf away from its mother too soon, and the law that one must not overburden a pack animal, are part of this overarching principle. The Talmud, *Berachot* 40a states that we must feed our animals before we feed ourselves.

The story of the phoenix and the chameleon on Noah's ark appears in the Talmud, *Sanhedrin* 108b. The commentary *Me'am Loez* suggests that Noah was observing a divine commandment by feeding the animals on the ark at the proper times. We, too, can observe this commandment by caring for our pets and other animals in our lives before we take care of our own needs.

Both Maimonides and modern Jewish environmentalists read the commandment to care for animals as an instruction to preserve species and ecosystems, so that whole tribes of animals do not disappear from the earth. The phoenix, a mythological animal that appears in Jewish and other sources, reminds us to think about the future a thousand years from now as we make decisions about our world today.

Jill Hammer is the Director of Spiritual Education at the Academy for Jewish Religion, and the co-founder of the Kohenet Hebrew Priestess Institute. She is the author of five books: *Sisters at Sinai: New Tales of Biblical Women*, *The Jewish Book of Days: A Companion for All Seasons*, *The Omer Calendar of Biblical Women*, *The Hebrew Priestess: Ancient and New Visions of Jewish Women's Spiritual Leadership*, and a children's book, *The Garden of Time*. She holds a B.A. from Brandeis University and a doctorate in social psychology from the University of Connecticut. Jill received rabbinical ordination from the Jewish Theological Seminary. She lives in Manhattan with her wife and daughter. www.RabbiJillHammer.com

Study Guide: Questions, Sources, and Projects for Reflection, Discussion, and Action

1. Which *mitzvot* are illustrated by this story? Which additional *mitzvot* can you also relate to this story?

2. If you were an animal on the ark, which animal would you be and why?

3. The phoenix was used to being alone, but when she was on the ark she made friends. What did she do to make friends? How might you experiment with following her example?

4. Have you sheltered animals, birds, or other creatures that became lost in a storm or appear to be strays due to other misfortunes? Did you make efforts to find an owner and return the animal if it seemed to be a pet? Would you want to?

5. How does the phoenix manage to have a meaningful life without having a phoenix family of her own?

6. Would you take action if a person, or animal, nearby appeared ill?

Sacred Story and Text Connections:

Rabbi Yehudah said in the name of Rav: "It is forbidden for a person to eat before feeding his [her] animal." [This is derived from the fact that] the verse (in Deuteronomy, *Devarim* 1:15) states, "I will give grass in your fields for your cattle," and then concludes, "and you shall eat and be satisfied."—Talmud, *Berachot 40a*

If you have animals in your family, whether raised for food or as pets, when are these animals fed? Why do you think Judaism's sages put feeding them as a first priority?

Project: Choose an endangered animal to learn about and discover what you can do to help.

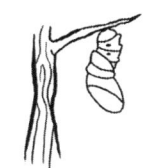

Chapter 14
Teeg, The Tiger
by Nancy Handwerger

Teeg was a handsome tiger. He liked to play games, write his name, and draw pictures. He played the piano for the other animals when they had jungle parties. He sang along with them.

Teeg lived with *Ima* (his mother), *Abba* (his father), and his younger brothers and sisters. An older cousin, Ari, had grown up and left the family to wander and find food on his own. On special occasions he returned to say, "Hello .....R- r-r-roar," and play with Teeg.

Sometimes Teeg's *Ima* invited him to find food and treasures with her. They would walk through the jungle and watch the monkeys swing from the trees. They dug in the ground to find tasty roots and nuts for snacks.

They played hide and seek. When it rained, they shook their bodies to dry their fur...and sprinkled each other with the water. That was fun!

Ima taught Teeg which animals to hunt. Teeg particularly liked to eat red deer steak. When there was no deer meat, they ate rabbit, or birds, or fruit from the trees. He didn't like those tastes so much. However, if he was hungry, that's what he and *Ima* would eat.

When Teeg tired of walking, he would cuddle next to *Ima* Tiger. He would listen to a story and fall asleep. He felt good being with *Ima*. If you listened carefully, you could hear him purr-r-r- like a kitten.

Teeg grew bigger and stronger. Now it was his turn to go off on his own. He played with friends in other parts of the jungle. When he came home, his younger brothers and sisters were eager to play with him. Even though they sometimes messed up his projects, they admired him and loved being with Teeg.

Often *Ima* and *Abba* Tiger traveled many miles away to find enough food for the family. Teeg missed them. He felt happy when they came home. He eagerly looked to see what goodies they brought home...maybe deer meat or buffalo brisket or chicken.

Sometimes, however, if he felt tired...or hungry...or angry, Teeg would start thinking that *Ima* didn't love him enough. He would scream or hit her. He hit things nearby. He felt mean. He acted nasty. Teeg became a loud, yelling, anger machine.

One day when his older cousin, Ari, came home for a visit, Teeg was crying. *Ima* had just come home from a hunting trip and was preparing supper. Teeg was angry that *Ima* had been away so long. Teeg wanted an ice cream cone. He was starving! *Ima* offered him a sausage of deer and rabbit meat or a falafel ball until supper was ready.

What did Teeg *really* want? Ice cream? A banana chocolate shake? A cupcake? What did he really, truly want??????

Teeg wanted *Ima* to pay attention to him…to listen to his feelings! She had been away a long time! He felt afraid and angry!

Teeg wanted *Ima* to love him and hug him…then give him something tasty to eat.

Cousin Ari took Teeg aside. They had a private tiger-to-tiger talk.
Ari told Teeg, "I'm so proud of you, Teeg. You are growing up to be a smart and strong tiger. Soon you will go to school to learn to read books, write words, and sentences and use numbers in different ways.

Ari spoke to Teeg about growing up behavior.

"Teeg, you now need to use words instead of yelling and tears. You can say what you are feeling and ask for what you want. Like, 'I miss you when you're away, *Ima*. I want a hug. Let's hug.' Or, 'I'm so hungry. I will eat some fruit or a falafel ball, or drink a glass of milk.'"

Ari encouraged Teeg to be kind and to consider the other person. Maybe *Ima* was tired or hungry or sad about something, so she couldn't pay attention to him right away. However, because *Ima* loved Teeg, she would hug him as soon as she could. And she did.

The next day was hot and sunny. Ari, *Ima*, *Abba* and Teeg walked deep into the jungle.

"Where are we going?" asked Teeg.

Ima said, "You are growing up now and can do special activities. There is a lake a long run from here. Would you like to go for a swim?"

They did! It was a special day!

Provenance: This original story was written for a five-year-old boy who was acting out frustration and anger with his voice and with his fists. He was seeking affirmation of himself and his needs from his mother. In the initial story complementary pictures of tigers showing a variety of feelings and behaviors were pasted onto appropriate pages.

Nancy Handwerger is an ordained *Kohenet* (Hebrew priestess), and has studied Jewish shamanism, Kabbalah, and leads Jewish meditation programs. Her book, *The Hebrew Letters Speak*, includes her paintings of each letter and invites readers to become 'friends' with the letters through meditating with them. As a licensed social worker and graduate of the Barbara Brennan School of Healing Science, Nancy offered psychotherapy integrated with energy healing. Currently she also volunteers, leading *Shabbat* and holiday services at senior residential homes. Grandmother to five, she enjoys writing dialogues that celebrate the stories of biblical women.
www.HebrewLettersSpeak.com

Study Guide: Questions, Sources, and Projects for Reflection, Discussion, and Action

1. Which *mitzvot* are illustrated by this story? Which additional *mitzvot* can you also relate to this story?

2. When you don't feel listened to, what happens to your mood?

3. How does Cousin Ari help Teeg in this story? Do you have relationships with your extended family or your parents' close friends?

4. Sometimes it can be hard to listen to people when they are upset or angry. This is also true for adults. What are good ways to let people know what you really need?

5. When you are feeling upset or angry, it can be hard to find words. What can you do to make yourself calm and find the words you need? How can God help?

6. As we grow up, we become more responsible. In what ways have you become more responsible?

Sacred Story and Text Connections

B'shem Adonai Elohai Yisrael	In the name of the God of Israel
mi'y'mini, Micha'el	May on my right be Michael (God's angel of mercy)
u'mismoli Gavri'el	and Gabriel on my left (God's angel of justice)
u'mil'fanai Uriel	In front of me, Uriel (God's angel of light)
U'may-acharai R'fael	Behind me, Raphael (God's angel of healing)
v'al roshi Shechinat El	And overhead, *Shechinah* (God's Presence)

   a. Human experience is often described in four dimensions: physical, emotional, intellectual, and spiritual. In which of these does the traditional prayer above, so richly poetic and full of metaphor, fit? So, for example, while a person might say, "I feel sick," but not actually turn out to be ill, this helps us understand that the emotional dimension has a different truth. In the same way, imagining, or praying for mercy, justice, light, or healing, can affect our well-being.

b. A child's capacity for imagination often allows this prayer to work quite rapidly as a calming influence. They often see angels, invisible friends, or have a relationship with God that isn't interrupted by intellectual functioning that comes later in life. Try calling in the angels together in the way of the prayer and enjoy the child(ren)'s experience; they may describe the angels as having particular visible qualities, often colors, which is what adult males describe in Jewish sacred text as their experience, too!

Choose or create a "listening object" and use it in family circle. Anyone holding the object gets to speak while others listen without interruption. Together create a prayer for calming and centering in difficult situations, and use it when any family member, child, or adult needs it.

Project: Take out some family photo albums with pictures of aunts, uncles, cousins and friends. Put a piece of plastic wrap over pictures where there are people who you don't know or barely know, then circle several who look interesting or friendly. Now make a plan to get to know them, perhaps become a pen pal, or connect on the phone or computer, or visit them on vacation, or take a walk together; if they have a special talent, do a project together. Together with your family or class, create a list of subjects to talk about and questions you might ask. There are times when we really need someone who is not our parent to talk to; this is an easy way to start building those connections and strengthening your own relationship to family.

Chapter 15
The Surprise of the Butterfly Aurelia
by Alide Huyser-Frijda

It was wartime in Holland. World War II. An alarming time for a Jewish family. My parents told me that they would have to seek out a hiding place for themselves, for my little three-year-old brother, as well as for me. Being six years old, I didn't fully understand...

My mother brought me to a "safe house" owned by friends of my uncle. I can remember that day now, after seventy years, as though it was just last week. I thought my mother was just dropping me off for a sleepover. I had never met the host family before. They had two children, a boy slightly older than me and a girl a little bit younger. Mother asked me to "Please be a good girl," and then she left.

The house was in Delft, a nice town in Holland. The family received me lovingly, with real warmth. But the sleepover continued for days, then weeks, and gradually years. They treated me as one of their own children. For safety, I was given a different name to use, should someone ask my name. And when people asked me: "Where are your parents?" I was taught to tell them that "My mother has a psychiatric illness and is in a hospital and my father has died." I understood that my parents would be in great danger were I to tell the truth.

Even though I was afraid of what could happen to my parents and to me, deep inside I believed better times would come. But I was not certain whom to trust, and of whom to be afraid. Who might betray us? Who would not?

One day something really scary happened.

I was walking to school, as I did every day on the small streets along the canals in Delft, when a big truck ran into me right in front of the police station. I still could walk, though one leg seemed broken. Bystanders brought me into the police station.

Of course, the officer on duty asked me my name. I gave him my hiding-name. But when he couldn't find that name in the official books, he realized what was going on. He proved to be on the side of goodness and made the official incident papers disappear. Not only I, but also my "hiding parents" were saved by this action. If it had become known that the family hiding me was harboring a Jewish child, then they and I would have been picked up and sent to an internment camp.

My host family found a doctor willing to secretly take care of my broken leg. It was infected for a long time, but eventually healed. I was left with only a forever scar, as a reminder of the grace by which I was able to stay alive.

My family, I missed them so—my parents and my little brother! Were they all right? What was happening to them?

One day, an incredible surprise occurred. A letter arrived from my father with illustrations by my mother. Inside the envelope was a story:

> Between the nettle leaves, a caterpillar crawls—she is multicolored and hairy. Look, the caterpillar is shedding her skin—four layers are coming off. She will soon become a pupa.
>
> [Time passes and] one beautiful morning, out of the pupa, something is emerging—antennae, folded legs and wings—all so tightly packed together. Ah, the legs and wings are unfolding. The caterpillar has become a beautiful, colorful butterfly!
>
> Our butterfly is called Aurelia. She is small and she can fly! She is going in search of flowers. Flowers have honey deep in their hearts, and butterflies are fond of honey.
>
> Aurelia first seeks honey from the honeysuckle that is hanging over fences. Using her long, sucking tongue, she drinks the honey from each flower. Now she is going further out into, and beyond, the garden, towards the violets and anemone, the Cuckoo Flower and the Apple Blossom. This is how Aurelia first visits a forest where children are playing.
>
> "Look, look! How beautiful!" The children have noticed Aurelia. "Look! See the reddish-pink wings with black stripes."
>
> "I am going to catch the butterfly," says [a boy named] Fransje. "With my catching net I can succeed easily and quickly." He rushes towards Aurelia and slaps down [the net]. But no....."zoef, zoef"....the butterfly flies away!
>
> High on a branch in a tree, the butterfly sits by herself and cries. She is so sad. Very sad, for if naughty boys catch you, then you cannot fly any more.
>
> Fransje and his friends start eating. They have brought everything with them—cups and bottles with milk and lemonade, and sandwiches with cheese, and bread spread with jam. Fransje eats greedily and so fast that a large piece of bread with jam falls on the ground.
>
> When the boys start to play again, Aurelia flies down to the piece of bread with jam, thinking it will taste "mmmm, delicious, like honey." Aurelia licks it with her tongue, but it doesn't taste so sweet and delicious as honey. So she flies away and falls asleep in the forest.

> It gets darker, the sun is disappearing, and the moon appears—bigger than it was yesterday. The moonlight is shining a bit brighter. The rabbits, the ducks, the horses, and the cows, too, they all turn inward, closing their eyes and falling asleep. Everybody is silent. The moon is watching with a smiling face; watching and taking care that everything and everyone is silent, and at peace.

This letter became my touchstone, and Aurelia, a beloved friend.

***

Perhaps you are wondering what happened after the war. My life became blessed with further good surprises. After living in hiding for almost three years, my parents retrieved my brother and me from our "hiding homes." Towards the very end of her life, my "hiding-mother" admitted to me she secretly hoped that my parents would not return after the war. This was because she had become so attached to me. I was really shocked to hear this. It was very honest of her to tell me. Only then did I realize what it meant to her to hide a Jewish child and take care of me for almost three years.

> After the war my mother wrote another letter to me. In it she said:

> You were a good girl. You did not cry when I took you to sleep in that new home. You asked me when I would be returning. I did not know what to say and so I told you: "There are always surprises and we do not know when, but the surprise will be there."

> During those long years in Delft, but also while growing up, right up to this very day, that last sentence became my guideline for living. I live with the knowledge that there are always surprises, and I have not been disappointed during my whole life. The biggest surprise of my life? It was after the war. I found out that both of my parents and my brother had survived. They were all alive!

Alide Huyser-Frijda, born in 1936 in Utrecht, the Netherlands, was a hidden Jewish child during World War II. Upon being reunited with her family, they moved to The Hague where her parents joined a Protestant church and she was sent to Christian schools. Alide married a pastor and they had three sons together. On a trip to Israel in 1969, she reconnected to her Jewishness. Unfortunately she was not accepted by the Jewish community, despite having three Jewish grandparents, because her maternal grandmother was not Jewish. Alide's survey of more than 100 people between ages twenty-one and eighty with Jewish fathers and "non-Jewish" mothers, exploring what difficulties they faced and how they were experiencing their Judaism resulted in "I Jewish?!" a report that contributed to creating discussion and approaches to resolving the challenges posed by their uncertain status after the war. At age seventy, Alide became bat mitzvah in a synagogue in Amsterdam. Grandmother to eight, she now lives with her husband in southern France where she is greatly enjoying her reclaimed Jewish life and retirement.

Study Guide: Questions, Sources, and Projects for Reflection, Discussion, and Action

1. Which *mitzvot* are illustrated by this story? Which additional *mitzvot* can you also relate to this story?

2. What would it be like to live with a strange family and pretend to be someone else? Would you be able to be like Alide and never tell anyone the truth about yourself? What would make it especially difficult?

3. Sometimes we are helped through the kindness of strangers, by people who are not our friends or family. Have you ever gone out of your way to help someone you don't know either at school or in your community? Why has this been especially important for Jews?

4. Why do you think the story of the beautiful butterfly, Aurelia, was sent to Alide? Why a butterfly and not some other animal or insect?

5. Alide tells us that there are always surprises. We may not know when, but the surprise will be there. What does this mean? Have you ever experienced this kind of surprise? Where is God in Alide's true story?

6. As a family, discuss whether you would shelter someone who needed a hiding place? Under what circumstances? For how long?

7. How did the letter from her parents help Alide to survive the war?

8. PARENTS: This story can open a conversation about the Holocaust—the *Shoah*—with your child, especially if you have not had that conversation before. If you have, allow the story to help you deepen it.

Project: Write and illustrate a butterfly story of your own, shaped to help those who are confined in some way. Or write a butterfly story to send to Alide (send to rebgoldie@gmail.com). Imagine that for safety reasons you can't sign your letter. How does that feel? What are your hopes for your story's impact? What is it like not knowing whether the person ever gets to open it, or actually gets to read or hear it?

Sacred Story and Text Connections

1. The *Zohar* teaches that a soul needs two wings to fly, like a bird [or the butterfly Aurelia]. One wing is the mitzvah of *yirat hashem*—awe and respect gained through appreciation of the intricacy and power of nature, one of the many face(t)s of God in Jewish tradition; the other wing is *ahavat hashem*—love, as inspired by the great beauty and abundance within the natural world, another face(t) of God.—*Tikunei Zohar* p. 82b. Also see *Tanya* chap. 41 ff. p. 57b ff.

2. When a person contemplates the wonders of God's creations, that person is immediately moved to love and awe….—Rambam, *Hilchot Yesodei Hatorah* 2:2

    a. Find a beautiful place to walk outside with a friend or class. Show each other details large and small that nourish your spirit with feelings of awe and connection to all that is, which some call God.

    b. What does it mean that "we are loved by an unending love," as we find in the prayer book, *siddur*, in the *Ahavah Rabbah* prayer? Become conscious of your breathing—and realize that it is the gift of the breath of life. Find a pond, river, lake, or stream, and observe the life forms and reflections. Behold a vegetable garden or trees in their flowering or fruiting process—do they sometimes appear to be the face of an unending love? Notice how a cut, bruise, bump or cold will usually heal naturally. Is this part of the "unending love?"

    c. Can you find examples in this story of these two *mitzvot* of love and awe in action in the life of the main character?

3. Psalms, *Tehillim* 92:13-16:
    Tzaddik katamar yifrach
    a righteous [mitzvah-centered] person is like a flowering date tree
    k'erez ba'l'vanon yisgeh
    [and] like a cedar of Lebanon, becoming tall
    sh'tulim b'veit adonai
    [righteous people] are plantings in God's house [life]
    b'chatzrot eloheinu yafrichu
    flowering in the courtyards of our Godsense
    ode y'nuvune b'seiva
    even in old age they will bring forth fruit

d'sheinim v'rah-ah-nahnim yih-yu
they will be vigorous and fresh
l'haggid ki yashar adonai
to direct us straight toward God [i.e., living mitzvah-centered lives]
Tzuri—My Rock!
v'lo avlata bo
[Viewed] from [God consciousness] nothing is bent.

This prayer from Psalm 92 suggests that the righteous ones are our role models; through their actions, their reputations become tall, so that they visibly show us a Godly way forward on our path of service in this life. This prayer helps us to appreciate and use one of the Jewish names for God: "My Rock." A strong foundation of knowledge of Jewish values tethers us safely to the idea of the "Rock" as steady source of support, powering us towards mitzvah-centered living.

a. *Tzur*, "Rock" as a metaphor for God, appears widely in Torah, prayer, and other Jewish sources. Can you think of some more examples? How is this name of God potentially helpful for you?

b. What "fruit" will these righteous people continue to create in old age?

c. Bring this interpretation of the prayer with you next time you are at services. See if it "sings" differently in your soul than the interpretation given on the page. Explore the differences together in class, or as a family at *Shabbat* dinner.

d. Who do you know personally, or what living persons have you heard of, who are mitzvah heroes?*

Project: In Israel there is a grove of trees where each tree is planted with a special ritual to honor "righteous gentiles," non-Jews who helped Jews to survive the Holocaust. Create a plan to found a garden or grove at your school, camp or other appropriate place in your community to honor contemporary "mitzvah heroes" from all faiths and traditions around the world.

*Danny Siegel coined this phrase. See his books *Heroes and Miracle Workers* and *Mumbaz II and Other Mitzvah Heroes*

Chapter 16
The Stranger at the Passover Table
by Barbara Solomon Josselsohn

Most times a stranger is a person you don't know. But sometimes a stranger is someone you thought you knew very well.

That was the case with my aunt, who I thought was the meanest, most prejudiced person in the world. I thought she hated Jews, which is weird since she's married to my Uncle Dan, who's my mother's brother and definitely Jewish. I guess she decided to ignore that about him when she fell in love with him. But the rest of us were a different story.

Aunt Catherine and Uncle Dan came to our house every year for Passover Seder, and Aunt Catherine always made it clear from the moment she stepped inside that she didn't want to be there at *all*. She'd purse her thin lips and look down her pointy nose at us as my dad passed out the *haggadot* (ritual booklets), and she never once smiled or nodded when Uncle Dan began chanting Hebrew—and he's the best Hebrew chanter I ever heard. She'd constantly look ahead in the book to see how many pages were left, and she'd sigh impatiently when she saw there were still a lot. She didn't know any of the verses of *Dayenu*, and barely opened her mouth to sing when Uncle Dan poked her with his elbow to join in the chorus—and how could somebody pretend not to be able to sing the chorus of *Dayenu*? It was only that one word—"*Dayenu!*"

And she was always insulting the food. Like last year, when my mom handed her the platter of gefilte fish, she firmly said, "No, *thanks*," baring her lower teeth and leaning away from the table, as though she couldn't stand to be near the little gray logs one moment longer.

"I'm with you, yuck!" said my little brother Jake, as he transferred the platter from Aunt Catherine to my father. My mother immediately asked to speak to Jake alone in the kitchen. But no one said anything to Aunt Catherine.

The only time Aunt Catherine looked happy at Passover was when the Seder was over, and the meal started, because then she would talk about Easter. She'd tell us that her two teenage sons, who were out with friends and not at our dinner, had already outgrown their old suits and bought news ones for Easter Sunday. She'd tell us how much she loved the Easter service at her church.

"Oh, the lilies and tulips are spectacular," she'd say. "And the music is so beautiful! It makes you tremble."

"It sounds lovely, Catherine," my mother always said, ignoring that she'd taught us years ago you're not supposed to visit one place and spend the whole time talking about how you'd rather be somewhere else. My mom is a teacher, and she's big on consequences, so if Jake or I had talked about how much we'd prefer to be at a friend's house or a movie, we would have gotten no dessert for sure. But Aunt Catherine—my mom all but *rewarded* her for gushing over Easter while sitting at our table.

Plus, as if talking about Easter weren't bad enough, each year sometime after Passover, Aunt Catherine would have us over to her house on Long Island for a big Easter celebration. She invited lots of people from her side of the family—baby nieces and nephews, old aunts and uncles, and cousins of all ages. The highlight was a backyard Easter egg hunt, when all the kids would search for chocolate eggs wrapped in colorful foil, and little yellow marshmallow chicks in clear plastic wrappers. I wished so badly that I could turn down my mouth at the mention of Easter chocolates, or say a firm, "No, thank you!" when the decorated baskets for collecting candy were passed around. But I couldn't. The candy was too delicious and the hunt too much fun, and before I knew it, I was racing among the bushes and calling out, "Found one!" just like all the other kids.

The year I turned eleven, I decided—once and for all—to reject the Easter festivities. I didn't have to be so obvious about it that my mom would notice and get mad. I could simply stand around and maybe yawn a few times if Aunt Catherine happened to look over. Why not? After all, Aunt Catherine was *always* nasty about our holiday. Why did we have to be polite about hers? What was fair about that?

But as the time of the hunt approached, I worried: Would I be able resist? Could I really just watch Jake and the others gather all the treats, and not be tempted by all the candies waiting to be plucked from the tree branches or pulled out of the grass? Figuring my best weapon was distance, I slowly backed into the house when I saw the kids assemble at the starting line. My luck, Aunt Catherine was coming downstairs at that very moment, carrying the baskets to hand out.

"Why are you inside, Michelle?" she asked. "The hunt is about to start."

I wanted to tell her I wasn't interested in her Easter silliness, that I much preferred our more mature and serious Passover customs, but I could hear my mom in my head warning me not to be rude. So I said the only thing I could think of.

"I need to use the bathroom."

"The one down here is occupied," she said. "Go upstairs and use the one next to my bedroom. And hurry or you'll miss everything."

I found Aunt Catherine and Uncle Dan's bathroom, but since I didn't really have to go, I washed my hands instead, lathering up twice just to waste some time. Then I went back into their bedroom. I could see through the window that the hunt had begun, with big and little kids happily circling bushes and digging near tree trunks. Their baskets looked about half full, which I knew from experience meant there were about ten minutes more to go. I wandered to Aunt Catherine's dresser, which was crowded with photos of weddings and other family events. I ran my finger over the frames, trying to guess how long ago each was taken.

Then I noticed a small black-and-white picture in the corner.

It wasn't framed, just lying flat on the wood surface. I picked it up. Although the image looked old and faded, I could see a pretty young woman with shoulder-length, wavy hair, and a small girl with dark bangs cut straight across her forehead. Long ago, it seemed, someone had written two names along the bottom border of the picture: *Rivka and Chana*.

Now even though my mom taught Hebrew, I wasn't exactly the best student at our temple. Still, I did know that Rivka and Chana were Jewish names, which made me totally confused. If Aunt Catherine hated Jewish things so much, why did she have an old picture of a Jewish lady and a girl on her dresser, next to all her important family photos? Who were these people, and why did they belong here?

I was so curious that I slipped the photo into my jacket pocket, thinking I could ask my mom about it and return it to the dresser without Aunt Catherine knowing. But when I got downstairs, I was suddenly hungry, and jealous of all the kids munching on chocolate eggs and sticky marshmallows. Running over to see if I could persuade Jake to share some of his stash, I forgot all about the photo until two afternoons later, when I was getting ready to do homework and dug into my jacket pocket, looking for my favorite mechanical pencil.

My shoulders fell, as I thought about how much trouble I was going to be in for taking the picture from Aunt Catherine's bedroom. But since I couldn't wait all the way until next Easter to put it back, I decided to confess and get it over with.

My mom was sitting at the kitchen table, going over some of her students' homework.

I put the photo on the table in front of her.

"Who are these people?" I asked.

She picked it up. "Rivka and Chana? That's Aunt Catherine's mother and grandmother. Where did you get this?"

I couldn't believe what she said. "You mean...Aunt Catherine is *Jewish*?"

My mom took off her glasses. "You didn't answer my question. Where did you get this?"

I looked down. "From Aunt Catherine and Uncle Dan's bedroom," I said softly.

"From their bedroom? What on earth were you doing in their bedroom?"

"I had permission—really, Mom," I told her. "Aunt Catherine told me to go up there and use her bathroom. And I saw this on her dresser and wanted to ask you about it. But when I got downstairs and saw all the candy, I...sort of forgot that I put it in my pocket."

The Stranger at the Passover Table | 127

My mom sighed. "Oh, Michelle, what were you thinking? You know not to take things from someone's home without permission."

"It was an accident," I said. "I just meant to show it to you. But she's so mean! She gets me all mixed up. And with the candy and everything, I wasn't thinking straight."

"You're going to have to return it. And tell her what you did."

"I know, and I'll say how sorry I am. But really, Mom—how can she be Jewish? It doesn't make sense. She hates Jews."

"She doesn't hate Jews."

"She hates Passover. She hates seders. She only loves Easter. She only loves Christian things."

My mom motioned to me to sit down. "Michelle, do you know what the Holocaust was?"

I nodded. "It was when the Nazis tried to get rid of all the Jews."

"And do you know what the Kindertransport was?"

This time I shook my head no.

"It took place around that time, when many Jewish families weren't able to leave Germany and other countries. So some parents sent their children off to England, so they'd be safe. Catherine's mother—that's the little girl in the picture, Rivka—she was a Kindertransport child. Rivka's mother, Chana, and her father were killed in the Holocaust."

I suddenly felt so sad. I couldn't imagine being sent away from home and never seeing my parents again.

"Rivka was raised in England by a family that wasn't Jewish, and when she went to America, she married a man who wasn't Jewish," my mom said. "When Catherine was born, they decided to raise her as a Christian. You see, Rivka associated Judaism with sadness and death. She didn't want to pass that on to Catherine."

I felt my eyebrows press together. "But doesn't Aunt Catherine *have* to be Jewish? Because her mother was?"

My mom shook her head no. "You see, it's clear for us—Daddy and I are Jewish, and you and Jake are Jewish, too. And we're happy that way. But it's not always that simple. Some people struggle to figure out how religion fits into their lives, or even if it does. And we need to respect their choices."

"But Aunt Catherine married Uncle Dan," I said. "If she didn't want to be Jewish so badly, why would she marry someone who was?"

She raised her shoulders to show she didn't have an answer. "Maybe because she loved him so much. And maybe she was searching for a part of herself that was missing. Maybe she's still searching now. Who knows?"

I rolled my eyes. "So that's why we have to be nice to her when she's mean to us on Passover?"

She reached out for my hand. "Michelle, do you remember the Torah story of Abraham and the three strangers?"

I shook my head no.

"Well, Abraham encountered three strangers one day, and he welcomed them into his home. He and his wife, Sarah, made them a good meal, and took care of all their needs. And as it turned out, these men weren't just strangers. They were angels—messengers sent by God. And Abraham and Sarah were blessed for showing them so much kindness and hospitality."

She put her hand under my chin. "I hope we're like Abraham and Sarah to Catherine. I like to think we're a blessing to her. And even though things are sometimes strained, I think she's a blessing to us, too." She stood up. "Now, go get your jacket, while I make sure Jake can stay next door until your dad gets home. You and I have an errand to do."

An hour later, we arrived at Aunt Catherine and Uncle Dan's house. Aunt Catherine was just getting out of her car, carrying two bags of groceries. I got out and walked up driveway.

"Aunt Catherine?" I called.

"Michelle?" she said. "What are you doing here? Why's your mom still in the car?"

I took the photo out of my pocket. "I took this picture from your house by mistake," I said. "I saw it when I went up to your bathroom, and I was curious. I brought it down to show it to my mom, but then I forgot about it, and I just found it in my pocket today. I'm really sorry."

My aunt put down the grocery bags and took the picture from me. "Thank you," she said stiffly. "No harm done."

I breathed in deeply. "And I'm really sorry about what happened to your family in the Holocaust," I said.

She looked away, her eyes skyward.

"And I'm really sorry I didn't participate in the Easter hunt this year," I added. "It's a really fun activity. It's nice that you include my family."

She looked at me. Her lips were a straight line. She was acting like she didn't feel anything, but I think she was feeling a lot. "It's nice for us to come for Passover, too," she said.

She slid the photo into one of the grocery bags and picked them both up, one in each hand. "Your mom is probably anxious to go. Thank you for coming by to return this." She waved briefly at my mom and continued into her house. I watched her close the door firmly behind her, and then I went back to my car.

Provenance: This story was inspired by the work of my home congregation, Westchester Reform Temple, and many other congregations, to foster tolerance, celebrate inclusion, avoid prejudgments, and demonstrate that open dialogue is always the key to understanding.

Barbara Solomon Josselsohn is a Jewish educator and freelance writer whose articles appear in *The New York Times, Consumers Digest, American Baby, Parents, Westchester Magazine*, and other publications. She also teaches in the Religious School of Westchester Reform Temple in Scarsdale, N.Y. Barbara also conducts children's writing workshops at the JCC of Mid-Westchester, also in Scarsdale. She is currently working on a picture book about Rebecca and Isaac, as well as on her first middle-grade novel. www.TorahandTweens.blogspot.com

Study Guide: Questions, Sources, and Projects for Reflection, Discussion, and Action

1. Which *mitzvot* are illustrated by this story? Which additional *mitzvot* can you also relate to this story?

2. Is there a relative you don't know well, or around whom you feel uncomfortable because you don't understand why they behave the way they do? What can you do to be welcoming to them?

3. Is it possible someone as close as family can be a stranger?

4. Are there aspects of your life that no one, or almost no one, knows? Why? How do you feel about keeping something secret? What effects do these secrets have on your relationships?

5. Why is Passover an important time to host strangers at your table?

6. Is it a good idea to have a non-Jewish family come over for Passover? If you are invited to their house to experience one of their holidays, is it a good idea to go? Why? Why not?

7. Look up the word "tolerance" and the word "respect." Find examples of these in your life and the world around you. Which is better: respect or tolerance?

Sacred Story and Text Connections

1. "All of the souls were present at the making of the covenant even before their physical bodies were created…"—*Midrash Tanchuma, Nitzavim 3*

   Keep in mind that not only Israelites were enslaved in Egypt; those who fled into the desert are called "a mixed multitude—*eirev rav*" in Exodus, *Shemot* 12:38. So when did they become part of the Jewish people? When they reached Sinai and experienced the giving of the Torah, they were all welcome. And we are also told to welcome the stranger to our Passover table. If you were the stranger, how would you want to be treated?

2. A student decided to volunteer at a soup kitchen run by a local synagogue and church together. A soup kitchen provides hot meals to people who do not have sufficient funds or well being to make meals for themselves. The student became very worried as her first day of service approached. She asked, "How will I know what to say when they arrive?" "Well," said her rabbi, "what are you thinking of saying?" "Oh, I'll ask them how they got into such trouble and what kind of work they used to do, and what music they like and…" "Hmm," the rabbi replied. "Now imagine that you are the hands of God and that the doorbell just rang at the soup kitchen and you go to answer it. What will you say?" The student closed her eyes and imaged the *Shechinah*, the feminine presence of God slipping on her like a pair of gloves. "I would open the door and say, 'Welcome! We are so glad you are here. There is a hot meal line right over there on the right side of the room. Welcome!'"

Which answer do you prefer in this story?

Project: Become involved in planning the details of your Passover meal, and in the cooking and other preparations for the *seder*, such as creating your own family *haggadah* by inserting illustrations, readings, songs, plays, and other things that you create or find. Ask about inviting someone who has no *seder* to attend and make them welcome.

Project: Add to the generations present by signing your family up to attend and help out at a *seder* at a residence for the aged. Help serve, give the elderly residents your loving attention and whole-hearted participation. During the *maggid* section, where the story is told of leaving Egypt, whether you are at the senior residence, or at home, invite elders to share about a difficult time in their own lives and how they were able to get through. In doing this you will gain some wisdom for living, while also giving others a powerful *shema*—listening, which is also a mitzvah!

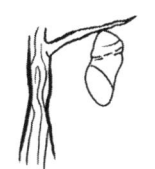

Chapter 17
Dimes for David
by Jennifer Voigt Kaplan

David dove to catch Mrs. Kohan's runaway strawberries. He missed, but somehow his knees caught every nook in the cement sidewalk. David watched the berries' insides ooze out as his fruit cart rolled over them on 165th Street in the Bronx.

"Gotcha!" screamed David's little sister Judy as she grabbed the cart before it rolled down the steep hill. The fruit in the cart was saved, but that wouldn't keep *Zayde*'s important customer happy. The handpicked strawberries were ruined.

"You're lucky I'm here today," said Judy. David and Judy's grandfather, *Zayde*, had wanted Judy to go with him so she could learn about deliveries.

Judy said, "I told you to stop eyeing that convertible. Mrs. Kohan will never give you a dime tip now."

"A dime?" David laughed. "Mrs. Kohan never tips. No, the only reason I make sure her deliveries get done right is so she won't take her business to the Adelmans. Besides, Mrs. Kohan never tips."

David noticed Larry Adelman watching from across the street. Larry yelled something David couldn't hear and then darted away. Larry helped his grandparents at the Adelman Fruit Store, which was next door to Goldberg's Fruit Store, owned by David's family.

Judy said, "You tripping is bad enough without Larry seeing! He probably called you a klutz."

"I'm sure he wasn't calling me names," David said, thinking about his old friend Larry. Last year, their grandparents had argued about who would make deliveries to the new family in the neighborhood, the Kohans. When their grandparents had stopped speaking to each other, Larry and David had stopped, too. No one had asked David to give up Larry, but he'd thought he should for his grandparents. David's *Bubbe* always said, "Family is everything. We're *mishpucha* (family)!" And *Zayde* always talked about honor. "*Kavod*," he would say as his voice turned gruff and rich.

"How can we get more strawberries?" asked David.

"Let's go back to the store and get some," suggested Judy.

"We can't. *Bubbe* picked out the best ones for Mrs. Kohan before we sold out." said David. "Maybe... Maybe we could go to the Adelman's store."

"We can't!" said Judy. "*Zayde* said that the Adelmans might put him out of business."

Judy plopped down on the sidewalk under the August sun. David could tell she didn't like being out of the store. She liked packaging fruit. And helping *Bubbe* schmooze (chat up) customers. Not making deliveries to ritzy ladies who lived on top of big hills.

David felt the rough edges of the dimes in his pocket. They were his delivery tips.

"I'll go to the Terminal Market." David said finally. That's where *Zayde* and David buy fruit in the early morning.

"I'll wait here with the cart," said Judy. "But you need to hurry! It's late and they'll sell out."

He ran so fast, the city's colors streaked together, and sweat rolled down his cheeks. The best fruit was sold at 4:00 A.M., so David wasn't sure what he'd find now.

David smiled when he smelled the market's thick, sweet air, but the smile vanished when he saw that Mr. Steinhardt was the only vendor left.

Panting, David blurted, "Strawberries, please."

Mr. Steinhardt said, "Nice to see you, David, but I just sold the last batch."

David turned to see where Mr. Steinhardt pointed. It was Larry Adelman. *Judy was right*! thought David.

"I raced here to get them!" said Larry.

David couldn't believe how Larry had turned on him. And they had once been best friends!

"Well, here you go," said Larry, and he handed David the berries.

"What..." David stuttered, feeling his cheeks burn.

"When I saw you fall, I knew you'd come here," said Larry. "I wanted to make sure they didn't sell out. I tried telling you, but I guess you didn't hear me."

"Thanks," said David. He suddenly felt like Larry was *mishpucha* (family), too.

David fished the dimes out of his pocket and handed them to Larry. He wondered what *Zayde* would think.

David said, "We need to get our grandparents talking again. I bet they don't even remember why they're fighting."

"You're right." Larry laughed. "What's the plan?"

"We'll make a plan later. I have to run."

David shook Larry's hand, and knew his grandparents could solve this problem like they did so many others. David thought maybe this was what *Zayde's kavod* really meant.

David sprinted back to meet Judy. By the time they trekked up the rest of the hill, the sun had lost some of its bite.

Mrs. Kohan swung the door open before David knocked.

"You are late," she said. She picked up the berries and frowned. "Those are not Goldberg strawberries."

Judy gasped.

"I want an explanation," said Mrs. Kohan.

David had no choice. He gulped and told Mrs. Kohan everything. The shiny convertible, the splattered strawberries, the run-away cart, and the market. He even told her he had used his dimes to pay Larry.

Mrs. Kohan smiled. She said, "The apple does not fall far from the tree. You are as honest as your grandfather."

Mrs. Kohan took out a dollar bill and handed it to David. She said, "Take your sister and Larry out for ice cream. And tell your grandfather to put the best strawberries aside for me tomorrow."

Provenance: This story is fictional, but based on family experiences. It depicts what life was like for the Jewish working class in the 1950s Bronx. The idea for this story is based on my father-in-law's childhood experiences. His grandparents' fruit store proudly served the local Jewish community in the Bronx until 1967, when emerging supermarket chains put it and many other mom-and-pop food stores out of business.

Jennifer Voigt Kaplan started her career as a management consultant and research analyst. She is now a full-time mother of three, founder and leader of a municipal public arts council, and writes children's fiction, including picture books, short stories and novels. Her middle-grade Holocaust novel, *Crushing the Red Flowers*, was awarded the 2012 Letter of Merit for the Society of Children's Book Writers & Illustrators Work-in-Progress Grant. Her stories appear under the aegis of a variety of children's magazines including *Hopscotch for Girls* and *Knowonder!* Jennifer holds degrees from the University of Pennsylvania and the London School of Economics.

Study Guide: Questions, Sources, and Projects for Reflection, Discussion, and Action

1. Which *mitzvot* are illustrated by this story? Which additional *mitzvot* can you also relate to this story?

2. Is Yiddish part of your background? Or do you have a different Jewish origin language such as Ladino, or Judaeo-Arabic? What other languages were spoken in your home? How is your Jewish culture part of your identity? How does your background enrich your cultural experience as a Jew?

3. Have you ever made a substitution like David did? Were you caught? Is this an ethical principle that you could hold onto more tightly? Do you hope others do so, as well?

Sacred Story and Text Connections

1. The sages believed there are seven types of thieves and, of these, most egregious is the one who "steals the minds" of people.—*Tosefta Baba Kama 7:3*

   What does it mean to steal someone's mind or consciousness? Can you think what the seven types of thieves might be? One example would be when a store blows an artificial aerosol scent (e.g., popcorn) out onto the sidewalk area to draw you in. The tradition's answers can be found in the *Talmud Tosefta* for *Babba Metzia* 3:15.

2. R. Jeremiah b. Abba said: Four types will not receive the presence of God (*Shechinah*): scoffers, flatterers, liars, and slanderers.—*Talmud, Sotah 42a*

   How is this true? How can a person undo this decree?

Chapter 18
The Secret Ingredient
by Alex Lazarus-Klein

Grandma Rose's Rosh Hashanah dinner was always noisy. Ten adults and eight children gathered together to celebrate the Jewish New Year in Grandma Rose's tiny Bronx apartment. There was Rose and her husband Jack, Rose's brother Lou and his wife Sussie, and Rose's four children and their spouses. And, of course, Rose's eight grandchildren, four boys and four girls, all under the age of thirteen: Sophie and Hannah, Yael and Eden, Rueben and Zev, Josh and Jacob.

Spread out on Grandma Rose's dining room table would always be a feast fit for a king and queen: the mandatory matzah ball soup, savory brisket and turkey, carrot and sweet potato tzimmis, moist noodle kugels, and brown rice and lentils for the vegetarians. And, most important, in the center of the table was Grandma Rose's Rosh Hashanah challah bread, round and fluffy, symbolizing the roundness of a new year.

The challah was important not only because of how good it tasted, but also because of who helped baked it. The night before Rosh Hashanah, all of Grandma Rose's grandchildren would gather in her apartment for a sleepover. Dressed in their multi-colored pajamas, they would carefully place the eggs and flour, yeast and water on their grandmother's kitchen table.

Listening to her instructions, they would measure the exact amount of each of the ingredients needed to make the dough. This was the messy part, and clumps of flour would end up in all of the grandchildren's hair and cheeks. Somehow, Grandma Rose would always keep herself neat, so that at the end you could never have known that she had participated at all. When they were through, they would put the dough in bowls in the refrigerator to rise.

The next morning the children would come sleepy-eyed in the kitchen to finish what they had started the night before. They would spread out puffs of flour and then roll the dough into long snake-like pieces. Then they would wind these snakes of dough into perfect circles ready for the oven. When they were finally ready to bake the challah, Grandma Rose would stop and look around.

"Did we forget anything?" she would say, almost absent-mindedly.

Her grandchildren would look at each other smiling, knowing exactly what was coming next.

"I think we forgot the secret ingredient," Grandma Rose would say.

"What could that be, Grandma?" her grandchildren would say. Then they would turn to each other and mouth the word, *love*, silently to one another.

Grandma Rose would open the oven, and a warm burst of air would fill the room. As the challahs baked the next few hours, everyone would play quiet games, savoring the joy of each other's company.

***

One year Grandma Rose was in the hospital before Rosh Hashanah and was not able to prepare the customary meal. All the adults and children gathered together for a family meeting to decide what they should do. Everyone agreed right away that they would have the meal exactly in the same place they always did. After all, what was Rosh Hashanah if it wasn't at Grandma Rose's apartment! They then divided up all of the different items needed for the meal.

Everything went smoothly until they got to the challah. None of the adults knew the recipe, or felt brave enough to improvise. While the adults were looking down, all of the children popped up their heads and said in unison, "We know the recipe. We can make the challah."

So, just like in other years, they all came for a sleepover in their grandparent's apartment. Grandpa Jack tried his best to keep them in order, but he was tired from the long nights caring for his wife. He finally just collapsed on the couch snoring.

The older kids, Shai and Sophie, began giving out instructions and taking out the necessary ingredients. They tried to do it exactly as Grandma would have done, but something seemed wrong. The children began fighting with one another about what they should do next. Shai said one thing, Sophie another, Hannah another thing altogether, all the way down to tiny Eden, who, at five, was just old enough to voice her own opinion. After a half-hour they were all screaming at each other, and the kitchen was a mess.

They went to sleep miserable, but woke up the next morning determined to continue the work. Unfortunately, when they looked in the refrigerator, the dough had not risen properly. They spread the flour and tried their best to roll it, but it was too sticky and did not have the usual consistency. When it came time to put the challahs in the oven, they looked like big blobs of dough, very different than the perfect circles they usually had. And, of course, they left the challah in for too long, so it came out as black as the inside of the oven.

By the time of the Rosh Hashanah meal, the children could barely look at one another, each of them blaming one of the others for what had transpired. They dreaded the moment when the challah would be uncovered, and their sins would be revealed.

Other than Grandma Rose not being there, everything seemed just about right. The same types of foods, the same smells, but there was an emptiness that filled the room. The usual banter between family members was absent, and it was clear that Grandma Rose was dearly missed.

After blessing the wine, everyone huddled off into the kitchen to fulfill the ritual washing of hands. Eden was assigned the duty of blessing the challah, and she tried to do it with as much spirit as possible. But, even her cheerful voice was swallowed by the sadness shown on everyone's faces.

"How can we call this is a challah!" they all seemed to say, when Eden finally took off the challah cover she had made for Grandma Rose the year before. After the blessing, all the children pointed at each other as the child most responsible for what had happened. The adults sat speechless, trying their best to chew and swallow the dry, tasteless bread.

Suddenly, Grandpa Jack cried, "Shah! Stop eating, at once!"

Everyone turned to him, stunned that he had spoke up.

"We need to save this challah. We obviously can't eat it. I think I have the perfect use for it tomorrow."

No one knew what he was talking about, but following his order, they quickly gathered together all of the pieces of challah and put them into a plastic bag.

The next day after services, Grandpa Jack had all of his grandchildren follow him to a nearby park, where a creek ran quietly behind the trees. There he opened the bag and had each of them take a handful of the dry, burnt crusts of challah.

"On Rosh Hashanah," he said, "challah is not just for eating. We also use it to rid ourselves of all the bad feelings we have about each other. We do this in a ceremony called *Tashlich*. I want you to take your pieces of bread and drop them in the water. As you do, try hard to let go of whatever bad feelings you have, so that you can start the new year fresh."

One by one, the children went to the creek and tried to follow Grandpa Jack's instructions. As they did, they quickly realized what they had forgotten in baking the challah.

Turning to one another they mouthed the words, "I'm sorry," and then, "I love you."

***

The next year, Grandma Rose was well enough to prepare the meal again. But, this time when her grandchildren gathered at her apartment, they had a new task. Not only were they going to make the challah that would serve as the centerpiece for their Rosh Hashanah meal, but they also were going to make the bread for *Tashlich*. This did not have to be made out of perfect dough, with the perfect consistency. They had fun poking and prodding the selection of dough marked for *Tashlich* in a way they would never have done for the main challah.

In the morning, after they had formed the dough into two separate challahs, they put the *Tashlich* challah in the oven first. And, before putting in the second challah, Grandma looked around and said, "I think we forgot the secret ingredient."

"What is it Grandma?" her grandchildren asked in unison. Then they turned to each other and mouthed the word, love, silently to each other. Grandma Rose opened the oven, and a warm burst of air filled the room. And as the challahs baked, everyone played quiet games, savoring the joy of each other's company.

Note: Bird and fish food have proven to be healthier than bread crumbs for wildlife found in and around water and so are preferable for casting in Tashlikh *rituals. Tashlich typically involves finding something about yourself or your life that you feel needs changing—to be released or transformed. Imagine embedding this awareness into something for the fish to eat and then cast it away from you into living waters.*

Alex Lazarus-Klein is a storyteller, author, chaplain, and rabbi, ordained by the Reconstructionist Rabbinical College. He currently serves Congregation Shir Shalom in Amherst, New York, where he lives with his wife and three young children. Alex holds a master's degree from the Jewish Theological Seminary. He has also served as rabbi of Temple B´nai Abraham in Bordentown, New Jersey, and directed the Community Partnership Program for the Jewish Federation of Greater Philadelphia. He currently serves as the president of the Network of Religious Communities of Western New York.

Study Guide: Questions, Sources, and Projects for Reflection, Discussion, and Action

1. Which *mitzvot* are illustrated by this story? Which additional *mitzvot* can you also relate to this story?

2. Do you have family memories from Rosh Hashanah and other holy days? What makes these memories so special?

3. What activities do you do as a family that have become traditions?

4. Is there an important difference between doing a mitzvah or prayer "by the book" and doing it with love?

5. How does the tradition of making challah affect the family? Would it be the same eating it at Rosh Hashanah if they just bought the challah at a store?

6. On holy days the challah is shaped like a spiral—what might that symbolize? And on *Shabbat* challah is braided—what might that symbolize about the importance of having family, community, and connection?

7. How did this family interpret the ritual of *Tashlich*? What does it mean to you?

8. At *Taschlich*, we cast our bad feelings, experiences, and behaviors into moving water so that they may be washed away from us and we can begin the New Year afresh, but we don't have to wait until Rosh Hashanah to do this. When, and in what other ways, can we put aside those feelings and behaviors and start again?

Sacred Story and Text Connections

1. The word challah is said to come from the word *chol*, meaning "everyday or common." Just as matzah isn't intended to be eaten when it isn't Passover, challah isn't intended to be eaten when it isn't *Shabbat*. Why is that? How do these foods help to turn a common day into a hol(y)day?

2. "…It shall be that when you eat the bread of the land, you shall set aside a portion [of dough] for God."—Numbers, *Bamidbar*, 15:17-21

In antiquity, the Israelites would go to the Temple bringing offerings of gratitude, atonement, and celebration (of births, holidays, etc.). Some of what was brought would be burnt as a sacrifice; most went to feed the *Cohanim* (priests), Levites (temple workers) and their families. As a way of remembering our history and how Judaism has evolved from using burnt sacrifices to communicate with God to using words and *mitzvot*, Jews continue to practice the mitzvah of *hafrashat challah* when a large quantity of challah is being made, breaking off a small piece of the dough, wrapping it in foil, and fulfilling the mitzvah by deliberately burning it to a black crisp.

a. In some families those kneading the dough will pray for their families, for our people, for the peaceful restoration of the Temple, or for anyone who is in need. Who would you pray for, if doing this right now? How might such a prayer practice affect you and others?

b. Why is *hafrashat challah* done only for a large quantity of challah (5 pounds/2.2 kilo of flour according to Ashkenazi custom, or 4 pounds/ 1.8 kilo according to Sephardic custom)? This blessing is said before removing the piece of dough:

Baruch ata Adonai, Eloheinu melech ha-olam, asher kidishanu b'mitzvo'tav, v'tzivanu l'hafrish challah min ha-issa.

Blessed are You God, Ruler of the Universe, for making us holy through *mitzvot*, instructing us to separate [a bit of] "challah offering" from the dough.

Project: Learn to bake challah. Work as a family, school, or community team and remember to include the special ingredient from our story. What happens to the quality of spirit in your home or school by doing this?

Project: In some communities, volunteers bring over to new members' homes a welcome packet, *Shabbat* candles and a freshly baked challah on a Friday before sundown. What other times, and types of people and situations, might also be appropriate for challah delivery?

Chapter 19
Treasure from Grandpa
by Melissa Klein

Grandpa's heart stopped while he was sleeping, and he didn't wake up the next morning. Jacob was in third grade. He and Mom drove the two-hour trip to Chicago barely talking, with the radio off. Mom had yelled a few times while they were packing their clothes and getting ready to go, and Jacob knew that it was best not to ask her to turn on the Lemony Snicket music he had checked out from the library the day before. He mostly looked out the window and played the alphabet game, finding each of the letters of the alphabet in order on signs and billboards and license plates. He got through the alphabet sixteen times.

They arrived at Grandma and Grandpa's apartment, and Grandma looked at Jacob with tear-filled eyes and pulled him to her warm, soft body and held him tight.

"I'm so glad you're here, Jakey," she said as she kissed him gently on the top of his head.

Jacob loved her soft kisses and the smell of his favorite chocolate chip cookies, which she always baked for him when he came to visit. There was no sweet smell of cookies baking today.

"He wasn't supposed to go first," Grandma said to Mom, shaking her head, before she let go of Jacob.

Jacob drove with Grandma and Mom and Uncle Fred to the cemetery in a black limousine. When they got there, he saw a group of men lifting Grandpa's wooden casket out of the back of another limousine and carrying it to the spot where a metal contraption with big fabric straps was covering a big rectangular hole. There was a big pile of dirt next to the hole and Jacob secretly wished that he could jump down into it. He wondered what it would feel like to be down there and whether he could climb out without help.

When everybody was gathered around, the rabbi started chanting the sad melody that Jacob recognized from *Shabbat* afternoon gatherings back home. Mom had explained that we chant a sad melody on Saturday afternoons because we're sad that *Shabbat* will be leaving soon. Hearing the familiar melody helped Jacob to relax a little and feel his sadness about Grandpa dying, and he hummed along with the rabbi.

The rabbi then invited Uncle Fred and Mom to talk about Grandpa. Jacob mostly watched the birds flying overhead as the adults talked and cried. He did perk up when Mom spoke about how happy Grandpa was the day Jacob was born.

"I have never seen my Dad happier or more hopeful than the moment he took his newborn grandson into his arms, ever so gently, and gave him a kiss."

The rabbi then invited everyone to recite some Hebrew words after her: "*al m'komo yavo v'shalom.*" Jacob repeated the rabbi's words as best he could.

One of the men who worked at the cemetery, who looked stronger than any man Jacob had ever seen, started rotating the metal rods, and Grandpa's casket slowly descended down into the hole. After the casket was lowered, Jacob waited his turn and shoveled some dirt onto the casket. He wondered whether Grandpa could breathe in there. He liked the sound of the thud as the dirt landed on the wood, so he took a second shovelful. Then Uncle Fred helped him place the shovel back into the dirt pile facing backwards.

Everyone who wasn't from the family lined up in two rows, and Grandma, Uncle Fred, Mom, and Jacob walked down the middle back to the limousine. The adults stopped to get hugs, and Jacob tried to keep his body behind Mom's because he didn't want the hugs.

After the burial, everyone returned to the apartment.

"Can I still call this Grandma and Grandpa's apartment?" Jacob wondered. He poured some water over each hand before he went inside, just like the woman in front of him. He wanted to ask what this was for but felt too shy to ask. A stranger came up close to Jacob and told him that everything was going to be okay, but he could tell that she didn't really mean it from the way her eyes darted around.

Jacob ate four of the butter cookies with rainbow sprinkles that cousins whom he had never met brought on the plane from a bakery in New York City. Nobody seemed to care that he was having more than two.

Jacob found Mom and pulled at her arm, and when he finally got her attention, begged, "Mommy, can we please go home now?"

She looked at him with sad, distant eyes, and said, "Not now, sweet boy, not now."

Jacob felt confused. He wanted to scream or slam a door or at least jump on and off the couch, which always made him feel better, but the room was too crowded for that. He went into the bedroom to be alone and started playing with Grandpa's radio. He wanted a bear hug from Grandpa. The bear hugs were always a little too tight for Jacob, but that didn't matter now.

Jacob sat down in the straight-back chair where Grandpa put on his sneakers before they went out on their monthly visits to the Art Institute of Chicago. Grandpa walked a little funny, leaning to the right before bringing forward his left leg, but he had no problem keeping up with Jacob. Grandpa did sometimes want to stay longer than Jacob did in front of a particular painting—his favorite was Sunday on La Grande Jatte by Georges Seurat—and Jacob would get bored and didn't understand what was so interesting about lots of people standing and sitting by a river, but that didn't matter now.

Jacob went into Grandpa's bathroom to explore, and he wet the Ivory soap and rubbed the shaving brush into it and covered his face with lather. Mom found Jacob in the bathroom and helped him wipe the soap beard off his face. She led him back to the chair and wrapped her arms around him, and they both cried.

At Jacob's next visit to Grandma a few weeks later, he asked her to give him a treasure from Grandpa. He wanted something special for his treasure drawer. Jacob's treasure drawer, the bottom drawer of the big wooden dresser in his room, was filled with all sorts of things: buttons, broken necklaces, the gold-filled pen from Mom's Bat Mitzvah, seashells from the beach, the lucky turtle coin from their vacation to Maine, tags from favorite toys, colorful scraps of cloth, bouncy balls, and many other treasures he had collected since he was about four.

Grandma asked, "Do you want to look through Grandpa's treasure drawer?"

Jacob had not realized that Grandpa had also had a treasure drawer, and he was delighted by this invitation to explore. Grandma brought in the step stool from the kitchen so Jacob could get a good view of the contents of the top drawer of Grandpa's dresser.

Jacob searched first with his eyes and then with his hands, and he found pennies and dimes, and even a 120-year-old silver dollar with the picture of a woman in a long flowing robe. He found the small, green and orange rubber dragon that Grandpa used to let him play with. He found brown shoelaces and two tape measures. Jacob began to make a pile on the bed of the treasures to take home: a wind-up watch with a worn leather band, a small spiral notebook with Grandpa's record of how much he paid for gas each time he filled up his car from 1975-1979, a bronze belt buckle from Jerusalem that said "*Shalom*" in Hebrew letters, which Jacob was proud to be able to read.

Grandma interrupted Jacob's search to tell him that lunch was ready, and she said, after a loud sigh, to nobody in particular, "He couldn't part with anything."

Grandma spent many hours that year sorting through Grandpa's things. She had no desire to work with tools, so she gave all the tools to the building's maintenance man, Frank, who was always cheerful and helpful and who she knew would find a good use for them. Jacob got mad that she wasn't saving the tools for him. Mom reassured him that they had the tools they needed at home, and anyway, they didn't have space to store them.

Jacob continued to collect treasures from Grandpa on his visits. He usually chose items that could fit in his drawer; however, he was able to convince Mom to let him take the old movie camera from the 1970's that had once been Grandpa's pride and joy. He'd used it to take videos of Mom and Uncle Fred when they were little. The camera didn't work anymore, but Jacob was happy pretending that it did.

The years passed, and Jacob spent less time collecting objects for his treasure drawer and more time acting and practicing piano and learning to edit his own videos on the computer. He missed his grandfather dearly, particularly when he went to an art museum. He would linger in front of each painting, the way Grandpa used to, as a way to feel that Grandpa was there, and he began to enjoy staying with a painting and really looking at it. He wished Grandpa were there to talk about what he saw.

The Friday night before Jacob's Bar Mitzvah, after the relatives had all gone to their hotels, Mom handed Jacob an almond-white envelope with gold trim that read, in Grandpa's handwriting, "To my grandson, Jacob, to be opened on the occasion of your Bar Mitzvah."

Jacob wondered what was inside. Mom looked at him expectantly, as if she were waiting for Jacob to open the letter and share it with her, but he decided to wait and open it when he was alone. He brought it to his bedroom and placed it on his nightstand as he got into pajamas.

"What did Grandpa write to me?" he wondered. He had last spoken to Grandpa when he was just eight years old. "How amazing that Grandpa wrote this letter to me and that Mom kept it a secret all these years," he thought.

After brushing his teeth, he climbed into bed and carefully opened the letter with the carved wood letter opener from his treasure drawer. He read the letter and cried a lot, and as he was reaching for a tissue, he got an idea.

The next morning, when it was time for Jacob to deliver his Bar Mitzvah speech, he slowly climbed the stairs up to the bimah (platform), holding the gold-trimmed envelope in his left hand. He was less nervous than he had expected he'd be, though his hands were a little clammy. Jacob smiled, knowing that he didn't have to stand on the stool behind the reading table like his mother did, as he was already six inches taller than her. When he had positioned himself behind the reading table, facing the community, Jacob scanned his eyes across the sanctuary to take in the smiles of all his friends and family. He then began to speak:

"I wrote a list of thank you's to begin my Bar Mitzvah speech, and I do appreciate all of you being here, but I have to start with something else. My Grandpa died suddenly when I was eight. We never said good-bye. We've all missed him a lot, and I know that Mom and Grandma are especially sad that he's not here today. I want you all to know that he may not still be alive, but he's still here with us. He wrote me this letter, which I just read last night, and I want to share it with all of you—

My Dear Grandson Jacob,

You are a source of great joy for me. The moment you were born, I felt hope and joy and a sense of wholeness in my life. I don't know how long I will be alive—I hope it's long enough to celebrate at your Bar Mitzvah—and I am comforted knowing that you, Jacob, a boy who is so full of love and light, are carrying on our family traditions.

Your mommy has been encouraging me to write this letter to you, and I am finally sitting down to do it. She wanted me to tell you about my values—what has been important to me as I have lived my life.

Here's what I have to say:

1. Put family first. They may not always be nice to you, they may get on your nerves, but they are your family. Stay connected to them. Celebrate with them. Show up.
2. Be generous with your time and money. Notice what help other people need. Do what you can. That's why God put us here—to be helpful to each other.
3. Let other people help you. I'm not always good at this one. I can be stubborn, especially with your Grandma. But things go much better when I let her help me out.
4. Read to learn. I didn't have books in my house growing up. That may surprise you, given how many books are in our home now, but my parents were poor immigrants, and they did not read. My father worked all day in a factory, and my mother could not read English. I'm so proud of you that you're learning to read. Let this open up worlds to you!
5. Be honest. Tell the truth, even when it's hard to do, but make sure to find a nice way to do it.
6. Forgive: forgive yourself for the mistakes you make and forgive others, too. None of us is perfect. God created us with the ability to be patient with each other and to forgive each other's mistakes.
7. Be loyal. Grandma and I have been married for forty years. We don't always get along, don't always agree, but we do love each other, and we take care of each other.
8. Exercise! I played squash for many years and now do yoga and tai chi. It's really important to stretch and move and take care of your body.
9. Go to museums and get to know the paintings. They will become your

friends and will tell you their secrets.
10. Celebrate your Judaism. Celebrate the Jewish holidays, light candles on Friday nights, invite family and friends over for Seder, learn Hebrew, study in Israel. Celebrate who you are while also being open to learning about others.

> I bless you, my dear grandson, with a life of learning and joy (laughing at yourself when you make mistakes), a life of health and loving relationships, a life of meaningful work, and a life of connection to the Holy One. *Mazel tov* on your Bar Mitzvah!
>
> Love,
>   Grandpa

There was not a dry eye in the sanctuary as Jacob finished reading the letter from Grandpa. Jacob was not yet ready to move back to the script of his Bar Mitzvah speech. He continued: "I loved collecting treasures from my Grandpa after he died. But by far, this letter was the best treasure he left me. This letter helps me to know what was important to him, which helps me to think about what's important to me. This letter tells me how much my Grandpa loved me. Thank you, Mom, for asking Grandpa to write this letter to me. I think it's time for everybody here to go home and write one of these letters."

Jacob smiled. He looked up and sensed that Grandpa was smiling too.

Provenance: One of my callings is helping to facilitate the writing of ethical wills (also called a spiritual will), and I have been struck by how many people say, "what a wonderful idea" and yet don't get around to writing theirs. Both of my mother's parents died suddenly, without the opportunity to say good-bye, and my hope is that this story will offer an extra nudge to those who have been contemplating writing their ethical/spiritual will. Even in our modern era that tends to devalue elders, the wisdom of the elders really does matter to the children and grandchildren. We live on through our values. The ethical/spiritual will is an offering of love to those most important to us. May we all be blessed with ever-opening channels of love within our family systems.

Melissa Klein facilitates spiritual writing groups, serves as a *mashpi'ah* (Jewish spiritual director), and leads rituals and healing services. She is an activist working on raising awareness around climate sustainability and mass incarceration. Melissa graduated Harvard University with a degree in chemistry and physics and received rabbinical ordination from the Reconstructionist Rabbinical College. She served as spiritual leader of Congregation Am Haskalah in Allentown, PA, for seven years. Melissa and her family presently reside in Philadelphia, Pennsylvania.

Study Guide: Questions, Sources, and Projects for Reflection, Discussion, and Action

1. Which *mitzvot* are illustrated by this story? Which additional *mitzvot* can you also relate to this story?

2. Has one of your relatives died? Did you want to be part of the funeral and *shiva*? How does Jake help his grandmother just by being there during these times? Does it seem important for him?

3. Which relatives and friends that you don't get to see often are you looking forward to seeing the next time there is a death in the family? What does it mean to the mourners when you are there at a funeral or *shiva* in their family?

4. Type out the letter from the grandfather and change each instruction into a blessing. How are these different approaches and how do they feel to you?

5. Write a blessing for a grandparent, or another close relative, and share it with this person. What effect does your giving someone a blessing seem to have?

6. Is there something that belongs to your grandparents that you would cherish having after they die, as a part of how you remember them and that you will commit to pass on through the generations? What would be a loving way to let them know?

Sacred Stories and Text Connections

Open a *Chumash* (The Five Books of Moses) to Genesis Chapter 49. Here you will read of Jacob, at the end of his life, blessing his twelve sons by summarizing a key issue or characteristic affecting each and predicting some of the implications.

   a. Jake's grandmother comments that her husband "couldn't part with anything". How is the story's author paralleling Chapter 49 by sharing this? Do people only leave us with positive memories?

   b. Why did the author of our mitzvah story name the grandson Jake?

Project: The grandfather's letter is similar to a Jewish practice known as an ethical or spiritual will. In such a document, you write down what you love and are concerned about for the people you are leaving when you die. In an ethical will, you also describe the values that you hope will support them as they grow and carry on after you. Parent(s) or guardian(s) and children: Discuss or begin to jot down an ethical will of your own, then compare and contrast one of the points you choose to make from your current vantage point in life.

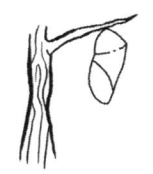

Chapter 20
Where's Derek Ericks?
by Geri Kolesar

Gabby and Max always agreed.

Except when they didn't.

"See, I told you. We don't have a new kid in our class," Max said, sticking his nose in Gabby's face.

"But I heard Mrs. Sirkin say she was going to introduce Derek Ericks today. I bet she's coming later," Gabby said right back in Max's face.

"She? Whoever heard of a girl named 'Derek', anyway?" Max held his head high. Gabby didn't like when he did that.

"Well, even if it's a boy, I'm getting ready," Gabby said, putting her hands on her hips.

Max didn't like when she did that. But Gabby was usually right, and so Max decided to get ready, too.

Gabby straightened her cubby so Derek would have a place to put *her* things.

Max sorted his markers into two piles so Derek could color *his* pictures.

Gabby wiped off the table so Derek would have a clean place to eat *her* lunch.

Max organized the coat rack so Derek could hang *his* jacket.

Gabby colored a special picture so Derek would feel welcome when *she* arrived.

Max pulled up an extra chair for Derek so *he* would have a place to sit.

Then Mrs. Sirkin said it was snack time, and she passed out yummy *hamantaschen*.

Gabby broke her cookie in half. She wrapped the bigger piece in a napkin to save for Derek.

Max picked up his cookie and licked his lips.

"There's no room for Derek. Move over," Gabby said, nudging Max's shoulder.

Max's *hamantaschen* tumbled to the floor.

"I'm sorry," Gabby whispered, but Max didn't hear. He was too busy staring at his broken cookie.

Gabby got the broom, and they swept up the crumbs. When they sat down again, Gabby took her half-cookie and slid it toward Max. She made a crinkly-nose smile.

Max loved when she did that. He gobbled up the cookie and winked at Gabby.

Gabby loved when he did that.

Then, finally, Mrs. Sirkin asked if anyone knew about Derek Ericks!

Max and Gabby raised their hands high in the air.

"Max thinks it's a boy," Gabby said.

"Gabby thinks it's a girl," Max said.

"Well," said Mrs. Sirkin, "you are both right."

Gabby looked at Max, and Max looked at Gabby. How could Derek Ericks be both a boy *and* a girl?

"And," Mrs. Sirkin continued, "we are lucky to have a lot in this classroom."

Gabby and Max looked at each other again. How could there be a lot of Derek Erickses in the classroom when they didn't see even one?

"But where *is* Derek Ericks?" Gabby and Max asked at the same time.

"Over here," Mrs. Sirkin said, walking across the room to the table Gabby had cleaned.

Gabby peeked underneath. No Derek Ericks.

"And over here," Mrs. Sirkin said, standing near the coat rack.

Max looked under the jackets he had straightened. No Derek Ericks.

"And over here," said Mrs. Sirkin.

There was a clean cubby. But still no Derek Ericks.

"And right here," Mrs. Sirkin said, putting her arms around Gabby and Max.

"Our names aren't Derek!" cried Gabby.

"True, but you have both done a great job of introducing us to the important Jewish value of respect and good manners. And it has a special name," Mrs. Sirkin said, as she wrote some words on the board.

Gabby and Max sounded out the Hebrew letters: ארץ דרך. Max looked at Gabby, and Gabby looked at Max.

Together they said, "*Derekh eretz!*"

And then they smiled at each other.

Mrs. Sirkin loved when they did that.

Geri Kolesar taught environmental education in Maine, worked for a U.S. Senator on Capitol Hill, and practiced law in Manhattan before moving to Cincinnati, where she now lives with her husband and three children. She has cultivated creative ways of bringing the joys of Judaism to secular classrooms and is an active member of the Isaac M. Wise Temple Board of Trustees. Her writing has been published in a variety of periodicals, including *Highlights Magazine*. Geri has earned a JD from Georgetown University Law Center, an MS from the University of New Hampshire in Natural and Environmental Resources and a BA in Social Work from the University of Wisconsin.

Study Guide: Questions, Sources, and Projects for Reflection, Discussion, and Action

1. Which *mitzvot* are illustrated by this story? Which additional *mitzvot* can you also relate to this story?

2. What is it like to be the new person in a group, school, or camp?

3. What kinds of things did the children do to prepare for "Derek Ericks"? It is a mitzvah to beautify or enrich another mitzvah. This practice is called *hiddur mitzvah*. What might you do that you haven't done before to make a new classmate feel welcome?

4. Why is kind and generous behavior toward strangers so important? Have you experienced this from others? Have you shown this toward others? How?

5. What are some examples of behaving with "good character?" Make a list of things you can do to be kind and helpful to your family and friends.

6. *Derekh eretz* refers to respect and good manners; it literally means the "way of the land"—the pathway of healthy human connection. Can you see a place where this is missing in your life?

Sacred Story and Text Connections

1. Open a *Chumash* (The Five Books of Moses) to Genesis, *Bereishit* 18:1-8. What are the elements of hospitality in Abraham's tent? What cultures share these practices today? What are the elements of hospitality you want to be known for in your life, home, dorm room, bunk, or classroom?

2. The phrase *derekh eretz* is originally found in *Ethics of the Ancestors, Pirkei Avot*, 2:2. Look up three different English versions of this verse either on-line or in a Jewish library. Compare the three versions. What are the differences? Which is most meaningful to you? Would you say each one is a translation or an interpretation? What is the difference? Create and share your own version as a family, class or group, based on the discussion so far and if you are able, working from the original Hebrew. What interpretation comes through you? How does this exercise fulfill the spiritual intent of this very chapter of *Pirkei Avot*?

3. Torah often has metaphors that help us picture an idea in a way that makes it easier to understand and appreciate. Look for the term *derech hashemesh*, "sunset road," in Deuteronomy, *Devarim* 11:29-30. How does this phrase in its context connect to the concept of *derekh eretz* in our story?

   Notice how the *derekh*, road, is a metaphor for the journey called life, just as the term *halachah*, often translated as "Jewish law" or "pathway," also means the ever-evolving process of updating Judaism for ever-changing times. "Walking the talk" of Jewish practice, i.e., living our path, is also a mitzvah, which you can find in Deuteronomy, *Devarim* 26:17.

4. "You shall love the stranger for you were a stranger in the land of Egypt."—Deuteronomy, *Devarim* 10:19.

Project: Meet to create and implement a class, bunk, or youth group welcome plan for someone new joining you.

"…My house shall be a house of prayer for all peoples."—Isaiah 56:7

Project: Has a new temple, mosque, church, or meetinghouse recently opened in your community? Create a plan to welcome and begin to create a healthy community relationship with your new neighbors.

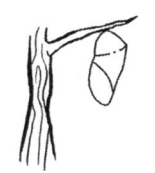

Chapter 21
Adira's Pocketbook
by Janet Madden

What Adira Silverblatt's seven grandchildren remembered most about their grandmother was her pocketbook. Whenever their grandmother came to their homes or they came to hers for *Shabbat*, she asked them to help her by carrying her very large pocketbook to the kitchen table. It was so heavy that every child in the family had to pitch in to help because it was almost impossible for only one child to carry it. As the children struggled to carry the pocketbook and lift it onto the table, they were reminded that this was no ordinary pocketbook: this was her *tzedakah* pocketbook.

Adira told her grandchildren that she needed their help with something very important in Jewish families—helping her to decide what to do with the treasure her pocketbook contained. When the children eagerly opened her very large and heavy pocketbook, they could see that it was, indeed, filled to the brim with treasure—quarters, dimes, nickels, and pennies. With one last struggle, the children spilled the pocketbook's contents onto the table. Their grandmother helped them sort the heap of coins into piles and count them. Then they rolled up the piles of coins in paper sleeves, returned any extra coins to the bottom of the pocketbook, and counted up the total amount of money. Finally, before sitting down to *Shabbat* dinner, the family decided together where to give the treasure that was now transformed into the mitzvah of *tzedakah*.

As the grandchildren grew older, the pocketbook was easier to carry and lift, and the coins could be sorted and counted and rolled much faster. The grandchildren discovered that when their grandmother's friends came to her home, they reached into their pockets and pocketbooks and contributed to the *tzedakah* pocketbook. The children's parents kept a *tzedakah* jar into which parents and children put change all week long. On Fridays, when they gathered together for *Shabbat* dinner, the grandchildren added the pennies, nickels, dimes, and quarters that they had put aside during the week to the coins in the *tzedakah* pocketbook.

When they were all grown up, Adira's grandchildren often talked about the hours they had spent with their grandmother learning about the power of *tzedakah*. They agreed that they would never forget what she had taught them. They understood that the value of the *tzedakah* pocketbook was not the amount of *tzedakah* that their family had given over the years but the example that their grandmother had given them of how *tzedakah* enriches the lives of those who perform it.

Provenance: As a hospice rabbi, one of the ways that I serve my patients and their families is by engaging with them in the holy activity of telling their stories. Most of the dying people I work with want to tell the stories of their lives—with very little prompting, they talk about their childhood memories, about falling in love, about when their own children were small, about their passions, their achievements, their failures, their hopes, and their fears and what they hope their legacy will be. As I get to know the children of my patients, they talk with me about their parents and tell me stories about their own lives. They share their sadness about their parents' approaching deaths, their memories of growing up with their parents, the lessons that their parents taught them and how proud their parents are of their grandchildren.

The opportunity to share grandchildren's stories most often happens when I am asked to officiate at a funeral. Then, as I sit with the family in the aftermath of death, I am privileged to see how it truly is possible to make a life into a blessing. The story that Adira Silverblatt's grandchildren told me is one of the greatest examples of how an adult can lovingly teach a mitzvah that will be a lesson in holiness that is passed from generation to generation.

Janet Madden earned her Ph. D. in Literature from The National University of Ireland and her rabbinic ordination from The Academy for Jewish Religion-CA. A four-time fellowship recipient of the National Endowment for the Humanities, she has published in areas that range from 19th century fiction to Jewish lifecycles. A spiritual director, GreenFaith Fellow, and graduate of Kol Zimra, she has served as rabbi to the Progressive Jewish community in Poland. Currently working on a book-length study of *Perek Shira*, Janet is Rabbi of Temple Havurat Emet, Visiting Rabbi of Saint John's Health Center, and Rabbi/Chaplain at Skirball Hospice.

Study Guide: Questions, Sources, and Projects for Reflection, Discussion, and Action

1. Which *mitzvot* are illustrated by this story? Which additional *mitzvot* can you also relate to this story?

2. Why is *tzedakah* a mitzvah?

3. Why does the author remind us that *tzedakah* enriches the lives of those who perform it?

4. What other *mitzvot* have you learned from your parents and grandparents?

Sacred Story and Text Connections

1. If there is poor person among you… within any of the gates in your land…do not harden your heart, nor close your hand to your impoverished [ones].
   —Deuteronomy, *Devarim* 15:7

2. A teacher of Torah and Jewish spiritual practices was rushing to catch a train to the airport. She was pulling two suitcases full of clothes (to wear and give away), and program supplies, and she also had a knapsack on her back and front. She came upon a beggar, an old woman to whom she would always give a subway token, and apologized for not having time to stop. "Where are you going?" asked the woman. "To teach a mother-daughter retreat in the Ukraine where it has only just become permissible to practice Judaism in the wake of the collapse of the Soviet Union and disbanding of laws that disallowed the practice of any religion there." "Oh my!" responded the woman, as she unwrapped a bandana tied to her wrist. "The people over there are so very poor. I, too, want to help them." And she took her begging bowl and emptied the coins and bills into the bandana, tied it in a knot, and placed it into the teacher's coat pocket. "Take this to them for me, please." All the way to the airport the teacher cried.

   How does this story affect you? What ideas do you take from it? Why do you imagine the teacher cried?

Project: In class, camp, a youth group, or perhaps during *Sukkot* or Hanukkah when it is not *Shabbat*, have friends and family gather with newspaper clippings about causes that need support. Also have them bring their *tzedakah* boxes. This is for coins and bills designated for charity. It is traditional to have such a box easily accessible in a Jewish home. Open and pool the funds contained in the *tzedakah* boxes with everyone present. Share stories about the causes you discover and select which to support from these funds.

Chapter 22
Painting
by Cindy Marshall

At first, I was jealous of Sophie. I went over to her house for a play date, and her grandma was there. I found out her grandma wasn't just visiting—she lived with them.

"Sophie's grandma is an artist—a painter! She has all this cool stuff," I told my dad later. "Why do my grandparents have to live so far away? We only see them a few times a year."

"I know, Avi," my dad said. "I wish we lived closer. But, you can Skype…"

"That's not the same," I pouted.

Sophie's grandma had all of her paints set up in their basement. She let us go down there after school. She didn't paint stuff that you can recognize, like people or houses, just these big blotches of bright colors. She said it's all right to get messy. She gave me and Sophie and Sophie's little brother, Daniel, some big paper so we could paint, too. It was awesome! So I thought Sophie and Daniel were really lucky.

That was before their grandma got sick.

One night I heard my dad on the phone talking to Sophie's mom. Then I heard my parents talking. It was something about cancer. It sounded pretty bad.

I was supposed to go over to Sophie's later that week, but I told my parents, "I don't want to go. I don't want to catch the cancer."

"Oh, honey, cancer is not contagious," my dad said.

"Well, I don't want to catch the sadness," I said.

"Avi, why don't we invite Sophie over to our house for the next few play dates?" suggested my dad. "It will help out her family anyway."

So Sophie came over and we played and everything was just regular.

A few weeks later we gave Sophie a ride home from Hebrew School. When we pulled up in front of her house, I noticed a man helping Sophie's grandma get out of another car.

"Doesn't he go to our temple?" I asked my dad. "He looks familiar."

"Yes, I think he does," my dad said.

"Is he a friend of yours?" I asked Sophie.

Sophie shrugged. "A lot of people from our temple have been helping us out with rides, and bringing over food," she explained.

After Sophie got out of the car, I said to my dad, "Maybe we should make some food for them, too."

"That's a really nice idea, Avi."

That Sunday I helped my parents make two big pans of lasagna, one for us and one for Sophie's family. Then we brought it over to their house.

Sophie's mom was grateful. "This looks delicious! And now I can spend time with my mom instead of cooking. Thanks so much."

"Can you stay and play for a while?" Sophie asked.

"Yeah," Daniel chimed in, "can you?"

My dad nodded that it was all right. "Okay, I guess so," I said.

"Come on," Sophie said, and she and Daniel brought me into their grandma's room. She was sitting in a comfy chair, and she looked kind of tired, but she smiled when she saw me.

"I'm not in the mood for painting today, but you kids can do some watercolors on the table near me if you'd like," she offered.

I dipped my brush in water and then in the blue. I added black. I thought the dark colors looked kind of sad. Then I added some bright yellow and orange.

Sophie's grandma said, "Oh, that's dramatic!"

"Would you like it?" I offered.

"I would. It would brighten my wall."

She admired Sophie's and Daniel's paintings, too, and we hung them up on the wall near her chair.

After that day my family helped out by giving rides to Sophie, and she came over to my house a bunch of times.

One day I noticed that Sophie was absent from school. When I got home I found out that her grandma had died. I felt kind of strange when I heard that. I didn't know what to do or say.

The funeral was going to be on a school day. I told my parents, "I don't want to go. I don't want to be around all that sadness."

"You don't have to go to the funeral, Avi," my parents said, "but it would be nice if you came with us to the *shiva* at their house in the evening. It's a way to show our support."

I wasn't sure what to expect but I thought if I was in Sophie's place, I'd kind of like to have a friend there, so I said I'd go.

We brought a plate of brownies with us, and I got to eat one in the car on the way over. When we walked in, the house felt so different than usual, with so many people standing around, talking. The table was full of food. I followed my parents over to say hi to Sophie's mom. They both gave her hugs and said, "I'm sorry for your loss."

She saw me and said, "Thanks for coming, Avi."

I gave her a hug, too, and said, "I'm sorry for your loss."

"Sophie and Daniel are in the back room with their cousins. You can go find them," she said.

It turned out there were a couple of other kids from our temple there, too. They were all hanging out together, playing cards on the floor. I sat down and joined them. We heard the grownups getting started with a service out in the living room.

Sophie said, "We don't have to go out there if we don't want to."

So we stayed back there, quietly playing cards. We could hear the grownups singing and saying prayers. We heard some talking and some laughter and some quiet.

When it was over, my parents came to get me.

As I stood up, I said, "I liked painting with your grandma. She was really nice."

Sophie nodded. Her mouth was smiling, but her eyes looked sad. Then she went to whisper something to her mom. They motioned for me to come with them. They brought me into Sophie's grandma's room. All of her stuff was still in there, but it felt kind of empty.

Sophie took the painting I had made off the wall and gave it to me. And her mom opened a box and took out a paintbrush. "Here, I think my mom would like you to have this, Avi. She liked your paintings."

"Wow, thanks," I said.

When I got home, I hung my painting on the wall in my room. I thought about how it had both dark and bright colors, was sad and happy, and how Sophie's grandma had called it "dramatic". I guess she really did like my paintings.

I looked at the paintbrush and thought, "I'm going to remember her. And I'm going to keep on painting."

Provenance: I was a consultant for an innovative project at a synagogue in the Boston area. Children and parents from the 4th grade Hebrew school class formed a Caring Corps to learn from the Caring Committee about ways that the synagogue community supports its members during life cycle events like the arrival of a baby, a death, or a time of illness. They made baby blankets, cards, and baked cakes for the Caring Committee to distribute. Several of the 4th grade families attended a *shiva minyan* when their classmate's grandfather died. I created this story to tell to them at our final meeting.

In crafting this story, I also drew upon my experiences of attending *shiva minyanim* with members of my own congregation. I was particularly moved by the experience of one family with a daughter, age seven, and a son, age five, who lost their dad to cancer. Their mom invited me to come over and tell stories to their daughter, to help her settle down before bed. It made me think a lot about how children experience loss and how a community supports a family in mourning.

As I developed the story, the detail of making the grandmother an artist came from my own imagination. To my surprise, after the Caring Corps session where I told the story for the first time, a girl approached me with a big smile on her face. She told me, "My family had a friend who was a painter. She was a friend of my great-grandmother's, and she died a couple of months ago. And I got one of her paintbrushes!"

Cindy Rivka Marshall is a professional storyteller who uses story to build community and consult with organizations. She performs Jewish folktales and *midrashim* for all ages in visits to synagogues and schools across the United States. Her award-winning audio recordings include "Challah and Latkes: Stories for Shabbat and Hanukkah" and "By the River: Women's Voices in Jewish Stories." She co-chairs the Jewish Storytelling Coalition. She has an MA in Communications. A former filmmaker, her credits include *A Life of Song*, a portrait of Yiddish folksinger Ruth Rubin. www.cindymarshall.com

Study Guide: Questions, Sources, and Projects for Reflection, Discussion, and Action

1. Which *mitzvot* are illustrated by this story? Which additional *mitzvot* can you also relate to this story?

2. What kinds of things can you do to support friends and family who are experiencing an illness?

3. It can feel difficult or awkward knowing that someone is ill or dying—so awkward that we sometimes choose not to go see them. How can we be sure to fulfill this mitzvah? What might you buy, bring, learn, or practice in advance?

4. Have you ever experienced mourning for someone you care about? If it is not too painful, try to recall what your feelings were. Judaism offers many rituals to help deal with loss and mourning. Which have you experienced and in what ways were these helpful to you?

5. Judaism embraces a whole way of living, from birth through death, and doesn't shy away from hard times. Sitting *shiva* is a core practice. Unless a mourner speaks to you first, or asks for a hug, traditional Judaism discourages touching, hugging, or speaking to mourners unless absolutely essential during the time before burial, the funeral and the week of *shiva*.

    a. Why do you think this came to be? How might it be helpful both to be present *and* to give the mourners a "bubble" of personal space? Traditionally, the mourners sit lower than the visitors, often by removing pillows on a couch, or by sitting on a box or lower chair than others. How might this affect their experience of mourning in a house full of guests?

    b. The original custom is to have a week of full-time mourning. The term *shiva* shares a root with *sheva*, the Hebrew word for seven (though lately, some families have only three days of *shiva*). What is the value of mourning at home, with the community coming over for services (save for on *Shabbat* and Holy Days, when mourners go to synagogue), rather than going to work or to school for the week? Do you think of this as more or less helpful in the long run?

Sacred Story and Text Connections

In Genesis, *Bereishit* 50:1-14, Joseph mourns for his father Jacob. They have had a very complicated relationship. In her workshops and her book, *Mourning and Mitzvah: A Guided Journal for Walking the Mourner's Path Through Grief to Healing*, (Jewish Lights Publishing) Rabbi Anne Brener helps mourners to identify and process complicated feelings as the year of mourning unfolds. She suggests looking at a picture of the deceased and letting feelings emerge. She also offers several pages of starting lines to trigger helpful writing and reflection such as:

"When I feel the need to communicate with you, I usually feel…"

"When I think of you, I remember…"

"What I always wanted to hear you say was…"

"What I wish you could have understood is…"

"What I will do differently in my life from what you did in yours is…"

"Despite the things that separate us, the things we share are…"

"I hope that you now are…"

Do you or someone you know well have complicated feelings about a deceased relative, teacher, or friend? Try journaling in this way and perhaps discussing with a skillful mentor or support group.

Project: Be aware when a friend or family member is experiencing a loss and support them by visiting, bringing food, helping to keep their place neat (check the bathroom for toilet paper, and clean hand towels regularly) so they don't need to think about such things at this time.

Chapter 23
The Mime's Rosh Hashanah
by Goldie Milgram

Look! thinks Ashley to herself. There's Daring Dan setting up his street show. It would be so great to have enough talent to do a gig like his—people piling money into his hat. He says as soon as three people put in money, then soon everyone else just starts doing it.

I sure miss my sisters, how we used to text each other funny or annoying things all day. If only that guy hadn't filched my cellphone while I was sleeping on a bench at the bus station. But I had no choice but to leave home. Mom and Dad were so furious with me all the time. I thought I'd be arrested, or that they'd kill me. Well, they have their life back now that their almost-always-in-trouble daughter is out of the picture. But really, I didn't mean for Dara to set the kitchen on fire during that unofficial birthday party when they weren't home…I wasn't even in the room when it happened.

Today must be the first or second day of Rosh Hashanah. I saw a sign in a store window. "Happy Rosh Hashanah." I wonder how you get forgiveness for nearly killing your friends and destroying your home and your parents' most precious possession? *Teshuvah, tefillah u'tzedakah*, they say, riiiiighhht…repentance, prayer, and charity—brings forgiveness. That must be for the small stuff.

I could sure use a slice of my grandmother's honey cake. I used to love making it with her every year. She was the only one who almost believed me about what happened that night. Well, no point dwelling on the past, I'd better get out there and hustle. It will be dark all too soon.

"Hello, lady! My name's Ashley. Can I carry your suitcase for you for a small tip? I'm homeless, and I'm happy to work for something to eat…"

"Sir, do you need help working that new ticket machine? Confusing, isn't it? For a small fee I can…"

Darn, why do most of them just ignore me? I'll try this next fellow. No, he's walking the other way.

Incoming targets at two o'clock! Two tour buses are stopping to let people out on this square. That professor-type woman looks like a good prospect…

"Hi! Can I help you with that? It looks so heavy, for just a small tip or a few of those nacho chips you are carrying?"

Why am I begging? I look like a nice girl, you say.

Oh, people. Listen to me people!!

Ashley moves into the center of the square where Daring Dan has just performed and begins her show. She notices someone watching her with sympathy, or is that pity? No matter. As long as she coughs up some money when her show is done.

***

I notice the homeless girl—someone tells me her name is Ashley—loitering at the edge of the crowd, watching a man collecting money in his outstretched hat. She must be about my daughter's age. I can't seem to stop watching her, wondering if I could help her parents find her. Now what's she doing? She's stamping her feet and shouting. She must be losing it. I sure would, in her position. That other guy, the one who just put on the street show, he's glaring at her like she's horning in on his territory. Wait, she's starting her own show.

I watch her raise her hands in the empty space in front of her as though feeling for something…she's moving too quickly. Whump! She's run into a wall that we can't see in the middle of the square. People are laughing at her stunt. Now she's setting out invisible wine and cake—she's holding a party! And…now she's lighting candles on the cake, and beginning to dance wildly. People are joining her—but, no, she doesn't want that.

Wait, our little mime is stopping. She's holding up her hand like a policewoman at an intersection. She's shaking her head. Something is wrong.

Reaching for an imaginary bag that has been hanging on the wall, she opens it and pulls out…what might it be?…It's a…huge saw. Oh, she's nicked herself on its sharp teeth. Someone in the crowd passes her a bandana, must be an accomplice. She's quickly returned to the saw, using it to cut a window in the wall. Through the window she's tugging at something heavy, a tight fit. She's struggling to bring it through the opening.

Done.

She's pulled through a rolled-up carpet and is carrying it on her shoulder to the other side of the circle. She puts it down onto the street and begins kicking it to make it unroll.

The air is filling with invisible stuff she's plucking from inside the rolled carpet! A glowing gemstone, a butterfly still folded in its chrysalis, a huge tasty lollipop, a frisky puppy, a portrait of her grandmother…now something is heavy, she is lifting it up high, like holding a chair by its legs…no, wait, she's turning her hands like she's unrolling it—could it be… a Torah scroll!? Yes! Look how lovingly she rerolls it and cradles it in her arms and begins a joyful waltz.

A crowd has gathered. A few coins land where she's dancing with the scroll held like a beloved child in her arms.

Her mood is changing. Something subtle is shifting in how she holds her shoulders. Holding the Torah with one hand, she uses the other to open a door in the wall. She's tapping around the space inside and confirms a shelf upon which she gently settles the Torah. She closes the door firmly and stands contemplating the door. The tilt of her head and pressed lips show she is remembering something. It is not good.

She's slowly walking around the edges of the carpet; now faster and faster as though on a train heading out on a journey, moving her hands in a chug-a-chug-a train wheel motion. She opens the window and begins pulling something else in. It's one, no, two entwined people, and they are resisting coming through with all their might.

Ashley puts her right foot up against the wall for leverage. She tugs fiercely. Once more, and again with all her strength. The crowd is groaning audibly with each of her efforts. Splop! She, they, all tumble, falling backwards onto the ground. The crowd roars with laughter.

Dusting off her hands, Ashley executes a perfect plié, pirouettes, reaches into the air and sets one chair upon the carpet, and then another; grandly gesturing for her two new guests to take a seat.

Comically, on point like a ballerina, but very wobbly, she walks around and around the chair until she stops beside it, and begins silently mouthing words, gesturing as though apologizing, but her two guests clearly don't accept the apology as sincere. She tries harder and harder. Finally she reaches into a pocket, fumbles around and finds a remote control—to judge from how she is clicking her thumb down onto her other fingers. She hands it to the couple.

With each click, she enacts what her guests are angrily recalling: a house ruined by water from the firefighters' efforts to stop the flames, her father furious at her, and she's now down on all fours—showing a puppy unable to breathe, falling over. Finally, and, it seems for her to be the hardest of all—she mimes a volume of some sort of Russian literature, the only thing that her mom has left from her father. The book is ruined beyond recognition. The pages appear to shred in her hands.

The guests won't budge. They don't accept her devastation, her profound apology.

Ashley slides down the wall, coils up in a ball, holding herself tightly, wailing silently.

The crowd is stone silent. I think they are waiting for something funny to happen again. The little mime gets up stiffly, picks up and hugs the gemstone and the chrysalis to her chest. A leash from the puppy is twisted around her ankle. She trips on it and then unravels it. Poignantly, she kisses her hand and then places the kiss on her grandma's cheek in the portrait.

She walks tensely, rapidly around the edges of the carpet and begins thumping her chest with one fist. She turns and walks the other way—the action becomes part

The Mime's Rosh Hashanah | 169

of a passionate, desperate dance of apology—around and around and around. She stops, closes her eyes and she rips her shirt at the neckline.

An old woman, who has been watching in the crowd, walks onto the carpet and stands, leaning on her cane, in the empty space of the imaginary couple. When Ashley sees her, she gasps audibly and backs away, tripping over the edge of the carpet, and falls sprawling on the floor. The crowd laughs in relief; that's better! This is all part of the show. Right?

The old woman thumps her own chest in the way the mime has done and walks around the sprawled girl. Gently tapping Ashley's shoulder to get her to look up, the woman shifts from thumping her chest to flattening her hand into a soothing, circular rubbing. Ashley sits up and copies the soothing movement, her eyes riveted on the old woman. Soon Ashley appears to be crying very real tears.

"How does she do that?"

"Very impressive acting," whispers the woman beside me.

"A world-class mime," says a man who has been watching the entire time.

"Very European, so serious," says a student holding a philosophy textbook.

The old woman watches Ashley cry, as do we, and at a certain point offers her a real tissue and points at the darkening sky. The sun is setting. The mime pulls from her bosom the invisible gemstone, the chrysalis, and the puppy—offering these to the woman in thanks. The crone shakes her head no, touches her heart and steps back into the crowd.

The applause is very strong. But if this is entertainment, why are so many of us also in tears?

Ashley retrieves the coins multiplying near her feet, since she has no hat to pass, and takes them over to a beggar who has been gradually working the crowd the whole time. He kisses her hand.

Ashley takes her jacket and backpack, and heads away from the dispersing crowd, down toward a side road, politely avoiding attempts by people to engage her. She appears very disturbed. Perhaps she is displeased with her performance. She cranes her neck from side to side, as if searching for something or someone.

***

I step out of the crowd and follow her. Two blocks later we are beside each other on the sidewalk at a red light.

"That was a really good show," I tell her. "Here are three fives to split with your partners." I notice tears in her eyes. "But what's wrong? Weren't you happy with the show?"

"They weren't my partners," she says. "I don't know them. They just hang around here, so I gave them the first part, *tzedakah*. What I need now is a synagogue. Is there a synagogue in this town?"

"My dear, your street show was amazing. What more could a synagogue provide?"

"I need to seal my hopes of doing *teshuvah*, of making amends with my parents, by an act of *tefillah*, of prayer, and by hearing the *shofar* blown. And I don't want to be alone on Rosh Hashanah. It feels totally wrong. I need to find a synagogue."

Without the illusion created by her miming, I now realize that she is much younger than the college student I'd taken her for at our first encounter. Maybe a high school junior. Could that really have been a true story she acted out?! And now she wants a synagogue. As it happens, I do know where a few are. Time was, I used to go. I could blow off my bus for now. It's pulling up but there's no rush. I'm sure my brother will understand, when I explain the reason for my delay.

"I can walk you to a synagogue," I offer. "And though I hadn't planned to attend, I'll join you, if you don't mind. You see, I haven't thought of myself as Jewish in a long time, and the holidays normally mean nothing to me. But because of you, somehow today they do. But first, I need to call my brother to let him know I'll be catching a later bus. And I'd be happy for you to use my cellphone after I reach him—it's all charged up. You are welcome to call anyone, anywhere you wish."

Provenance: Unbeknowst to my parents, the year I was to attend what was then called The Brandeis Camp Institute, I managed to book my flight to arrive a week early. With $75 earned tutoring *b'nei mitzvah* in hand, sixteen-years-old, I hitchhiked up and down the coast of California before arriving on time at BCI. I did nearly get killed twice by some pretty wicked characters. I also had a run in with a puma (no kidding), when the bus couldn't continue south due to a massive fire in the Santa Barbara area. It was in the Santa Barbara bus station that I met the main character of this story. She was holding a crumpled United Synagogue Youth brochure as we were chatting. A run-away for different, far more serious reasons, she told me she was the president of her USY region, usually kept kosher and wanted money so she didn't have to keep dumpster-diving. Who could make up a story like that! My story, however, beyond my brief meeting with her, is spun out of pure imagination woven through many years of experience as a social worker before becoming a rabbi.

Goldie Milgram founded and directs Reclaiming Judaism and she serves as dean of the Jewish Spiritual Education and Maggid-Educator ordination programs. A rabbinical graduate of the Reconstructionist Rabbinical College, she also holds the honor of *maggid, mashpi'ah* (storyteller/spiritual guide), and rabbinic *smichah* (ordination) from her teacher Rabbi Zalman Schachter-Shalomi. The Covenant Foundation and National Jewish Book Awards have honored Goldie's work. A widely published author, professional storyteller, and speaker, some of her new works are *Seeking and Soaring: Jewish Approaches to Spiritual Development and Guidance, Reclaiming Bar/Bat Mitzvah as a Spiritual Rite of Passage* and *Mitzvah Stories: Seeds for Inspiration and Learning.* www.ReclaimingJudaism.org and www.Bmitzvah.org

Study Guide: Questions, Sources, and Projects for Reflection, Discussion, and Action

1. Which *mitzvot* are illustrated by this story? Which additional *mitzvot* can you also relate to this story?

2. Most of us get it wrong sometimes and do things for which we are sorry. In this story, Ashley believes that what she did is so terrible that her family will never forgive her. Do you think she is right? What would you do if you were Ashley? What would you do if you were her parents?

3. At the end of the story, it seems that Ashley is beginning to be able to forgive herself. Have you done something for which you haven't been able to forgive yourself? What could you do to move towards healing?

4. Can you imagine what it might be like to be homeless? What are the things you would most miss if you had to live on the streets? What dangers might you face? How would you survive?

5. Two strangers stop to help Ashley. If you lost your wallet or purse, had no money suddenly and needed help, how would you get people to help you? Under what circumstances might you feel safe helping a stranger? When not?

6. Have you ever erred in judgment in a way that affected important relationships? How did you handle the situation? Discuss options for such circumstances as a family, in class, and with friends.

Sacred Stories and Text Connections

1. "When do we say that *teshuvah* alone can atone? This refers to a mitzvah-related mistake between human[s] and God...] However, regarding transgressions between someone and a friend, such as wounding someone [physically, socially and/or emotionally], stealing from someone, or causing damage in any way, either physically or through speech—these are not forgiven through *teshuvah* [expressed to God] alone. Rather, one must first return to the friend whatever is obligated to return, and then the relationship can begin to heal."
—*Sefer HaChinuch* 364

What needs to be returned to the friend when the damage you've done is emotional or social? What if the damage you did is physical to the person or something precious to them? Or an object or money? Before the mitzvah of *teshuvah*, where another person is involved, can actually begin to take place, Judaism requires going to the person you hurt. Why?

2. The process of *teshuvah* must develop from identifying our mistakes to also focus in on the factors that caused the reaction. From here we learn that it is praiseworthy for one who is engaged in *teshuvah* to channel remorse towards not just abandoning the behavior, but also addressing those internal pressures that gave rise to it.—Rabbi Yitzchak Hutner, *Pachad Yitzchak, Rosh HaShanah, Ma'amar* 6-A, pp 61-2

    Ashley misses her family. She regrets what happened. This quote suggests more is needed to return and have a *teshuvah gemorah*, a complete healing with herself and with her family. What would that be? Can you think of a behavior you are trying to shift? What is triggering you when it comes up? What deeper understanding is possible that can help you strengthen your ability to change?

3. Obtain a copy of Psalm 69. Could you imagine Ashley's miming as an expression like these words? The biblical psalms are rich sources for venting strong emotions in prayer. It is very important to lament a difficult situation, for lamenting is part of the human healing process that empties out the pain and allows new hope and possibilities to come in. Did this happen for Ashley? Learning how to express and respond to a lament is an important life skill. You can learn more in "The Lament: Hidden Key to Effective Listening" by Barry Bub in *Seeking and Soaring: Jewish Approaches to Spiritual Guidance and Development*

4. "On the first day of the seventh month, you shall rest, with remembrance [inspired by] a blasting sound, so holiness happens."—Leviticus, *Vayikra* 23:24

    How does hearing the shofar affect you? What adjectives would you use? Why was it important to Ashley? How had even the sight of a shofar changed her path in life?

5. Why does awareness more often arise when a person is in silence, like on a solo walk in the woods or while in the shower, or during the silent *Amidah* prayer at services? Do you organize your life to have the time you need to reflect and get better consequences from thoughtful actions and reactions?

"My children, open to me the gate of *teshuvah* as minutely as the eye of a needle, and I will open for you gates wide enough for carriages and wagons to enter through them.—*Shir HaShirim Rabbah 5:2*

What are the elements of personal opening within the story for Ashley?

Project: Collect toiletries for those living in a homeless shelter or volunteer to teach literacy and other vital skills.

Project: Encourage the adults you know to carry small bills and change to give to people asking for money on the street. How do we really know the difference between who is a con artist and who is in need and afraid or unable to seek more conventional sources of help? When offering money, it helps reduce isolation to ask the person if they would be interested in telling a story or hearing a story, perhaps one from this volume. Being homeless can be very isolating, especially for children. There are also tent cities where homeless families live near some major cities. Consider going over to tell stories to a teenager that you see on a corner begging, or offering a show like in this chapter's story; they might really appreciate a listening ear.

Project: Create a ritual with a friend to be "best friends forever", one that includes a promise that if you ever hurt each other, you will create a *teshuvah* process until your friendship is back on solid, happy, healthy ground.

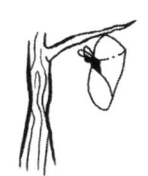

Chapter 24
Finding Peace
by Lynnie Mirvis

Once a king tossed and turned in his royal bed. In the morning, he summoned his advisor.

"I am so upset! I need to find peace," the king cried. "At night, I twist in my bed covers and can't sleep at all, and during the day, all I do is pace up and down the halls. I need peace!"

"Send out a proclamation!" the king commanded his advisor. "Whoever brings peace to the king will be rewarded with up to half of my kingdom!"

The proclamation went forth to all parts of his kingdom as the king had commanded.

Now in this kingdom, there was much poverty. Little ones dazed from hunger roamed the countryside, looking for a scrap of bread, but none was to be had. Farmers worked the land, which was often barren from lack of rain, and the meager crops that somehow survived were heavily taxed to fill the royal treasury.

But the king never noticed how his people suffered.

When the proclamation went forth, many of the king's subjects were too broken in spirit to pay it much attention.

But the royal palace was abuzz with ideas about how to bring peace to the king.

The royal baker decided that he had just the thing to bring the king peace. With a flourish and numerous bows, he entered the royal chambers, carrying on his shoulder a tray of freshly baked croissants. All the nobles in the court were overcome with the delicious aroma of the royal baker's offering.

"Your Majesty!" said the baker, "Take just one bite from these delectable croissants, and you will experience true peace. They are like manna from heaven, made from a recipe passed down to me from my ancestors of old."

The king bit into the delicacy and was transformed. He closed his eyes and felt as if he had indeed found peace. But as soon as he had swallowed the last crumb, the feeling disappeared.

"Perhaps I need more," said the king, and he promptly consumed the entire baker's dozen. Instantly, he was seized with a rumbling in his innards, which didn't subside for a full day and night.

Next came the royal juggler, dressed in purple and red, carrying in one hand a set of golden balls.

"Please, Your Majesty," he said, "watch as I spin these golden spheres in the air. See them sparkle and shine! Watch and you will know true peace."

Up and down, up and down, the royal juggler threw the balls and caught them effortlessly. At first, the king was mesmerized and felt tranquil. But the more he watched, the dizzier he felt. Soon he fell into a swoon, with his head spinning, spinning, spinning, so that he was forced to retreat to his royal bed where he endured a night of vertigo—the walls of his chamber going round and round like a carousel.

Next came the royal dancer accompanied by three fiddlers.

"I beg your indulgence, Your Majesty," said the royal dancer, bowing low. "Allow us to perform before you. You will see that peace can be found in my dance."

And with these words, the dancer glided and pirouetted and spun and leaped high into the air, keeping time with the fiddlers' melody. The king was so delighted that he stood and joined the dancer, and they twirled around the room. Faster and faster, the music played until the king lost his balance, his crown precariously askew. He slipped on the marble floor and would have hit his head on the edge of the throne had not his advisor caught him just in time.

"Why does peace run from me!" raged the king. "Is there no one who can bring me peace? "

Suddenly an old woman, dressed in rags, appeared at the end of the hall. The guards tried to bar her from entering the throne room.

"Let her approach!" the king called out in a desperate voice, for something in the way her eyes searched his face captured his curiosity.

"Your Majesty," the old woman said as she drew near the throne, "I know you desire peace more than anything in the world." The king nodded wearily. "Perhaps I can help. Look deeply into my eyes."

The king peered into her dark eyes, as bottomless as two deep wells. Then she cast her gaze around the vast room.

"All who are gathered here, I beseech you to look deeply into the eyes of the person next to you!"

People gasped, unsure about what to do. For the truth was that they had never really seen each other. Then the king did as she commanded, and the courtiers and ladies-in-waiting followed his example. They all looked into the eyes of the person next to them. And as they did, a hush filled the palace. No sound was heard for miles around. The moment seemed to last for an eternity, as if the whole kingdom were suspended in space.

Each one saw a reflection of themselves in the eyes of the other.

"Ah," said the old woman, "what you see is the *Tzelem Elohim* that resides in each of you, the spark of the Divine image. And when you see that, you understand that the gift of peace—*shalom*—has been inside each of you all along—if only you can see the other."

The king took a deep breath, and for the first time felt peace enter him like a pure, white light. When he looked up, the old woman had disappeared. Yet the special glow inside of him remained very present.

Everyone in court was silent and filled with wonder.

Then the king ordered his servants to bring the royal carriage, for he wanted to see his kingdom.

And as he rode through the countryside, he saw for the first time his own reflection in the eyes of all his people, and they saw their reflection in his eyes. Rich or poor—it didn't matter.

And for the first time, he saw his people's hardships, and vowed to help them. And if I told you all the good he did, and the kindness he bestowed throughout his kingdom, that would be another story. But I can tell you this: from that time on, the King rarely had a sleepless night. He lived in peace and harmony—shalom, shalom—'til the end of his days.

As far as the old woman was concerned, some say they saw her feeding soup to the hungry. Others, that they saw her at the gate of the city, mending the clothes of the poor. And others whispered that she was the *Shechinah*—The Divine Presence—who always hovers over the earth, if only there are eyes to see.

Provenance: When the Early Childhood Department at the Memphis Jewish Community was doing a unit on Peace, they invited me to share a peace story. I created this story that uses the motif of a King's search—my character is reminiscent of Ahashveros of the Book of Esther. I remembered a Buddhist story about a quest for peace that ends with self-discovery, and I realized that the Jewish idea of *Tzelem Elohim* fits with that concept. I am also fascinated by the idea of the feminine aspect of God—the *Shechinah*—and wanted to incorporate that into the story.

When telling this story to younger audiences, I invite them to mime with me eating the baker's delicacies, juggling, dancing, and spinning our heads round and round in sympathy with the King. For all audiences, I invite participants to turn to the person next to them and look into each other's eyes—a very powerful experience.

Lynnie Mirvis creates narrative images through story, painting, and poetry. She is a storyteller in Memphis, Tennessee, who shares midrashic tales, Jewish folk tales, and original stories with audiences of all ages. Lynnie hosts GHS TV's award-winning *Story Time* show and gives tours at community art museums that encourage young people to respond to art by using their imaginations. Her stories and poetry have appeared in *Storytelling Magazine, Mitzvah Stories: Seeds for Inspiration, Tennessee Voices Anthology: the Poetry Society of Tennessee* and *Grandmother Earth*.

Study Guide: Questions, Sources, and Projects for Reflection, Discussion, and Action

1. Which *mitzvot* are illustrated by this story? Which additional *mitzvot* can you also relate to this story?

2. How do Jews greet each other in Hebrew?

3. Peace in Judaism is so important that the word *shalom*, which means "peace" is used both to welcome and leave people. Peace and wellness are also interwoven in Hebrew. The adjective for feeling whole, *shalem*, comes from the same root as the Hebrew word for peace. Why might this be?

4. The ruler in our story was trying to find *shalem* through peace. To be a *rodef darchei shalom*, someone fulfilling the mitzvah of pursuing pathways of peace, is a mitzvah. This story illustrates a way of seeing oneself in the eyes of the other.

   How many ways can you think of that help to find the divine spark in the other?

5. Genesis, *Bereishit* 1:26-27, 5:1-3, and 9:6 teach that we are made in God's image. What does this mean to you?

6. Would your gift of peace for the king be the same as the old woman's or would you offer him something else?

7. How do you experience the *Shechinah*, the spark of Divine presence, in your life? Nachmanides suggested that this spark is your soul and that your soul is immortal; for much of Jewish history there has been the option of believing in reincarnation. Could that be? Would that affect your work for peace?

Sacred Story and Text Connections

1. Depart from evil, seek peace, and pursue it.—Psalms, *Tehillim* 34:15

2. Rabbi [Yehudah haNasi] said: "All manner of lying is prohibited, except it be to make peace between one and one's neighbor."—Talmud, *Derekh Eretz Zuta 10:7*

3. "Be among the disciples of Aaron—a lover of peace (*ohev shalom*) and a pursuer of peace (*rodef shalom*); a lover of all people, bringing them closer to the Torah."—*Mishnah Avot 1:12*

4. *Rodef shalom.* "This teaches us that a person should be a pursuer of peace among people, between each and every one. If a person sits in his/her place and is silent, how can s/he pursue peace among people, between each and every one?! Rather, one should go out from one's own place and go searching in the world and pursue peace among people.—*Avot d'Rabbi Natan, version A, ch. 12*

5. When two people had a dispute, Aaron went and sat near one of them and said to him: "My son, see what your friend is doing? He is beating his heart and tearing his clothing saying: 'Woe is me! How can I lift up my eyes and look at my friend? I am ashamed of myself since I was the one who offended him.' Aaron would sit with him until he removed the hatred from his heart. Aaron would then go and sit next to the other and say to him: "My son, see what your friend is doing?! He is beating his heart and tearing his clothing saying: 'Woe is me! How can I lift up my eyes and look at my friend? I am ashamed of myself since I was the one who offended him.' Aaron would sit with him until he removed the hatred from his heart. So, when the two met, they hugged and kissed each other.—*Babylonian Talmud, Avot d'Rabbi Natan* 12:3, *Talmud, Perek HaShalom*

   What does it take to remove hatred from your heart? Was the way the rabbis imagined Aaron, Moses' brother, who served as the first *kohen ha-gadol*—high priest, the way you'd have expected his role to be described? What might it have been like to be Aaron? What skills might you seek out to better promote peace? Does helping others find peace help us, too?

Project: Invite several peace workers to your school, camp, or organization. Develop a list of questions for them that will help you understand how they function and when and how they succeed. How do their approaches differ? Is there training available that might be of interest to you?

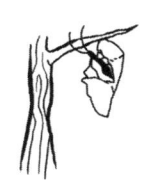

Chapter 25
Two Candles for Maria
by Seth F. Oppenheimer

The black horse surged beneath him. Rifle shot rang out from his companions as they charged the fixed lines of the Federal troops.

"Too soon, too soon," he thought as he fired his own rifle. Where were the other units?

The Fourth Mississippi galloped forward around him, fewer and fewer gray uniforms ahorse. He holstered his rifle as it ran out of ammunition and pulled out the first of his two pistols, his actions automatic after three years of battles. The Federal line was becoming clearer. Perhaps they would be able to take the line. The roar of gun and cannon fire filled his ears along with the thunderous pounding of hooves. But piercing the overwhelming wall of sound, the screams of horses and men. Gunpowder smoke filled his nose, tinged with his own and his horse's sweat; the copper tinge of blood added its odor along with the fecal stench of those with belly wounds.

Where was the support from other units? The enemy fire, rifle shots, and canisters exploding, came thicker in the air, sixty yards as he pulled out his saber, taken from a dead Federal cavalryman, lighter and more effective than the one he started the war with. Suddenly the big black horse screamed and reared. The young officer tried to jump free, but screamed as the horse fell on his leg, breaking it in several places.

Screamed and screamed...

And sat upright in bed. His room. He was in his own bedroom.

There was a knock on the door.

"David? *Mein heartzela* (my heart)? The dream again?"

His mother's soft German accent meaning home as much as anything.

"I'm okay, Momma. Not so bad this morning."

And it was morning. The light coming in the window showed that the sun had just broken above the horizon. He had learned in the field, in the absence of clocks, to judge time from the quality of light, the height of the sun, and the position of stars. So many unexpected skills from four years in the field. Things a merchant's son from Columbus, Mississippi might not be expected to know. Things not taught in his one year at the University of Mississippi. That one year in Oxford, now a distant dream.

"Come have breakfast. Your father is up. I am getting your brother and sister up for school. Your father wants you to help close the month's books today."

"I will be out soon, Momma."

David Roth, former First Lieutenant, CSA, eased himself out of bed. His leg hurt in the mornings, but it was still attached to the rest of him. He could walk and, while not at skilled as before, he could still ride a horse. Only his good fortune in being evacuated back to Columbus and being nursed by his own mother had saved his leg. He vaguely remembered the small woman urgently arguing with a surgeon as he drifted in and out of a fevered sleep.

The War Between the States had ended while he was still recovering. The battles in the north of Mississippi had spared Columbus the fate of some other cities. Blessedly, his city was not pillaged. It was left unburned and intact. As trade resumed with the end of the war, the Tombigbee River brought goods that the torn-up railroads could no longer carry. Roth's Dry Goods Store was prospering. David's parents made clear that he could return to university whenever he chose. As a decorated and wounded veteran of the late war, there would be no question of his re-admittance to the university when his original acceptance had been no means assured.

Breakfast called. With a slight limp, the overly pale young man joined his family at the table. His sister, Ruth, 16, and brother, Leon, 14, were sitting down, and all were joined shortly after by their father and then their mother, bringing a skillet of eggs to join the bread already on the table. There would be no bacon in this house for the Friday morning meal. The family spoke about the schoolwork of the two younger children, and Ruth continued her long-term campaign to be allowed to apply to one of the women's colleges in the Northeast. David sat mostly in silence, only occasionally lending a word of support to his sister, but not too much lest his parents resume their pincer attack on the question of his return to Oxford.

Leon and Ruth went off to school while David and his father went to the store. The two of them worked in a companionable silence until they opened the store to a steady stream of customers. In the afternoon the two of them discussed the end of month accounts between customers and then, with his father's complete confidence, David went to the back room and finished the detail work to close the month's accounts. Father and son shut down an hour earlier than on other weekdays and hurried home to clean up for the Sabbath. Joined by Leon, the three Roth men went to Isaac Zeigler's home to join other Jewish men of the city for a Friday evening service. They lingered a short time afterwards to contribute to the discussion about founding a formal congregation and the costs and logistics of buying a building and hiring a rabbi.

At home, the whole family gathered around the large dining table. It was only as he watched his mother light and bless the *Shabbos* candles, drawing the light into her eyes, that David finally felt the tension drain from him that dogged him every other moment of his life.

Then his father blessed the wine, and together the family blessed the challah. After passing around the braided bread sprinkled with salt, they finally sat down to eat.

As the chicken was being passed around, David spoke. "Momma, Poppa, I need to leave Columbus."

His father smiled. "So you will be continuing your studies!"

"No. I am not going back to the university. I am filled with restlessness, haunted by old ghosts. I need to leave Columbus, leave Mississippi. I need to travel for a bit."

Momma and Poppa looked at each other.

The eldest Roth cleared his throat. "If you wish to visit Europe, we may be able to help you with the passage...." He looked at his son expectantly.

"No. I think I want to go west. They need horsemen on the ranches. I don't know cattle, but I know horses better than I know people."

"When would you go?"

His father was stoic while his mother's eyes welled with tears. Four years before, both parents had learned the uselessness of arguing with their eldest child when he had come to say goodbye, wearing his new gray uniform.

"After Passover."

And so it was. Two months later, David hugged his parents and siblings amidst tears and promises to write. He mounted the strong brown horse with four white stockings that his father had helped him buy and started west. He would sleep in Starkville down the road with family friends, and then he would head off into the unknown.

***

With intense curiosity, Maria Carmella Lopez watched the cowboy walk with a slight limp down the wooden sidewalk. He was not much taller than she and had dark brown hair. He fascinated her. Not as a man, of course. Her mother, Rosalinda, and her father, Dr. Juan Antonio Lopez, had made clear to Maria that her husband would be found for her from an appropriate family, as had been done for generations in their family. Maria had already rejected two suitors sent from New Mexico in the last year. Her parents' displeasure was clear. Still, she would never consider as a potential suitor the dust-covered man who had come to town to get supplies. She had made quiet inquiries and knew he was both the business manager and stable master for the Wilson spread—a large ranch running the longhorn that could make a profit in the arid and hot world that was West Texas. Her interest was piqued by the fact that he appeared to be the only other person who usually had a book with him when he was walking around town.

Maria smiled to herself. It would never do to talk to the man in public, but she could meet him in a way that would not get her in trouble. She opened her Cervantes and feigned reading the volume as she walked down the sidewalk and ran right into the cowboy as he stared unseeing into the middle distance, his book held loosely in his right hand as he walked. Both books fell to the ground with dusty thumps.

"I'm terribly sorry Ma'am! I didn't..."

The cowboy paused, and then looking at her, blushed. He blushed! "Excuse me senorita, er..."

"I speak English quite well, sir. My grandfather served with the Army of the Republic of Texas when we gained our independence."

"I beg your pardon ma'am, I wasn't watching where I was going. Miss?"

"Miss Lopez. My father is..."

"Dr. Lopez! Yes, I have met him. He has come out to the ranch several times. He is very skilled and..." He paused again. "Gentle. The boys at the ranch like to be strong when they are hurt, but we all get frightened when we think that our strength and livelihood could be taken away. Your father is a healer."

"Thank you, Mr...?"

The cowboy looked stricken. "Roth, David Roth. I am so sorry. My mother would be appalled at my manners."

Maria let out a light laugh. "It would seem that our mothers have some similarities. My mother is always going on about how I am not proper enough or seemly or careful."

David suddenly noticed the two books lying on the wooden sidewalk at their feet and hastily bent down to collect them, handing one of the volumes to Maria.

"Well, a great pleasure to meet you, Miss Lopez." He tipped his hat. "I hope I might run into you in the future."

She smiled and nodded, and they each went their way. Maria could not help but notice that the cowboy—David, she corrected herself—was whistling to himself, a behavior she had never observed in him in the past.

Maria continued on her way home. The two-storey white house with blue shutters was mirrored in the carefully tended beds of newly blossomed blue and white flowers behind the wooden fence that bordered the front yard. The house was situated on the main street of the small ranching town. On the gate was a small plaque designating the house as the place of practice of Dr. Juan Antonio Lopez. The front part of the first floor served as her father's office and, when necessary, surgery.

Coming through the door, Maria saw her father sitting at his desk, reading one of the medical journals that had arrived on a recent stagecoach.

"Good morning, Father."

"Good morning, my treasure. Did you have a good walk?"

"An interesting walk. May I read for a bit before I do my chores?"

"Reading too much is the best of the vices." He smiled. "Ask your mother. If I release you from work without her leave, I will suffer for it."

Just before Maria had gone to town that morning, Mrs. Lopez had decided that this spring day was a perfect one for flipping the feather mattresses on the beds so it was not until late afternoon that that chore and several others—changing the linens from winter weights to those more appropriate for spring as well as the usual round of sweeping and dusting—were finished by the mistress of the house and her reluctant daughter. Fortunately for Maria, Rosalinda Lopez was very vain about her cooking and, except for those times that she felt an obligation to teach her daughter, preferred to keep her kitchen to herself. So as her mother bustled about the kitchen preparing the evening meal, her daughter slipped back into the quiet of the backyard.

Maria settled herself on her favorite bench in the small back garden, under her mother's carefully nursed lemon tree, fragrant with new blossoms, and set about finding her place in the book since the slender piece of paper she put in as a bookmark seemed to have fallen out. She was confused until she realized that the book was in English, certainly not her Cervantes. She looked at the spine. She had heard of Gibbon's history of the Roman Empire, but had not read it. Looking in the front cover, she saw a name inscribed in a fine clear hand: Ruth Roth.

She was suddenly vexed. Could the bookish cowboy be married? Why did that bother her? No, no. She knew from asking around that that man was single. It was a puzzle, though.

In any case, this was a book she had heard that she should read so she decided to take advantage of the opportunity. If Mr. Roth was a gentleman, he would soon come by with her book.

That Sunday, Maria was uncharacteristically antsy. She was a bit sharp with her few friends and had difficulty feigning paying attention at the small Catholic church where her family prayed. Two days before, she had finished *The Rise and Fall of the Roman Empire*. Now she really wanted her Cervantes back so she could finish reading it. For some reason, her father's large library did not hold any new book to tempt her as it usually did. Mr. Roth was certainly very irritating!

When she returned home from church, Maria seriously considered borrowing her father's buggy and going to collect her book herself.

But, before she could ask permission, her mother called from the bottom of the stairs: "Maria, you have a visitor!"

Maria quickly checked her appearance in the glass. She started to run to the stairs and forced herself to slow down.

David was chatting with her mother in the front room, her father being out on a house call. When Maria came in, David said, "Good morning, Miss Lopez."

Her mother turned to her and raised a disapproving eyebrow.

Maria put on a slightly puzzled expression. "Yes?"

"David Roth. We bumped into each other last week."

"Oh, yes. I had forgotten."

Maria felt no guilt at the lie and experienced a surprising satisfaction in the slight dimming of the cowboy's smile. She suddenly noticed that he was not wearing regular work clothes, but something a bit nicer.

"Well, I fear I accidentally switched our books when we dropped them. I have to admit that I did try to read yours, but my bit of Latin did not give me the skill to read Spanish."

Maria smiled. "I had no such difficulty with yours. I will go get your wife's book."

"Oh, not my wife. My sister's. She is in her last year at Wheaton Seminary. She knows I love history, so she sends me books when she is done with them, though I must return them."

"She attends a college?"

Maria was suddenly very interested, though at nineteen, she knew she was too old to attend college. Visions of libraries far exceeding her father's leapt into her mind.

"Yes. And my brother as well, at the University of Mississippi. I fear my higher education was interrupted by the late war."

The conversation paused, and David and Maria looked at each other for a bit before Maria's mother broke the silence. "Maria, perhaps you should get Mr. Roth his book."

Maria felt her face heat up.

"Of course, Mother. I will be right back with your Gibbon. I trust you have brought me my Cervantes."

Maria quickly went upstairs and recovered the book. She exchanged books with the cowboy, who now stood in awkward silence beside her mother.

He cleared his throat "I have other books you might want to borrow."

Trying to forget her mother standing there, Maria said, "My father has many books in English, as well as Latin and Greek."

"I fear my Greek was never really up to reading for pleasure, but I enjoyed reading Latin in school. Perhaps we can make trades?"

"That would be very nice."

"I come into town on business every Monday. I will bring you something then."

"And I will choose something for you. I am sure my father will not object."

The cowboy tipped his hat both to her and her mother, and took his leave.

Maria's mother sighed.

"To the exchanging of books, your father will not object. To your spending time with this man is another story. Take care. You know he is not appropriate for you."

"Oh, Mama, he is just another person who likes to read. You know there are not many people I can discuss books with in this town."

Her mother shook her head. And returned to her sewing.

That evening there was a tense discussion in the Lopez home.

Dr. Lopez slowly wiped the lenses of his spectacles with a white cloth and spoke. "It is best not to take a chance. You know this man is not suitable for you. He is not of our religion or of our people. Since you were a girl, you have known that you must marry an appropriate man."

"Yes, Papa, I know." Maria looked at her hand in the light from the oil lamps that lit the family sitting room. "But I would like to talk to him. Only for walks in public, so we can talk. I am very lonely. My girl friends did not grow up with parents who think it appropriate for a girl to have so much education, even if you did most of the teaching yourselves."

"You blame your interest in this cowboy on your education?"

"You know I do not mean that, Papa. What harm can there be?"

At this her mother spoke out: "There can be much harm!"

"Mama!"

Dr. Lopez sighed.

"Tomas Garcia's youngest son is studying in Oberlin College," he said, "and intends to follow his father into the law. He is an educated young man with good prospects who is one of us. His father has asked if he might come visit us when he returns to Austin for the summer. The train ride is only a few hours, followed by two on the coach."

Maria looked up at her father. "I will be happy to meet with Judge Garcia's son this summer. But that does not mean I cannot discuss books with this man. I understand my duty."

Her parents looked at each other. "You may meet in this sitting room, and you may walk on the main road."

Maria was careful not to react too strongly, "Thank you, Papa, Mama. It will be good to have a friend who also reads books."

**

That Monday afternoon, David arrived at the Lopez house with a copy of *Moby Dick* and was greeted with Marcus Aurelius's *Meditations*. However, Maria wanted to discus Gibbon's book. The conversation started civilly enough, but Maria's great admiration of the Romans sparked an unexpected response from David.

"Yes, they were great engineers and soldiers, but look how they amused themselves! They made men fight to the death for sport! Torturing people for amusement! I do not admire the Romans."

"What side did you fight for in the War?"

"I fought for my state, Mississippi."

"For a man who defended slavery, you have an odd attitude toward the Romans."

"My family did not hold slaves, though I must admit it may have been because we could not afford one to help in the house. But still, I was fighting to defend my state, not for slavery."

With a delicately arched eyebrow, Maria replied, "My father stood with his state by standing with Governor Houston".

The debate on the relative moralities of the slave-holding South and the Roman Empire continued until David had to return to the ranch in the late afternoon.

And so it continued. Books exchanged and returned, arguments, and agreements.

And spring moved on.

***

One hot Monday late in May, David and Maria continued their walk far too late. Late enough that Maria knew she would be having a talk with her parents before the end of Tuesday. The sun was starting down.

David and Maria stood quietly and watched the shadows lengthening. Standing very close, their hands almost touched, but they did not, of course.

"If things were different, I would ask your parents for permission to call on you," David said.

"If things were different, I would beg them to say yes."

Maria felt her eyes well up.

David turned to the west and shaded his eyes against the setting sun. "I love the sunset. It reminds me of home."

"Why?"

"Well, it reminds me of Friday evenings. My father would close the store early, and we would welcome the *Shabbos*. At home, my mother would light the candles and bless them. I think I am ready to visit home again. You would like it. It is so green compared to here. The magnolias would be filled with white blossoms now. My father has a library too, you know. But there are a fair number of German books that neither of us could read." He laughed.

Maria looked at him oddly. "What does your mother do on Friday evening?"

"She lights the *Shabbos* candles and blesses them. Are you all right, Maria?"

"And you, what do you do on Friday evenings?"

"Me? I actually have an agreement with Mr. Wilson to have Friday afternoons off. I have my own room off the stable, and I try to make my own *Shabbos*. I have my prayer book, my candles, some bread and the awful stuff they call wine from the saloon."

"Could you come to town this Friday, Mr. Roth?"

"Why so formal, again *Miss Lopez*?"

"Please, David, meet me outside my house Friday evening. I know that will mean giving up your ritual, but please."

"Of course, Maria. But why? You are probably going to be in trouble for being out so late. And I am going to have to explain why I am back at the ranch so late with the mail and the bank receipts."

"Just come."

"For you, I will."

Friday, as the sun descended, David walked up to the Lopez house. Maria came out of the house quietly. She held her index finger up to her lips.

"Be very quiet."

David followed her into the house and entered a side room he had never been in.

Maria whispered, "Be silent. Do not take the turn on the stairs into the room. You will be able to see over the wall."

David was confused, but watched Maria pull a hanging aside to reveal a stairway going down. Lamplight flickered from around the bottom of the stair and through a small gap above the wall on the right hand side of the stair.

Maria strode down the stairs. David crept down three stairs where he could peer over the wall. He saw Maria kiss her mother on the cheek and then slide under her father's arm.

Rosalinda Lopez pulled a lace shawl over her head and gazed down on a pair of candles in silver candlesticks. She took some matches, lit the candles, and drew the light into her eyes. As she began to chant the blessing, David gasped.

Rosalinda, startled, flung her arms out, knocking over the candlesticks and extinguishing the flames.

David came slowly down the stairs. Maria's mother ran to her husband, her eyes wide with fear.

Dr. Lopez stared at his daughter. "Maria, what have you done!"

David walked, as if in a trance, to the small table on which the candles lay askew. He righted the two silver candlesticks and, with great deliberation, put the candles into the silver cups. He picked up the matches and paused. He looked up at the family tableau and said quietly, "The pronunciation is different than my mother's, but I think the words are the same."

David lit the candles and drew the light into his eyes. He took a shuddering breath and said the ancient Hebrew blessing he had learned from his mother.

Juan Antonio Lopez stared at David Roth, his forehead a mass of furrowed lines. "But, but you are not Converso!"

"No, Dr. Lopez, but I am, as I think you are, a Jew."

Seth F. Oppenheimer is a rabbinical student studying in the Aleph: Alliance for Jewish Renewal Ordination Programs. He serves Congregation B'nai Israel in Columbus, Mississippi. Dr. Oppenheimer is also a Professor of Mathematics and Director of Undergraduate Research for the Shackouls Honors College at Mississippi State University. He has also served as interim head of the Department of Philosophy and Religion. Father of two, Seth is also an accomplished poet.

Study Guide: Questions, Sources, and Projects for Reflection, Discussion, and Action

1. Which *mitzvot* are illustrated by this story? Which additional *mitzvot* can you also relate to this story?

2. We have some stereotypical ideas of what a Jew can be. Was it a surprise that a Jew was both a Confederate soldier and a cowboy? What other stereotypes are there? How can we let people know that we can be anything we choose?

3. What do you know about Conversos? Do you ever hide your Jewishness?

4. What would it be like to be raised as a Christian but then discover that you were Jewish? This is the experience of many Conversos. What might you feel? What would be your concerns and questions?

5. When and why does *Shabbat* bring together Jews from different cultures? What differences in culture and practice do you know about within Jewish life?

Sacred Story and Text Connections

1. Turn to Isaiah 58 for reflection and discussion. Which of Isaiah's concerns remain current? Why does he end with *Shabbat*?

2. There is a realm of time where the goal is not to have but to be, not to own but to give, not to control but to share, not to subdue but to be in accord. Life goes wrong when the control of space, the acquisition of things of space, becomes our sole concern.—Abraham Joshua Heschel, *The Sabbath*

3. Six days you will labor and do all your work, Exodus, *Shemot* 20:9. Is it possible for a human being to do all his[one's] work in six days? Does not our work always remain incomplete? What the verse means to convey is: Rest on the Sabbath as if all your work were done. Another interpretation: Rest even from the thought of labor.—Abraham Joshua Heschel, *The Sabbath*

Some find the idea of *Shabbat* confining and others find it liberating in a way that makes room for pleasure. The original idea was to obtain freedom from slavery, stop working, and start renewal of body, mind, and spirit one day out of seven. This is becoming important again, as employers, schools, and highly pressured sports teams try to utilize more and more hours of a person's life.

How would you ideally shape your *Shabbat*?

Project: *Shabbat* can become a conscious time for appreciation and incorporation of differences in culture and practice. There are different Sephardic and Ashkenazic prayer books, Torah casings, synagogue-styles and foods, for example. If your family has only Sephardi roots, try holding an Ashkenazi *Shabbat* dinner and vice-versa.

Project: With your family or class adapt the "*Shabbat* Manifesto" found in *Reclaiming Judaism as a Spiritual Practice: Shabbat and Holy Days* by Rabbi Goldie Milgram to reflect a current oppression that you plan to stand up to!

Project: Draw your family tree. Where do your ancestors come from? Were they always Jewish, or do your family have a mixture of cultures and faiths?

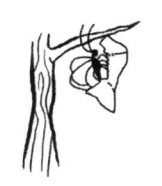

Chapter 26
A Minor "Profit" in the Land of Israel
by Marden David Paru

What could possibly make young Jewish teenagers homesick when traveling in their homeland, the State of Israel? You won't believe this, but it is true: yearning for Coca-Cola.

In 1959 the infamous Arab Boycott against the new young State of Israel was in full effect. During our youth group pilgrimage—travelling by air and ship—Coke products were as abundant as at home, in the air and in port: Goose Bay, Amsterdam, Nice, Marseille, and Naples. However, once we arrived in Israel, none could be found anywhere. What a disappointment this was to our American contingent!

The summer of 1959 was a particularly hot and dry time in Israel. We were constantly thirsty. Remaining hydrated became a medical necessity, we were told, particularly when involved in physical activity: hiking, picking melons, conducting kibbutz chores, etc. We always kept our canteens filled with water but were constantly in search of more exotic beverages. But there simply was no Coke to be found.

Then came the first of our getaway weekends.

"You are free to visit with relatives as long as you leave an address and phone number where you will be staying," explained one of our *madrichim* (counselors).

Ouch! I had no *mishpacha* in Israel; none of our family had made it to safety there....none had survived the *Shoah*. My buddy Nate invited me to "piggyback" with him and travel north from Jerusalem to Haifa for a *Shabbat* weekend in early July to visit his non-English speaking *mishpacha*. Before we arrived at the address on Har HaCarmel (Haifa's upper heights), we entered an import-export store to buy house gifts for our hosts: wine and candy. Shock of all shocks: I saw a gallon jug of Coca-Cola syrup on the counter. Wasn't the Arab boycott still in effect? Our only snack choices up to this time had been Tempo—a weak lemon-lime soda—or Strauss Cola, which didn't taste like any cola with which this American was familiar.

I asked the proprietor of the gift store, "How is it that during a major Arab boycott, you have Coke syrup?"

He replied, "A merchant friend in Cyprus from whom I purchase my imported goods sold it to me. This one bottle has been here for a while and serves more as a conversation piece and decoration than a serious seller."

My next question—you guessed it—was: "How much are you asking for the gallon of Coke?"

He said, "$10, in US currency."

When I told him I was in Israel on a scholarship, he lowered the price to $8. We had a deal! I really wasn't sure what I would do with this rare commodity. All I knew was that I would have to *schlepp* it up the mountain to our hosts' home and then back to Jerusalem.

As a younger teen, I had once sold encyclopedias, but I was never an entrepreneur. At this moment, coming as I did from modest means, I knew I certainly could use a few shekels to buy gifts and mementos to take home for my family. Also, I thought it would be a mitzvah for me to break the Arab boycott by selling Coke in *Eretz Yisrael*, the Land of Israel. For a brief moment, I imagined myself a Maccabean hero of sorts.

So, upon my return to Jerusalem, I made arrangements with the head cook at our "home base" (a local teacher's seminary) to purchase a dozen cases of *gazoz*— one liter bottles of carbonated water (quite a cheap commodity in Israel at that time). For a small fee, the cook supported my endeavor by providing paper cups and chilling the carbonated water. And after dinner most evenings, when our group wasn't travelling, I set up a kiosk and sold my American compatriots cups of Coke for twenty-five cents a shot.

Delighted by even a sip of this familiar flavor of home, all the various youth group participants flocked to my stand. Soon I was selling perhaps fifty glasses an evening, three to four times a week for about a month, until I ran out of Coke syrup. I not only recouped the original $8 investment in syrup, but also the $25 for all the chilled carbonated water, the cook's fee and the cups. In fact, I made a profit of about $200. (I probably still owe Israel a few shekels in income tax, but I've more than made up for that in contributions since then.) That was a lot of money in 1959.

Thus I can claim—and no one has contested my assertion—that *I was the first seller of fountain Coke in the new State of Israel*. I hope this story will encourage you, too, to find your own way of taking a stand for Israel, our homeland.

L'chayim!

Provenance: My first of many trips to Israel took place in the summer of 1959. Sponsored by the B'nai B'rith Youth Organization (BBYO), a scholarship made it possible for me to visit and experience the land of our ancestors through the prism of my youth group. We toured the new state from Metullah to Eilat in a period of eight weeks. What a life changing experience it was! We took in every excavated site known at that time.

I was fully prepared for what I was to see, for I consistently chose "Israel" as the theme of many term papers I'd researched and written for high school class assignments. I knew a lot about the economics, politics, and social climate of this new country. My family background gave me the Jewish bug for learning and Zionism, so it was quite reasonable that I found myself perched on a camel in Jerusalem one summer day. This lengthy tour included two weekends designated for family visits, and this experience I describe began on one.

Marden David Paru is Dean, *Rosh Yeshiva*, and co-founder of the Sarasota Liberal Yeshiva, a Sarasota adult Jewish studies institute; a former instructor at the Melton Adult Mini-School and now a faculty member of the Lifelong Learning Academy at the University of South Florida. He previously trained as a social worker and long served as an executive of five Jewish Federations and other non-profit organizations. He attended Yeshiva University, the University of Tulsa, and the University of Chicago. Additionally, he was a doctoral fellow and faculty member at Brandeis University.

Study Guide: Questions, Sources, and Projects for Reflection, Discussion, and Action

1. Which *mitzvot* are illustrated by this story? Which additional *mitzvot* can you also relate to this story?

2. The author stood up against the Arab boycott by selling Coca Cola—and made a good profit on a small investment. Is there anything wrong with making a profit from doing a mitzvah?

3. Why is Israel important? What does it mean to you?

4. Research "boycotts" versus "promoting products in the marketplace". Which strategy seems the most mitzvah-centered and why?

Sacred Story and Text Connections

1. *Aliyah l'regel* (visiting Israel and going up to Jerusalem) following the destruction of the Temple is an expression of the Jewish people's great love for the Land of Israel.—*Shu"t Maharit, vol. 1, no. 114*

2. Justice, justice, you will pursue.—Deuteronomy, *Devarim* 16:20

Project: Begin discussions about a trip to Israel; look at travel books and websites, read the history of the country, ask Israelis and those who have stayed for long visits, and the Israeli Embassy representatives in your town known as the *shaliach*, emissary, for planning assistance. It's especially interesting to go with a Jewish youth group or dynamic Jewish organization with good contacts that will show you Israel in her glory as well as her troubles. It is fascinating to be there during major holidays and festivals. You can also fulfill the mitzvah of *aliyah l'regel*, by making a pilgrimage to Jerusalem on *Sukkot, Pesach* (Passover), and *Shavuot*. See if you can find a way to stay on to do volunteer work. Next time you have to do a report on a country for school, choose Israel.

Project: While some countries are over 200 years old, Israel, the modern state, is just sixty-six years old at the time of publication. Israel, the Jewish homeland, is precious for our thousands of years of history in it. Even so, modern Israel is no more perfect than any other modern country. Learn about the inventions and discoveries developed by Israelis, and also about some of Israel's challenges. Select a challenge to work on. This, too, is part of the mitzvah of *ahavat tzion*, loving Israel.

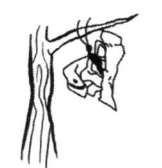

Chapter 27
Asmodai in Portland
by Gail Pasternack

Why did I come to Portland? I should have stayed in Los Angeles. There were plenty of Jews ripe for temptation there. You would think that I, Asmodai, King of Demons, would feel at home there. But I didn't. It was the sunshine. That infernal sun keeps even the most downhearted hopeful. How depressing. Even the smog couldn't cheer me up. So I left my henchmen in L.A. and made my way north to Portland, Oregon, the place they call "The City of Roses." I must have been desperate; I hate roses.

It was a weekday when I got there, so I cast an illusion over myself to give the appearance of a businessman. I wouldn't be able to persuade people to go astray if I approached them in my true form—a magnificent charcoal-black, winged demon with a dashing goatee. However, Portland wasn't like the other cities I had visited. I quickly realized I was overdressed for the place.

Anyway, that wasn't the worst thing about the city. It was way too clean—and green. Instead of litter and grime, the streets were lined with trees. How unnatural.

I shook off my disgust and started searching for Jews. Finally, I saw a bagel store, so I dashed inside. And then I saw it: a display case full of enormous hams and rounds of cheese—in a bagel shop! I walked out.

True, many Jews don't follow the kosher laws, and maybe this shouldn't have surprised me, but I needed to find pious Jews. After all, where was the challenge in tempting a person who was already questioning the faith to abandon that faith entirely? But convincing a devout Jew to question the faith and go astray, now that would be a victory. After failing so miserably in Los Angeles, I needed to prove myself. My followers respect me because I can tempt those whom no other demon can. And I couldn't afford to lose that respect.

Disheartened, I slogged through the puddles until I saw a cafe with a *mezuzah* on the doorpost and a sign advertising dairy-free items. Dairy-free. Surely, that must be a place for meat-loving Jews. Perfect! Pious Jews ripe for temptation. I licked my lips.

I entered a high-ceilinged, rectangular space with paintings by local artists hanging on pumpkin-orange walls. A chalkboard menu listed egg dishes, vegetarian dishes, pastries, all sorts of coffee drinks, but no meat. No meat—and dairy-free? How strange. Curious, I approached the counter and took my place at the end of the line.

A slight, gray-haired woman stared at the pastries in the display case for what seemed like an eternity.

"I'm allergic to dairy," she finally said. "Which are dairy-free?"

After the curly-haired teenage boy behind the counter indicated the pastries clearly marked "dairy-free," she added, "And they're gluten-free, too?"

The teenage cashier smiled. "Everything here is gluten-free. My father is gluten intolerant." He indicated an older gentleman cooking an omelet.

The woman bit her lip. "Do you have anything without eggs?"

I started drumming my claws on my leg.

"Yes." The cashier pointed to several items. "Those are vegan."

The woman stared at the pastries, taking her time. The other customers in line shuffled their feet, but no one said anything. The cashier waited patiently. He smiled when she ordered an apple-cinnamon muffin and ginger tea. As she sidled to a table across the room, I lifted my hand and pushed the air in her direction, causing her to trip and spill her tea. After all, she had made me wait.

Finally, it was my turn. I ordered black coffee and found a seat by the window. I turned the chair to face the counter so I could watch the father and son work while I sipped my coffee. Several customers chatted with the father as he cooked. They whined about their allergies or preached environmental mumbo jumbo. He listened to them patiently, and even nodded enthusiastically from time to time. This man seemed too good to be true. I needed more information to be certain he was my ideal target.

The next day I brought a laptop, parked myself at a table at the cafe, and typed in the password for the cafe's WiFi. I did a little research and discovered that the cafe owner, Joseph, had participated in an online discussion about how the ancient Jewish idea of eating conscientiously meant something different in the twenty-first century. He had said that today it also meant buying food from local farms that didn't use pesticides and other such nonsense. It reminded me of that Dr. Seuss story…what is it called? *The Lorax*, right. Anyway, a number of people in the discussion had agreed with Joseph's comments. This man was more than pious; he was influential. I couldn't believe my luck.

When the cafe closed, I left my laptop and walked out. I entered an alley next to the building and lingered in the shadows close to the cafe's rear door. I waited for more than an hour, growing more and more impatient. Eventually, the boy emerged and hopped onto a bicycle with a cart attached to it.

"Wait, Ben," Joseph said as he stepped into the alley. "We also need mushrooms. And remember to bring back receipts. We have to track our expenses very carefully, especially now."

"I'll try, but you know these farmers don't always give receipts."

Joseph sighed. "Just try." As his son took off down the alley, he whispered, "Go safely and return in peace."

Worry creased Joseph's brow, and I suspected there was more bothering him than just the safety of his son. I followed him into the cafe. He entered a room that served as both pantry and office and sat at a desk at the rear. I hid behind shelves of coconut milk, rice flour, and other unusual ingredients. Despite seeming to resemble human hands, my hands are really claws, so when I passed my sharp nails over the bag of rice flour, the bag split and flour trickled onto the floor. All right, it was petty, but it made me happy to see the waste.

Joseph stared at his computer screen for a long time, flipped through a stack of papers, and stared at the computer again. Then he flipped through the papers over and over. Finally, he groaned and put his head in his hands.

I stepped forward. "Money trouble?"

Joseph jumped.

"Sorry. Didn't mean to startle you. I knocked on the front door but no one seemed to hear, and when I tried the entrance from the alley, it was unlocked." He seemed disturbed by this, so I gave him a sheepish grin. "Normally, I wouldn't just come in, but I left my laptop here, on the table by the window. It's not there now."

"My son found it. It's behind the counter."

He led me into the cafe and grabbed the laptop from behind the counter.

I took it from him. "What a relief! I'd be ruined if I lost this."

"What do you do?"

"I'm a freelance accountant. I work out of cafes because it's cheaper than renting an office. I need to keep my costs down."

Joseph sighed. From his expression, I knew I had hit a sympathetic chord. I leaned across the counter. "My name is Amos."

"Joseph." He shook my hand.

"Are you having financial problems?" I waited for him to nod, and said, "I owe you for saving my laptop. Let me look over your records and see what I can do to help."

His face lit up. "Sure."

I sat at his desk and looked over his accounts. I saw right away that his food costs were too high, and to make matters worse, his rent was going up soon. "You seem to be missing some receipts here, but from what I can tell, it looks like you get all of your food supplies from local farmers and artisans."

Joseph, who had just finished inventorying supplies in his walk-in refrigerator, closed the large metal door. "That's right."

I leaned back in my chair. "That's the problem. You should buy food from a discount restaurant supply warehouse. Get rid of all these organic products and fair trade coffee, and you'd save a ton of money, especially on coffee."

Joseph sat in a chair next to the desk where I sat.

"My coffee supplier is a little expensive, but his product is excellent and he only uses beans grown on environmentally friendly farms."

"Forget about the environment!" I leaned forward. "You need to worry about saving your business."

He ran his hands over his stained apron. "I just want to provide a place where people who have food allergies or feel as deeply as I do about protecting our earth can come, relax, and enjoy good food."

I focused my eyes on him, willing him to believe every word I uttered. "Nice ideals, but is it worth going bankrupt for them?"

Joseph stared into my hypnotic eyes but said nothing.

"With such high costs…" I shook my head. "I don't see how you can continue paying your bills—unless you raise your prices, and in this economy, you'll lose customers and go out of business within a year."

Joseph's eyes glazed over. "What should I do?"

I knew I had him. I just needed to complete the deal.

"Forget about the environment," I said. "Let others worry about that. If you stop buying food from local farmers and artisans, and buy from large, discount warehouses, you'll be rolling in dough."

"Are you kidding! Our customers would have a fit."

Ben had just entered the pantry and dumped bags of produce from the farmer's market on the floor. I tried not to let Ben's sudden entrance disturb me. He was just a youth.

"They wouldn't have to know," I said to Joseph.

Ben stepped closer to me. "You're going to lie?"

Joseph's shoulders sagged.

I had underestimated Ben; I couldn't just ignore him. I fixed my hypnotic eyes on the child. "His business is in danger. If your father doesn't do what I say, he'll go bankrupt."

Ben met my penetrating stare, but unlike most people, he seemed completely unfazed. He turned to his father.

"Who is this guy, and why are you listening to him?"

"He's an accountant. I asked for his help," Joseph said in a monotone.

Ben opened his mouth to speak again and stopped, looking curiously at the floor. He pointed to the spot where the rice flour had spilled.

"What's this?"

Joseph snapped out of his trance and walked over to his son. My heart sank. There were non-human prints in the flour where I had walked earlier.

Joseph rubbed his forehead. "My grandmother used to tell me stories about demons. She said that you could detect demons by the bird-like footprints they leave behind. I never believed her." He faced me. "Amos, why don't you walk over there? Let's see what kind of footprints you leave."

"Why would I do something so ridiculous? Besides…" I showed him my feet, which were talons but appeared as normal human feet inside a pair of dress shoes. "I'd hate to get my shoes dirty."

"Take them off then."

Obviously I couldn't take off my shoes.

"This is silly," I said to the son, hoping to get him on my side.

"Dad, you are talking kind of crazy."

"How else do you explain the footprints?"

Ben examined the prints in the flour. "No idea." He glared at me. "But only a demon could convince my father to give up his ideals."

I could see the dread in Joseph's eyes, but when he turned to his son, he stood up straighter and squared his shoulders. "I can't give in to him, even if he is as dangerous as I've heard demons can be. I'd rather face his wrath." Joseph took several deep breaths before stepping closer to me. "I'll figure out how to save my business—without compromising my principles."

I was beat, and I knew it. If only the son hadn't returned so soon. I'd almost had the father. I dropped the illusion of human form and reverted to my true self. I relished the terror on their faces. Lifting my claws, I prepared to tear them apart, but then changed my mind. Instead, I flew through the window to the dark alley, breaking the glass in the process. At least I knew the family would have to pay to replace the window, a small price for embarrassing me.

I don't know why I let them off so easily. Maybe it was all the trees in Portland. That despicable beauty made me soft.

Gail Pasternack is a writer and educator who has a passion for Jewish folklore, food, and the environment. After earning her master's at Columbia University, she taught high school environmental science, worked for Cornell University Cooperative Extension, and homeschooled her children. She currently lives in Portland, Oregon, where she writes Jewish folklore-inspired fantasy fiction, including a new novel. To merge her love of food with her love of storytelling, she and her husband create cuisines for her fantasy world in her blog, *Crossing the Demons' Threshold*. www.GailPasternack.com

Study Guide: Questions, Sources, and Projects for Reflection, Discussion, and Action

1. Which *mitzvot* are illustrated by this story? Which additional *mitzvot* can you also relate to this story?

2. "The body is the instrument on which the soul plays life for God."—Hassidic aphorism as reported by Rabbi Zalman Schachter-Shalomi

   What does this phrase mean to you?

3. "Eco-kosher is not only concerned with the origin of the things consumed—what animal the meat came from, say, or what dishes it was cooked in, but also with the results of our consumption, such as the environmental and human toll of our actions…According to tradition, the fruit of oppressed labor is just as tainted as meat from an animal that was slaughtered without mercy…Are fruit and vegetables picked by underpaid migrant workers kosher?"—Rabbi Zalman Schachter-Shalomi, *Jewish with Feeling: A Guide to Meaningful Jewish Practice*

   How would you answer Rabbi Schachter-Shalomi's question? How might keeping eco-kosher connect to text #1 about your body and soul? What do you do that goes with or against these ideas in your daily life?

4. Joseph is a man who walks the principled path, and the demon tries to unseat him. Do you have principles that you would adhere to regardless of the pressures brought to bear upon you?

5. What is your practice regarding food ethics? How is keeping kosher related to food ethics?

6. It doesn't take a demon to tempt people to turn away from Jewish practice. What are some of the temptations you see around you? How do you deal with them?

7. The laws of *kashrut* (kosher) are to help you eat consciously—to separate meat, where life has been taken away, from milk—the earliest nourishment of a baby's life. Do you know where your family buys its food? If not, go food shopping with your family and engage with the process, read labels—what's healthy? Look for kosher certification symbols or at the ingredients—what's kosher? Is there also a *Tav Hayosher* symbol that shows the company pays attention to proper working conditions and earnings for its employees or one of the several green kosher or other environmental symbols to show care for animals and nature?

8. Are you now, or have you considered becoming, kosher? Why or why not? If not, what other things can you do to eat ethically and consciously?

9. If Asmodai visited you, what Jewish practice would he try to make you stop? How would you deal with him?

Sacred Story and Text Connections

Project: Take a class trip to the local farmer's market or natural foods store and bring with you a box or bag of a favorite food from a regular supermarket in your area. Compare options for your favorite products in the farmer's market or whole food store and interview the vendors about why they have chosen this path over the major supermarket scene. What do you learn that might affect your practice of the mitzvah of caring for your body, *shmirat haguf*?

Project: Choose to add one new element of eating "ethical kosher," for at least one week, if you are not already. How does this affect your interest, quality, and experience of life?

Chapter 28
The Magic Soup
by Geela Rayzel Raphael

Once upon a time, an old, old woman named Maraka lived in a cottage in the woods. She was so old she didn't know how old she was. She was so old her wrinkles had wrinkles, yet she had a sparkle in her eyes, and the light of her soul shined forth. Her daily passion was making soup. She carefully gathered wild ingredients from the forest: roots, onions, and mushrooms; as well as dried spices and herbs each season: dill, basil, and rosemary. She was careful not to pick too many of them, to ensure they would grow back each year. She knew the most delicious recipes, and yet she never followed them. Her true talent lay in what she invented. Her secret ingredient was her magic.

In Birzai, Maraka's hometown, she was one of the *kesefot*, women trained to make Jewish amulet scrolls and recite incantations to help those in need. Such incantations are a form of prayer. She would also pray over the soup. Holding her hands over the kettle, she blessed it with her secret words. She added her love to the process, for she knew that without love a soup could only turn out "so-so." She then called on the Angel of Spices, Saminiel, to add blessings, and also summoned forth the spirits of the plants to contribute their healing energy.

These were no ordinary soups. Each had the power to heal everything from heartaches to backaches. Her specialty was chicken soup, for it had the yearning for the Sabbath in every bite. Every night Maraka would secretly take containers of her soups and leave them on the stoops of those who were sick. Because she didn't want anyone to know, she went at night: it was her private *mitzvah*. This went on for years. Everyone thought well of his and her neighbor, because no one knew who was doing the *mitzvah*. After all, it could be anyone... No one imagined it was the old woman, because they thought she couldn't walk far.

One night, a young girl of the village was having a bad dream. She woke up, looked out the window, and saw a gnarled, old woman waving her hands over a pot of soup on their stoop. Frightened by this sight, she started screaming, waking her mother.

"Momma," she cried, "a strange women is casting a spell on our doorstep! I think it's an evil witch, not one of the wise *kesefot* from our synagogue. I have never seen this woman before. Perhaps it is her spells that make people sick."

Her mother ran to inform the authorities, who came and asked the girl to describe the evil women. The authorities took the pot of soup away as evidence for the "witch" trial. The rabbi was then called in to check the *mezuzah* and to make sure the house was safe.

Surprised and frightened, Maraka ran home in fright. She entered her house and collapsed from fear. Maraka offered some *tzedakah* (charity) that would prevent the worst from happening. Then she lit candles and prayed to *Shechinah* to help her. She fell into a deep sleep and dreamed of a beautiful temple in heaven, filled with a great light and three dancing Hebrew letters. A sense of calm soon came upon her soul, and she knew all would be all right. Awakening before dawn, she sat quietly, and thought of what she would need for this final journey—for this might be the last time she saw her home again. She knew the authorities would soon come for her, and she wanted to take three things with her to represent the dream.

As she looked around her humble home, she wondered what to take. Her eyes fell on her *Shabbat* candlesticks. Her grandmother's grandmother had lit those lights. She had to take them. She would need some herbs as well—for they were her tools and were not hard to conceal. But she would have to leave her mezuzah, for it was forbidden to take a *mezuzah* from one's home in case another Jew moved there. What else was needed?

Finally she decided to take her red thread, for red thread was a powerful amulet of protection for women. Tamar had wrapped it around her eldest twin when he appeared first out of her womb; Rahav had used red thread to show Joshua her house; and red thread was wound around Mother Rachel's tomb and then used for fertility blessings. Yes, the candlesticks, the herbs, and the red thread would go with her.

The next day the king's authorities searched the kingdom far and wide for an old woman making soup. They found Maraka at home and overheard her "casting a spell" over a cauldron. They marched right in.

As they prepared to seize her and the pot as evidence, Maraka said to them, "You must be hungry. Would you like a bowl of soup before we go?"

The soldiers were flabbergasted—and hungry—and the soup smelled delicious, so they looked to one another and said, "Why not? This old woman can't hurt us."

They sat down and ate, and entered a much better mood after that. Thus when Maraka asked to take her few belongings with her—the candlesticks, the herbs, and the red thread—the soldiers did not object.

Loading her onto their cart, they traveled to the royal dungeon. Maraka was terrified, for she knew that all too often the good intentions of a lone woman were misunderstood. She could be burned at the stake over a pyre of hot coals! She prayed to *Shechinah*, the Divine Great Mother who went into exile with her people, to help her as she went into this exile, asking her to guard her and send angels for protection.

Under the castle, the dungeon was many levels deep. It was a cold and damp place where many cried for help. Maraka's magic was powerless here, not being the kind of magic that could release the imprisoned. Her magic was a form of prayer to God. The dampness crept painfully into her old bones, as the dungeon guard marched her deeper and deeper away from the light.

Maraka was forgotten in her cell for seven weeks. Yet she never gave up hope. She was content to die, for she knew that she had led a good life and done only good deeds. She waited in her cell for the end to come, while singing songs to *Shechinah*, calling upon angels, and praying for a miracle. Her ancestors' candlesticks and the red thread were her faithful companions.

One day one of the young guards named Gabriel stood outside her door, sneezing and wheezing. Maraka said to him, "God bless you! I know what herbs might help. I can advise you."

The young guard was curious but unsure whether to trust her guidance. Maraka told him what remedy he needed, gave him a chicken soup recipe and some of her sacred herbs, and told him to eat the soup for three days. And she told him to have someone say, "*Ana Ayl na r'fa na lo*—Please, God, heal him." It was the proper incantation to summon Raphael, the Angel of Healing.

Gabriel went home and told his wife everything Maraka had told him. She agreed that following Maraka's advice might be worth the risk. So she made the soup and recited the incantation. And lo and behold! Gabriel was cured in three days.

His wife said, "This reminds me of Abayeh's mother, who was cited in the Talmud for her knowledge of healing herbs. She used to say that a cure should be taken for three, seven, or twelve days. I think that this old woman in the king's dungeon is a good Jewish witch!"

Gabriel, too, realized that an injustice had been done, that Maraka was no threat to anyone. In fact, she reminded him of his *Bubbe*. From that day on, he felt pity for her and would often sneak his cape and cup of tea into her cell to warm her. The cloak didn't help very much with the cold. But the hot tea probably saved her life. Maraka asked him for some candles and fire so she could light her candlesticks, and he smuggled them in to her as well. Maraka was so grateful to be able to do the *mitzvah* of lighting *Shabbos* candles. The light sustained her faith, and the warm glow of the candlelight illumined her dank cell. Maraka also tied knots in the red thread to mark her days in prison.

In the meantime, people in the region were getting sick and staying sick. There was no longer any healing soup appearing on their stoop as there once had been.

The townsfolk began squabbling with each other, accusing one another of stealing the other's precious healing pots of chicken soup! There were squabbles and riots. The rabbi was besieged with complaints.

The princess of the castle also fell ill. The queen was beside herself, for this was her only daughter. She pleaded with the king to seek a cure. So he offered a purse of gold for a cure. His officials crisscrossed the land to find someone to heal the princess. Many tried in vain. They used leeches, cupping, and concoctions, but the young princess continued to languish and began to waste away toward death.

Finally, the plight of the princess came to the attention of the guards serving in the dungeon. Gabriel, hearing the story of the princess, thought of the old woman. He sent a secret message to the queen about her. The queen didn't know what to do. She had never been down in the dungeon before and knew that the king might imprison her if he suspected that she was consulting a prisoner. So she summoned her most trusty maidservant, Azriela.

She sent Azriela to the backdoor of the kitchen where the beggars usually gathered, asking for scraps. Azriela gave a beggar woman a few coins and bought some rags for the queen. She brought the tattered clothing to the queen, who changed into the clothes and swore Azriela to secrecy. She told the maidservant that if she wasn't back in three days, to inform the king.

Then the queen descended into the dungeon dressed as a beggar. She was horrified at how the prisoners were treated and by the filthy conditions.

Suddenly one of the guards grabbed her and said, "What are you doing down here, beggar woman?"

The queen was shocked at this treatment and demanded to be taken immediately to the king.

The soldier just laughed. "Why should a beggar be brought before the king?" and he threw her into the cell. It just happened to be Maraka's cell.

The queen fell to the floor. Maraka helped her up, brushed off her clothes, and offered her a cup of tea and Gabriel's cloak to keep warm. They huddled together through the night, the queen sobbing, Maraka comforting her. The queen had never slept in anything but a soft bed before, and here she was on the hard floor with rats. When she told Maraka that she was the queen, Maraka tried to soothe her spirit, for Maraka really thought this beggar woman was crazy. What would the queen be doing in the dungeon?

The queen let herself be comforted by Maraka. This was a new experience for her, being held in a woman's arms and gently rocked to sleep. Because she was the queen, she didn't have many friends, and no one was even allowed to touch her besides her family and servants. This was a new experience for her being held in a woman's arms and gently rocked to sleep.

When the queen awoke, she was in a much better frame of mind and was very hungry. Maraka asked her favorite young guard, Gabriel, to bring her some herbs so she could make some soup and a cup of tea for her "guest." Soon the three of them were trading tales and laughing as they sipped their steaming tea.

The queen was fascinated with Maraka's candlesticks and red thread. Her own mother had given her candlesticks but had never explained how to use them. She looked closely at the red thread, which had now become an intricate woven design with seven weeks of knots.

In the meantime, the king was frantic over the queen's disappearance. His soldiers and servants searched far and wide for three days but found no trace of her. The princess was still deathly ill, and now was sad as well. She spent her days in bed, very depressed. The king was beside himself. His wife was gone, and his daughter ill. He sent soldiers into the towns and villages, offering a reward for anyone with news of the queen. No one knew where she was. She had just vanished.

Down in the dungeon, the queen and Maraka were becoming fast friends. It was almost as if they had always known each other. They laughed and cried and told stories. Since the queen seemed to know so many stories about the court, Maraka slowly became convinced that maybe she was the queen after all. Who could make up such stories?

One night as the queen was sleeping, her rags slipped down off her shoulder and Maraka noticed she was wearing a gold necklace with a Hebrew letter, the royal seal of the kingdom. The queen had forgotten to take it off in her haste to get into her disguise. And she had even forgotten she was wearing it!

Maraka sat back stunned. This woman she had been cradling in her arms and amusing with stories really was the queen. She knew then that her prayers had been answered, that the angels had listened, that *Shechinah* had been with her all this time. Maraka fell to her knees in gratitude and treasured the quiet moment of relief. She knew then this might be her last calm moment, and she wanted to savor it. She let the queen sleep.

The next day Maraka called to Gabriel through the bars and told him that he was hosting the queen in his dungeon. She appealed to him to help free her.

Gabriel's first reaction was to fear for his life. If she was truly the queen, he would be imprisoned for imprisoning her. And if she wasn't the real queen, he would be killed for lying to the king. What to do?

Maraka handed him the woven red thread, tied like *tzitzit*—prayer fringes, and said, "Put this around you, Gabriel. It will protect you."

The queen came to the bars and said, "Do not fear. We have proof that what I am telling you is true. Take my necklace with the royal seal to the king right away. Honor my wishes and you shall live. Deny me and you will die."

At that moment, Gabriel knew she was speaking the truth.

He took the necklace and the red *tzitzit*, and ran all the way out of the dungeon. When he burst into the throne room, the guards instantly grabbed him. What was a guard doing wearing red threads? They dragged him before the king, thinking he had gone mad.

The king was in a foul mood that day. He was about to have the rude intruder beheaded when Azriela, seeing the necklace, threw herself at his feet.

"He knows the truth, your Majesty," she cried.

"Speak, young man," the king said, "but I warn you that I have little patience left."

So Gabriel told the story about the old woman and the soup, and the crazy woman in rags who insisted she was the queen…and then he showed the king the necklace. The king stroked his beard, and said, "Why not bring them up?"

So the guards were sent to the dungeon, and returned with the queen and Maraka. As soon as the king saw his wife, he let out a cry of joy. She ran to hug him and the royal couple was thus reunited.

The king then turned to Maraka and asked to hear her story. Maraka cleared her throat and said, "Could you take these shackles off first, and could I have a cup of tea…or perhaps a glass of wine? I'm an old woman, and my throat is parched. Your royal dungeon isn't as comfortable as the palace, and I'm thirsty. Our father Abraham ran to do a *mitzvah* for his guests—*hachnassat orchim*, welcoming the stranger. Surely a king should do the same."

The king was taken aback at her boldness and was ready to throw her back into the dungeon. But the queen stepped forward and said, "Let me remind you, my dear king, that this was once my throne alone. Though you married into my royal family, I remain the legal ruler. I insist that Maraka's every need be taken care of."

The king muttered, "Yes, dear," and then added, "All this talk about soup is making me hungry. When can I taste this miraculous soup you are all talking about?"

Maraka was then asked to make her famous soup. As soon as it was ready, she brought it to the princess, first surrounding her sickbed with the red thread *tzitzit*, and then spooning some of the broth into her mouth. Immediately she felt better and was soon nursed back to full health.

Maraka was installed as the royal soup maker and lived out her days in comfort in the palace. The princess and Azriela learned her recipes and incantations. The royal candlesticks were found and polished, and were lit regularly on Sabbath, feast days, and special occasions. All royal tablecloths were woven out of red thread from that time forth, and the king enjoyed wonderful soups at his table. And the queen finally had a real friend. The villagers stopped fighting and wore red *tzitzit*. Gabriel was promoted. The dungeon was cleaned out, and only good food was served from that point on to the prisoners. The rabbi was called in to make sure it was kosher. Every Friday, free chicken soup was available to anyone in town who needed it to make *Shabbos* or cure a cold.

And to think....it all started with the *mitzvah* of a bowl of soup.

Geela Rayzel Raphael is an "unorthodox" rabbi doing outreach, lifecycle events, and providing counseling in the Philadelphia area. She has served as a chaplain; worked for Hillel; and has been spiritual leader at three congregations—currently serving at Temple Israel of Lehighton, Pennsylvania. Rayzel received ordination from the Reconstructionist Rabbinical College and studied at Pardes, as well as at Indiana, Brandeis, and Hebrew Universities. She is recipient of a Wexner Graduate Fellowship. Rayzel is an award-winning songwriter/liturgist and artist, painting silk *tallitot* and creating a deck of *Shechinah Oracle Cards* through collage and paper. www.shechinah.com

Study Guide: Questions, Sources, and Projects for Reflection, Discussion, and Action

1. Which *mitzvot* are illustrated by this story? Which additional *mitzvot* can you also relate to this story?

2. Maraka has a private mitzvah of helping people without their knowing. What *mitzvot* could you do for others without their knowing? Try tomorrow to find some and do as many as you possibly can.

3. How is Maraka's life changed by the arrival of the new woman? What makes life meaningful for you? Do you prefer living alone or with others?

4. Are there Jews being held captive at this time? Explore their stories and join in the mitzvah of participating in protests and funding organizations aimed at securing their release. Also explore the stories of captives held unjustly by other cultures and nations. How can we be of assistance to them?

5. If you had to leave your home quickly, what three things would you take with you to remind yourself of your Jewish life?

6. Maraka prays to the *Shechinah* when she is in trouble. Why do you think she chooses this name of God from among the many?

Sacred Story and Text Connections

1. All Israel is responsible for one another.—*Talmud, Shevuot* 39a.

   This is known as the mitzvah of *arevut*. Is it ethical to be responsible first for ourselves and Jewish people? What do you think? Is there an order of priority for helping in your family?

2. In Numbers, *Bamidbar* 12:13, Moses prays to heal Miriam, "*el na, r'fa na la*— please, God, heal her." When you are deeply sad and concerned about someone, try repeating this verse many times with passion. How is this helpful to you? Many studies show such prayers are helpful to those who are suffering and their families. Is this surprising to you? If an effect is good, does it matter that it can't be explained? How might knowing you are remembering someone ill and their family be of support to them?

3. *Talmud, Bava Batra 8b* calls *pidyon shvuyim*, redeeming captives, a mitzvah *rabbah*—mega mitzvah, because captivity can feel worse than starvation and death. Based on this verse, why do the sages consider it important to rush and prioritize this mitzvah?

4. The Rambam (Maimonides) ruled that one who ignores ransoming a captive is guilty of transgressing many *mitzvot*.—*Mishneh Torah, Hilchot Matanot Aniyim* 8:10-11. Which ones seem to apply?

5. *Kesefot*, women with shamanic skills and talents, are widely mentioned in the Jewish literature of earlier ages, sometimes viewed as helpful experts and other times as evil and put to death. Maggie Anton has written several novels to help redeem this profession of Jewish women; *Rav Hisda's Daughter: A Novel of Love, the Talmud and Sorcery* is a good place for a class to begin reading and discussing.

   a. The daughters of Rabbi Nachman stirred a [presumably boiling] pot with their bare hands...they stirred the pot with witchcraft.—*Talmud, Gittin 45a*

   b. If two women sit at a crossroads, one on this side and the other on the other side, and they face one another - they are certainly engaged in witchcraft.—*Talmud, Pesachim 111a*

   c. You shall not suffer a witch to live.—*Exodus, Shemot* 22:17

   d. Abbaye's mother is cited in the Talmud for her expertise in healing, for example: "For a chronic fever, complicated remedies are required: take a black hen, tear it crosswise, shave the middle of the head of the patient, and place the hen there-on and leave it there until it begins to smell. Then the patient should get up and stand in water until he gets weak."—*Talmud, Gittin* 67b

   e. Rabbi Shimon bar Yohai performing an exorcism by removing a spirit which had entered into the body of the emperor's daughter—Babylonian Talmud, *Me'ilah* 17b, and in another text, he places an evil eye on his opponent and turns him into a heap of bones—Jerusalem Talmud, *Shevi'it* 9:1, 38d

   Why do you think it has taken so long to achieve more rights for women in general society and within Judaism? What made Shimon bar Yohai's behavior acceptable and the shamanism of women, not? If Moses turned his

The Magic Soup | 215

wooden staff into a snake, it was a miracle. If a woman did it, it was typically termed witchcraft, putting her at risk of being put to death.

Project: Learn how to make soup in a large quantity to freeze in small portions for two or three meals, and bring to those who might feel better from the human contact, and the soup's warmth and nourishment. How might your class organize to keep this project going from generation to generation?

Project: Create a short prayer inviting support in the name of Shechinah, to say when you feel you need help.

Project: Organize friends, family, and students to pray for those who need healing and/or to be freed from unfair captivity. How would you set this up and keep it going?

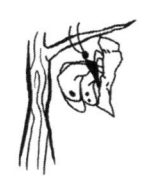

Chapter 29
The Story of the Magic Apple
by Jack Riemer

I am not a philosopher, and I am not a theologian; I am a storyteller. I believe that this whole Jewish business in which we are involved is one long, still incomplete story, to which each generation contributes its own chapter.

I love stories, and I think God loves stories, too. Otherwise, why would God have created the world? Was God short of aggravation? But if there were no world, there would be no stories, and if there were no stories, how dull and boring God's life would be.

So let me tell you the first story, the one on which all the other stories that make up the Jewish House of Stories are based. The story begins the way most stories begin: "Once upon a time..."

***

Once upon a time, there was a little boy named Israel, who ran away from home, because there was no food in the land where he lived, and he was very hungry.

Israel traveled south to another country, where he was treated well for awhile. But then a new king came along who was a very mean man. This king made little Israel work very, very hard. He made him get up early in the morning—before the sun came up—and work until late at night—when it was dark outside.

One night, little Israel came home from work worn out. He lay down on his bed, but was so tired that he could not sleep.

He called out into the night, "Help me! Somebody please help me!"

And then, all of a sudden, he felt the presence of Someone standing near him: invisible, yet very real.

"Who is it?" Israel cried out.

"Don't you remember Me, Israel?" said the invisible Voice, which sounded to the little boy just like the voice of his father. "I have seen how badly this mean, old king has been treating you, so I have come to take you home. But before I do, I am going to teach that mean, old king a lesson."

So the invisible Voice went to the palace and hit that bad king ten times in a row. And then the Voice guided little Israel out of the country, into the desert. Along the way, they had many adventures.

First they came to a big body of water. A giant hand appeared and stretched out over the water, and—presto! The water split. And down the middle ran a road, as wide as a superhighway! Israel walked down that road, without even getting his feet wet, and when he got to the other side, Israel was so excited that he did a dance right there on the edge of the water.

One day they came to a big hill. The Voice told Israel to climb to the top of the hill and fetch an apple from the tall, green tree growing there.

"My son," said the Voice at the top of the hill, "this is a magic apple. Always hold on to it, and never, never lose it."

"What is so magical about this apple?" asked the little boy.

"It is magical in four ways," answered the Voice. "First, the more you eat of it, the more there is of it. Second, this apple tastes delicious. Third, whenever you look at it, it will remind you to think of Me. And last, if you eat this apple, it will make you very, very smart."

"Can I taste it now?" asked Israel.

"Sure you can," answered the Voice, which now sounded to Israel just like the voice of his mother.

So the little boy took a bite of the apple and then another and another. And guess what happened?

The more bites he took, the more apple seemed to be left! At first, it was just this big, but after he took a few bites, the magic apple became this big. And when he took some more bites out of it, the magic apple became THIS BIG.

And sure enough, the apple tasted absolutely delicious. It tasted even better than an ice cream sundae—with sprinkles!

And when the little boy ate pieces of the apple, it always reminded him of the wonderful Voice, who had given it to him.

And eating this magic apple made the boy very, very smart.

Now let me stop here and ask you: Can you guess what this story is really about? Who was Israel? Who was the bad king? And what is the magic apple?

The little boy is the Jewish people.

The mean king who made him work so hard was Pharaoh, the king of Egypt.

And the invisible Voice who rescued him was God, who hit Pharaoh ten times with the ten plagues.

And the Magic Apple?

The Magic Apple is the Torah. The more we eat of it, the more there is to chew on. And how delicious the Torah is! Even tastier than a sundae—with sprinkles. And whenever we study it, we think of the special Someone who gave it to us. And if we keep studying it, we become very, very smart.

So this is the story of the Magic Apple. When I was a little boy, I heard this story—in a slightly different form—from my father, and he told me that he heard this story—in a slightly different form—from his father. So this is probably a very, very old story.

And do you know what my wish for you is? That someday you get to tell this story—in a slightly different form—to your children, and that they get to tell it to their children, too.

Jack Riemer is a rabbi, author, educator, and speaker, and has edited six books on modern Jewish thought, as well as *The World of the High Holy Days* and *Wrestling with the Angel*, and co-edited *So That Your Values Live On: Ethical Wills and How to Prepare Them*. He has travelled widely, conducting programs to help people learn about ethical wills. Jack served as rabbi for Temple Beth Tikvah of Boca Raton, Florida and as head of the National Rabbinic Network. He presently gives sermon seminars throughout the United States.

Study Guide: Questions, Sources, and Projects for Reflection, Discussion, and Action

1. Which *mitzvot* are illustrated by this story? Which additional *mitzvot* can you also relate to this story?

2. Something that unifies us as Jews is our common story of leaving Egypt and becoming a people. Are there stories passed through in your family about your Jewish story? Record the elders telling them so these don't get lost.

3. Why is it so important to retell "Israel's" story?

4. The author says the apple represents Torah. Could there be another reason to use an apple symbolically in this story?

5. What other stories about the Jewish people do you know?

6. Imagine that you are Israel—who would you give the magic apple to and why?

7. In what way do stories power learning and personal growth more readily than just memorizing information or being directed?

Sacred Story and Text Connections

The apple is a metaphor. Trees, water, stone, light, and earth are also very common metaphors in the Torah. For example, in the following prayer that is one of many early ways of saying Grace After Meals in Judaism, what does *tzur* (rock) stand for?

Tzur mi shelo achalnu
Rock from which we have eaten
bar'chu emunai
We faithfully bless
Savarnu v'hotarnu
Sated and satisfied
ki-d'var Adonai
in accord with the word of God.

Projects: Draw the story of Jack and the Magic Apple, act it out, make puppets and turn it into a play, put your drawings of the story into a book; take some lovely apples to *Shabbat* morning Torah service for people to share afterward, tell them this brief story by heart at the reception after services, the *oneg*, and invite discussion.

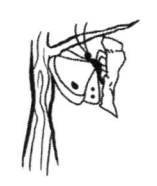

Chapter 30
The Reward for a Good Deed
by Barbara Rush

Do you know what a *luftmentsch* is?

The literal translation from Yiddish is an "air person." In actuality, it means a person whose head is in the clouds, who places hope in fantasies, and, who truly believes that his action–albeit outlandish and risky–will "make things better," not only for his family and himself but for society in general.

My father, Abraham Wishengrad, of blessed memory, was such a "mensch."

The story is told that in the early '30's, only a few short years after arriving in the United States from Poland, and via what was then Palestine and is now Israel, Abraham gave what little money he had to a fellow immigrant who was trying to manufacture a snow blower he had invented. "After all," Abraham thought, "the man is in need, and a man in need must be helped. And isn't this an opportunity to perform a mitzvah? And isn't a snow blower a machine that will make life easier for everyone?"

Who knows whatever became of this invention—or of Abraham's money?

Now, Abraham had arrived in the U.S. just in time for the Great Depression. During that time he resourcefully flitted from job to job: factory worker, house painter, peddler, and more, in an effort to eke out a living for his wife, Sarah, and his tiny daughter.

But it did not occur to Abraham not to do good deeds, and it did not seem to matter to him that his money, hard earned though it was, would never be returned, or that he might never see the stranger again. To Abraham "the reward for a good deed is the deed itself" (*Pirkei Avot* 4:2). Those words from the Talmud must have been ingested during his days as a young pupil in the Jewish schools of his early 20th century *shtetl* (village), after which they spread throughout every fiber of his body.

Nor did Abraham's *mitzvot* always involve gifts of money. During the Great Depression, or so the story goes, he found a young mother crying in the street. Her family, including a young child, had lost their home. Here were people in need! Here was the opportunity to perform a mitzvah! Yes, Abraham took them home, and, as the story goes, their one-year-old daughter and his recently born daughter, Barbara, shared the same bed. This arrangement continued for many months. At another time, only a few years later, Abraham adopted a mother and two sons, after the husband had been killed in New York in an anti-union riot. They came to live with Abraham and Sarah for a long time.

And so this pattern continued for many years. But now, decades later, most of Abraham's impulsive good deeds, and their recipients, have been forgotten. Only one mitzvah, one of his good deeds, remained alive for many years:

One day in the late '40's, Abraham met with his cronies, as was their habit, at a local coffee shop on Jerome Avenue in the Bronx, N.Y. While there, Abraham, being a jovial sort, struck up a conversation with an Orthodox Jew—Abraham assumed him to be a rabbi or a person of equal education—who told them that he had just written a commentary on a Talmudic treatise, and that he was seeking funds in order to get his work published. "Well," thought Abraham, "a man in trouble must be helped—and wouldn't an explanation of Talmud be helpful to everyone?" The man's plea reawakened memories of his own childhood and youth in Poland, and of his studies at *cheder*. And so, Abraham, always a great lover of books, promised the man a loan of $200 (a considerable sum in those days). Other friends, as well, were encouraged to lend money toward the publishing venture.

In the summer of 1948 Abraham suffered a massive coronary, and soon Sarah and Abraham and Barbara moved to Florida to provide him with a warmer clime. (Another daughter had recently married and now remained in New York.)

But, despite all medical efforts, Abraham died in the spring of '52.

Sarah and Barbara returned to New York, the place where they had lived for so many years and where they had friends and family. It was there that Sarah heard from fellow "investors" in the publishing venture that the author of the book was now living in Canada, that somehow a connection had been made with him, and that their loans had even been repaid.

Sarah immediately wrote to the man. "Do you remember my husband, Abraham Wishengrad, who lent you $200 toward the publication of your book?" And Sarah added that she was now a widow and could really use the money.

The man replied at once: "Yes, I do, indeed, remember the kindness of your husband, and I am, indeed, sorry to hear of his death, and I do, indeed, intend to return the money. However, I am short of funds at the moment and will send the money as soon as I can."

Months passed. Years passed—first one, then two, then three. No money arrived, and the man from Canada was forgotten.

***

On a Sunday afternoon in January, 1956, Barbara was married. On Saturday, the day before the wedding, a letter arrived from Canada–from the man who had borrowed the money. It was an apology—and a check for $200.

Sarah beheld the check, and tears welled in her eyes, "This is a wedding present from your father," she cried. "This is a present from your father."

Coincidence, you say? Perhaps! But, until this very day, Barbara continues to believe that it WAS her father's special gift—and his performing the mitzvah of helping a stranger–that had come full circle—back to her!

Provenance: This is a true story.

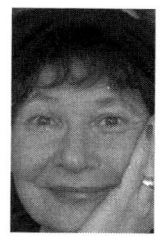

Barbara Rush is an author and former librarian, teacher, and storyteller resides with her family in Durham, North Carolina. She has a Master of Arts in Jewish Studies, and has authored/co-authored more than two hundred stories, translated into many languages and collected in thirteen books, including *The Diamond Tree*, winner of the Sydney Taylor Book Award; *The Book of Jewish Women's Tales*; *The Kids' Catalog of Passover*; *Mitzvah-Stories: Seeds for Inspiration and Learning* and three volumes on Jewish art. Among the first to bring Sephardic tales to American audiences, Barbara also helped develop the first course for professional storytellers in Israel. As an ALA Book Fellow, she has also taught abroad.

Study Guide: Questions, Sources, and Projects for Reflection, Discussion, and Action

1. Which *mitzvot* are illustrated by this story? Which additional *mitzvot* can you also relate to this story?

2. Look up the Great Depression online. Was it as hard for people economically as the story describes, or was it even harder? What is a socioeconomic safety net? How many of the *mitzvot* are fulfilled by creating these in a society?

3. Look up the problems that are caused by credit card debt. What is interest and how does it work? Why is it a mitzvah for Jews not to charge each other interest on personal loans, and to share profits rather than charging interest in business scenarios? Would it be a difficult task to expand this practice to the entire business world? Who would you need to seek out to research the matter? Look up the term *landsmanschaften* and learn about how Jewish immigrants created ways to try to both save safely and "have each other's backs" in the event of emergencies or a capital crunch in a family or business.

4. What mitzvah did the story's character, Abraham, fulfill by coming to the United States from Poland via Palestine? Look into the historical record to see other reasons why he may have gone that route, including what Palestine was like in those days, to understand why he didn't remain.

5. Was it ethical for the person given the loan to ignore the request of the widow for an immediate return of the funds?

6. The $200 being returned the day before the wedding is a phenomenon called synchronicity. Do you see the hand of God in this?

Sacred Story and Text Connections

1. You shall not ill-treat any widow or orphan. If you do mistreat them, I will heed their cry as soon as they cry out to Me, and My anger shall blaze forth and I will put you to the sword, and your own wives shall become widows and your children orphans.—Exodus, *Shemot* 22:21-23

2. Uphold the rights of the orphan; defend the cause of the widow.—Isaiah 1:17

3. If you mend your ways and your actions; if you execute justice between one [hu]man and another; if you do not oppress the stranger, the orphan, and the widow.—Jeremiah 7:5-6

4. Job protests his innocence by saying: "I saved the poor man who cried out, the orphan who had none to help him. I received the blessing of the lost, I gladdened the heart of the widow."—Job 29:12-13

What connects the poor, the orphan, and the widow? Why are they singled out?

Project: Raise funds towards a micro-loan to help a business or family. Go to the website of an organization such as the Jewish Free Loan Association in Los Angeles and select a category that is meaningful to you, e.g., emergency car repair loan, adoption loan, home health care loan, graduate school tuition loan, and more.

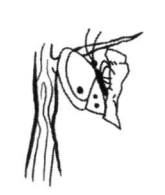

Chapter 31
Each Bird Must Carry Her Own Light
by Cassandra Sagan

At the edge of a lake in the Rift Valley known as the Hula, lived *Tzipor* Rina, an earnest bird with a goofy grin. Humble, and a bit bumbling. If Rina had a sleeve she would wear her heart on it. Instead she wore a shaggy blue-yellow fire of feathers, flung like a boa over her shoulder with a flick of what would be her wrist, if she had one.

Hula is in Israel, and it is a favorite vacation spot for millions of birds as they migrate through the Middle East on their way to Africa, Europe, and Asia. Rina ran a bird lodge called the Edge of the Field. She kept one eye trained on the distance, looking for travelers just as Father Abraham did, and one eye turned toward the worm stew she was preparing for her guests, just like Mother Sarah. Watching and worming.

More than anything, Rina loved to listen to the *sipurim*, the stories, being told by the *tziporim*, the birds, who lodged at the Edge of the Field. Eyes opened wide on the sides of her head, Rina once leaned so far into the storytelling of a Yemenite bird that she fell over her own feet and into the soup she was preparing. Rina always turned each stumble into a dance, laughing until her round bird belly shook so hard it almost knocked her off her feet again.

The stories Rina loved most were those the *tziporim* told about a time when there would be enough light in the world to recycle all sadness and suffering into joy.

***

"Each bird must carry her own light into the future!" mumbled a guest from Jerusalem. She carried so much *or tzipor*, Birdlight, in her beak that it was a little hard to understand her.

"What? Each bird must marry her own kite into furniture?" said Rina, a little confused.

The Jerusalem Bird tucked her bulging bundle of *or tzipor* carefully under her wing. "I said, we must gather and carry the sparks of Birdlight, *or tzipor*, into the future. And when that big bird's nest in the heaven-sky is filled with light, there will be peace in all the worlds, *shalom be-khol ha-olamim*!"

The nutria, giant rodents who lived on the boggy shores of Lake Hula, loved to entertain travelers by telling and retelling about the time when Rina rolled backwards off a log into the lake, her feet kicking up, up, up, as if she was in a chorus line. Then, instead of flying away, she fell onto her tail feathers and splashed into the water.

Rina knew the nutrias mean no harm in telling this story at her expense, so she played along with them, kicking her legs and flapping her wings wildly, spoofing her own fall. She would much rather be teased than have anyone find out her secret. A secret she had kept her whole life.

Rina couldn't fly!

Rina couldn't levitate. She couldn't anti-gravitate. She couldn't hover or lift off. Rina couldn't even stop falling once she had started.

Yet Rina longed to feel the joy of flight, the wind beneath her wings of which every bird sings. Each morning she *davenned* (prayed) with the *minyan* (quorum) of birds who lit their candles of song at dawn. She pulled an early worm out of the earth-bed, brushed the moon from each of her eyes, and watched sadly as her friends and guests flew off into *ha-shamayim*, the heaven-sky. She watched the birds swoop in V's and frolic in flocks, gathering *or tzipor*—Birdlight.

"Hey, friends, don't wait for me," called Rina each day, sneaking backwards into the bulrushes. "I'll catch up with you in a bit!"

Then, after all of the birds had soared across the valley toward the blue, distant hills, Rina would try to fly. She took a running start, thrust her full, fluffy front out farther and farther until—whomp—she bounced on her beak.

Determined, Rina scrambled up a cornstalk, flapped her wings, let go of the stalk, and tumbled to the ground with a thump.

She back-flipped off boulders and tried leaf-parachuting in wind storms. She balanced on tippy-toes while gazing at a rainbow, but nothing worked. Rubbing her bruised bird rump, Rina flicked the dust from her feathers, then skipped off to do her favorite mitzvah, greeting guests at the Edge of the Field.

***

A *tzipor* arrived at the inn from Ethiopia.

"Shalom!" said *Tzipor* Rina, for that is how she greeted her guests. "What do you hear on the wind?"

If the Ethiopia Bird had a mouth she would have smiled, because she had a story to tell.

"In Ethiopia," she said, "we say that the past is right in front of you, because you can see it, and the future is behind you, because you can't. That is why the *tzipor* is the only creature who may ascend to the heavens. Through the eyes on the sides of our heads, we are able see halfway backwards. So it is that every now and then, we receive a glimpse of the future."

"If that is so, then why don't birds fly backwards into the future?" asked Rina. "Why fly headfirst into the past? Everyone knows that the future needs us to carry the Birdlight, the *or tzipor*, forward."

The Ethiopia Bird tilted her head, opened her beak as though to speak, but then, perhaps because it was too complicated to explain, she suddenly flew away.

Rina's heart felt a little droopy in her chest. Why couldn't she rise up to carry her *or tzipor* into the future?

At the Edge of the Field, Rina listened to *sipurei tziporim*, bird stories, from *kol ha-olam*, the whole world. She heard the *sipur* of the Syria Bird about a bird weighted down by her own tears, and the Lebanon Bird's tale of being forced to live behind the copper bars of a cage. Then there was the Persia Bird who told Rina about the Conference of Birds who traveled seven months across seven treacherous hills and valleys in search of the legendary Simorgh, reputed to carry messages between earth and sky. Only thirty birds arrived at the lake where this magical bird was rumored to perch, but instead of finding the Simorgh, they found only their own reflections in the water.

Rina listened to bird stories until she felt as if her whole bird-boned body was made out of stories. She could feel them sloshing around inside her like *mayim*—water, and tickling her like *ananim*—the clouds above. Sometimes, out of the corner of her eye, Rina thought she could see the future coming towards her. She could hear laughter and the gentle thrum of birdsong. She saw hidey-holes and cozy columbaria like the ones in the stories the birds told about the future time. In the distance, far, far behind her, was a nest. She couldn't quite see what was inside, but she could tell that it glowed.

One day an Old Bird stumbled down from the sky on unsteady legs, staggering to a wobbly landing at the Edge of the Field.

"*Shalom*, friend!" said Rina. "Let me help you."

"*Baruch Hashem*—Blessed be!" said the old bird. "You would be doing a *mitzvah gedola*, a really great deed, to help me. I am old and tired, and this flight will be my last. I feel the future coming towards me, and there's not much left. I can barely see anything behind me."

Rina arranged a pile of bulrushes and grasses, gesturing for the Old Bird to rest there.

"Would you like some worm soup? I just made a batch in this puddle of tears left by a Syria Bird. Nice and salty! Here, let me ladle you a leaf-full."

The two birds pecked at their meal together, sharing stories that each had gathered over the years. When the old bird was fed and settled in her feathers, she began rocking back and forth gently, humming *L'cha Dodi*, a *Shabbat* song she knew from her home in Tzfat.

"Tell me, Old Bird, what do you hear about the future time?"

Old Bird opened one eye and looked Rina over, up and down, front to back. Outside to inside.

"You have a good heart, so I know you won't let it go to your head when I tell you that where I come from in Tzfat, there are people called Kabbalists, and they call the future time *y'mot ha-Mashiach*. They say that in the time of *Mashiach* there will be enough light to transform all sadness and suffering into joy."

Old Bird leaned in even closer. "And the Kabbalists say that *Mashiach* (messiah) is a *tzipor*!"

Rina's beak fell open.

"*Mashiach* is a bird, a *tzipor*!" Rina said. "Sometimes I can see a glimpse of a nest behind me—do you and all the birds see it, too? Is it the nest of *Mashiach*?"

Old Bird nodded. "So it is."

"And the light in the nest must be the *or tzipor* which each bird gathers and carries into the future."

"Indeed, that's what we birds do," said Old Bird. "We gather light like worms and twigs. Crack the dark seeds and pull out the sparks of Birdlight."

Slowly Rina said, "And of course… then….*Mashiach* can fly?"

"Yes, how could *Mashiach* be a bird without flying?"

Rina drew very close to the old bird from Tzfat. They looked at each other, eye to eye, side by side. One bird facing the mountains, the other bird facing the lake.

"Old Bird, something troubles me greatly," Rina said.

Neither bird blinked.

"Why would *Mashiach* fly toward the past to become the future? What is the future, if not the fullness of the *or tzipor*?"

"Aha, I am glad you asked," said Old Bird. If she had a pair of glasses, she would have taken them off and wiped them on her apron.

"*Mashiach* is flying towards us because that's what the future does. It comes towards you. You just have to head in the right direction, and you will meet the future somewhere along the way."

Then Old Bird waved Rina off with a wing. "Speaking of the very near future, I'm tired and it's time for my nap. Why don't you fly away to sing the sunset song with the other birds? I've slept through every sunset for weeks." Her head began to sink forward into her chest…

…and Rina's heart sank like a pebble to the bottom of a leaf-full of worm stew. If her feathers had been petals, they would have wilted.

Always the perfect hostess, Rina didn't want to disturb her honored guest, but she just couldn't help herself. "Oh, I wish I could fly away, but I don't know how!"

For a moment the world was still. The wind paused, and the tall grass quit rustling.

Old Bird opened her eyes slowly and turned to look at Rina. "Well, you could have fooled me. With all your exotic stories I assumed that you were well traveled."

"I entertain a lot of guests," said Rina. "I ask a lot of questions."

Old Bird eased up from her nestbed and headed unsteadily to the shore. "I've straightened out a lot of flight problems in my day: weight balancing, flap rhythm, and the like." She gestured with what would have been her chin, if she had one. "Go ahead and show me what you've got."

Rina shook out her feathers and circled her hips, rehearsing in her mind's eye the little dance number she would make of her inevitable stumble. Then she took a deep breath and let it out with a sigh, and with a running start and a beat of her wings, leaned forward, forward, forward until she fell on her front with a thump.

"Hmmmm," said Old Bird. "You weren't kidding."

"I'm sorry," said Rina. "My mother hated the way she flew, and so she refused to teach me anything about it."

Old Bird nodded kindly. "Well, I've never encountered this particular issue before, but your problem seems pretty simple to solve."

"Really! Old Bird, do you think there's hope?"

Old Bird shook her head. "Hope? The future is coming and it's right in front of your face! You'll be flying in just a few minutes."

The dream of her lifetime was about to come true.

Rina froze.

Who will greet the guests and make the soup?

What if I forget the instructions and plummet to my death?

What if I love flying so much that I never stop to listen to a stranger's story?

Who will I become? How will I recognize my own reflection when I get to the lake where the Simorgh lives?

What if I learn the secret of flight, and still can't do it? Will failing to fly break my heart into a thousand pieces?

"It's simply a matter of aiming in the right direction," Old Bird was saying. "What I observed you doing is leaning into it, but what you need to do is to lean back."

Old Bird rocked on her wobbly legs to demonstrate.

"Lean back, into the future, lean back until you feel that little pull, the dynamic tension. It's the difference between pulling on a slack rope, or pulling on a rope that has another *tzipor* pulling on the other end of it."

So Rina leaned back until she felt the arms of the future holding her. She began to rise, to lift, to levitate off the ground.

"Now what?" sang Rina, for she could not contain her joy.

"Aim for the nest," said the Old Bird, her head drooping to her chest. "But don't go too far. Best not to overdo it on your first day."

"Wheeeee!"

The top of Old Bird's head seemed smaller and smaller as Rina rose into the great blue. A cloud kissed her wing as she dipped and swirled and flipped and whirled. It seemed like an eternity, but it was actually only five minutes before Rina got a cramp in the place where her armpit would be, if she had one. She skidded in for a landing, a tear falling off the tip of her beak.

"There, there now," said Old Bird, patting Rina with her wing.

"It's so....glorious up there. But my whole world is down here, at the Edge of the Field."

Old Bird wiped away Rina's tears. "Not every *tzipor* has the ability, or even the longing, to do the full migration. Millions of birds live in the Hula Valley all year round."

"I didn't know that!" said Rina. "Every bird I meet is in the middle of the big migration."

"That's the innkeeper's dilemma, isn't it?" said Old Bird. "You only meet birds who are traveling."

"But the *or tzipor*! I must gather and carry my Birdlight into the future. Now that I know how to fly, I can't just stay here all the time."

"Silly bird!" said Old Bird fondly. "You have been carrying your light into the future all along. When you listen to stories, you gather *or tzipor*, and when you tell stories you carry Birdlight into the future. You're famous! Migrating *tziporim* tell and retell the stories they learn from you everywhere they go."

Rina's blinked. "Famous?"

"I have heard the stories of *Tzipor* Rina of the Hula Valley told all over the East. I have listened while perched in the branches of a cypress in Lebanon, and I have heard your stories while hunting worms among the twisted willow roots of Morocco."

If Rina had cheeks, she would have blushed.

***

The next morning, Old Bird waved from the Edge of the Field as Rina leaned back into flight.

"I'll just be a short while," she said, heading for the tops of the bulrushes, then the low branches, the high branches, the steep boulders, and beyond.

"Don't worry," called Old Bird. "I'll be sure to stir the worm stew."

Just ahead, a V of *tziporim* soared through the perfect clouds towards the Syrian hills.

"Wait for me," Rina sang. "Do you know any good stories?"

And they did.

Cassandra Sagan is an ordained *Maggid* (storyteller/teacher/preacher), a poet, mosaic artist, InterPlay leader and ukelele player. She developed and offers workshops in InterPlay Torah study, a playful approach to personal midrash, insight, and embodied Torah. Cassandra has long taught as a "Poet in the Classroom," across all age groups and populations, producing almost 100 volumes of student writing. She is also a faculty member of the Jewish Spiritual Education and Maggid-Educator Ordination Programs at Reclaiming Judaism. A songwriter and performer of original and traditional music, her poetry and essays have appeared in numerous anthologies and journals. www.UkeMama.com

Study Guide: Questions, Sources, and Projects for Reflection, Discussion, and Action

1. Which *mitzvot* are illustrated by this story? Which additional *mitzvot* can you also relate to this story?

2. Rina hides her lack of flight from the other birds. Have you ever hidden something about yourself because it makes you feel as though you are different from others? Do you think other people do this as well?

3. Describe Birdlight, *or tzipor*, in your own words. What Jewish concept does it symbolize? Why "must every bird carry her own light"?

4. What was Rina's true gift? Sometimes, trying to be like others, we forget about our real gifts. What are your gifts? How do you share them with others?

5. Have you ever tried to do something and failed? How did it feel? Did it make you give up or become more determined to try again?

6. Who do you think you will become in the future? How will it be different from who you are now (not counting that you will be older)?

7. What are your special talents? How might you apply your talents helpfully in the Jewish community on a regular basis?

8. Sometimes we want to become one thing when we are really another. How will you know when you have found the right thing?

Sacred Story and Text Connections

1. When Rav Huna had a meal, he would open the doors of his house and say, "Let whoever is in need come and eat."—Talmud, *Ta'anit* 20b-21a
   And Rav Dimi of Nehardea said: "the welcoming of guests takes precedence over [time in] the house of study"...Rav Judah said in Rav's name: "the welcoming of guests takes precedence over welcoming the divine presence—the *Shechinah*."
   —Talmud, *Shabbat* 127a

   How might Rina relate to this text? How do you view having guests? What kinds of preparations do you tend to make for them? Some people have the custom of taking on one mitzvah that is their very special practice that they do the best of all. A powerful story with a surprising twist about this is by Benji Levine, and is titled "The Escort." The story begins in Israel during the British occupation, and can be found in *Mitzvah Stories: Seeds for Inspiration and Learning* (Reclaiming Judaism Press).

2. The Jewish concept *mashiach*, comes from the root *mem, shin, chet*, meaning to anoint, or paint. The kings of Israel in the biblical period were anointed as part of their ritual of appointment and called *mashiach*.

    Times of war and suffering often bring a yearning for a single individual, a leader, who could fulfill the later ideals for *mashiach* expressed by the prophets Isaiah, Jeremiah, and Hosea. These, for example, include bringing about the political redemption of the Jewish people, restoring us all to living in Israel, establishing a world government in Jerusalem, rebuilding the Temple, restoring the sacrificial system and Jewish law as the law of the land. The expectation was that the ultimate evolution of human civilization, the "world-to-come", would be the result of this, and the entire world would be at peace (Isaiah 2:4); even the animals would cease to eat each other. (Isaiah 11:6-9)

    At various times in Jewish history specific individuals were believed to be this sort of superman *mashiach*. For example, Rabbi Akiva believed that the military commander Bar Kochba would turn out to be such a *mashiach*, but he was wrong. Jesus's followers believed he was such a *mashiach*, and he, too, did not fulfill these prophecies during his lifetime. Nor did Shabtai Tzvi, who lived in medieval times and who was initially regarded as having potential. And there were many more.

    Why is the idea of a messiah attractive to so many?

3. The actual work of redeeming the world is turned to us in history, and is done by all of us, day by day… Rather than messiah redeeming us, we redeem messiah.
    —Rabbi Arthur Green, *Seek My Face, Speak My Name: A Jewish Mystical Theology*

    How does the author of our story re-envision the idea of *mashiach*? What would it mean for you personally to live in relationship to the approach she takes?

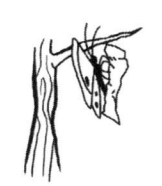

Chapter 32
Bringing Joy to Others
by Peninnah Schram

On the first day of Rosh Hashanah, Aaron sat in synagogue thinking how he could keep reading his book of favorite Calvin and Hobbs comics without anyone seeing him. As he had often done before, he "hid" the book inside the *machzor* (High Holiday prayerbook), and slouching slightly in his seat, pretended to be engrossed in his prayer book so his father wouldn't catch him. But every once in awhile, Aaron would laugh, and his father would glance over at him. Then Aaron would sheepishly say, "I just thought of something funny. Whatever." A tall and lanky fifteen-year-old, Aaron was forever trying to get out of going to synagogue, and some of the time he succeeded. But he was smart enough to know he would not be nearly as persuasive with his parents when it came to the High Holy Days.

Suddenly, he heard coming from the *bimah* (synagogue stage) a voice he had not heard before. It was not the voice of the regular rabbi. He looked up and saw that a guest rabbi, a *maggid* (storyteller/guide), was talking about people being kind to one another and reaching out to perform *mitzvot* to those in need of help. Then the *maggid* began telling a story about a rabbi named Kalonymus Kalman Shapira, who came from a Polish town near Warsaw. Slowly, Aaron began to tune into the story, hearing about this beloved rabbi who was known as "the Rebbe of the Warsaw Ghetto". Before World War II, this rabbi used to especially enjoy teaching young people in his school, called a yeshiva. He was constantly saying to them: "Children, precious children, remember, the greatest thing in the world is to do somebody a favor."

Hearing this, Aaron leaned over to his father and whispered, "Hey, *Abba*, could you do me a favor and loan me two hundred bucks for a new iPod? You'd be doing a really big mitzvah!"

His father's withering look made Aaron's smile vanish. Maybe it would be wiser just to sit quietly and listen—or pretend to listen.

The guest rabbi went on to describe how an American rabbi named Shlomo Carlebach had heard about this inspiring Polish rabbi and his mitzvah message. Reb Shlomo wanted to continue his mission of teaching people "to do somebody a favor". Wherever he traveled, always with his guitar on his back, Reb Shlomo would sing and tell stories about Rabbi Kalonymus Kalman Shapira and his teachings.

Aaron loved Reb Shlomo's songs so he began listening even closer to the story. At the end of the story, everyone sang a Carlebach *niggun* (wordless melody), and then the Rosh Hashanah service continued with the blowing of the *shofar*.

***

On the second day of Rosh Hashanah, Aaron continued to read his comics. Since the book he was reading this time was a bit smaller than the *machzor*, it fit neatly inside. During the *Kedushah* prayer, he happened to glance at the right hand margin of his prayer book. The note in the margin said something about angels turning to each other, "acknowledging each other and recognizing their mutual responsibility". Whatever that meant. Aaron shook his head and turned back to his comic strip.

Suddenly, like an instant replay, Aaron pictured in his mind two lines of angels turning to each other, bowing or making a curtsey to each other, like doing a dosey-doe in a square dance. Aaron snorted. His father's angry look reprimanded him for being disrespectful in synagogue. Aaron was careful to remain quiet for the rest of the service.

On his way home, Aaron kept thinking about what it meant, "to do somebody a favor", and puzzled over what "mutual responsibility" meant. Responsibility of what–for what–to do what? He soon gave up trying to figure it out. Who cared, anyway?

When the story and its message came up later at lunch and then again at dinner, Aaron said, just to be annoying, "Hey, guys, listen, you can do me favors anytime you want. You'd be doing a really big mitzvah!" When he saw how irritated everyone got, he began to repeat the words as often as he could. To his sister and brother, he would say, "Oh, by the way, would you do me a favor and lend me your iPod? It's a mitzvah!" Or "Do you want to do me a favor? Can you lend me ten bucks?" Of course, his siblings knew him too well so they didn't fall for any of his "shtick".

Then he decided to juice up his new routine with another of his talents— speaking with different accents. He could imitate an Indian accent very well, and could put on a very credible Arabic, Moroccan, Greek, French, Spanish, or Italian accent. He was so good that sometimes he even answered the phone in these accents, and the people at the other end would think they had dialed the wrong number. People who heard him do these accents laughed with astonishment, even his sister and brother.

Now he began asking for favors in his various accents. After awhile, Aaron's family would just sigh loudly every time he said anything about doing a "favor" in any accent. Finally, at dinner one night, his sister said, "Aaron, let it go! O.K.? Enough! It's not funny any more, you know." His brother said, "Shut up, Aaron.

You're not funny!" His mother, trying a different approach, asked, "Aaron, what does 'doing someone a favor' really mean? Can you explain why the Polish rabbi emphasized this teaching with his students?" Aaron just shrugged his shoulders and turned his attention to his food.

But Aaron found himself pondering his mother's questions. As he thought more about it, the angels he had envisioned at services returned to his thoughts. They seemed to be echoing his mother's questions.

"So what does 'doing a favor' really mean?" he asked himself.

A few days later, he was in the school library. He located the biggest dictionary he could find and looked up the word favor. He read: "a. A gracious, kind or friendly attitude. b. An act evidencing such an attitude; an act of kindness. c. An act requiring sacrifice or special generosity." Aaron now realized that doing him a favor didn't mean for someone to give him money or something else just because he had asked for it or just because he wanted it, especially when he didn't really need it for something urgent or important.

"Boy, what a selfish bully I've been!" Aaron thought to himself. "But how can I do 'acts of kindness' or an act of a 'special generosity'? I can't give money away to the poor or homeless. I barely get an allowance and I really need that money myself."

From then on, Aaron stopped doing the "do me a favor" shtick at home (although he kept doing his foreign accents to get laughs). And he couldn't stop thinking about doing the kind of favors he'd read about in the dictionary. Thoughts kept churning in his mind, like the wheels of a machine turning around and around.

***

Aaron belonged to the drama club in his high school. At one of their meetings, they were discussing what their next play would be. One of the teachers told some stories about Elijah the Prophet, the Master of Miracles, to see if any of these tales could be turned into a dramatic script for the group to perform.

In some of the stories, Elijah appeared in disguise.

"Hey, it's like 'Where's Waldo?'" someone called out. "That sounds like fun!" The students became enthusiastic about writing a play based on a series of Elijah stories. They began collecting Elijah tales and putting them together as a "Story Theatre" production.

One of the scenes was based on the story the teacher had told the drama group at its planning meeting. In this story, Rabbi Beroka asks his friend Elijah: "Who deserves to live in Paradise?" In response, Elijah gives a most unusual answer that had truly intrigued the teens.

Narrator: Rabbi Beroka was walking in the crowded marketplace with his friend Elijah the Prophet.
Rabbi Beroka: Tell me, for I am very curious to know certain secrets that only you could know, Elijah. Is there anyone in this busy marketplace who will deserve to live in Paradise?
Narrator: Elijah remained silent for awhile as he looked around at the crowd. Then he said to his friend, Rabbi Beroka:
Elijah: Ah, yes, those two jesters over there—they will inherit a place in Paradise.
Rabbi Beroka: Jesters! They are often so crude in their jokes and make fun of people. Why would they deserve such an honor?
Elijah: Well, let's ask them and hear their answer.
Narrator: So Elijah the Prophet and Rabbi Beroka walked over to the two jesters to talk with them.
Elijah: Jesters, tell us: what do jesters do?
Narrator: The two jesters answered together.
Two Jesters: What jesters have always done…
Jester #1: When we hear that someone is ill or suffering…
Jester #2: Or when someone is in mourning or distress…
Jester #1: Or when two people have been quarreling…
Jester #2: Or when someone is broken-hearted…
Two Jesters: We go to their homes and try to console them.
Jester #1: We sigh with them and we listen.
Jester #2: We talk and remain silent, all the time trying to bring some joy back to their dark life.
Jester #1: We tell stories and sing songs and create laughter until we see there is harmony in that person's soul and gladness in his heart.
Two Jesters: We are peacemakers—for we remember what Hillel said, "Love peace, and pursue peace".
Narrator: At this point, the jesters spun around—one clockwise and the other counter-clockwise—and together turned cartwheels all the way to another part of the marketplace.
Rabbi Beroka: Elijah, this is amazing to hear…
Narrator: But Rabbi Beroka realized that Elijah was no longer there–for Elijah had disappeared. That was often his habit—to disappear. So Rabbi Beroka said aloud to himself…
Rabbi Beroka: What deserving companions those jesters will be in Paradise!

When the entire play was scripted, the teens auditioned for parts. Aaron got the part of one of the jesters and rehearsed with his jester-partner, especially the lines they had to speak together as well as the lines that had to be spoken in rapid counterpoint as though it was one character speaking them. And he practiced his tumbling as well, especially to make sure the two jesters wouldn't bump into each other.

When Aaron had learned his lines and his blocking on stage, he started to think about what the jesters were really saying. Suddenly, he realized that what they were doing were favors for people in need. They were lifting the spirits of sad or sick or heart-broken people. All of a sudden, Aaron knew what he wanted to do. He ran home as fast as he could. Just as he bolted through the open door, he saw his mother. Totally out of breath, he blurted out,

"*Ima! Ima!* I want to be a jester! Can I join a circus? How can I become a jester and make children who are sick laugh or entertain people who are old and need someone to talk to?"

"Aaron, Aaron, slow down! What a wonderful idea! Let's talk more about this after the play is performed in school. We'll have more time then."

Reluctantly, Aaron agreed to wait three weeks to talk more about this idea. Besides, he was busy rehearsing and trying to decide what kind of jester costume he would wear in the play.

***

A few days later, Aaron received a Facebook message from his pen pal in Israel. Ilan was sixteen and had been at the same American summer camp as Aaron. Since they both loved basketball, they had joined the same team at camp and had become good friends. After camp was over, they promised to stay in touch on Facebook. This was only the second message that Aaron had received from Ilan, and he was excited to read it.

Ilan wrote about learning Arabic and Chinese at school since he loved languages and hoped to become an interpreter in the Israeli Army. He also wrote about being in the Scouts. Then Aaron read something that made his eyes grow bigger. It was as if Ilan had been reading his thoughts:

> *Yesterday the Scouts made a visit to a hospital to watch high school students entertaining sick children. They juggled and made animal characters out of balloons. Some of the students played a kazoo and did card tricks. Some sang songs and told jokes. The children were laughing and had great smiles on their faces even though they were very sick, some with cancer and many of them had lost their hair. I was thinking maybe I could take this training to become a Medical Clown. It's pretty amazing to bring such joy to kids who are so sick. You should also think about doing this. Do they have such programs where you live? If not, then come to Israel and we could do this together.*

The next day, Aaron went to the guidance counselor's office to ask if he knew anything about medical clowning. The guidance counselor told Aaron that he knew that Israel was a pioneer in this field. There were some internship programs in Israel and in the U.S. for training people in methods to entertain sick children in various hospitals and also elders in nursing homes.

"I'll look into this for you, Aaron," he said. "With your talents, you would make a very effective medical clown. I'll let you know what I find."

Whenever he had time, Aaron Googled "clowns" and "medical clowns" and read whatever he could find. He was hoping that he could find some good ideas for his jester costume for the play. He was surprised to discover that there had been Jewish clowns as early as the 1600s in Central Europe during Purim festivities. In those times, there had been parades of clowns, including one clown in a green costume named 'Pickleherring,' who was also a character in the *Purimspiels* (plays). Aaron loved that idea, and thought that the clown's name was really funny. Then he read about a clown who wore a blue cape on which pastries would hang. As this clown would ride through town on a wooden horse, he would eat bits from the pastries and make horn sounds, pretending that he was playing a horn. Aaron liked that one even better, especially the idea of eating cake while performing. Another clown had kitchen utensils hanging on his costume with an upside-down pot for a hat. Then Aaron found another clown called, "The Half-Fool." This clown was dressed like a buffoon on one side of his body and a wise man on the other. He liked "The Half-Fool" so much that he laughed aloud for a few minutes. By now, Aaron's head was spinning with ideas and confusion.

Aaron tried drawing these clowns as he imagined them and showed his drawings to his parents and to the guidance counselor. Everyone was very impressed and excited to see Aaron taking this so seriously.

***

A few days after the play was performed at school, Mrs. Mizrahi, the drama director, announced that because the Elijah production had been so successful, the students had been invited to perform the play at a senior residence. Then she asked Aaron, "I understand that you are interested in becoming a medical clown. Did I hear this correctly?"

"Yes, that's right, Mrs. Mizrahi," replied Aaron.

"Well, how would you like to stay in character as the jester, and after the play, do some 'jester entertainment' on your own with the elders at the Residence? Would you like to try out some of your own clowning talents?"

Aaron was deliriously happy and couldn't wait to tell his parents—and to write about it to his friend, Ilan.

After giving it a lot of thought, Aaron finally decided on the nature of his jester character for the visit, a combination of some of the ideas he had read about. He would be a clumsy silly-fool on one side and a wise-fool on the other side. He would also wear a two-sided crown: on one side, a floppy jester hat, and on the other side, a royal crown; the two halves would be sewn together. These two contrary sides would always be debating with each other. One side would always be bumping into things in a clumsy way while the other side would dance and walk gracefully. One side would bow like a silly jester while the other side would bow like a gentleman. One side would speak with a strange made-up accent and the other in Aaron's own voice. Aaron decided not to wear any make-up or mask and only use his own facial expressions.

The elderly residents walked slowly into the hall. They seemed tired and sad, and Aaron wasn't sure if anything he would do could change their demeanor.

After the applause at the end of the production, when everyone was getting up to leave, Aaron wove his way through the crowd, beginning his "debate" with the two sides of himself. Slowly, the people in the senior residence realized that the entertainment wasn't over yet. Everyone sat down and watched what the two-sided clown was doing. At first they were quiet, but when they were surprised by a quip or play on words, they laughed in delight. When Aaron finished his act, the residents applauded with great appreciation, their faces smiling and alive. Everyone in the cast took another bow with Aaron in the center of the line. Aaron could see that he had truly brought joy to their lives, even if only for that afternoon. When the students left the social hall, the audience again burst into applause.

For the first time in his life, Aaron understood that he had truly done everyone a favor. He knew what doing a mitzvah for others felt like—better than anything he had ever experienced before. And he wanted to keep having those good feelings of bringing joy to those in need.

Provenance: The reference to the story of Reb Kalonymus Kalman Shapira comes from Shlomo Carlebach's story, "The Holy Hunchback" and "Rav Kaloinimus Kalman" on his audiocassette, *The Best of Shlomo Carlebach*, Volume I (1960-1990). This story can also be found in print as, "The Ghetto Rebbe and 'His Kingdom of Children'" in *Chosen Tales: Stories Told by Jewish Storytellers*, edited by Peninnah Schram (Jason Aronson, an imprint of Rowman & Littlefield, 1995, pages 70-75).

The episode of Elijah the Prophet meeting Rabbi Beroka is from *Ta'anit* 22a. It was adapted from "Beroka and Elijah the Prophet" in Peninnah Schram's *Tales of Elijah the Prophet* (Jason Aronson, an imprint of Rowman & Littlefield, 1991, pages 23-24).

The descriptions of the Purim clowns in the 1600s are from Nahma Sandrow's *Vagabond Stars: A World History of Yiddish Theater* (Harper & Row, 1977, page 1).

Peninnah Schram, Professor of Speech and Drama at Stern College of Yeshiva University, has authored twelve books of Jewish folktales, including *The Apple Tree's Discovery*, and a recording, *The Minstrel and the Storyteller* (with musician Gerard Edery). Her story and storytelling essay also appear in *Mitzvah Stories: Seeds for Inspiration and Learning*, a volume published in her honor. Recipient of outstanding educator awards from the Covenant Foundation and NewCAJE, Peninnah has also been awarded the National Storytelling Network's Lifetime Achievement Award. She is a faculty member of the Jewish Spiritual Education and Maggid-Educator Ordination Programs at Reclaiming Judaism.

Study Guide: Questions, Sources, and Projects for Reflection, Discussion, and Action

1. Which *mitzvot* are illustrated by this story? Which additional *mitzvot* can you also relate to this story?

2. Do you empathize with Aaron reading a comic book during synagogue? How might Aaron's father and his community have helped him to become more present during a service?

3. Why does Aaron bug people with his fake requests for loans and accent imitations? What might be a better way to respond to him?

4. Having the capacity for humor and clowning is a great talent. To this day there are some *badhanim*, who offer the mitzvah of insight by satirizing Jewish life, juggling for children in hospitals, and much more. Do you know someone who would make a good *badhan*? Where could their talents be put to good use instead of experiencing the misfortune of being regarded as annoying?

5. Rabbi Naomi Steinberg wrote a story, "Queen Esther's Joy" about a person whose connection to being Jewish primarily involved his role in a Purim *shpiel* (play). You can find this in *Mitzvah Stories: Seeds for Inspiration and Learning* (cited above). Having a meaningful role in the life of your community makes for a more joyous, interesting, supportive, and supported life. What role(s) could you play?

Sacred Story and Text Connections

1. Rabbi Beroka Hoza'ah used to spend time in the market at Bet Lapat where Elijah often appeared to him. Once he asked him, "Is there anyone in this market who has a share in the world to come?" He replied, "No." Meanwhile, he caught sight of a man wearing black shoes and having no thread of blue on the corners of his garment. [Elijah] exclaimed, "This man has a share in the world to come." Rabbi Beroka ran after him and asked him, "What do you do?" The man replied, "Go away and come back tomorrow." The next day he asked him again, "What do you do?" He replied, "I am a jailer and I keep the men and women separate by placing my bed between them so that they will not sin; when I see a Jewish girl upon whom the non-Jews cast their eyes, I risk my life and save her...." Rabbi Beroka asked the man, "Why have you no fringes and why do you wear black shoes?" He replied, "So that those who are not Jewish amongst whom I constantly move may not know that I am a Jew, so that when a harsh decree is

made against Jews I inform the rabbis and they pray to God and the decree is annulled." He further asked him, "When I asked you what you did, why did you say to me, 'Go away now and come back tomorrow?'" He answered, "They had just issued a harsh decree and I said I would first go and advise the rabbis of it, so that they might pray to God." While they were talking, two men passed by and Elijah remarked, "These two have a share in the world to come." Rabbi Beroka went to them and asked, "What do you do?" They replied, "We are jesters. When we see men depressed we cheer them up; furthermore when we see two people quarreling we strive hard to make peace between them."
—adapted from the AJWS translation at www.On1Foot.com

a. What did Rabbi Beroka Hoza'ah view as the qualities that make one merit the world-to-come?

b. Why did the jesters merit the world-to-come/paradise? How do they save people?

c. Why were Jews and girls at such great risk during this time?

d. Why is the story of the "jailer" set before the story about the jesters?

e. In folklore, the 9th century B.C.E. prophet Elijah, a master of disguise, also becomes a master of miracles and a bringer of hope. Find Elijah stories online or in the book *Tales of Elijah the Prophet* by Peninnah Schram. What unifying factors about Elijah's role in Jewish life can you find in these stories? Whenever Elijah is mentioned in study or prayer, the words "*zachor la-tov*" are added, "may he be remembered for the good". Why might that be? For whom else might you want to add this phrase after their names?

f. Did you notice how the absence of a "thread of blue" seems to be significant early on in the tale of Rabbi Beroka? Look up Numbers, *Bamidbar* 15:38 to see the biblical reason why.

The Rabbinic explanation of describing the precise color blue is found in *Midrash Sifre*, where Rabbi Meir explains: "What makes *techelet* different from other colors? *Techelet* is similar in color to the sea, and the sea is comparable to the sky, and the sky to the throne of Presence." For the Kabbalists' explanation you can look online for the commentary in the Zohar on *Parshat Shelach Lecha*.

How might you creatively adopt this sort of color to help you and perhaps those in your family, class, or bunk to remember to live a mitzvah-centered life?

2. Rav Chelbo became sick, so Rav Kahana went around announcing, "Rav Chelbo is sick." But no one came to visit him. Rav Kahana then said [to the sages and students], "Did it not once happen that one of Rabbi Akiva's students became sick, and none of the sages came to visit him." So Rabbi Akiva went to visit and because they swept and washed the floor, the student recovered. Indeed, the student said, "My teacher, you have given me new life!" And right after that incident, Rabbi Akiva went out and taught, "Whoever does not perform the mitzvah of visiting the sick—It is as though [s]he spilled someone's blood."—*Talmud Nedarim 39b-40a*, translation by Danny Siegel from his book *Where Heaven and Earth Touch*

   a. What is your diagnosis of the student's illness?

   b. Who is the "they" in "they scrubbed the floor?"

   c. Why is it like "shedding blood" not to visit and help those who are sick or elderly? What could happen?

Project: Research Jewish stories about healing—physical, emotional, intellectual, and spiritual types of healing. Pick six to tell at an evening of storytelling and small groups where people talk about healing they've experienced and share healing wisdom together. Consider making this an inter-generational program, or one for people in treatment or recovery from illness, trauma, or addictions. Incorporate inspiring music and perhaps some appropriate humor and text study as well.

Project: What clown character would you design for yourself? Why? What clown characters might fit others in your family or friends? Discuss. Using an art medium illustrate, write about (perhaps in a poem), or make a costume. Research places for training as a medical clown. What do you communicate through your make-up, mask and/or costumed appearance?

Project: Suggest to your teacher or counselor that your class visit an institution where you can listen to the stories of the residents' lives. What questions might you ask them? For example, what were their experiences as young people listening to the radio? Or going to the movies or watching television? What was a *Shabbat* or holiday like in their homes? Where were they during major world events?

Chapter 33
Tzedakah in the Market
by Rebecca Schram-Zafrany

It was only eight A.M. on a day in August but the sun was already blazing, and twelve-year-old Rachel was beginning to sweat. The plastic baskets she was carrying, tucked one inside the other, were scraping against her leg as she walked toward the *shuk* (market), and her fingers were cramped and sweaty around the handles. All this didn't really bother Rachel. She loved going to the *shuk*, which was held every week in the parking lot at the beach in Ashdod. Farmers from *moshavim* and *kibbutzim* (collectives) from all over the country came to sell everything from fruits and vegetables to sandals, clothes, toys, and even music CDs.

Even though Rachel had wanted to stay in her cool bedroom a little bit longer this morning, she had gotten up eagerly, proud that she was the only one of her brothers and sisters whom Mamma trusted to go shopping in the *shuk*. She enjoyed hearing the vendors calling out to attract customers to buy their products, and she loved the colors, sights, and smells of all the different fruits, vegetables, and spices mixed in with the salty sea air. She would also have a chance to visit her favorite stall, which was at the very end of the *shuk*. The seller at this stall sold an assortment of hair accessories. It thrilled her to see the different colored ribbons, bows, and barrettes all arranged by size and color, and she often lingered at this stall almost mesmerized by the array. She always looked forward to visiting this stall after she finished Mamma's shopping.

By this time it was beginning to get even hotter. Rachel knew that the only relief from the heat that she could expect would be the slight breeze coming off the water and the shade from the tarps covering the individual stalls.

Today Rachel was especially excited about going to the *shuk* because this shopping trip was going to be little different. Rachel was anxious to finish buying all the produce her mother needed as quickly as possible. She wasn't going to stop to look at all the stalls, admiring the sight of the colorful pyramids of fruits and vegetables and savoring smells of the spices as she did every week. Rachel wanted to do something she had been waiting for all week. Last week at her favorite stall, she had seen the most beautiful rhinestone barrette. It was different from any other barrette she had ever seen! The rhinestone beads had sparkled in the sunlight and glimmered with all the colors of the rainbow. It had seemed almost magical. Today she had five extra shekels in her pocket, saved from babysitting her little brother, and she planned to buy that rhinestone barrette. She had been hoping all week that it hadn't been sold and would be waiting for her today in its small white plastic box. As she walked into the *shuk*, she imagined how she would point to the barrette, watch as the man put it into a small paper bag, and how she would slip that paper bag into her pocket, paying for her new purchase with her shiny coin. She planned to keep her new treasure wrapped up in her dresser drawer and wait to wear it on the first day of school next month. Rachel imagined all the girls in her class oooohing and aaaaahing in admiration and envy over her new barrette as it sparkled in her hair, nestled on the back of her head.

Rachel was suddenly jolted out of her reverie as she approached the first vendor calling out to attract people to buy his goods. She began making the rounds from one stall to another. She chose carefully, asking the prices of each product, making sure to stay within the budget her mother had carefully counted out before she left. Finally, when Rachel's baskets were full and very heavy, filled with everything her mother wanted her to buy, she knew it was the time she had been waiting for. She asked permission from the woman who sold fresh herbs to leave her heavy baskets in a shaded area behind the long, narrow table laden with mint leaves, parsley, and dill. She then walked as fast as she could toward the object of her desire, trying not to appear too nervous.

Rachel arrived at the stall and immediately eyed her treasure, twinkling in the sun among all the other colorful objects. Suddenly, an old woman wearing tattered clothes, her gray hair pulled back sharply into a small bun, practically blocked Rachel's path and said, "Excuse me. My bags are so heavy. I can't carry them any more in this heat. Could you please help me carry them to the bus stop?"

Rachel didn't want to postpone buying the barrette. She was sure someone else would buy it, and it would be lost to her forever. Also, the bus stop was at the entrance to the *shuk* all the way at the other end. She looked at the old lady's bags. They were plastic bags filled with potatoes and onions and melons–so heavy for her thin little arms to carry. She looked longingly at the sparkling barrette, and sighed. She knew she could not refuse this woman's request. She had been brought up to respect her elders and also to help anyone in need. How often had she seen Mamma helping others, even strangers? Her mother always told her: "*Tzedakah* is not just charity, but doing something beyond your duty. It means helping someone else in this world. We help people in the hope that they will pass on this tradition and help others who need it." Then she always ended with "…and don't forget what Rabbi Elazar says: '*Tzaddikim* say little and do much.'" (Talmud, *Baba Metzia* 87a)

Rachel gave one last look at the shiny barrette on the vendor's table, looked kindly at the woman, and picked up her bags. She carried the bags all the way to the opposite end of the *shuk* and set the bags down at the bus stop. The old woman thanked her and blessed her with success in her studies, health, and finding a good husband. She ended with the blessing of "May you grow up healthy *l'Torah, l'huppah, u'l'ma'asim tovim*—to the study of Torah, the wedding canopy, and doing good deeds!"

Rachel wished her a good day and good luck, and because it was Thursday, the day before *Erev Shabbat*, she also wished her *Shabbat Shalom*. She knew she had been helpful, but she was also eager to get back to the vendor and buy that barrette before someone else had the chance.

Just as she was turning to go back into the *shuk*, the old woman asked her, "Do you, by any chance, have five shekels to give me for the bus? I spent all my money on food to feed my family, and I can't carry these heavy bags all the way home."

Rachel shivered despite the heat. She didn't know what to do. She had saved her five shekels so carefully, resisting any temptation to spend it on candy or little toys in the local stores. She had been dreaming about this barrette–*her barrette*–all week, hoping it would still be there this week. She didn't know when she would ever have another five shekels to spend. Then slowly, the image of the barrette seemed to fade, and she knew what she had to do.

Without any further hesitation, she reached into her pocket and handed the woman the five-shekel coin. The woman hugged her and continued to thank and bless her profusely. She even went so far as to say that Rachel's kindness helped her to feed her family. Rachel thanked the woman for her blessings, wished her *Shabbat Shalom* again, and helped her drag the heavy bags onto the bus. She then watched the old woman pay the bus driver, and stood there feeling forlorn and disappointed until the bus had traveled around the bend in the road and was out of sight.

Suddenly Rachel realized she wasn't upset about not being able to buy the barrette at all. She had done something more important than having that shiny piece of glass in her hair. She had actually helped someone. She had done what Mamma had been teaching and doing ever since she could remember. Rachel felt good—in fact she had never felt such satisfaction in her whole life! She walked back to the herb seller's stall where she had left her baskets, picked them up as if they were not heavy at all, and thanked the herb seller for watching over them. To her surprise, the heat no longer bothered her. She felt like she was floating. She walked home and set the plastic baskets down in the kitchen.

Her mother walked in and asked, "So, anything interesting happen in the *shuk* this week?"

Rachel just smiled.

Rebecca Schram-Zafrany is head of the English department at the Ginsburg Ha'Alon High School in Yavne, Israel. She holds a BA in English Literature from Hebrew University and an MA in Applied Linguistics from Tel Aviv University. Rebecca is also a storyteller, performing and leading workshops in the United States and Israel. Her story "The Miracle of the Black Pepper" was published in *Chosen Tales: Stories Told by Jewish Storytellers*, and her story "Elijah's Yellow Balloon" in *Mitzvah Stories: Seeds for Inspiration and Learning*. Rebecca resides with her family on Moshav Shdema, Israel.

Study Guide: Questions, Sources, and Projects for Reflection, Discussion, and Action

1. Which *mitzvot* are illustrated by this story? Which additional *mitzvot* can you also relate to this story?

2. Rachel is given the responsibility of going to the market for her mother. Do you have any responsibilities at home? What are they and how does it feel when you do them? Where do the *mitzvot* regarding obeying parents fit into this story? Is it okay for her to be late returning with the groceries because she did *mitzvot* along the way?

3. Imagine that you have saved up for something special. Would you give it up in order to help someone? Why is this considered a good thing?

4. Sometimes we think of rewards as prizes we receive. What other kinds of reward might Rachel have felt inside of herself for her decisions?

Project: Find ways to do more for others. Try to "stop and help" at least once a week, and increase your frequency until this mitzvah becomes a personal habit.

Sacred Story and Text Connections

1. The *Megillah* (scroll, or book) of Ruth illustrates many interpersonal situations and *mitzvot* of helping someone who emerges in your life asking for assistance with their needs. Take a look and see which are possible in our times.

2. Hillel taught, "If I am not for myself, who will be for me? But if I am only for myself, what am I? If not now, when?"—Ethics of the Ancestors, *Pirkei Avot* 1:14. Hillel's statement raises the question of whether it was necessary for Rachel to give up her barrette. Could she have instead said, "Wait a minute! I'll just finish this purchase and then I'll be glad to carry your bags"? How would this effect the rest of the story? What would you most likely do in her situation?

Project: Do you have any investments? One contemporary way of leaving the "corners of your field," to be gleaned by the poor in an age when few of us have farms, is to give the first interest payment on each investment, each year, to a charity that feeds the hungry, or a percentage of the costs of the party for a rite of passage, or to tithe the cash presents we receive. Or to give at least one of each thing you create with your own hands or business to a charity auction. How much would you have to give based on earnings or items from the beginning of this year?

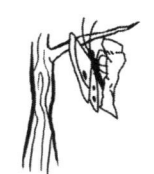

Chapter 34
Three Wishes
by Sandor Schuman

"I will grant you three wishes," said the Old One, "but each wish must meet all of the following conditions:

"First, each wish must be possible. I can't do magic. If you ask for something that's not possible, I can't grant it, but it will count as a wish anyway.

"Second, your wishes must be for things that will last you your whole life. So, for example, you can't wish for some kind of food, because that won't last. If you ask for something that won't last for your whole life long, I can't grant it, but it will count as a wish anyway.

"Third, each wish must provide something that you can learn from. As with the other conditions, if you ask for something from which you can't learn, I can't grant it, but it will count as a wish anyway.

"So tell me, what is your first wish?"

The child, trying to be clever, replied, "I wish to know the difference between what is possible and what is not."

"Sorry, I can't grant you that wish. Although it is something that would last your whole life long, and from which you would learn a great deal, it's not possible. We never know if something is possible or not until we try, sometimes over and over again. What's your next wish? You have two left."

The child thought, and then replied, "I wish for a great big house where all of my family and friends can live."

"Sorry," replied the Old One, "I can't grant you that wish. Although it is possible to build such a house, and you would learn a great deal from living with all of your family and friends, I cannot grant this wish because the house might not last your whole life long. Fire, floods, earthquakes, war, all these things can destroy a house. But your family and friends will be with you always. Even when they die, your relationships with them continue. What's your next wish? You have one left."

Thinking carefully, the child, not wanting to waste the last wish, struggled to find something that was possible, would last a lifetime, and involved learning. After long and careful thought, the child asked, "Teach me to understand everything you know."

"Sorry," said the Old One, "I can't grant you that wish. Although I can teach, you might not understand, for understanding is something that you must do, not I. Although perhaps you would learn a great deal, such learning would not last your whole lifetime, because knowledge is created continuously, and you must go out and learn for yourself beyond what I might know."

The child began to cry, for now all three wishes were gone.

"No, child, don't be disheartened, for you have received three great things."

The child, looking up in surprise, asked, "What are they? What have I received?"

"You have learned to try what can't be done, for it may turn out that you can make it possible, even though others have failed.

"You have learned that your relationships with others are most valuable because they will always be with you.

"And you have learned that knowledge is ever changing, and you must be responsible for your own education.

"To learn these three things is possible, and you have learned them, and they will last you your whole life long. Now go, and grant these three wishes to others."

Sandor Schuman is a group facilitator, collaborative process advocate, and storyteller. He uses storytelling in his consulting work with government and not-for-profit organizations to help them create shared meaning, make critical choices, and build collaborative relationships. Sandy has been a featured storyteller on television and radio, at storytelling festivals, numerous conferences and for a wide variety of congregations. He is the author of *Adirondack Mendel's Aufruf: Welcome to Chelm's Pond*, where the stories of Chelm meet the tall tales of the Adirondacks, and he blogs at *Another Side to the Story*. www.tothestory.com

Study Guide: Questions, Sources, and Projects for Reflection, Discussion, and Action

1. Which *mitzvot* are illustrated by this story? Which additional *mitzvot* can you also relate to this story?

2. If you had three wishes, what would you wish for? Do not wish for more wishes.

3. If your wishes had to be realistic, possibly last your whole life, and be ones you could learn from, what would you wish for?

4. Have you ever wanted something but received something else, and only later realized that what you received was better than what you wanted?

5. Who does the Old One symbolize?

6. At the end of the story, the Old One told the child to pass on the same three wishes he received. How might this be done?

Sacred Story and Text Connections

1. Then Moses went back to Yitro (Jethro) his father-in-law and said to him, "Let me return to my own people in Egypt to see if any of them are still alive". Yitro said, "Go, and I wish you well."—Exodus, *Shemot* 4:18

   Is a wish different from a blessing or a hope? Is it different from praying for what you want for yourself or another?

2. Open a *Chumash* (Five Books of Moses) to 1 Samuel, *Shmuel* 1:4-18 where Hannah expresses her wish for a child in the temple. Think of your own needs, as well as what you know of the needs of people in your life. What would you wish for that is so important you would want to do it in a sacred space?

Project: Choose one realistic wish. Write it on a piece of paper and hang it up in your room. Read it every day and devise ways to make it happen. See if focusing on the wish in this way (making it the prayer of your heart) eventually causes it to come true.

Project: Visit the website of the Make-A-Wish Foundation to find out how you can help a wish come true for others.

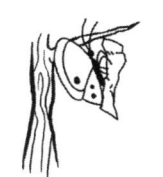

Chapter 35
Here's to Healing!
by Cherie Karo Schwartz

Once upon a time, not too long ago, and not too far away, there was a young girl named Ariella who loved to give gifts to people. She had a particularly kind heart, and unlike many of the girls her age, she especially liked helping people. Her parents *kvelled*—they were very proud of her—when they saw how she loved to give, but they also had to watch out so that she didn't give *everything* away!

One day, Ariella's *Ima* (mother) took her to a crafts fair in the neighborhood where people were raising money for groups that help people.

They stopped at one booth, and *Ima* cried out, "Look, Ariella! A sock monkey just like the one I had when I was your age!" She picked it up and hugged it.

A nice lady named Dotty came over, smiled at Jan hugging the monkey, and said, "I make these sock monkeys, just like I made them for my daughters when they were young. Now I sell them to raise money to help people with arthritis. And sewing helps my arthritic hands feel better, too."

"Well, we just have to buy this monkey, Ariella," said *Ima*. "Dotty, thank you! This is one wonderful monkey, and he will do good for many other people."

Dotty thanked them, and then asked, "What are you going to name him?"

Ariella thought for a minute, and then her face lit up. "I know! I'll call him the Hebrew word for luck, *Mazel*, because I know he will bring me luck."

Ariella loved her new monkey. It was made from socks! It had long beige arms and legs, a red stocking hat, red bows on its hands and feet, and even a red *tushie*! (bottom)

A few days later, Ariella's best friend Steve got sick. Ariella went to visit him at home, and she brought Mazel with her. After all, *Ima* had said it would do good for lots of people. Steve's eyes lit up when he saw Mazel, and he looked so happy that even his Mom was smiling. Ariella knew just what to do.

"Mazel really, really likes you. I can tell. Here, Steve. You keep Mazel, okay?" Ariella went home beaming, knowing that Mazel would bring her friend happiness and hope.

When her *Abba* (father), asked where Mazel was, Ariella just smiled and said he was with Steve.

And guess what?

A week later, Steve came to Ariella's house, and he was all better. He brought some cookies that his Mom had made, and he also brought Mazel!

"Did Mazel come to visit?" asked Ariella.

"No, silly! Mazel knows his own home. He came back to you."

"But I gave him to you!" said Ariella.

"Look," said Steve. "You gave me Mazel so I could get better. Now that I am feeling great, I'm giving him back to you so that you can give him to other people who need cheering up or are sick. Maybe his luck and his bright red smile will help them, too!"

Ariella and Steve laughed and played games all afternoon.

The next month, one of Ariella's grown-up friends was in the hospital. *Abba* and Ariella went to visit her, and guess who came along? Mazel! Ariella held up her Mazel monkey for Shayna to see.

"Mazel is here to cheer you up," Ariella said. "I gave him to my friend Steve when he was sick, and when he got well he gave him back to me. He said that Mazel could go to someone else who needed him…for a while…."

With her bright blue eyes, Ariella looked up into Shayna's smiling face. Then, Shayna finished the sentence:

"So he can keep me company…for awhile. And when I am all better, then Mazel can go back to you, right?"

"Right!" smiled Ariella.

And that is just what happened. Shayna got all better, and Mazel came home again.

Mazel monkey was gaining quite a reputation! And everywhere he went with Ariella, he just made people feel better.

Then one day, Ariella got a letter from Jan, her pen pal in Israel. Jan wrote that she had had an accident. She had fallen out of a tree and broken her leg! Ariella remembered the big tree in her friend's yard. The two of them had climbed high up in the branches when Ariella and her family had visited Israel last year. Ariella and Jan were so happy to have the chance to meet after being pen pals for so many months. They had shared almost every day together, laughing and playing. And now her friend was hurt and had to stay home from school, and away from the rest of her friends!

"Oh, I feel so sad about Jan," Ariella said to her parents. "And I am not even there to keep her company. Israel is so far away! I know how much my arm hurt when I broke it, and it was in a cast. And this is her whole leg. She can't even move very much. What can I do to help?"

Well, it did not take Ariella long to figure out what to do. She got down a big box from a closet shelf, wrapped Mazel in a pretty blanket, placed him carefully in the box, and then talked to him to calm him down. He looked a little afraid even though he was still smiling his red smile.

"Don't be afraid, Mazel," Ariella told him. "You are going on your biggest trip ever. And you will get to meet my super-good friend, Jan. She has a broken leg, and she needs a close friend right there beside her. I can't go all the way to Israel now, but you can go for me! Give Jan big hugs, lots of love, and maybe she will get better so much faster with you there to take care of her. Be a good friend for her, and bring her good luck, please."

Then, Ariella took Mazel into the living room to *Abba*.

"*Abba*, we need to send Mazel to Jan in Israel. Can you help me put the address on the box and get it to the post office?"

Ariella's father picked her up, sat her on his lap, and gave her a huge hug.

"Ariella, this is a very wonderful thing that you want to do for your friend Jan. But Israel is very far away, and Jan will be in her leg cast for a long time. She may not be able to send him back to you. Are you sure you want to chance that?"

Ariella's bright blue eyes got misty.

"But *Abba*, I don't want her to ever send him back. Mazel will be in Israel! I'll bet he will want to stay there and be Jan's friend. It's okay. I will really, really miss him, but I understand. He will be happy there, and Jan will love him."

So, off they went to the post office, and off went Mazel monkey half way around the world to help make someone else feel better.

The days went by. Ariella had so many stuffed animals: bears and doggies and a zebra and kitties and a hippo and so many more stuffed friends. But it just wasn't quite the same without Mazel.

Then one day, just before Hanukkah, *Ima* was looking at a catalogue, and there was a picture of a sock monkey! It was a kit that people could put together. What a grand idea! She talked with *Abba*, and he agreed, so they ordered it. The next week, when *Ima* came back from school with Ariella, there was a package addressed to Ariella sitting on the front porch.

"Whatever could that be?" asked *Ima*, with a sparkle in her eye. That night, after they lit the Hanukkah candles together and said the blessings, Ariella opened the box and there inside was the sock monkey kit!

"*Todah rabba*! Ooh, thank you, *Ima* and *Abba*! It's another Mazel! Wow! What a perfect present. Thank you!"

So over the next few days, *Ima* and Ariella sewed the new Mazel together. This sock monkey had the same long beige legs and arms, the same red smile, red hat, red bows, and even the same red tushie!

As they put the last bow on the sock monkey, *Abba* asked, "What are you going to name the new member of our family?"

Ariella thought for a moment, and then knew the perfect name.

"She will be *Mazel Tov*, because she will do so many good, lucky things for people, just like her brother Mazel."

And everyone laughed together, knowing that she was right.

During Hanukkah, Ariella received a box all the way from Israel. It was from her pen pal Jan! Ariella had told her all about her new sock monkey, Mazel Tov. Had Jan sent her Mazel back to her?

Ariella opened the box and read the card first.

Shalom to my wonderful friend Ariella and her family,

Happy Hanukkah! This is a time of miracles, and I want to tell you that Mazel has been a miracle for me. I am now all better. My leg cast is off. I am so happy to be able to walk, and soon I will be able to run again. I will be much more careful in trees, too.

Your friend Mazel really loves Israel. He has now seen more of it, because he has kept doing his job! I remembered what you had said about him traveling around. So, when one of my friends is sick or sad or hurt, I send him over to stay with that friend until he or she is better and then "Mazel" comes back to me again.

One day I came up with an idea. Ima and I made some things for Mazel to wear. No, not clothes, but special things depending on where he is going and what has happened. We made crutches, a Band-Aid, an ace bandage, a thermometer, a cast, an eye patch, a hot water bottle, and a hanky for colds or tears. Each of these things has a rubber band to attach it onto Mazel's leg or arm or head or tummy. Everyone loves the little ornaments! So, we've made an extra set for you so you can put them right onto your new sock monkey Mazel Tov when you send her out to help heal someone.

Enjoy these little presents in the best of good health for you and your friends! We send love from us here in Israel to you and your family.

Shalom,
Jan

And that is the story of Mazel and Mazel Tov, the miracle monkeys, and the joy and healing that they brought to Ariella's friends…and now to you!

Cherie Karo Schwartz is a storyteller, author, and educator living in Denver, Colorado. She has shared stories with audiences of all ages throughout North America and abroad for forty years and is a master teacher in methods and repertoire for Jewish storytelling. Cherie has produced five recordings of Jewish folklore and is the author of *My Lucky Dreidel* and *Circle Spinning: Jewish Turning and Returning Tales* and co-author of *The Kid's Catalog of Passover: A Worldwide Celebration*. A co-founding coordinator of the CAJE Jewish Storytelling Network, Cherie's stories and teachings appear in many anthologies including *Mitzvah Stories: Seeds for Inspiration and Learning*. www.HamsaPubs.com

Study Guide: Questions, Sources, and Projects for Reflection, Discussion, and Action

1. Which *mitzvot* are illustrated by this story? Which additional *mitzvot* can you also relate to this story?

2. What is luck?

3. Have you received something helpful when you've been ill? How did it affect you? What could you do that might work similarly for someone else?

4. Would it be hard for you to share a precious thing, like a beloved toy? How might remembering the *mitzvot* of *yirah* and *ahavah* (see mitzvot 49 and 50 on page 318) help you to do so?

Sacred Story and Text Connections

1. "*Mitzvah gorreret mitzvah, aveirah gorreret aveirah.*"—*Ethics of the Ancestors, Pirkei Avot* 4:2

   One mitzvah leads to another mitzvah; one sin leads to another sin.

   Mazel the monkey was passed on like *mitzvot*, one good deed leading to another. Can you think of a mitzvah that you have been involved in that led to another mitzvah? Done by you or someone else? What about troublesome behavior? Does getting away with something once, tend to lead to doing it again?

2. "The people came to Moses, and said, "We have sinned, for we spoke against God, and against you. Please have God take away the serpents from us." Moses prayed for the people. God then told him to make a fiery-looking serpent and set it upon a pole. All who would look at it would be cured of their snakebites. Moses made a serpent out of brass and it came to pass that if someone bitten looked at it [that person] would live."—Numbers, *Bamidbar* 21:7-9

   How does the story of Mazel help us to try to understand this story about people being healed by looking at a brass metal serpent?

Project: Find or make something special that you, too, can give to a friend or family member who is suffering in some way.

Chapter 36
Saving Lives BIG TIME
(As Humbly Told by Elisheva, The Hero of Our Story)
by Danny Siegel

Let me tell you about my family.

There's my *Abba*, Aminadav, who must be somebody important because we keep getting invited to come over to Miriam's and Aaron's, who are two of the most important elders of our people. My *ima* is Ruthie, a very gentle and kind woman, though most people don't know it because she does her good things so quietly. And then there are the four kids: my big brother, Nachshon, who's six years older than I, and in between, Yirmiyahu ("Yir" for short), Batsheva ("Shev"), and then me, the youngest. I'm Elisheva (or just plain "Eli").

Since I've decided to tell you the Story of Myself, you should know that this is really about me and my big brother, Nachshon. Ever since I can remember, he's always taken care of me and watched out for me. All of this happened a long, long time ago, when the Israelites were slaves in Egypt. These were hard times for us Jews, but even though we had such a hard life, kids will still be kids—having fun, getting into trouble, and ignoring most of the things that worry grown-ups so much. And picking on certain kids who are a bit different from everyone else. Now, I don't think I'm particularly cute—and certainly not adorable—but I'm not so chunky or funny looking that other kids should be calling me names like "geek" or "nerd" or "doofus." But they quickly learned not to do this when my big brother Nachshon was around. If they did, he would always step in and get the others to back off.

And even though it's usually your parents who tell you stories or sing to you at night to help you go to sleep, as long as I can remember, it was my brother Nachshon who put me to bed, telling me the most fantastic, wonderful tales and sometimes singing—even though his voice was a little raspy, and sometimes he was off-key—fun songs and funny songs and lullabies, which helped me drop off into *very* sweet dreams.

Nachshon is fourteen now, and I'm eight. For the past year, he had to go to work like all the adults and slave away because of Pharaoh's horrible laws. And still, even with all that hard work and coming home exhausted, he would always find time to play with me. Since he spent the day making bricks from clay and straw, he managed to make little bricks for me so I could build anything I wanted.* He played with me for hours, no matter how exhausted he was. Who could wish for a better big brother than Nachshon? Now, you should know that you wouldn't particularly pick Nachshon out of a crowd. Although he's beginning to grow tall, and even though he has gorgeous blue eyes and thick, dark black hair, he's not all that special to look at. But he is *so* special to me. Even though he's so young, he's already a *mensch* (good person).

As I said, life was pretty difficult because of the horrible Pharaoh. That's how my early childhood was lived—until things suddenly began to change. One day, Miriam's and Aaron's brother, Moses, suddenly showed up after having run away a few years ago. (He had a price on his head for killing an Egyptian taskmaster. The Egyptians were after him and wanted to throw him in prison, or worse, kill him.) But here he was now, out of the blue, telling Pharaoh that God wanted him to let us all go to be free of slavery. All kinds of crazy things happened once he started to give God's message to Pharaoh: the Nile turned blood-red, frogs by the millions began hopping around everywhere in Egypt (but not in our homes), storms, hail, darkness for days (though not in our homes), scary things, ten of them in all.

Finally, Pharaoh had had enough. Moses told us to get ready—that we were finally going to leave Egypt.

We could hardly believe it. After so many years as slaves, we were going to be free! One night, after a strange meal of lamb and some very sharp vegetable that stung your mouth, we got up and left.

Just like that.

Thousands and thousands of us.

Out into the desert.

We walked and walked. (At first we ran because we didn't really believe the Egyptians were going to let us go "just like that", but when we got a long way over the border, we slowed down.)

After a while I got very tired, and, you guessed it! Nachshon picked me up and carried me for miles and miles…until we got to this *big* stretch of water, with no bridges or ferries or anything like that. And worse: Pharaoh and his Egyptians finally woke up to the fact that we were gone, and they were plenty sorry he let us go. So right behind us and gaining on us was this huge army of screaming soldiers and neighing, snorting horses and incredibly noisy chariots. It was terrifying!

They were behind us—and in front of us was this water—I mean, it was *right* in front of me and Nachshon, because he had carried me to the very front of all those crowds of people, put me down when we got to the water's edge.

It was scary, *very* scary.

I figured that maybe if somebody stepped into the water, it really would open

---

*   An historical note: This is the true origin of Legos.

up a nice, dry pathway for us all to escape, just like God told Moses would happen. So I did the only thing *I* knew how to do. I looked up at Nachshon and said, "You can do it."

And not five seconds later, he plunged right in. Instantly.

Not too long after that amazing day, Nachshon was having dinner in a tent with Moses, Miriam, and Aaron. Aaron must have been listening very carefully to Nachshon's account of our escape, because to this day Aaron likes to tell the story Nachson's way. How I, Elisheva, standing beside Nachshon right in front of the water, looked up at him (he was at that time a full eight inches taller than I was) with admiring eyes, and an expression on my face that said, "Thank you" for all the years he had been so good to me. Aaron accurately reports that I only said four words, "You can do it!" And then, without hesitation, realizing that he couldn't let me, his "kid sister" down, Nachshon jumped in—the waters parted and all the escaping slaves, every single one of us, followed him across the river bed. The Egyptians pursued with their chariots and foot soldiers. But once we reached dry land, the water crashed down on the heads of the Egyptians, and they all drowned. Nachshon had saved us.

Aaron must have kept that story in the back of his mind. He had always thought of me as a kid until years later when he saw how much I had grown. Then he blurted out: "Oooh, Elisheva, ever since I heard Nachshon's story, I have been thinking about you. I would very much like to spend years and years with you as husband and wife. I admire you so much, I am sure it is an easy step from there to loving you."

And I, by then not-so-little Elisheva, thought this was a fine idea. Not because Aaron looked so dazzling in the outfit he wore to do all those rituals in the Tabernacle (although I have to admit he did look awfully splendid in those special clothes). I agreed to his proposal immediately, because as the daughter of Aminadav, I had attended dinners in Moses' tent with Miriam and Aaron, and had seen and heard for myself that he is a good man, or as we say nowadays, a real *mensch*.

***

And that's one way to envision how a little eight-year-old girl, barely mentioned in the storybooks, made Jewish history Big Time.

Provenance: Based upon the midrash about Nachshon being the first to enter the waters that is found in Talmud, *Sotah* 37a.

Danny Siegel, author, lecturer, and poet, is a recipient of the prestigious Covenant Foundation Award. For thirty-nine years he has served as the Tzedakah Resource Person for USY Israel Pilgrimage. Among his many books are *Danny Siegel's Bar and Bat Mitzvah Mitzvah Book: A Practical Guide For Changing the World Through Your Simcha; Heroes and Miracle Workers,* a collection of essays about everyday people who are Mitzvah Heroes; *Who, Me? Yes, You!*; and *Danny Siegel's Workbook to Help You Decide Where, When, Why, and How You Can Do Your Best Tikkun Olam.* He has also published several collections of poetry and children's stories. Danny is also a faculty member of the Jewish Spiritual Education and Maggid-Educator Ordination Programs at Reclaiming Judaism. www.DannySiegel.com

Study Guide: Questions, Sources, and Projects for Reflection, Discussion, and Action

1. Which *mitzvot* are illustrated by this story? Which additional *mitzvot* can you also relate to this story?

2. What qualities do both Nachshon and Elisheva have that made it possible to do something so frightening?

3. What are your strongest qualities? How are these qualities of yours assets and when do they get you in trouble?

4. Can you think of other situations where women may have been actively engaged in facilitating something important in the Israelites' wilderness crossing, but that we simply don't get to read about it because the Torah was finalized during a time of patriarchy?

Sacred Story and Text Connections

Open a *Chumash* to Exodus, *Shemot* 1:15-21 where the midwives defy Pharaoh. Who are the modern day Pharoahs? Who stands up to them? What approaches are being used in the world today for resisting oppression? If you were being oppressed by a government or religious policy or employer, what would you do?

Project: Refugees are on the move all over the world, many desperate for a safe haven, clean clothes, water, food, medicines, replacement eyeglasses, and so much more. Find an organization that focuses on this issue and ask them for a specific project you, your family, school, business, or camp can take on.

Chapter 37
The Wall
by Shoshana Silberman

"Attention everyone!" shouted Rabbi Berenstein into the microphone. "It's time for the raffle! I'd like to call on Cantor Roth to come up and select the winning number."

Cantor Roth bounded up to the front of the room and put her hand into a large bucket full of folded sheets of paper. She pulled one out, opened it up and read the number in her lovely alto voice. "Number 118! Who has number 118? You've just won a trip to Israel for two!"

"That's me! That's me! I can't believe this!" exclaimed a very startled Jessica Brenner. Then she ran up to receive the gift certificate, as her equally surprised family looked on and cheered. As the Brenners were leaving the Purim Carnival, their friends rushed over to congratulate them. These friends seemed genuinely happy for them, even though they themselves had obviously lost the raffle.

When they got into the car, Josh, who had recently turned thirteen, interrupted the laughter with a question. "If there's only two tickets, who will get to go on the trip? One ticket should be for me," he stated in an authoritative voice, "since now I can have an *aliyah* at the *Kotel*.*

"That would not be fair," pleaded Leah, age ten. "You just had a bar mitzvah with all the fuss and attention on you. It should be my turn to do something special."

Their mom calmed everyone down and said, "We'll discuss this tomorrow night, after Dad and I have had a chance to think about it."

The following evening after dinner, Mom made an incredible announcement.
"We've decided that with two trips being sponsored by the raffle, we will have sufficient funds for both of you to come with us, provided we all watch our spending over the next few months."

Smiles broke out on both children's faces.

The trip was arranged to begin two days after school ended. Until then, the entire family was busy, planning, packing, listening to conversational Hebrew recordings, and dreaming about the adventure ahead. All had agreed that as soon as

---

* An *aliyah* is the mitzvah of witnessing the Torah reading, and the *Kotel* is the western wall built by King Herod around King Solomon's Temple in Jerusalem, known in Hebrew as the *Kotel* and at this time to English speakers as "The Wall".

they were settled in their Jerusalem hotel, their first outing would be a trip to The Wall.

The Brenners felt that this holy place would connect them to their ancestors and to their history. Since the 1967 war, The Wall had become a symbol of national unity, a place of pride. Praying there would be a way of showing their gratitude, that finally the Jewish people had a country of their own.

They also liked the custom of writing a prayer on a piece of paper to be put into a crevice in The Wall, and decided to write their own prayers in advance. Dad had joked that the last time someone in their family put a folded piece of paper and placed it into something, they were very lucky. Perhaps they'll be just as fortunate this time as well.

And so it was that on the day after they arrived in Jerusalem, the Brenner family took a cab to the Old City and made their way to the *Kotel*. As they approached the ancient site below, the family became very silent, each engrossed with his or her own thoughts. It was hard to believe that they had finally come here. Leah broke the silence by wondering out loud if it was real or a movie set. Josh pointed out that it was a busy place with such a diverse crowd of people, everyone pouring out their hearts. Mom and Dad, with tears in their eyes, just held hands. Finally, Mom suggested that they recite the *Shehecheyanu* prayer for reaching this special time together.

Dad then requested that they sit down so he and Mom could explain how they would proceed. Mom said that Dad and Josh would be going to the men's side to pray, and Mom and Leah would be going to the women's side.

"There's just one other thing, Leah," Mom noted. "Women are not allowed to sing their prayers out loud."

Leah was stunned, but it was Josh who spoke up first. "But that doesn't make any sense! Women always sing the prayers at our synagogue."

"Yes," acknowledged Dad, "but there are rules here that are very different from home."

Leah then posed a question. "What if I decided to sing *Adon Olam*? I really like that prayer."

"Well, some people may get very angry and even try to hurt you."

"What?" shouted Leah. "Why would anyone want to hurt someone who is praying?"

"I don't know," said Mom, " but we need to follow the rules. I don't want you to get hurt."

"I'm not sure I really want to go now," said Leah, "unless we could go to The Wall together as a family."

"I understand how you feel," said Dad. "I wish it were different, too. You should be aware, though, that there are many people around the world working to make changes so that men and women can pray together, with all of their voices heard. I hope that when we return as a family—and I hope it will be soon—there will be changes."

"Leah, I won't make you go to The Wall," said Mom, "but I want to put a special prayer in a crevice. It's a healing prayer for my friend Hannah, who is sick. You know," she said, like she was thinking out loud, "I have some paper and pencil in my pocketbook. Maybe we all could add prayers to the ones we already wrote, asking for a way for women to pray as they wish at this holy place."

"I like that idea," said Leah, and the rest of the family nodded in agreement. "I'd like to do that, so I'll join you, Mom."

Yet as they walked towards The Wall, Leah was still sad that her *Adon Olam* could not be sung. Her Dad and brother parted with them and went to the men's section, where the sound of the *davvening* (praying) could be heard. Mom and Leah entered the quiet women's section, where tears seemed to substitute for song.

The ancient stones kept beckoning to Leah to come closer. Her hand trembled as she placed both of her prayers in a crevice. As she stepped back, she noticed that there were many tiny birds that had come to the women's side. They flew about between the cracks, as if gathering up blessings. Their chirpy bird voices were loud and clear. Leah knew at once that they were singing her song—her *Adon Olam*!

She burst into tears as she cried out, "Thank you, birds. Thank you so much! When I come here next time, I pray I will be able to join you in prayer."

Provenance: This story is based on my own experience at the *Kotel* more than twenty years ago. It is re-imagined as a child's experience.

Shoshana Silberman has been a teacher, educational director, and consultant, who has led workshops and teacher training across North America. She holds bachelor's degrees from Columbia University and Gratz College, a masters from the University of Chicago, and a doctorate in education from Temple University. Her articles have appeared in numerous journals, newspapers, and books. Among her many books are *A Family Haggadah I & II, The Whole Megillah (Almost), Tiku Shofar (machzor), Siddur Shema Yisrael*, and *Active Jewish Learning*. Shoshana presently lives in Montclair, New Jersey, where she facilitates a Lilith Salon, enjoys grandparenting, and continues to study, teach, and write.

Study Guide: Questions, Sources, and Projects for Reflection, Discussion, and Action

1. Which *mitzvot* are illustrated by this story? Which additional *mitzvot* can you also relate to this story?

2. Why is the Wall such a powerful symbol for Jews? Other religions have a powerful historical connection to the Temple Mount as well. Do you know which ones and why? If you were to put a written prayer into a crack in the wall, as is the local custom, what might your prayer be?

3. In what other ways are some women and some men restricted from specific Jewish practices? How do you feel about this?

4. Where do you stand on matters of gender equality? Traditions usually emerge for a reason, so why might male and female roles have become so differently organized? Studies do not show an improvement in human behavior because of religious practice or gender-based separations and restrictions, so why do societies and groups still exist that forbid men to hear a woman lead prayer or to see the bare arms or legs of a girl or woman on the hottest day of the year? What responsibilities are perhaps being avoided or enforced by these practices?

Sacred Story and Text Connections

1. You have seen what I did to the Egyptians, and how I bore you on eagles' wings and brought you back to me.—Exodus, *Shemot* 19:4.

   Who or what does the eagle symbolize here, and throughout Jewish scripture, prayer and poetry? Why did the birds' songs make such a difference to Leah?

2. While pregnant, Rabbi Geela Rayzel was among those attempting to read Torah at the *Kotel*, at a planned women's service there. From the men's side a chair was thrown at all the women.

   What emotion do you imagine led the man to do such a thing? How, might you imagine, was Rabbi Rayzel and the women's prayer experience impacted by this kind of violence?

3. Learn more about the *Kotel* and original Temple and its artisans and rebuilding, in I Kings 6:1-13, Talmud, *Bava Batra* 4a and Josephus, *The Jewish War*, page 304.

Project: In the Talmud, *Shmuel*, a decisor of Jewish law (*halachah*), declares "*kol b'isha ervah*," the voice of a woman is *ervah*, overly attractive for men.
—Talmud *Berakhot 24a, Kiddushin 70b* and *Sotah 48a*

Similarly, in Victorian times, catching a glimpse of the ankle of a woman was considered scandalously alluring. Look up how long it took women in the United States and abroad to secure the right to vote, to secure the right to train and serve as doctors, lawyers, rabbis, and cantors. What might you do to support inclusion in Jewish practice and leadership across the full spectrum of gender?

Project: Anthropologists and scholars do not find evidence of gender segregation during the offering of sacrifices in the ancient Temple that once stood on the site of the Wall. This seems to be a practice that entered Judaism at a later time. It is not until the nineteenth century that a ruling by Rabbi Moshe Sofer of Slovakia prohibited all women's singing at religious services, and this then began to be adopted by other men of the Orthodox rabbinate. Visit womenofthewall.org to learn more about the many sides of this issue, for even among women there are passionate differences on how to proceed with this cause. See how you might best lend your support.

Project: Experience undisturbed sacred space. Ask your rabbi, cantor, *maggid* (storyteller/guide), or classroom teacher if each person in your class can have time to quietly be before the open ark. When you feel ready, ask a question that is important to you or express something you've needed to say. Then wait quietly and listen for a message for you that could be a feeling, a memory, a voice in your head, a symbol that comes to mind. Sometimes you will hear back later; and either way you will have had a very special private experience with the Torah.

Project: Make a silent sacred space in the back of your synagogue sanctuary or in a spot in your school, camp, or home where you can go for rest and reflection. You might do this by hanging silk scarves or creating panels to enclose the space.

Chapter 38
Bending The Laws of Physics
by Anna Sher Simon

October 15, 1982

5:03 pm

The strange metal box opens with a squeak. Pushing aside a plain envelope, I pull out a large plastic cassette. Nervously, I insert it into our new VHS machine. The screen of the bulky, little television is black, and then slowly comes to life with the words, "A message for 13-year-old Anna," appearing in the center. I inhale sharply with surprise and sit, transfixed, in front of the flickering screen as the music begins, and the picture begins to take shape.

***

(Earlier that day)
12:13 pm

I didn't think life could get much worse than seventh grade, but then eighth grade happened.

I unwrap the oddly shaped PB&J I made that morning on sliced challah, sitting alone on the cold cement in an unclaimed spot. The leaves are just beginning to turn, and I zip up my jacket against the chill. Around me on the vast front steps of the school are large and small clumps of students talking and eating. They remind me of troops of baboons I've seen on Mutual of Omaha's *Wild Kingdom*, chattering and picking lice out of each other's fur in groups of two or more. I can't see my old clique from where I am sitting, but I imagine them laughing and gloating over the look on my face when they finally announce, in no uncertain terms, that I am not welcome to eat lunch with them any more. Or worse, and more likely, they aren't even giving me a second thought.

Who could blame them, I sigh. Those stuck-up girls I went to elementary school with were sick and tired of my "not getting it"—I wear the wrong clothes, don't spend my weekends learning tennis at the country club, and boys don't make me blush or giggle. I figure I was tolerated for a whole year simply out of allegiance to our shared history at our private, German elementary school. This year, they must have decided that they are no longer obligated to shelter me at this huge, new middle school. We had been convening each day at a prime spot under one of the maple trees on the front lawn where they ate the neatly wrapped ham sandwiches, Oreo cookies, and potato chips that their mothers packed for them each morning. I'm not going to miss being the butt of their jokes, but I am going to miss the soft grass and that tree…and I now I have to eat alone.

I search the steps for a familiar face, and think I see Karen just before she abruptly turns her back and skips down the stairs. How naive I was to think that things would be different this year. Just a few weeks before, at my Bat Mitzvah, she and my other Hebrew school friends, Adam and Jonas, were my bosom buddies. As soon as the final prayers were done, they all followed me upstairs to my room (we had the service in our grand front room, the same place my parents had been married) where I changed into my cutest cut-off shorts, ripped through the pile of gifts from people with names I didn't recognize, firmly said no to more family photos (I am an adult now, right?), and set off with my friends to find some fun.

That late summer afternoon, my Hebrew school clan and I walked the mile to the commercial strip, un-chaperoned for the first time, to play Pac-man and Galaga in the back of a greasy spoon café for a quarter a game. As both my hands operated the controls, I felt Adam begin to gently "feel me up" with his hands. I noticed that Tirtza and Jonas were doing the same and was deeply pleased by the normality of it all. Boys have never interested me in that way, but I knew him for as long as I could remember and trusted him completely. I liked it that he saw me as a "real girl," even if this kind of touching seemed mostly like a waste of time. With these kids, I felt more than acceptable; I felt like I belonged—as if I were neither a religious minority nor a freak for being attracted to girls instead of boys. I had thought that maybe my "Jewish rite of passage" was the beginning of a new life for me.

However, at the start of the school year, my comfortable Jewish clan dissolved at this predominantly gentile junior high. We all just seem to understand that we can't be friends here, but I don't know why. I will have to assimilate the best I can on my own.

As I begin to peel my orange, I mentally go through all the girls I know. Rebecca and Deborah go to the Conservative synagogue and always come to school well dressed, wearing nice jewelry. They seem nice enough, but the girls I went to elementary school with call them "JAPs". I'm not sure what that means, but I know it can't be good from the way they wrinkle their noses when they say it. No, I sigh to myself, I can't hang out with them. Then I think about the girls in my various classes and feel that familiar, painful clenching in my gut, remembering the events of last week. Knowing that my days with the stuck-up group were numbered, I had found Gwen and her friend Laura one lunch period and ate with them instead that day. They didn't make fun of me, and I was excited to have found an alternative to the snarky girls I usually ate with. But then the dreaded note arrived on my desk in

American History last Tuesday: "I'm sorry, but we just don't want you to eat with us." I taped it in my journal that evening after crying my eyes out. It was proof positive of my loser status.

I sigh again and work on getting the straw into my Capri-Sun pouch. Sticky fluid sprays over my corduroy pants. "Dang it!" I groan under my breath and wonder why I can't get the knack of it. Most of the time, I feel like everyone knows what to do and what is going on…except for me. Furthermore, I am fat and ugly (just look at the stretch marks on my expanding hips and unevenly developing breasts, to say nothing of the acne!), awkward, and worst of all, stupid. I am a fraud in the honors classes, but I study hard and hope no one will find out that I don't really belong there. It's the one thing that makes me feel a little special and it would be the end of the world if I lost it.

No, I'm not smart like Isaac. My little brother tested as brilliant, but I know better than to want to switch places with him; he's having a rough go of it at the Hebrew Day School where the teachers seem at a loss as to what to do with him. And his only friend seems to be that boy who is so nasty to him. I'm so worried about my brother and have no idea how to help him.

Heck, I can't even help myself. At least I have green eyes and a button nose and so can pass as gentile, not to mention that no one knows the secret, horrible thoughts I have about Samantha. I think about the reply to the letter I sent to *Young Miss Magazine's* advice column about what I was going through with her. Instead of a personal answer, they sent me a copy of a previously printed response to a girl who had written about her feelings for a female gym teacher. The advice columnist wrote that it was "normal to be attracted to authority figures" and her "feelings would most likely pass with time." What did that have to do with me? I wonder to myself. Sam isn't an authority figure; she is in my grade. And, I reassure myself, this isn't a juvenile "crush"; I love her, deeply. I am attracted to her in a way I could never imagine feeling about an adult I barely know. No, I decide, the two situations are completely different. The people at *Young Miss* must not have even read my letter, or at least didn't bother to understand it.

At least I know enough to pick a boy to "have a crush on" when asked, while avoiding him like the plague. I decide that Rick could be my choice for the year; a normal kid who didn't give a lick whether I lived or died. I made the mistake of asking Christian to a dance last year because everyone else was going, and then he actually wanted to kiss me. Gross. I shudder. I'm pretty sure that wouldn't happen with Rick. Could there be a boy I would actually want to kiss me? I pose the question to myself. Maybe the right boy just hasn't come along yet. I can't picture my future, nor, frankly, do I want to think about it much—it takes enough effort to just survive each wretched day.

My sack lunch finished, I look at my watch: still twenty minutes to go. I take out my planning book for the tenth time that day and review where I am to go and when. In a rush, I realize that I had almost forgotten that I had cross-country practice after school that day.

I had discovered running by joining my mother on her jog each morning before school my fifth grade year. I loved the time alone with her, how strong my body felt, and listening to nothing but the sound of the birds and my pounding feet. Often, when I couldn't contain my joy and mounting energy any longer, I would sprint ahead for the mile home. Just before the final turn, the high school kids waiting for their early bus would cheer me on, the little kid, as I rushed past, red-faced and breathless. I didn't know anyone else my age who ran every day and couldn't wait to get to middle school where there was a real team.

I continued on my own for awhile after my mother stopped her daily practice when I was twelve, looking forward to the next year when I would be able to run with kids my age. But being on a team isn't anything like I expected. No one is cheering me now. I am always the slowest, always last, and my coach seems perpetually annoyed by me. My short legs mean that I seem to work twice as hard to get the same speed as the tall girls. I don't understand why different kids seem to be there each day; in fact, some only appear at meets. It seems to me that either you are on the team and come to practice or you don't. I want so badly to score for my team, but I always seem to get a stich in my side or have to go to the bathroom in the middle of the race.

My mother and father barely seem present these days; my father working in the back room on his TRS-80 computer and my mother busy with a million different things or in meetings. I can tell that they are under a lot of stress, dealing with the stuff involved with being a grown-up. It seems terrible to be an adult, especially in light of everyone always saying that I should consider my current existence "the best years of my life." I shudder, wondering what deeper misery the future will bring.

5:00 pm

I'm finally home, sweaty and tired from running. I almost miss the small package sitting next to the front door. It is army-issue gray metal, the size of a shoebox and dented in several places. I see no stamp, but it is addressed to me on a tattered paper label. Intrigued, I take it upstairs.

5:04 pm

The scene on the screen is that of a formal event with sparkling chandeliers and white tablecloths; the room is filled with laughing, happy people in festive dress. Dance music pumps energetically in the background. The camera pans across the crowd, settling on one table near the front. I make out the silhouette of an elegantly dressed couple flanking a small boy, no older than six, expectantly turning their heads toward a stage in the front of the room. The words "Power Awards: The Simon Family" are projected on a screen above the stage.

"While so many contributed to the passage of the bill, one family went above and beyond the call of duty. Time and time again, they were testifying, speaking at rallies and answering requests for interviews. They won the hearts and minds of Coloradans. From all of us here, thank you for showing what a modern family looks like."

The family rises from their seats and makes their way to the stage, hand-in-hand. The camera sweeps the crowd, which is now on its feet, applauding. Viewed from the back, I can see the parents and the child walking up the stairs and across the stage to the podium. The woman leading the way has beautiful, curly, long, brown hair and her hourglass figure is accented by a floor-length, red velvet dress. Her partner is in a smart, black suit, and the little boy is wearing a vest over his button-down shirt. There are cameras flashing all around. The music swells as the family on the stage turns to receive their award.

With a jolt I can now see that the parents of the boy are both women! I gasp with surprise upon discovering the one in the dress is… ME. I'm older, but the faint scar on my right cheek is unmistakable, as are my distinctive green eyes. Bewildered, I look around for an explanation and remember there was an envelope with the tape in the box. I quickly retrieve it and tear it open with trembling hands. I read the following letter:

Dear Anna,

>I hope the tape has made it to you safely, as it has travelled a long way. On it, you will see a glimpse of your future self, a look into a real crystal ball. I know that it's hard to believe, but consider how deeply true M. L'Engle's *Wrinkle in Time* felt when you read it in fourth grade. Know that you are worth bending the laws of physics. You need this message; you need to know the truth, and so I have found a way to get it to you.
>
>The truth is this: as bad as things feel now, the pain will not last. I will not describe to you all of the amazing things that will happen to you because you will not believe them, and you need to understand that this is real. Instead, I will explain to you that your tenacity and heart will carry you farther than you ever thought possible. I cannot give you advice; you will do what you will do, but I can give you reassurance that it will all work out.
>
>Remember when Mother gave you the little astrology book and said that you were still a Leo? You dismissed her, but remember when you

were five—the brave, outspoken, and happy girl who climbed trees every chance she got? The one who basked in attention and praise and wasn't afraid to laugh out loud? You are still that proud lion, Anna, and you will find her in yourself again.

I know this will be hard for you to accept, and that is why I have sent the video. You can see with your own eyes how beautiful you are (not so changed from now), and that you are deeply, deeply loved and appreciated. Furthermore, you will be loved and appreciated for who you are—you do not have to bend yourself into something else. You are blessed in so many ways, even now, and with time you will be able to harness those blessings to be able to make a positive difference in the world. And every once in a while, as I show you here, you will be bowled over by love and thanks in return.

Life will never be perfectly easy, nor should it be. There will be difficult times ahead that make what you are going through now seem like nothing at all. But don't believe for a second that you are now experiencing "the best time in your life". With each challenge, you will get stronger and wiser. Out of this strength and wisdom will come the sweetest experiences you can ever imagine, including a meaningful and prestigious career, the satisfaction of raising a child, and yes, a partnership based in love and respect.

I have come to believe that the God you spoke of in your Bat Mitzvah speech exists, and not just in the symbolic, humanitarian form you currently think is acceptable. I know I risk losing you at this point in my letter, because this particular concept of God seems immature or inherently Christian to you now, but as a Jew, you, too, have a right to our people's tradition of a personal relationship with the divine. For now, understand that your Judaism is your tribe, and no one can deny you that. Let this be a source of strength—consider the fact that our people have outlasted the Egyptian, Roman, and Ottoman empires!

What I want for you, my dear tenderhearted self, is to not fear being alone so much. The world is changing in wonderful ways, and you will be a part of that change, with a multitude of others like you working together to make it happen. Don't worry; you will find the love of your life, when you are ready for such a serious relationship and have learned how to stand on your own two feet.

You will seek and honor the truth, even when it frightens you, which it often will. You will discover that the most powerful thing you can do in this life is to fully and bravely be yourself. When you are able to do this, with your life-partner at your side, incredible things will happen. And you will know happiness beyond anything you have experienced.

I promise.

With great love and admiration,
Your 44-year-old self

Anna Sher Simon and her family have fought for marriage equality in Colorado by testifying at the capitol multiple times and making numerous public statements and appearances. They have been honored for this work with awards from the Denver LGBT Chamber of Commerce, the University of Denver where Anna works as a tenured biology professor, and *Out Front*, a publication for the LGBT community in Colorado. Anna and her wife, Fran, were the first couple in Colorado to receive a civil union, which was performed by the Mayor of Denver. Anna loves running and recently completed her first half-marathon.

Study Guide: Questions, Sources, and Projects for Reflection, Discussion, and Action

1. Which *mitzvot* are illustrated by this story? Which additional *mitzvot* can you also relate to this story?

2. What activity done by a majority of your friends have you tried out and discovered that is just wasn't the real you?

3. What is it like to be different, to not fit in?

4. Anna wants to assimilate—not be singled out as Jewish or lesbian. Is assimilation a good or bad thing?

5. Anna says, "I feel everyone knows what to do and what is going on except me." Do you or have you ever felt like that? What can you do to change the way you feel?

6. Does it matter to whom you are attracted?

7. Take a look at the author's bio. What in the story gives you a clue that she might become a social justice leader? What characteristics do you have that you can apply to working for liberty and justice for all?

8. How can you be more welcoming to those who are different from you?

Sacred Story and Text Connections

1. You shall not wrong a stranger or oppress him, for you were strangers in the land of Egypt.—Exodus, *Shemot* 22:20

2. Ben Zoma says: Who is honored (*mechubad*)? One who honors (*mechabed*) every human being (*habriyot*), as it is said: 'For those who honor Me [God] I will honor, and those who scorn Me shall be degraded' (Samuel I 2:30). —*Mishnah, Avot* 4:1

   In what way would treating someone scornfully be degrading to the person who is being scornful? Why would your treating every human honorably bring honor upon you?

3. "[Empathetic justice] seeks to make people identify themselves with each other—with each other's needs, with each other's hopes and aspirations, with each other's defeats and frustrations. Because Jews have known the distress of slaves and the loneliness of strangers, we are to project ourselves into their souls and make their plight our own."—Rabbi Emanuel Rackman, "Torah Concept of Empathetic Justice Can Bring Peace," *The Jewish Week* (New York, 3 April 1977), page 19

4. Ben would often wonder, "Why aren't there pictures in synagogue with families like ours? Or like Sarah and Sam's two dads?" One day he asked his parents this question during the break between services on Yom Kippur. The two mothers looked at each other thoughtfully and his *Ima* Lara replied, "Good question! We'll look into it."

   During the months leading up to Hanukkah, Ben and his mommies began to design a present for the synagogue based on the practice called *hiddur mitzvah*. This means it is a mitzvah to make something that is already part of a mitzvah even more beautiful than it already is. The two mothers are two weavers, so, with Ben helping as apprentice weaver, they made magnificent new covers for the tables where the Torah is placed and chanted during services, and also for the *shtender*, the service leader's reading stand. Embedded into the design of the cloth, including on the edges that hang over right where the congregation can see it, are images of all kinds of families. Families like Ben's mommies, and Sarah's and Sam's daddies are included in the pattern, and also families with only one mom or dad and a single child, families with some members in wheelchairs and with canes, and families with children and parents who looked like they came from every people in the world! Ben bounced in joy as he carried it to synagogue. Now many of the families that had been left out would be right there—in front of everyone on a cloth touching the Torah!

   "But why," asked the rabbi, as they brought it up front to present their gift to everyone. "Why is there an empty oval embroidered right where the Torah would be placed on the fabric? "That was my idea!" exclaimed Ben. "That will be where we embroider a verse to be chosen by the congregation."

   What is your reaction to Ben and his parents' gift? Would your community be receptive? What verse(s) would you offer as an option for the oval?

Project: How many different kinds of families are there in your community? Do the synagogues and other organizations, textbooks, other print media and websites in your area have photographs, art, posters, and sacred objects that reflect the diversity of individuals and families? Where might you get started on *tikkun olam*, repair of the world, on this aspect of just inclusion where you live, pray, work and learn?

Project: It has recently become illegal to discriminate based on gender in many states and a number of countries—but many people, countries, and religious denominations still maintain such practices. Do your school, camp, and community each have a social justice committee where youth and adults plan and serve together? Ask to join, or create one. Make sure that issues of full inclusion and respect for diversity for all kinds of people are on the agenda. Be sure to check online for the kinds of programming that work, because sometimes what we think helps in reality just pushes people further into their prejudices. There is so much to be done in every generation for justice!

Chapter 39
Lost In God's Hand
by Devorah Spilman

At 6:40 A.M. on that Sunday morning, I went out for my customary walk. I downed a big glass of water before leaving so I didn't bring any extra along. There was no cellphone service in the area, so no point in pocketing a cellphone. Anyway, my whole family was asleep; I assumed I'd be back at camp before they woke up. Was I ever wrong about that! Following the beautiful and well-marked Liahona Horse Trail, I came out at the camp entrance. Posted there was a trail map. I saw that the horse trail wound around in a long, meandering loop back to camp. But I saw that there was another path, which provided a shorter, more direct way back. I decided to take the shorter, more direct route home.

After a lovely hike, I came to an intersection, and took the shorter way back. Following the logging road for a bit, I came to a fork. One branching path led into the forest and was marked with a small horseshoe symbol. It wasn't clear whether this path was designed for foot traffic or only for riders, but I decided to try it. I was not sure if it was the right way. I didn't remember seeing such a fork marked on the map.

After walking for quite some time without seeing any sign of camp, I turned around, returned to the fork, and tried the other way. This path brought me to an old metal gate, its two sides swung open, which led to a dirt road.

Surely a gate must signal the way back to camp, I thought, so I went that way.

The dirt road led to another junction with three more forks, none posted with signs leading back to camp. By now I had been walking for about an hour and a half, and I really wanted to get back. If I turned around and walked all the way back via the long horse trail, it would take another couple of hours to get back. I was not fit for such a long walk. What I needed was to find someone soon who would give me a ride back to camp. A small sign at the junction read: "Rolling Timber Sale", with an arrow pointing toward one of the three routes. I thought, "A sale means people and civilization, and maybe even someone who will give me a ride back to camp."

Sometimes a sign can reveal God's hand miraculously acting on our behalf in the world. But sometimes we misunderstand the signs along the way. On this particular day, when I came to the end of the path, I discovered that there was no sale, no civilization, and no person to give me a ride. All I found was timber that perhaps had once been for sale there. And looking out from that spot, I saw only more dirt roads and forest, extending endlessly in all directions. The idea of going back to the original road seemed farther away than ever. In fact, I wasn't sure I could even find my way back to it anymore. Still I had no choice but to go on, hoping for both a sign and a miracle—a road sign directing me to a place with real people who could help me get home.

I began to pray in earnest: "Please God, help me to get back to camp." When I came to yet another junction, with a road marked with one of those small horseshoe signs, I thought, "Yes, it's a sign! The camp *must* be this way."

So I continued on with a bit of hope. Exhausted and parched, I hiked uphill, and as the trail topped out, I arrived at a memorial of sorts. A white wooden cross with pots of plastic flowers surrounding it.

"How long ago did people put this here?" I wondered. "And where are those people now?" Looking out from the hilltop, I couldn't see any sign of Camp Wilkerson, nor any other evidence of human civilization.

At that moment, I felt all hope evaporate. There was no way back. I despaired, envisioning the intersections of miles and miles of unmarked roads throughout the forest. I was completely and totally lost in the wilderness. Desperately I began calling out for help. Maybe someone would hear. But there was no response.

"Perhaps someone can find me here," I thought. "This high clearing is a visible spot in the landscape." And besides, I needed to rest.

After about fifteen minutes, I began to pray intensely, reciting Psalms and voicing my own personal prayer for God to send someone in a car or on a horse, to bring me back. I knew people at camp would be starting to worry about me and that I would be really hard to find. I had to keep trying to find my way back. And I needed a miracle.

I kept walking. At one point, I fashioned an arrow out of rocks to show which direction I was taking, in case someone might try to follow my tracks. I did this twice. Then I came to a junction where there was already an arrow made of sticks on the ground. So I followed it, hoping to find someone else's trail. But at the next junction there was no arrow, no sign of any kind, just three different roads. I went a little way on each to try to see if I could discern which way to go. One way led to a path under giant power lines. The clearing under these giant structures formed a huge open strip through the forest, but I still didn't know where I was in relation to Camp Wilkerson. I was so tired. It was now about 11:00 A.M. and I had been walking since dawn, without food or water.

I knew I had to rest, so I spread my sweater on an even patch of ground, and lay down upon it. I just couldn't go on. A short distance away, I saw a small bear. It looked at me, and I looked at it. As I'd been taught, I lay still. Eventually it turned and walked slowly back among the trees. We were two quiet souls in the forest, only *he* probably wasn't lost.

I kept thinking that I heard a motor, but it was always only the wind. And then… it wasn't. It was definitely a motor, loud and close. That meant human beings! I ran toward the sound coming from the path under the power lines. And I saw them! My personal miracle: a father and his two children, out riding their off-road motorbikes.

I called to them—"Help me! I'm lost."

They stopped. The father had a small child in front of him on his bike.

The other child, a young boy, had his own bike. I explained, "I'm trying to get back to Camp Wilkerson, and I've been walking for almost five hours."

"The road back to camp is at the top of the next hill," he told me.

"Is it far?" I asked.

He said it was, so I asked him for a ride out. *B'ezrat HaShem* (with God's help)—Thank God! And it was so.

On the way back I told this man that he was the answer to my prayers. He said that he hadn't been planning to go this way as it was so steep and might be hard for his younger son, but for some reason he suddenly felt that today they should take the path on which they'd met me.

It took us only fifteen minutes to drive out of the forest. Then we saw a car coming towards us. It was a group from camp looking for me.

After we all profusely thanked the man for saving me, I was whisked back to camp. I began to hear their stories, as they elicited mine. When I hadn't returned from my early morning walk, they had concluded that I had lost my way. First they had honked all the horns at camp so that I could use the sound to find my way back. Eventually they stopped the honking, gathered together all the children, and began to chant *tehillim* (Psalms) and to offer their own personal prayers for me. Finally they had set out to search for me in the car. It turned out that I had shown up just in time to prevent their calling 911 for a search and rescue team.

So it was that I was rescued by the power of prayer and through the hand of God. To this day, I feel grateful to all those who were involved in this awesome miracle.

Provenance: Two of my greatest passions are walking alone in new places and storytelling. I love the quiet and the usually small, sweet adventure of it. It is a comforting thought to remember that in hard times maybe someone else is praying for us, and we are not alone. My husband later told me the prayer he offered for me that day: "God, I know everything you do is for the good. I also know that nothing is beyond you. Please bring my wife back to me." I had become overconfident going into the woods without telling others where I was going, not even bringing a companion, communication tool, or water. In the end I emerged a humbled, small, scared, and thankful human, grateful for the immense kindness of others, the unpredictable possibilities of this world, living in awe of God's role in my life and my place in this vastness.

Devorah Spilman is the owner of Spilman Storyselling, an international training and consulting firm dedicated to training businesses and entrepreneurs to master the power of story in their sales and marketing. Devorah has been a professional storyteller for more than thirty years, creating and telling stories to all age groups. She has a one woman show called, "Is God a Man in the Sky?" She has performed throughout the US and in Israel. Her original story, "The Candle Maker of Light," is published in *Chosen Tales: Stories Told by Jewish Storytellers*. Devorah lives in Portland, Oregon, with her family, and trains people all over the world in the art of Storyselling over the internet.

Study Guide: Questions, Sources, and Projects for Reflection, Discussion, and Action

1. Which *mitzvot* are illustrated by this story? Which additional *mitzvot* can you also relate to this story?

2. Have you ever been lost? What feelings did you have during this time?

3. How did you find your way? Or did someone find you? Did you see a "sign" indicating which way to go?

4. Does praying for help make a difference in difficult circumstances? In what ways?

Sacred Story and Text Connections

1. So I decided there is nothing better than to enjoy food and drink and to find satisfaction in work. Then I realized that these pleasures are from the hand of God.—Ecclesiastes, *Kohelet* 2: 24

2. So in God's hand, I set my soul, both when I sleep and when I wake and my soul, my body too. God is in me, I will not fear.—Rabbi David Wolfe-Blank, interpretation in his *Meta Siddur* of the last verse of the *Adon Olam* by Shlomo Ibn Gabiriol

    What does it mean to sense "the hand of God" in your life? To go to sleep and entrust your soul into the Godfield? How do you relate to the story's main character viewing "the hand of God" as having made the rescue possible? If your Hebrew skills are up to it, make your own translation of the *Adon Olam* and notice how this medieval prayer echoes many of the concepts of modern physics.

Chapter 40
Heavenly Soup
by Susan Stone

Whining is not pretty. And when my six-year-old complained about her birthday present I was fed up. She needed a story...

It was her bedtime and I plopped down on her bed, my head on the pillow next to hers, only streetlight peeking through the shades to illuminate the room. I could see the outline of her tiny nose. I stroked her silky head. She requested another story about her grandfather, the one whom she had never known. I knew just the right one.

Your grandfather, my father, was a *tzaddik*, a holy person; a person who does good things for others—mitzvahs. At the end of his life, when you were very little, he was very sick.

"Dad, is there anything I can bring you?" I would ask him. "You barely eat. There must be something you would like."

He was very old by this time. He had been sick for many months, and I didn't know what else to do for him. The doctors had given him all the medicine they could think of but it wasn't working. He looked pale and grizzled and tired. I was scared. Very sad and very scared. He had always done so much for me, for our family. I wanted so much to give back to him.

I asked him again, thinking he hadn't heard me. "What can I bring you to eat?"

With a sad smile your grandfather replied weakly, "I wish I could eat, but my body rejects all things of this world. Ah! But one time, during my years of wandering, before I was married and had children, I stayed at an inn and ate there a delicious soup. If I could only get a bowl of soup, the kind I was served by a young Jewish woman at that little gray inn so long ago, I would eat. It was as if it was from the Garden of Eden. Oy," he lamented, "what I would like, just one more time, is to taste this soup again." His eyes closed over his memories.

Well, I have to tell you I couldn't imagine where this inn was or even if the woman would still be in the little gray inn from so long ago. The whole idea was preposterous! I was so sad! I couldn't grant your grandfather's request, I was sure.

Now you know I like to cook. I even thought I could concoct some soup and try to fool him into thinking it was from that same inn! No, I thought, that wouldn't work. But I didn't know what to do.

My journey then began. I went off in search of the inn, convinced that the quest was futile. I knew he had travelled from this town to that town along the Raintree River in his youth, so I consulted maps. I went online—very helpful. There were three towns along that tiny river.

I drove through the first village. Two restaurants, one gas station, but no inn. The second town had an inn but it was new. It was in the third town that I found the right inn! The paint was peeling and faded but it was gray still. And still, the same woman my father had named worked there, much older, of course.

To my surprise, the wizened old woman remembered my father. I told her how he had recalled this wonderful soup.

"Please," I implored, "prepare the exact same soup that you prepared for my father years ago, so that I can take it to him." (It was probably her first request for "take-out"!). She put a pot of water on the stove, adding a few beans and some pepper.

"But what is so special about this soup?" I asked.

"Many, many years ago, when your father first entered my inn, I knew immediately that he was a holy person. I don't know how I could tell. My heart opened to him the moment I experienced his presence. I could tell he was kind, generous, and learned. I wanted to do something for him but what could I give? We had just opened our little inn, and your father stopped there because he knew we were Jews, and the meal would be kosher. 'We are poor people,' I told your father. 'We have no food. I can offer you nothing but a place to sleep for the night.'

"Your father sensed my despair. 'What is your name?' he inquired kindly. I told him. Then he ordered soup! 'Put everything you have in it,' he said, 'and it will be wonderful.' But I had nothing. Nothing. Have you ever had ....nothing? I boiled water and put in a few beans and some pepper. Secretly I prayed, 'Creator of the Universe...You have provided me with the mitzvah of preparing a meal for a special guest. If only I had spices or meat to put in....' And then I cried. I cried and cried as I prepared the so-called soup. I had so little to give.

"I brought it to him. With the first taste his eyes lit up.

"'*Es lost zich essen*! I can't resist it...the taste of the Garden of Eden!' He slurped it down.

"I thought he was making fun of the soup, and me, but he motioned for me to taste it as well.

"'*Ess gezunterhait*—eat in good health,' he whispered.

"Without a doubt—I couldn't believe it, it was heavenly soup! Your father," the old woman told me, "gave me the greatest gift—he received with love what I had to give—which was nothing but this soup. He thanked me, and I never saw him again." Wistfully she added, "That was a long, long time ago."

The ancient woman covered her face with her bony fingers. She and I both began to cry. She at the memory of the moment he ate the soup, and I, thinking about my dying father. Into the pot of water these tears went, tears of love. And in this way we made a pot of soup for your grandfather. The soup…well, he ate it as if it were from heaven. It was the last thing I did for him. He died the next day, may his memory be for a blessing.

I looked at my little girl. She had fallen asleep, perhaps visiting her grandpa in her dreams. As for her birthday present…well, I never heard her complain about it—or any other one—again.

Provenance: This is a story I adapted, which is told of the holy Rebbe Elimelech of Lizhensk from Poland and his son Rabbi Eleazar. I first told it on Yom Kippur.

Susan Stone is an award-winning storyteller. Her recordings have received the Parents' Choice Gold and Storytelling World Awards. She has taught at the Piven Theatre Workshop and directed for the Chicago Jewish Theatre. She served on the adjunct faculty of National-Louis University, and her stories appear in numerous anthologies including *The Voice of Children: A Siddur for Shabbat* and *Yom Kippur Readings: Inspiration, Information and Contemplation*. www.susanstone-storyteller.com

Study Guide: Questions, Sources, and Projects for Reflection, Discussion, and Action

1. Which *mitzvot* are illustrated by this story? Which additional *mitzvot* can you also relate to this story?

2. Millions of people have almost nothing to call their own in this world, yet they, too, want to give gifts to others as opposed to solely receiving food and other support for themselves. This is true in our story. Are you good at accepting gifts and compliments? Are you good at giving them?

3. What did the grandfather do and how do you imagine he did it so that the soup maker remembered their brief encounter so clearly?

Sacred Story and Text Connections

This example of dark humor may help with soul searching and future reactions:

Upstairs in bed during what doctors declared would be the last days of his good, long life, a *zayde* (grandfather) smells the most delicious aroma wafting up the steps. "Cheese blintzes!" he declares to his grandson who is playing by his side. It must be *Bubbe* (grandmother) making cheese blintzes! They are my favorite food in the world. My sweet one, please run downstairs and ask her to send some up for me." The grandson runs down and not too long after returns empty-handed, saying, "I'm sorry, *Zayde*, *Bubbe* says they are for the guests who will be coming for *shiva* (memorial visits) later in the week."

Have you ever assumed something about someone who is sick and overlooked something important s/he was trying to tell you? What was it like when you realized this? What does it take to change patterns of assumptions and behaviors toward those who are frail?

Project: Bedtime is a precious time of day. Parents, grandparents, counselors and children share what can be whispered that might not have come out earlier in the day. Memories arise that lead to passing important stories from generation to generation. Are there bedtime stories that have been precious to you in your life? Does this story remind you of family stories that may not yet have been shared? Make a list and begin to share them.

Chapter 41
The Wine of Paradise
by Marc Young

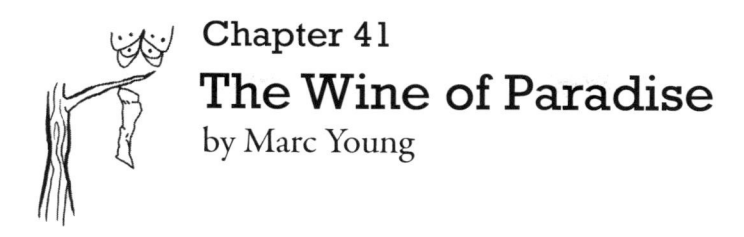

Rebbe Elimelech of Lizhensk taught his disciples, "In the beginning, the Holy One created countless worlds, each with its own gate. When at last our souls return to Him, the merit of our deeds in life determines which gate we pass through. Only while we live can we transform ourselves, rising from the lower to the higher realms. Given such great liberty to wander, it's important not to be a fool."

Rebbe Elimelech hosted a gathering each month to bless the arrival of the new moon. Before the *birkat ha-mazon* (Grace After Meals), the Rebbe would lead his followers in a toast, during which he introduced his topic for the evening. On one such occasion, the Rebbe said: "Behold our many blessings! Tonight we all received enough to eat and drink. Now we are gathered in joyous fellowship to nourish our spirits with words of Torah, to tell the stories of our righteous teachers, and to sing praises to our Creator. Truly, is there anything we lack?"

Seated in the rear of the hall that evening was a young student named Menachem. This was the first time Menachem had been permitted to hear Rebbe Elimelech teach, and he was dizzy with excitement. Or perhaps he was simply dizzy; for it was also the first time he was permitted to drink strong spirits. Whatever the cause, Menachem shouted out a merry response to the Rebbe's question.

"We only lack the wine of Paradise, which the Sages drink in the World-to-Come."

A shocked hush fell over the assembly. Who dared to interrupt Rebbe Elimelech with such impudent nonsense? A hundred pairs of disapproving eyes fastened upon Menachem. The lad blushed red as borsht and prayed to sink through the floor.

From his place at the head table, Rebbe Elimelech spoke to Menachem, as though the two of them were alone in the room.

"So young man, you wish to taste of the wine of Paradise, eh? *Nu*, perhaps you are ready. Go out back to the well and get the buckets. Carry them through the woods, down to the old cemetery. After you enter the gates, turn around and take three steps backward, no more. Look at the new moon and say, 'Elimelech sent me to fetch wine for his guests.' Then return immediately with the wine of Paradise. Don't dare spill a drop! Above all: do not speak a word to anyone on the way, no matter what is said to you. Go now!"

Menachem lurched from the study hall and crossed the dark yard like a man being led to the gallows. By the old stone well he found two wooden buckets and a sturdy pole. Menachem hung a bucket from either end of the pole, slung it across his shoulders, and set off toward the woods.

Two ancient hemlock trees marked the footpath to the old cemetery. They grew close together, so it was difficult for Menachem to squeeze through carrying the buckets and pole. After banging and clunking and spinning in circles, he finally slipped sideways through the narrow gap and started down the path.

Beneath the heavy canopy of the trees, Menachem could see neither the sky above nor the ground in front of him. A cold wind moaned through the creaking branches. Menachem stumbled half-blind down the overgrown track, stubbing his toes on tree roots. As he walked, he thought, "Oy, what a fool I am! Why didn't I keep my mouth shut? How am I supposed to find the wine of Paradise in an old graveyard? I should turn around and go home right now. They'll probably expel me from the yeshiva anyway for my disrespect, so what difference will it make?" But after he'd walked a little farther, Menachem thought, "It's true that I am a great fool, but Rebbe Elimelech is a great *tzaddik*, a wise and righteous man. Who knows what deep purpose he might have for setting me this impossible task? I will do as the Rebbe instructed, and have faith that it will turn out for the best."

At the very moment Menachem decided to complete his fool's errand, he emerged into a weed-filled clearing facing the cemetery. He gathered his courage and pushed upon the rusty gate, which opened with a bloodcurdling Kve-e-e-e-e-tch! Menachem entered the graveyard, immediately spun around, and stepped three paces backward. There he stopped and carefully set down the pole and buckets. Then Menachem tipped his head back and gazed up toward the heavens. And do you know what he saw there?

Gornisht! Nothing.

A thick veil of clouds covered the entire night sky. Neither a glimmer of starlight nor the least hint of a moon could be seen. Menachem was dumbstruck. How could he deliver Rabbi Elimelech's message if the new moon did not appear? He thought, "Wonderful! I'll just stand here among the dead all night, then return empty-handed and disgraced in the morning."

From the corner of his eyes Menachem saw tombstones tumbled in the weeds, while others jutted up like teeth in an old skull. The wind moaned among the broken stones like a sorrowful voice. Menachem shivered and thought, "What am I doing alone in this dismal place? I wish I were back at the light and warmth of the Rebbe's table, with all that cheerful company. What use is the wine of Paradise to the living?"

After what seemed a long while, Menachem glanced up again. This time he saw the silver sickle of the new moon shining through a break in the clouds! With a pounding heart, Menachem stammered out his request.

"Excuse me, um… if you please, er, Rebbe Elimelech sent me to fetch wine for his guests. Ummm, if it's not too much trouble…?"

For one dizzy instant the new moon appeared to tilt like the delicate rim of a *kiddush* cup. Then Menachem heard a remarkable sound. It was liquid music, like the song of a mountain brook dancing across a springtime meadow. It took Menachem a moment to realize that this sound arose from the buckets at his feet, which were being filled from an unseen source.

"It's a miracle," he marvelled. "Blessed be the Holy Name of God."

When both buckets were almost full, Menachem carefully eased the pole back onto his shoulders. The buckets were heavier now, so he had to move slowly to avoid spilling the contents. Dark wine sloshed gently against the sides of the containers as he walked, releasing a complex aroma of wildflowers, incense, and pomegranates, with a lingering finish of chocolate and tobacco. This heavenly fragrance lifted Menachem's spirit and gave him fresh strength to bear his burden.

As Menachem began walking back through the woods, the wind also gained new strength. Fierce gusts pressed against him, driving him back. Dead leaves swirled around his head, battering his face. In their rustle hissing voices pleaded and threatened. Menachem quaked with fear, for he realized that hungry ghosts had followed him from the graveyard. These parched souls were condemned by their earthly sins to wander the bleakest realms of the afterlife, forever denied the rewards reserved for the righteous in Paradise. The fragrance of the wine of Paradise inflamed them with desire. Menachem did his best to ignore their entreaties and plodded on towards his goal.

Suddenly unseen fingers twisted Menachem's nose, while a rasping voice spoke into his ear.

"In life I was a greedy miser. Blessed with great wealth, I pretended to have nothing, so no one would ask me for anything. Now I truly have nothing: even my pauper's shroud has turned to dust. Give me one drop of the wine of Paradise, and I will tell you where my secret hoard of gold and jewels is hidden."

But Menachem knew the spark of God that lives in all things is a treasure more precious than gleaming metal or glittering stones. He remained silent and continued along his path.

Before Menachem walked much further, from out of nowhere bony knuckles rapped him on the head. Another voice issued from the darkness and said, "In life I was a gossip and spoke wickedly about my neighbors. Now beetles gnaw on my withered tongue. Give me one drop of the wine of Paradise and I will make you fair of speech, a great preacher, a *maggid*. All who hear your words will be spellbound and believe."

But Menachem now realized that although any fool can speak, only the wise truly *know*. He determined to guard his tongue better in the future, said nothing, and continued along his path.

Overhead the branches angrily tossed and groaned, as if in a gale. Every step was more difficult than the last. Menachem bent nearly double, trying to push his way forward without spilling any wine. Suddenly he felt a warm breath upon his ear, stirring his side-curls. An intimate voice whispered, "In life I was a famous beauty, and had many rich and handsome lovers. But when I grew old and sick they abandoned me and left me in the dirt to rot. Even the worms no longer caress my dry bones. Give me one drop of the wine of Paradise, and I will make you irresistible to women. All the pleasures Solomon knew with his thousand wives were not a tenth part of what *you* will enjoy."

It is barely possible that Menachem paused for an instant; he was an inexperienced young man, after all. But a night in the graveyard had taught him that pleasures of the flesh are fleeting, gone in the space between two breaths. They weighed less than a feather measured against the eternal embrace of the Torah. Menachem put this temptation behind him and continued along his path.

Finally Menachem saw the two hemlocks that marked the end of the trail looming ahead. He trudged toward them with all his remaining strength. But only a few steps away from his goal, cruel invisible hands clutched Menachem's throat and forced him to his knees. A bestial voice growled, "In life I was a murderous bandit. I left a trail of blood wherever I went, and bathed in the tears of widows and orphans. Give me the wine of Paradise, and I will spare your wretched life. Refuse and I will drag your soul down to *Gehinnom* (the underworld), to devour it in the flames."

But tonight Menachem refused to be bullied by a mere demon. His soul came from the Maker of All Things; and God alone would dispose of it, not some blustering phantom. The wine he carried was sent from Heaven to honor Rebbe Elimelech. Menachem would not surrender a single drop. Ignoring the dire threats of the ghost, Menachem struggled back onto his feet, threaded his way between the two great trees, and was out of the woods at last.

Staggering with fatigue, Menachem crossed the yard, illuminated by the candle-lit windows of the study hall. He rested for a moment at the foot of the steps, soaked with sweat and panting for breath. From the forest blew a last, roaring wind, fraught with the shrieks and curses of thwarted ghosts. Then the night grew tranquil and still, and the new moon shone serenely overhead. Menachem shook a trembling fist toward the scene of his recent trials, and hoarsely shouted, "*Mamish* (indeed), I've overcome you all!"

And in the instant that he spoke, the oak pole across Mendel's shoulders broke in half with a loud CRACK! The buckets filled with the wine of Paradise spilled out upon the ground, which greedily sucked them dry. The whole business was finished almost before it started, leaving Menachem to stare in astonishment. The door to the study hall opened, and Rebbe Elimelech stood there framed against the light.

The Rebbe looked down the steps at Menachem and the empty buckets. Menachem looked up the steps at the Rebbe, spread his arms and shrugged. Rebbe Elimelech shook his head and said, "Come inside, fool, and sit at our table."

For the second time that night a shocked silence descended upon the celebrants, as Rebbe Elimelech reentered the hall arm-in-arm with the rude yeshiva *bocher* (student) he had sent away hours earlier. The young man's clothes were muddy and torn, his eyes were haunted, and his dark hair had turned white as milk. Rebbe Elimelech pulled out a chair at the head table, and to everyone's amazement, he poured the youth a glass of plum brandy with his own hand.

"Reb Menachem," said Rebbe Elimelech, "Would you honor us with the final toast of the evening?"

For a long moment Menachem stared into his cup, as if it held a hazy glimpse of his future. Then he stood and raised his glass high in a silent salute. Rebbe Elimelech immediately did the same, and everybody else rushed to follow his example. Menachem swept his gaze slowly across the room, intently studying the faces of his companions, as though he wished to memorize them all. Then he offered this toast:

"*Yidn*, Jews, listen to me! Don't fret about the World-to-Come. *HaShem* (God) will take care of it, in His own time and wisdom. Neither fear of the day of one's death, nor hope of rewards after life, can arouse a person's heart to serve God. Instead let us rejoice while we are together, raise each other up, and give thanks for the countless blessings we receive while we live. Truly, we lack nothing at all."

"*L'chayim!*" (To life!)

"*L'chayim!*"

"*L'chayim!*"

Provenance: I first encountered this story in Martin Buber's volume, *Tales of the Hasidim: Early Masters* (NY: Schocken, 1947). It appears there under the title, "The Wine of Life," in the section devoted to Rebbe Elimelech of Lizensk. Buber did not provide sources, so its ultimate provenance is obscure. Buber's book ignited my interest in Rebbe Elimelech's teachings, which eventually led me to his mystic Torah commentary, *Noam Elimelech*. I have attempted to convey a tiny glimpse of his teaching at the start of the story and, with greater chutzpah, an impression of his presence as recalled by his *hasidim*. The ghosts in my version of the story 'came alive' and found their individual voices with the help of master storyteller, Noa Baum. I am indebted to her expert coaching. Menachem's final toast, in which he disparages concern with the next world as a basis for true service in life, is built upon a statement attributed to the Baal Shem Tov in a letter by one of his disciples.

Marc Young is the Chief Learning Officer for a federal agency. He was storyteller-in-residence for the Columbia Jewish Community School for ten years. Marc has performed at 'Tellabrations' in Baltimore and Washington, at the national conventions of several Jewish denominations, at the Washington Folk Festival, Limmud Baltimore, LimmudPhilly, and the Hans Christian Andersen Storytelling series in NYC's Central Park. He is a performing member of the National Storytelling Network and the Jewish Storytellers' Coalition. Marc lives in Columbia, Maryland.

Study Guide: Questions, Sources, and Projects for Reflection, Discussion, and Action

1. Which *mitzvot* are illustrated by this story? Which additional *mitzvot* can you also relate to this story?

2. What might Menachem mean by the "Wine of Paradise?"

3. Wine is part of many Jewish rituals. Make a list of those occasions when it is used. What does wine symbolize in Judaism?

4. Why did the Rebbe send him to the graveyard? Have you ever been in a graveyard at night? What was it like for you? Have you ever experienced someone communicating with you who has died? Many people report such experiences and wonder if they were dreaming.

5. What did Menachem learn from his experience? Do you ever want things or get to have experiences that you probably weren't ready for?

6. Take a look at Menachem's final speech. What does he mean: "We lack nothing at all?"

Sacred Story and Text Connections

1. Four went into *Pardes* (mystical world of Torah experience)—ben Azzai, ben Zoma, Elisha ben Avuya, and Rabbi Akiva…Ben Azzai looked and died, and of him it is said, "Precious in the eyes of God is the death of his faithful." Ben Zoma looked and was struck [with madness]…Elisha ben Avuya cut the shoots [which means in Talmudic language that he became a heretic]. Akiva entered in peace and departed in peace.
—*Talmud, Chagiga* 14b

    How does this text helps us understand why Menachem was being considered foolish for wanting the wine of paradise?

2. Turn not to ghosts nor familiar spirits, nor seek them out to be defiled by them. I am the Lord your God.—Leviticus, *Vayikra* 19:31

3. There shall not be found among you any one that…uses divination, or an observer of times, or an enchanter, or a witch, or a charmer, or a consulter with familiar spirits, or a wizard, or a necromancer, for all that do these things are an abomination unto the Lord.—Deuteronomy, *Devarim* 18:10-12

Jewish ghost stories abound. What attracts us to them? How did Menachem protect himself from the spirits he encountered? There are many references in Torah and Talmud discouraging contact with dead spirits. Why do you think this is? Have you ever experienced what seemed to be a real ghost? If yes, what did you do?

4. Young women are like vines. There is a vine whose wine is red. A vine whose wine is abundant and a vine whose wine is sparse. Rabbi Judah said: Every vine has its wine…*Gemara*…Reb Hiyya taught: As leaven is wholesome for the dough so is blood wholesome for a woman. One taught in the name of Rabbi Meir: Of a woman with an abundance of blood many children may come.
—Talmud, *Niddah* 64b

5. At a circumcision or *hatafat dam brit* (those who are already circumcised who convert to Judaism just have a tiny, symbolic drop of blood drawn), males are given a sip of wine immediately after the blood is drawn and blessed in the words of Ezekiel: "in your blood live".

    Wine is a major symbol in Judaism. What do the two texts above indicate that wine symbolizes? Look at the list of occasions you listed above for when wine is used in Jewish ritual. What do they all have in common, even the drops removed from the Cup of Blessing (*cos shel brachah*, the *Kiddush* cup) to symbolize the plagues?

6. "Can one make *Kiddush* over milk?" a rebbe was asked. Rather than responding, a large sum of money, enough to make a significant *Shabbat* meal, was provided to the questioner. When the students asked about this way of responding, the rebbe explained that a person wanting to bless over milk most likely could not afford a meal either.—classic tale from the oral tradition

    a. Many times when someone is posing a personal question, the real reason for it is hidden. Have you ever noticed this? How can you tactfully find out what is really needed, as the rebbe did?

    b. Is there another possible reason a person would want to bless over something other than wine?

    c. You will find a different approach to this story in "The Integration of Stories and *Hashpa'ah*" by Rabbi Marcia Prager in *Seeking and Soaring: Jewish Approaches to Spiritual Guidance and Development,* Reclaiming Judaism Press, 2014. Compare and contrast the stories. Why might Rabbi Prager have changed the tale in this way?

7. Wine gladdens the heart—Psalms, *Tehillim* 104:15

8. Wine causes a person to become sleepy, overconfident, and confuses their judgment—Bachya Ibn Pakuda

    How can we best respect the intent of both texts #4 and #5 in ritual in our communities and in our lives without experiencing or causing damage to ourselves and others?

The Wine of Paradise | 305

Chapter 42
Binah and the Broken Pieces
by Jennifer Rudick Zunikoff

"I will return in forty days."

Moses slowly spoke these last words to the Hebrews assembled before him. Binah watched as he turned and began to walk toward Mt. Sinai.

"Good-bye Moses!" she called.

Moses turned and smiled back at Binah. Moments later, he began his ascent. Binah watched for a long time, following Moses' steps as he climbed the mountain and disappeared into the mist. Moses was the leader of the Hebrew people. Binah was a ten-year-old girl from the tribe of Benjamin, the smallest of the twelve tribes. She and her parents and the other Hebrew slaves had followed Moses out of Egypt.

In some ways, Binah and Moses were much alike. It was difficult for Moses to speak. It was difficult for Binah to hear. Binah was not deaf, but she struggled to hear. Moses was not mute, but he struggled to speak.

Once Moses was gone, everyone stood quietly for some time, looking at the lonely mountaintop. Then the Hebrews returned to their chores: caring for their animals, preparing for meals, and keeping the camp in order.

As Binah and her parents walked back toward the camp, she stopped to look back at the mist.

"Moses is up there talking with God right now." She smiled at the thought. "God chose *him*.

"Did God choose him because he is intelligent, or because he is strong, or because he is kind? Or because Moses understands things that other people don't?" Binah, as always, was curious.

Back at camp, she and her mother took the sleeping mats out of their tent. As they beat one mat against another, a plume of dust formed in the air. The muffled sounds of their work allowed Binah to continue thinking about Moses and God. As she helped her mother, a new idea formed inside of her....

"Did God choose *me* for something? Moses struggles to talk, and yet he was chosen to speak with God on behalf of the people. My ears don't hear well," she thought. "Maybe then, God wants me to *listen* for something."

Binah knew that we hear with our ears, but we listen with our hearts.

***

After completing her chores each day, Binah walked to the base of Mount Sinai. She looked up at the top of the mountain and imagined Moses there, speaking with God. She looked down at the bottom of the mountain, at the sand, and at her own feet, and she listened. She did not know what she was listening for. Still, every day she went to the bottom of the mountain, as close as she dared. Every day she listened. Forty days passed.

On the fortieth day, Binah hurried to the base of the mountain. She felt an excited flutter in her stomach. Moses was coming soon!

In the distance, she saw Joshua, Moses' student and friend. Joshua was also waiting at the bottom of Mount Sinai. He, too, was waiting for Moses to arrive. He looked calm and peaceful and trusting. He listened and waited, listened and waited.

Far away, Binah did the same. Minutes passed.

The sun descended, but Moses did not.

Binah looked toward the camp, and she saw the people gathering around a fire. What was going on? She squinted. Men from the camp surrounded a tall man with a long beard—Aaron! It was Aaron, the high priest; Aaron, Moses' brother. The men around him held many pieces of gold in their hands. A misshapen pile of golden objects was growing at Aaron's feet.

Binah felt her stomach twist. What were they doing? What were the men doing? Why did Aaron have so much gold?

She continued to watch, as the men piled the gold into metal pots and set the pots inside the fire. She saw the men with wild, reddened faces as they wielded hammers, striking again and again. She watched, dazed, as some men pounded on drums, and others danced around a large shimmering object. She felt the vibrations of the discordant music inside her body. A beast of gold was growing out of the fire!

Binah quickly turned away. "Listen for Moses, not for the chaos," she told herself again and again. "Wait for Moses." She felt grateful that her poor hearing helped her to focus on the mountaintop, where Moses would certainly appear at any moment.

As she waited, the men danced wildly around the golden beast late into the night. Then, at last, Binah saw him.

"Moses," she whispered.

She could see him—there, at the top of the mountain. His face glowed with a light like none Binah had ever seen. It was the light of God.

Despite Binah's distance from the light, she felt its warmth. It glowed inside her body, through each of her cells. God's light was dancing inside of her. But the light was not only glowing from Moses' face. The light was in his hands. He was *holding* the light. He held two stone tablets, two tablets of light.

Time stopped.

Moses looked at the camp. He saw the dancing and the chaos and the fire and the gold. His face twisted in pain. Binah's head swung toward the camp. She, too saw the dancing and the chaos and the fire and the gold. The people had forgotten God.

And then, there was a sound—a sound so holy and so painful that Binah could hear it. The sound cracked the silence of God's light.

In an instant, the light flew from the tablets. Sparks shot into the air. Moses staggered. Within seconds, the tablets slipped from his hands.

The tablets crashed against the mountain. The light flashed and broke into hundreds of pieces. And then it was gone. The light was gone.

Binah didn't move. Her heart beat loudly.

"No!!!" she screamed inside her head. "No!"

Tears spilled from her eyes. They had been so close. They had been so close to receiving God's light. And they had ruined everything.

**

When Binah finally returned to the camp in the early morning hours, there was no dancing. There was no fire. There was no gold.

She crawled into her tent beside her sleeping parents.

When she awoke, she went to look for Moses. But Moses had left again. He had climbed back up Mount Sinai. Somehow, he had been given another chance. The people had been given another chance. *She* had been given another chance, another chance to listen. She still did not know to what she should listen, but she did know *where* she should listen—at the bottom of Mount Sinai.

She went to the base of the mountain every day that Moses was away. She walked back and forth, trying to discover what had happened, and why so many of the Hebrews did not trust in Moses and in God.

"I cannot understand," Binah thought. "I have to stop trying to. I just need to listen. I need to listen for God."

For more than a week, Binah walked back and forth before the mountain, praying, meditating, and listening. She heard no answers.

Then one day, her listening felt different. Her mind was quieter; she went deep inside herself. Binah meditated and walked. She was walking near the same spot where she had waited for Moses to descend the night the light had shattered.

Suddenly, Binah tripped and fell to her knees onto the sand. She was not hurt, but the fall had awakened her from her meditation. She looked down at the sand and saw that she had tripped on a small rock. It was the size of her fist, and it was odd-looking, dark and ancient and scarred. She leaned over to pick it up but struggled to lift it. It was so heavy, impossibly heavy for its small size.

Binah sat down. Slowly, she pulled the rock into her lap. She ran her fingers over the edges: some were jagged and some smooth. In a moment, Binah knew what she was holding. It was one of the broken pieces!

"This rock once held God's light!"

Binah stood up and walked back to the camp, holding the piece in both hands. It took a long time to arrive at her tent. She walked with slow, heavy steps.

Once inside, Binah set down the rock and began to dig into the desert floor. She dug and dug until she had created a deep hole in the sand. She rolled the rock into the hole and covered it with a length of cloth.

Now that she knew what to look and listen for, Binah returned to the base of the mountain every day. She searched for more pieces and picked up each one and slowly brought it to her tent. It was difficult, painstaking work. There were so many broken pieces.

As the days passed, Binah filled the hole. Some of the pieces were as big as a man's hand; some were the size of a small egg. Others were as tiny as crumbs. The day before Moses was to return again, Binah searched and searched, but she could find no more pieces of the dark, scarred stone.

Binah was there with the whole *kehillah* (community) when Moses appeared on the mountaintop. The Hebrew people were excited and anxious and alive with hope. Their leader's face shone with that extraordinary light once more. When he walked toward the people, many stepped back, afraid. But Binah held no fear at that moment. She knew Moses wore God's light.

When Moses arrived, he saw Binah among all of the Hebrews, and he took a long moment to smile into her eyes.

"I have been waiting for this moment," Binah thought as she looked at him.

***

Moses was busy in those first days after bringing the tablets to the people. He met with the elders and shared God's law and God's light with them. Moses would eventually share all of the Torah with everyone.

Binah was patient.

When it was time for the people to break camp, and continue their journey into the wilderness, Binah came to Moses late in the afternoon.

"Moses, I have something to show you," she softly said.

He followed her back to the tent. Once inside, she lifted the cloth from the desert floor. Moses looked at the broken pieces. He looked at Binah.

"I saved these," she said. "I think these pieces are a part of us. They are a part of our story."

He blinked and stood in silence, his eyes closed. After a long moment, he smiled.

"Thank you, Binah," he said. "You have listened well."

Before they left the camp to travel through the desert, Moses picked up each broken piece and gently placed it into the Ark of the Covenant. He set the scarred, broken pieces beside the smooth, glowing tablets.

Because a ten-year-old girl listened to God, and because Moses listened to her, our broken pieces are a part of our story.

Provenance: While the Torah indicates that only the second set of tablets were kept in the ark, the Talmud offers a different view, "The intact tablets and the broken tablets were both kept in the ark."—Talmud, *Berachot* 8b and *Baba Batra* 14b. From this comes the question: Who gathered up the pieces of the broken first set of tablets and put them in the ark?

Jennifer Rudick Zunikoff, storyteller, poet, and coach, encourages her students to imagine themselves inside the Torah, listening and voicing our ancestors' stories. Her story, "Rina and the Exodus" was featured in *Mitzvah Stories, Seeds for Inspiration*. Jennifer's CD, *The Growing Season*, commissioned by the Louise D. and Morton J. Macks Center for Jewish Education, contains original stories for Tu B'Shvat, Purim, and Passover. Jennifer facilitates the Storytelling Teacher Training project at Krieger Schechter Day School. For the past ten years, she has co-taught the Oral History of the Holocaust course at Goucher College. www.JenniferStories.com

Study Guide: Questions, Sources, and Projects for Reflection, Discussion, and Action

1. Which *mitzvot* are illustrated by this story? Which additional *mitzvot* can you also relate to this story?

2. What does it mean that we listen with our ears but hear with our heart?

3. Binah's poor hearing helps her listen better. Have you ever experienced the loss of something through illness or injury, which made you more aware of other things?

4. What is important about the broken pieces and why are they placed in the ark with the whole tablets?

Sacred Story and Text Connections

1. When Moses saw that the Israelites were rejoicing in the desecration that they had created, he became angry and despaired of his ability to correct this egregious sin.—Sforno

2. When Moses saw the calf, all of his strength failed him. He no longer had any energy and so he cast the tablets far away from him in order that they not damage his legs as they were falling. This is what people do when they can no longer bear their heavy burden. Such is the interpretation I saw in the *Pirkei d'Rabbi Eliezer* and this is the basic understanding of the text.—Rashbam

   a. The two texts above differ on how Moses felt. With which do you agree? Do you think Moses was angry or disappointed? How would you have felt if you were he?

   How has your relationship to Judaism and the *mitzvot* changed while reading *New Mitzvah Stories for the Whole Family*?

Project: Put aside time every day to listen. What do you hear? Can you hear God's voice? Some say that our dreams are the voice of God. What do you think?

Chapter 43
Finishing The Tale
by Howard Schwartz

There was a renowned storyteller who announced that he was going to tell his last tale. People came from all over to hear this story, certain it would be his best. The storyteller started the story, and from the first word all those who listened to it fell into a trance, where nothing existed for them except the words that he wove. The story seemed endless, and that is how they wanted it to be. But then the storyteller fell ill and died before he had completed the tale. And not only was there an uproar on earth, among all those who were waiting for the story to be finished, but also in heaven, for the angels had also been waiting to find out how the story ended.

Now, when the storyteller reached heaven, the angels crowded around him, anxious to hear the end of the story. But the storyteller was silent. He refused to reveal anything about it.

"Why not," the angels begged, for their curiosity is far more intense than that of any human.

"Because," the storyteller replied, "I must first complete it on earth."

"But that's impossible," said the angels, "for you are now among us, and there's no going back."

"That's all I have to say," responded the storyteller, and after that he was completely mute.

His silence lasted so long, it was like trekking through an endless desert. One century, two, three centuries passed. The angels saw that he meant what he said. And after three hundred years, they pleaded for the Holy One of Blessing, to send the soul of the storyteller back to earth, so that he could finish the tale, for they now realized that was the only way they could find out how the story ended.

So they sent him back to earth, where he was reborn as an infant. And that infant remembered everything of the storyteller's life and even knew how the last story had ended. And that child also grew to be a storyteller, and told every tale of the old storyteller—except for the last one.

This went on for many years. The storyteller grew to be an old man, and still the angels waited for him to tell the last tale.

At last, in his old age, he announced that he would begin to tell the unfinished tale. And as he began to speak, there was silence on earth and in heaven. And this time he finished the tale.

Howard Schwartz, a three-time winner of the National Jewish Book Award, is the editor of six important collections of Jewish folklore: *Elijah's Violin & Other Jewish Fairy Tales*; *Miriam's Tambourine: Jewish Folktales from Around the World*; *Lilith's Cave: Jewish Tales of the Supernatural*; *Gabriel's Palace: Jewish Mystical Tales*; *Leaves from the Garden of Eden: One Hundred Classic Jewish Tales* and *Tree of Souls: The Mythology of Judaism*. A children's book, *Gathering Sparks*, won a Sydney Taylor Book Award. His story "The Dead Sea" appears in *Mitzvah Stories: Seeds for Inspiration and Learning*. Howard's newest release is a volume of poetry, *The Library of Dreams*. www.HowardSchwartz.com

Study Guide: Questions, Sources, and Projects for Reflection, Discussion, and Action

1. Which *mitzvot* are illustrated by this story? Which additional *mitzvot* can you also relate to this story?

2. What do you think this story was about?

3. Why do listeners have a need to hear the ending of story, rather than be satisfied with an open-ended tale?

4. When a story, even with an ending, confuses us, how do we create meaning? How do you think the story ended? What happened when it was finished?

Sacred Story and Text Connections

...write this song for yourselves...—Deuteronomy, *Devarim* 31:19

Project: Now it is your turn to tell the story.

114 Mitzvot That Can Be Found in, or Related to The Reclaiming Judaism Mitzvah-Centered Life Series
Volume 1. *Mitzvah Stories: Seeds for Inspiration and Learning*
Volume 2. *New Mitzvah Stories for the Whole Family*

1. WELCOME AND HOST GUESTS	2. AVOID GOSSIP AND SLANDER
3. REFRAIN FROM TAKING REVENGE	4. REFRAIN FROM BREAKING PROMISES
5. STOP TO HELP	6. REFRAIN FROM WORK ON HOLY DAYS
7. TURN TO HEALING DAMAGED RELATIONSHIPS: DO TESHUVA	8. WALK THE TALK: CREATE A MITZVAH-CENTERED LIFE
9. PAY WAGES PROMPTLY	10. MEZUZAH: MARK THE DOORPOST OF YOUR HOME AS SACRED SPACE
11. GATHER ON THE NEW MOON: BLESS "MOONTHLY"	12. LIGHT SHABBAT AND HOLY DAY CANDLES
13. LOVE YOUR NEIGHBOR AS YOU MIGHT BEST LOVE YOURSELF	14. SIT IN A SUKKAH
15. JUSTICE, JUSTICE PURSUE	16. Spread THE LIGHT OF THE MENORAH
17. BE AN ACTIVE CITIZEN	18. WITNESS HONESTLY
19. VISIT THE SICK	20. RESEARCH AND CARE, AND PROVIDE ASSISTANCE FOR THOSE WHO ARE ILL
21. VOLUNTEER: ENGAGE IN DEEDS OF LOVING KINDNESS	22. WEAR A TALLIT TO HELP REMEMBER THE MITZVOT
23. REMEMBER THE EXODUS	24. GIVE GENEROUSLY TO THOSE WHO ARE SUFFERING FROM ACCIDENTS, WOUNDS, ILLNESS, AND DISEASE
25. SHIVA: VISIT MOURNERS IN THEIR HOMES; YOUR PRESENCE COMFORTS	26. STUDY AND TEACH TORAH
27. LISTEN TO THE SHOFAR	28. ACT AND SPEAK WITH LOVE FOR ISRAEL
29. PREVENT NEEDLESS PAIN TO ANIMALS	30. FEED THE HUNGRY
31. FREE CAPTIVES	32. PRAY DAILY
33. KOSHER: EAT CONSCIOUSLY	34. TAKE EXCELLENT CARE OF YOUR BODY
35. SEND THE MOTHER BIRD AWAY BEFORE TAKING EGGS OR HER YOUNG	36. YOU COUNT: SHOW UP TO ENSURE COMMUNITIES OF PRAYER AND CARE
37. SAY THE SHEMA. LISTEN CLOSELY, KNOW ONE	38. CREATE NO OBSTACLES

39. practice non-attachment to that which is not yours to have or hold	40. refrain from holding a grudge
41. eat matzah every day of Passover week	42. honor elders
43. honor parents	44. refrain from damage to nature
45. secure and savor Shabbat	46. refrain from deceiving others
47. help create peace in your home	48. live in awe and respect for the Divine nature of all that is
49. know God	50. live in love with the Divine nature of all that is
51. write a Torah	52. honor Torah scholars; make them your teachers
53. rest from work on Shabbat	54. be happy on the festivals
55. offer the traditional blessings over food and mitzvot and know you are blessed	56. refrain from leavened foods during Passover week; do not have them in your home
57. Maggid: tell the Exodus story	58. fast on Yom Kippur
59. eat in a sukkah	60. live in respectful awe of your parents
61. return stolen goods	62. engage lovingly with Jews
63. lend money without interest to Jews as we are family	64. engage lovingly with converts
65. return something borrowed promptly when it is needed	66. allow workers to eat food they are harvesting or producing
67. Hafrashat Challah: take and burn a piece when baking large quantities	68. lift the burden of a struggling animal
69. privately reprove someone who has erred in a mitzvah	70. remember Amalek who did great evil
71. enter into a Jewish marriage and create a Jewish home	72. put an end to evil behavior
73. refrain from murder	74. refrain from stealing
75. refrain from taking things by force	76. refrain from keeping something that belongs to someone else
77. refrain from denying a debt	78. refrain from hitting
79. refrain from delaying burial	80. refrain from cursing
81. refrain from cheating	82. refrain from verbal abuse

83. REFRAIN FROM INFLICTING SUFFERING ON A WIDOW OR ORPHAN	84. REFRAIN FROM DEMANDING PAYMENT OF A DEBT FROM ONE WHO CANNOT PAY
85. REFRAIN FROM BORROWING AT INTEREST FROM A JEWISH PERSON	86. REFRAIN FROM TAKING KITCHEN IMPLEMENTS AND A PERSON'S CLOAK AS SECURITY AGAINST A LOAN
87. REFRAIN FROM HARDENING YOUR HEART OR SHUTTING YOUR HAND TOWARDS A POOR PERSON	88. LEAVE THE CROPS AT THE SIDES OF YOUR FIELDS FOR THE POOR
89. BUILD A SANCTUARY	90. NIDDAH: CULTIVATE AWE FOR THE HUMAN POTENTIAL TO CONCEIVE LIFE
91. TAKE NO MORE THAN YOU CAN EAT WHEN WORKING IN THE FIELDS	92. JUDGE HONORABLY
93. REFRAIN FROM SORCERY	94. REFRAIN FROM HARBORING HATE OF PEOPLE IN YOUR HEART
95. REFRAIN FROM CHARMS OR SPELLS	96. REFRAIN FROM ACTING AS A MEDIUM
97. REFRAIN FROM ACCEPTING A BRIBE	98. REFRAIN FROM FALSE PREDICTIONS
99. REFRAIN FROM IGNORING LOST OBJECTS; IF YOU SEE IT, RETURN IT	100. CLEAVE AND COMMIT TO YOUR BELOVED
101. REFRAIN FROM PREVENTING A WORKING ANIMAL FROM EATING	102. REFRAIN FROM DAMAGING THE ENVIRONMENT
103. REFRAIN FROM DWELLING IN EGYPT	104. REFRAIN FROM SHAMING PEOPLE
105. REFRAIN FROM REPEATING THINGS SOMEONE TOLD YOU ABOUT SOMEONE ELSE	106. REFRAIN FROM JUDGMENT BASED ON ONLY ONE WITNESS
107. SAVE SOMEONE BEING PURSUED	108. DO NOT PITY THE PURSUER
109. REFRAIN FROM INQUIRING OF THE DEAD	110. FEED YOUR ANIMALS FIRST; EAT AFTER THEY DO
111. ATTEND FUNERALS AND OTHER RITES OF PASSAGE	112. CALL OUT TO GOD
113. WE ARE CREATED IN GOD'S IMAGE: TREAT EVERY HUMAN WELL	114. BRING HONOR TO GOD'S NAME: BE A BLESSING IN HOW YOU LIVE

NOTE: Beautifully printed Mitzvah Cards in their own matching box are available from ReclaimingJudaism.org, Bmitzvah.org and through many booksellers. In these high quality decks each mitzvah is presented in Hebrew, transliteration, with its source in Torah or Talmud, and described through the lens of spirituality and meaning.

Acknowledgments

Reclaiming Judaism Press is an almost 100% volunteer publishing house. We pay only for the physical/graphic layout, printing, and advertising.

The volume advisory and editorial teams included Ellen Frankel, Arthur Kurzweil, Goldie Milgram, Batya Podos, Peninnah Schram, Danny Siegel, Mindy Shapiro, and Shoshana Silberman. The Study Guide was primarily developed by Goldie Milgram and Batya Podos. Team members donated incredible amounts of time, reflection, creativity, and professional editorial review and labor. Over a dozen volunteers assisted with the final copy-editing and proofreading. We are also profoundly grateful to Susan Leopold for her magnificent butterfly image on the front cover and to Taylor Rozek for the beautiful lifecycle of the butterfly drawings. Each and all mitzvah heroes!

We are also grateful for the donations and grants for the Mitzvah-Centered Life Initiative received from private donors, as well as from the Jewish Federation of Cumberland, Gloucester & Salem Counties and the Makor HaLev and Generations Foundations.

All revenue from this volume, after expenses, goes into the Danny Siegel Fund at Reclaiming Judaism to ensure the transport and affordability of Reclaiming Judaism's Mitzvah-Centered Life programs for Jewish communities, educators, organizations, and seekers worldwide.

Recommended Reading

Artson, Bradley Shavit. *It's a Mitzvah: Step-by-Step to Jewish Living*. West Orange, NJ: Behrman House, 1995.

Artson, Bradley Shavit and Gila Gevirtz. *Making a Difference: Putting Jewish Spirituality into Action, One Mitzvah at a Time*. Springfield, NJ: Behrman House, 2001.

Artson, Rabbi Bradley Shavit and Rabbi Patricia Fenton. *Walking with Mitzvot*. Bel Air, CA: Ziegler School of Rabbinic Studies, 2011.

Chasin, Esther G. *Mitzvot as Spiritual Practices: A Jewish Guidebook for the Soul*. Northvale, NJ: Jason Aronson, 1997.

Chill, Abraham. *The Mitzvot: The Commandments and Their Rationale*. Brooklyn, NY: Urim Publications, 2009.

Cone, Molly. *Who Knows Ten? Children's Tales of the Ten Commandments*. Illustrated by Robin Brickman. NY: URJ Press, 1998.

Dorff, Elliot and Avram Kogen, Editors. *Mitzvah Means Commandment*. New York: United Synagogue of America Department of Youth Activities, 1989.

Frankel, Ellen. *JPS Illustrated Children's Bible*. Illustrated by Avi Katz. Philadelphia.: Jewish Publication Society, 2009.

Frankel, Ellen. *The Classic Tales: 4000 Years of Jewish Lore*. Northvale, NJ: Jason Aronson, 1989.

Golub, Jane Ellen and Joel Lurie Grishaver. *Zot Ha-Torah: This is the Torah—A Guided Exploration of the Mitzvot Found in the Weekly Torah Portion*. Los Angeles: Torah Aura, 2000.

Ha-Levi of Barcelona (Venice 1523), Aaron (ascribed to). *Sefer Ha-Hinnukh*. Jerusalem: Feldheim, 1978.

Isaacs, Ronald. *Mitzvot: A Sourcebook for the 613 Commandments*. Northvale, NJ: Jason Aaronson, 1996.

Jaffe, Nina and Steven Zeitlin. *The Cow of No Color: Riddle Stories and Justice Tales from Around the World*. Illustrated by Whitney Sherman. NY: Henry Holt, 1998.

Lipkin, Lisa. *Bringing the Story Home: The Complete Guide to Storytelling for Parents*. New York: W.W. Norton, 2001.

Maimonides. *Sefer ha-Mitzot—Book of Commandments, Volume I—Positive; Volume II—Negative*. Brooklyn, NY: Soncino Press, 1976.

Milgram, Goldie. *Meaning & Mitzvah: Daily Practices for Reclaiming Judaism through Prayer, God, Hebrew, Mitzvot & Peoplehood*. Woodstock, VT: Jewish Lights Publishing, 2005.

———. *Reclaiming Judaism as a Spiritual Practice: Holy Days and Shabbat*. Woodstock, VT: Jewish Lights Publishing, 2004.

Milgram, Goldie and Ellen Frankel, Eds. with Peninnah Schram, Cherie Karo Schwartz & Arthur Strimling. *Mitzvah Stories: Seeds for Inspiration and Learning*. Philadelphia, PA: Reclaiming Judaism Press, 2011.

Milgram, Goldie and Shohama Wiener, Eds. *Seeking and Soaring: Jewish Approaches to Spiritual Guidance and Development*. New Rochelle, NY: Reclaiming Judaism Press, 2014.

Podos, Batya and Martha Shonkwiler (Illustrator). *Rebecca and the Talisman*, Gleneden Beach, OR: Spirit Books / Portal Center Press, 2013.

Schram, Peninnah. *Classic Jewish Children's Stories*. Illustrated by Jeffrey Allon. NY: Pitspopany Press, 1998.

———. *The Hungry Clothes and Other Jewish Folktales*. Illustrated by Gianni De Conno. NY: Sterling Publishing, 2008.

———. *Jewish Stories One Generation Tells Another*. Northvale, NJ: Jason Aronson, 1987.

———. *Tales of Elijah the Prophet*. Northvale, NJ: Jason Aronson, 1991.

Schram, Peninnah, ed. *Chosen Tales: Stories Told by Jewish Storytellers*. Northvale, NJ: Jason Aronson, 1995.

Schwartz, Cherie Karo. Illustrated by Lisa Rauchwerger. *Circle Spinning: Jewish Turning and Returning Tales*, Aurora, CO: Hamsa Press, 2002.

Schwartz, Howard. *Invisible Kingdoms: Jewish Tales of Angels, Spirits and Demons*. New York: HarperCollins, 2002.

———. *A Journey to Paradise and Other Jewish Tales*. Illustrated by Giora Carmi. NY: Pitspopany Press, 2000.

———. *Leaves from the Garden of Eden: One Hundred Classic Jewish Tales*. NY: Oxford University Press, 2008.

Schwartz, Howard and Barbara Rush: *The Wonderchild & Other Jewish Fairy Tales*. Illustrated by Steven Fieser. NY: HarperCollins, 1996.

———. *The Diamond Tree: Jewish Tales from Around the World*. Illustrated by Uri Shulevitz. NY: HarperCollins, 1991.

Siegel, Danny. *1 + 1 = 3 and 37 Other Mitzvah Principles For a Meaningful Life*, Pittsboro, NC: Town House Press, 2000.

———. *After the Rain: The Book of Mitzvah Power for Adults and Teens*. Pittsboro, NC: Town House Press, 1993.

———. *Angels* (essays). Pittsboro, NC: Town House Press, 1993.

———. *Before Our Very Eyes: Readings for a Journey Through Israel*. Pittsboro, NC: Town House Press, 1986.

———. *Danny Siegel's Bar and Bat Mitzvah Mitzvah Book: A Practical Guide*. Pittsboro, NC: Town House Press, 2004.

———. *Family Reunion: Making Peace in the Jewish Community: Sources and Resources from Tanach, Halachah, and Midrash*, Pittsboro, NC: Town House Press, 1989.

———. *For Changing the World Through Your Simcha*. Pittsboro, NC: Town House House Press, 2004.

———. *From the Heart—Love Poems*. Pittsboro, NC: Town House Press, 2012.

———. *Giving Your Money Away — How Much, How to, Why, When, and to Whom: Danny Siegel's Practical Guide to Personalized Tzedakah*. Pittsboro, NC: Town House Press, 2006.

———. *Good People*. Pittsboro, NC: Town House Press, 1995.

———. *Gym Shoes and Irises: Personalized Tzedakah*. Pittsboro, NC: Town House Press, 1993.

———. *Healing: Readings and Meditations*. Pittsboro, NC: Town House Press, 1999.

———. *A Hearing Heart* (poetry). Pittsboro, NC: Town House Press, 1992.

———. *Heroes and Miracle Workers*. Pittsboro, NC: Town House Press, 1997.

———. *The Humongous Pushka in the Sky*. Pittsboro, NC: Town House Press, 1993.

———. *The Meadow Beyond the Meadow* (poetry). Pittsboro, NC: Town House Press, 1991.

———. *Mitzvah Magic: What Kids Can Do to Change the World*. Minneapolis, MN: Kar-Ben Publishing, 2002.

———. *Munbaz II and Other Mitzvah Heroes*. Pittsboro, NC: Town House Press, 1993.

———. *Tell Me a Mitzvah*. Minneapolis, MN: Kar-Ben Publishing, 1993.

———. *Where Heaven and Earth Touch: An Anthology of Midrash and Halachah Book One*, Northvale, NJ: Jason Aronson, 1995.

———. *Who, Me? Yes, You! — Danny Siegel's Workbook To Help You Decide Where, When, Why, and How You Can Do Your Best Tikkun Olam*. Pittsboro, NC: Town House Press, 2006.

Wengrov, Charles. *The Concise Book of Mitzvot: The Commandments Which Can Be Observed*. Nanuet, NY: Feldheim Publishing, 1990.

Index

A

abandon 199
Abayeh's mother 209
Abba 111, 112, 136, 237, 259, 260, 261, 265
Abraham 99, 129, 155, 212, 227
Adata 106
Adon Olam 272, 273, 291
adopt, adoption 247
Ahavah Rabbah 122
Akiva, Rabbi 104, 235, 247, 303
Aliyah 198, 271
Aliyah l'regel 198
angel(s) 114, 115, 129, 207, 208, 209, 211, 238, 239, 313
anger 37, 49, 64, 104, 111, 112, 224
animal(s) 14, 19, 46, 84, 85, 105, 106, 108, 110, 121, 124, 204, 205, 241, 261, 307, 317, 318, 319
apologize (also see *Techuvah*) 48
apology 52, 169, 170, 222
apple(s) 118, 135, 217, 218, 219, 220
Arab(s) 195, 196, 198
arevut 214
ark 53, 54, 56, 105, 106, 107, 108, 110, 275, 311, 312
Ashkenazi 66, 142, 194
aunt 125, 129
Australia 89, 91

B

Baal Shem Tov 69, 71, 301
baby 126, 164, 205
Babylon 99
Bamidbar (also see Numbers) 92, 112, 141, 214, 246, 264
Bar Kochba 235
bar mitzvah (also see *b'nei mitzvah*) 89, 90, 146, 147, 148, 271
barrette 249, 250, 251, 253
bat mitzvah 11, 14, 75-80, 120, 145, 172, 278, 282

bear 83, 84, 85, 87, 106, 288
bedtime 293, 296
beg, beggar, begging 31, 33, 159, 167, 170, 175, 210
Bereishit (also see Genesis) 79, 155, 166
bicycle 200
bike 289
bird(s) 69, 70, 85, 108, 110, 111, 122, 140, 144, 203, 227, 228, 229, 230, 232, 234, 273, 274, 280, 317
birth, birthday 53, 77, 142, 165, 167, 293, 295
Blessing(s) 17, 73, 77, 79, 80, 93, 129, 139, 142, 150, 158, 191, 192, 207, 208, 225, 229, 251, 257, 261, 273, 282, 295, 297, 301, 304, 313, 318, 319
blind 14, 101, 102, 104, 298
blintzes 296
blood 51, 183, 247, 266, 300, 304
b'nei mitzvah (also see *bar* and *bat mitzvah*) 11, 14, 79, 80, 171
body 50, 60, 70, 84, 99, 102, 143, 147, 194, 204, 205, 215, 221, 229, 242, 280, 291, 293, 308, 317
body language 60
breath, breathing 15, 32, 46, 47, 49, 63, 85, 95, 102, 122, 129, 144, 169, 179, 192, 203, 231, 241, 300
brit, bris 304
broken 70, 117, 118, 145, 153, 177, 183, 240, 241, 260, 261, 298, 310, 311, 312
broken, tablets 298, 310, 311
brother 15, 38, 117, 118, 119, 125, 137, 161, 171, 182, 184, 188, 238, 249, 262, 265, 266, 273, 279, 308
b'tzelem elohim 79
Bubbe (also see grandmother) 117, 133, 134, 209, 296
business 4, 14, 64, 95, 96, 133, 135, 185, 188, 199, 202, 203, 224, 225, 253, 269
butterfly 118, 121, 122, 168

C

calligraphy 58
camel 197
camp 28, 60, 68, 117, 123, 155, 160, 241, 286, 287, 288, 289, 307, 308, 309, 310, 311
cancer 161, 164, 241
candles, candlesticks 34, 47, 77, 84, 142, 148, 168, 185, 190, 191, 192, 208, 209, 211, 212, 228, 261, 317
captive(s), captivity 214, 215, 216, 317
Carlebach, Shlomo 237, 238, 244
caterpillar 118
cellphone 37, 40, 42, 64, 287
cemetery 143, 144, 297, 298
challah 47, 137, 138, 139, 140, 141, 142, 185, 277, 318
chant, chanting 60, 80, 101, 125, 143, 191, 289
chaplain 140, 213
chariot 99
child, childhood 14, 42, 69, 75, 80, 83, 88, 92, 93, 101, 102, 104, 115, 117, 119, 120, 121, 128, 135, 137, 139, 157, 158, 168, 185, 202, 221, 222, 224, 237, 241, 245, 255, 256, 257, 266, 271, 273, 281, 282, 285, 289, 305, 313
Chofetz Chayim 19, 51
Christian 120, 128, 193, 279, 282, 302
Christmas 47
circle 68, 69, 72, 76, 77, 81, 115, 168, 223
clarinet 22, 23
cloud(s) 33, 69, 70, 104, 221, 229, 232, 233, 298
clown(s), clowning 241, 242, 245
club 239, 277
Coke 195, 196
comfort 107, 212
computer 115, 146, 201, 280
congregation, (also see synagogue) 11, 53, 55, 75, 77, 130, 164, 184, 285
Converso 192
cook, cooking 15, 132, 162, 187, 196, 200, 204, 294
cos shel brachah 304
cousin 111, 112
covenant 31, 89
cowboy 185, 186, 187, 188, 189, 193

create, creator, created 14, 19, 60, 75, 79, 87, 92, 98, 101, 102, 115, 123, 131, 132, 147, 156, 164, 175, 179, 217, 224, 240, 253, 275, 286, 294, 297, 310, 312, 315, 317, 318, 319
cry, crying (also see tears) 46, 47, 49, 112, 119, 170, 212, 221, 224, 256, 279, 295
curious, curiosity 102, 127, 129, 178, 185, 209, 240, 307, 313

D

dance 27, 60, 168, 170, 178, 218, 227, 231, 238, 243, 279
danger 117, 202
darchei shalom 20, 181
date, dating 122, 161
Dayenu 125
deaf 101, 103, 307
death 39, 67, 128, 150, 158, 164, 165, 190, 210, 215, 216, 222, 231, 301, 303
demon 199, 203, 204, 300
depression (illness) 221, 224
Depression, The Great 221, 224
desert 105, 131, 217, 266, 310, 311, 313
Deuteronomy (also see *Devarim*) 58, 110, 156, 159, 198, 303, 315
Devarim 58, 110, 156, 159, 198, 303, 315
diamond 33, 34, 35
die, dying, died 32, 35, 38, 69, 117, 143, 146, 148, 150, 151, 158, 162, 164, 165, 209, 211, 222, 255, 279, 295, 303, 313
divine 19, 85, 88, 93, 99, 108, 178, 181, 208, 234, 282, 318
doctor 22, 118
donation(s) 43
Down syndrome 14, 15

E

eagle 274
Easter 47, 125, 126, 127, 128, 129
Eden 101, 293, 294
Egypt 104, 131, 132, 156, 218, 220, 257, 265, 266, 284, 307
elder(s) 23, 132, 148, 220, 242, 250, 265, 310, 318
Elijah 239, 240, 242, 244, 245, 246, 252, 314
Elimelech 295, 297, 298, 299, 300, 301
Elisheva 265, 267, 269

emet (also see truth) 158
environment 98, 202, 203, 319
equality 274, 283
ervah 275
ethical will(s) 148, 151, 219
ethics 27, 253
Ethics of the Ancestors (also see *Pirkei Avot*) 27, 253
eved 60
evil 46, 47, 67, 68, 70, 72, 181, 207, 215, 216, 318
exam 59
exist, existence 34, 59, 101, 102, 280, 313
Exodus (also see *Shemot*) 104, 131, 193, 215, 224, 257, 265, 274, 284, 311, 317, 318
Eybeschutz, Yonatan 68
Ezekiel 98, 99, 304

F

family 15, 21, 31, 34, 35, 36, 38, 42, 43, 47, 48, 56, 65, 66, 68, 81, 85, 87, 89, 90, 93, 103, 106, 107, 110, 111, 114, 115, 117, 118, 120, 121, 126, 127, 128, 129, 131, 132, 133, 138, 139, 141, 144, 146, 147, 148, 150, 155, 157, 158, 160, 161, 162, 164, 165, 166, 173, 174, 184, 185, 187, 189, 190, 191, 194, 195, 196, 197, 203, 205, 210, 212, 214, 220, 221, 222, 225, 238, 251, 255, 260, 261, 262, 265, 271, 272, 273, 278, 281, 287, 293, 296, 318
father 15, 23, 47, 48, 64, 72, 76, 88, 111, 117, 118, 125, 128, 129, 135, 147, 161, 162, 164, 166, 169, 184, 185, 186, 187, 188, 189, 190, 191, 200, 202, 203, 212, 217, 219, 221, 223, 237, 238, 245, 257, 259, 261, 280, 285, 289, 293, 294, 295
fear(s) 37, 40, 46, 49, 66, 70, 80, 84, 96, 158, 188, 191, 208, 211, 282, 291, 299, 301, 310
feather(s) 51, 105, 106, 107, 108, 187, 227, 228, 230, 231, 300
feel, feeling, feelings 23, 35, 36, 37, 38, 46, 48, 50, 52, 58, 64, 65, 67, 75, 80, 83, 84, 87, 92, 104, 106, 107, 112, 114, 121, 122, 129, 131, 134, 139, 140, 141, 143, 144, 146, 150, 153, 155, 165, 166, 168, 173, 177, 181, 193, 199, 202, 215, 216, 228, 229, 231, 234, 243, 251, 253, 259, 260, 261, 272, 274, 275, 278, 279, 281, 284, 289, 291
feminine 80, 132, 179
field(s) 69, 70, 71, 110, 183, 227-232, 242, 253, 319
fish 29
fly 69, 105, 108, 118, 122, 144, 228, 229, 230, 231, 232
food 14, 25, 29, 35, 36, 40, 43, 77, 84, 107, 110, 111, 125, 135, 140, 162, 163, 166, 200, 201, 202, 203, 204, 212, 217, 239, 251, 255, 269, 288, 291, 294, 296, 318
forest 69, 70, 71, 118, 207, 287, 288, 289, 300
fossil 63, 64
friend(s) 17, 21, 23, 24, 25, 27, 31, 33, 37, 38, 39, 40, 45, 46, 47, 48, 49, 56, 69, 77, 81, 85, 89, 90, 106, 107, 108, 110, 111, 114, 115, 117, 118, 119, 121, 122, 125, 126, 133, 134, 146, 148, 150, 155, 157, 160, 161, 162, 164, 165, 166, 167, 173, 174, 175, 182, 185, 187, 189, 195, 210, 211, 212, 222, 228, 229, 239, 240, 241, 242, 255, 259, 260, 261, 262, 264, 271, 273, 278, 279, 284, 308
fringe(s) 92, 211, 245
fruit 15, 107, 111, 112, 122, 123, 133, 134, 135
funeral 150, 158, 162, 165

G

garden 101, 109, 293, 294, 314
Garden of Eden 101, 293, 294, 314
gates 159, 175, 297
gefilte fish 29
gender 19, 79, 81, 274, 275, 286
generous, generosity 15, 31, 34, 36, 108, 147, 155, 239, 294
Genesis (also see *Bereishit*) 79, 155, 166
ghost 300, 304
giving 11, 22, 23, 24, 25, 38, 68, 77, 91, 131, 132, 150, 162, 191, 243, 260, 277, 296

God 15, 16, 34, 60, 69, 70, 71, 72, 73, 75, 76, 77, 79, 80, 81, 84, 88, 89, 90, 91, 93, 99, 101, 104, 106, 107, 108, 114, 115, 121, 122, 123, 129, 132, 136, 141, 142, 147, 173, 179, 209, 214, 217, 218, 220, 224, 246, 264, 266, 267, 275, 282, 284, 287, 288, 289, 290, 291, 299, 300, 301, 303, 307, 308, 309, 310, 311, 312
gold 32, 33, 81, 106, 107, 145, 146, 210, 211, 299, 308, 309
gossip 47, 299, 317
Grace After Meals 220, 297
grandfather 15, 21, 64, 133, 135, 146, 150, 151, 164, 186, 293, 295, 296
grandmother 15, 29, 30, 33, 38, 39, 120, 127, 137, 150, 157, 158, 164-168, 180, 203, 208, 296
gratitude 54, 60, 63, 65, 79, 93, 96, 126, 129, 142, 146, 186, 211, 259, 261, 267, 272, 273, 281, 310
graveyard 298, 299, 300, 303
grief 166
grudge 19, 51, 318
guard 48, 208, 209, 211, 212, 299
guest(s) 83, 165, 169, 211, 212, 227, 228, 231, 234, 237, 294, 296, 297, 299, 317
guitar 237

H

haggadah, haggadot 125, 273
hair, haircut, hairdresser 46, 49, 60, 69, 83, 98, 99, 127, 137, 185, 241, 249, 250, 251, 266, 281, 301
hakarat ha-tov, hakarat hatov 60
halachah (see also law) 156, 275
hand, hand of God 224, 289, 291
Hanukkah 83, 85, 87, 160, 164, 261, 262, 285
happy, happiness 25, 27, 33, 34, 35, 45, 60, 62, 87, 108, 111, 125, 128, 133, 144, 146, 163, 167, 170, 171, 175, 189, 201, 242, 259, 260, 261, 262, 271, 280, 282, 283, 318
Hashem 229
hate, hatred 90, 128, 182, 199, 203, 319
heal, healing 13, 50, 51, 52, 78, 113, 114, 122, 149, 173, 174, 207, 209, 210, 214, 215, 216, 247, 262, 273, 317
health 66, 148, 212, 225, 250, 262, 294

hearing 69, 143, 237
heart 19, 27, 33, 35, 48, 49, 50, 63, 70, 71, 72, 85, 93, 143, 159, 170, 182, 183, 203, 220, 225, 227, 229, 230, 231, 240, 241, 257, 259, 281, 294, 298, 301, 305, 309, 312, 319
heaven 95, 96, 177, 208, 227, 228, 295, 313
Hebrew 16, 29, 31, 57, 59, 73, 75, 79, 86, 89, 91, 109, 113, 125, 127, 144, 145, 148, 154, 161, 164, 165, 181, 192, 208, 211, 213, 252, 259, 271, 278, 279, 291, 307, 310, 319
heretic 303
Heschel, Abraham Joshua 52, 193
hiddur mitzvah 155, 285
hiding 32, 107, 117, 119, 121
Hillel 213, 240, 253
Holland 39, 117
Holocaust (see *Shoah*)
holy, holiness 12, 52, 54, 60, 87, 123, 141, 142, 158, 174, 272, 273, 293, 294, 295, 309, 317
homeless 14, 167, 168, 173, 175, 239
honest, honesty 23, 119, 135, 147
Honi 76, 77, 79, 81
honor 5, 11, 20, 25, 27, 28, 34, 59, 91, 123, 133, 172, 240, 244, 282, 284, 300, 301, 318, 319
horse 101, 183, 184, 185, 242, 287, 288
hospice 158
hospital 15, 22, 23, 38, 117, 138, 241, 260
hug(s) 89, 112, 144, 163, 165, 169, 212, 261
hunger, hungry 31, 33, 36, 40, 42, 43, 95, 106, 107, 111, 112, 127, 177, 179, 208, 211, 212, 217, 253, 299, 317

I

ill(ness) 68, 110, 114, 117, 164, 165, 210, 211, 214, 224, 240, 247, 264, 312, 313, 317
Ima 111, 112, 241, 259, 261, 262, 285
incantation 209
infant 313
inn 228, 293, 294
innkeeper 232
insect(s) 70, 105, 106, 121
interpret, interpretation 16, 59, 60, 76, 91, 123, 141, 193, 291, 312
isolate, isolation, isolated 23, 67, 68, 175

330 | New Mitzvah Stories for the Whole Family

Israel 14, 15, 16, 29, 57, 58, 59, 67, 69, 70, 71, 72, 86, 89, 91, 92, 93, 103, 104, 114, 120, 123, 148, 192, 195, 196, 197, 198, 213, 214, 217, 218, 220, 221, 223, 227, 235, 241, 242, 252, 260, 261, 262, 268, 271, 290

J

janitor 59
jesters 240, 241, 246
Jesus 235
Jethro (also see *Yitro*) 257
Job, book of 225
juggle, juggler(s) 177, 178
justice 66, 114, 198, 225, 284, 285, 286, 317

K

kadosh, kodesh, kedushah 53, 238
Kagan, Yisroel Meir (also see Chofetz Chayyim) 19
Kalonymus Kalman 237, 244
Kaplan, Mordecai 19
kavannah 19
kesefot 207, 215, 216
kibbutz, kibbutzim 249
Kiddush, Kiddush cup 299, 304
Kindertransport 38, 39, 128
king 14, 29, 95, 98, 179, 199, 271
kiss 144, 169, 191, 279
Kotel 271, 272, 273, 274, 275

L

labor (see work) 193
lake 48, 85, 99, 122, 227, 228, 229, 230, 231
law(s) (also see *halachah*) 47, 108, 156, 189, 199, 205, 235, 265, 275, 281, 310
leaving Egypt 132, 220
lesbian 284
letter(s) 55, 58, 63, 65, 67, 68, 75, 76, 113, 118, 119, 121, 143, 145, 146, 147, 148, 150, 151, 154, 208, 211, 222, 260, 279, 281, 282, 301
Levin, Aryeh 67
Levite(s) 142
Leviticus (also see *Vayikra*) 35, 51, 98, 174, 303
liar, lie, lying 32, 36, 37, 38, 47, 64, 99, 127, 181, 186, 188, 202, 211

light(s) 14, 21, 22, 23, 24, 25, 27, 31, 34, 53, 54, 84, 85, 93, 114, 147, 148, 170, 179, 183, 185, 186, 189, 190, 191, 192, 207, 208, 209, 220, 227, 230, 232, 234, 280, 298, 300, 308, 309, 310, 317
listen, listening 37, 39, 40, 53, 54, 56, 68, 69, 76, 90-96, 101, 106, 107, 111, 112, 115, 132, 137, 167, 174, 175, 200, 202, 211, 227, 229, 231, 237, 238, 247, 267, 271, 275, 280, 301, 308, 309, 311
lizard 105, 106
loan(s) 31, 222, 224, 225, 237, 238, 245, 318, 319
loneliness 285
lonely 21, 60, 189, 307
lost 37, 287
lo tikom 51
love 14, 17, 19, 21, 31, 36, 70, 81, 83, 89, 90, 92, 98, 111, 112, 122, 125, 128, 138, 139, 140, 143, 147, 148, 153, 167, 181, 189, 160, 207, 216, 217, 222, 227, 231, 238, 240
love your neighbor 98
luck 31, 38, 66, 96, 126, 133, 145, 154, 161, 200, 251, 259, 260, 261, 264, 272

M

maggid (also see storyteller) 20, 78, 172, 233, 237, 275, 299, 315
magic 30, 207, 209, 218, 220, 255
Maimonides 19, 43, 108, 215
market(place) 95, 134, 198, 240, 249
marriage 79, 283, 318
mashiach (also see *moshiach*) 230, 235
mayor 95, 96
mazel 148, 259, 260, 261, 262, 264
medical clowning 242
meditation, meditating 41, 113, 309
Megillah 253, 273
melech 73
memorial 288, 296
memories 14, 141, 150, 158, 222, 293
memory 14, 17, 27, 34, 40, 221, 275, 295
mercy 114
message, messenger 65, 79, 81, 84, 95, 96, 210, 237, 238, 241, 266, 275, 277, 281, 298
messiah (also see *mashiach* and *moshiach*) 72, 230, 235

metaphor 114, 123, 156, 220
midnight 77
Midrash 101, 104, 131, 246
mime 103, 168, 169, 170, 179
minyan 53, 54, 55, 56, 164, 228
Miriam 22, 23, 24, 214, 265, 266, 267, 314
mirror 47, 60, 81, 98
miser 35, 299
mitzvah hero(es) 14, 123
Mitzvah List 317-320
money 21, 23, 24, 31, 33, 34, 38, 42, 64, 65, 90, 147, 157, 167, 168, 171, 173, 174, 175, 196, 202, 221, 222, 239, 251, 259, 304, 318
monkey 106, 111, 259, 260, 261, 262, 264
Moses 16, 150, 155, 182, 214, 215, 257, 264, 266, 267, 307, 308, 309, 310, 311, 312
moshav, moshavim 249, 252
moshiach (also see *mashiach, messiah*) 235
mother, mom 15, 40, 45, 46, 47, 48, 49, 50, 61, 67, 77, 83, 84, 85, 92, 101, 108, 111, 112, 117, 118, 119, 125, 126, 127, 128, 129, 146, 147, 148, 159, 183, 184, 185, 186, 187, 188, 189, 190, 191, 192, 207, 208, 209, 211, 215, 218, 221, 231, 239, 241, 249, 250, 251, 253, 259, 271, 280, 285, 307, 317
mountain(s) 15, 85, 107, 196, 230, 299, 307, 308, 309, 310
mourn, mourning 34, 164, 165, 166, 240
museum 91
mystic(s) 80, 99, 301

N

Naamah 106, 107, 108
Nachmanides 181
Nachshon 265, 266, 267, 269
name 6, 22, 24, 31, 59, 63, 69, 70, 72, 76, 77, 93, 99, 110, 111, 114, 117, 123, 150, 154, 167, 168, 187, 201, 214, 216, 234, 242, 259, 261, 262, 294, 304, 319
nature 19, 72, 81, 99, 122, 205, 243, 318
Nazis 128
Netherlands 120
niddah 304
Noah 16, 89, 90, 105, 106, 107, 108
Numbers (also see *Bamidbar*) 112
nursing home(s) 242

O

olam ha-ba (also see World-to-Come)
old man (also see elder) 83, 85, 87, 101, 313
old woman (also see elder) 159, 170, 178, 179, 181, 207, 208, 209, 210, 212, 250, 251, 294, 295
orphan 224, 225, 319

P

paint, painting 145, 146, 161, 162, 163, 180, 213, 235, 294
paradise 239, 240, 297, 298, 299, 300, 303
Pardes 213, 303
parent(ing) 20, 80, 92, 115
Passover (also see *Pesach*) 125, 126, 128, 129, 131, 132, 141, 185, 198, 223, 263, 311
peace 20, 59, 91, 99, 119, 177, 178, 179, 181, 182, 201, 227, 235, 240, 246, 303, 318
Pesach (also see Passover) 29, 198
Pharaoh 218, 265, 266
phoenix 105, 108
phone 37, 38, 39, 40, 42, 115, 161, 167, 171, 195, 238
photo 115, 127, 129
picture 63, 64, 65, 90, 95, 127, 128, 129, 130, 135, 145, 153, 156, 166, 167, 261, 277, 279
pilgrimage 14, 268
pillow 51, 293
Pirkei Avot 5, 27, 221, 253, 264
place 72, 101, 102
pocketbook 157
police 38, 40, 63, 117
politics 197
pomegranate 107, 108
poor 31, 33, 43, 68, 70, 147, 159, 179, 225, 239, 253, 294, 308, 312, 319
Portland 199, 203, 290
pray, prayer 11, 15, 19, 35, 47, 58, 68, 75, 76, 93, 108, 114, 115, 122, 123, 141, 142, 156, 167, 171, 174, 191, 194, 207, 209, 211, 216, 220, 237, 238, 246, 257, 272, 273, 274, 286, 288, 289, 290, 291, 317
presence 12, 14, 83, 85, 89, 93, 132, 136, 181, 217, 234, 294, 301, 317
princess 210, 211, 212
prisoner(s) 61, 63, 64, 66, 67, 68, 91, 209, 266
Psalms, 92 35, 122, 181, 288, 289, 305

332 | New Mitzvah Stories for the Whole Family

Purim 68, 242, 244, 245, 271, 311

Q

queen 137, 210, 211, 212
question(s), questioning 23, 24, 25, 59, 61, 62, 67, 77, 79, 81, 88, 89, 101, 102, 196, 199, 231, 239, 247, 253, 271, 272, 275, 279, 285, 297, 304

R

Rachel 3, 16, 37, 38, 39, 40, 61, 66, 75, 78, 208, 249, 250, 251, 253
rainbow 89, 90, 107, 108, 144, 228, 249
Rambam (also see Maimonides) 19, 122, 215
Ramban (also see Nachmanides) 52
ransoming 215
Raphael, Geela Rayzel 3, 114, 207, 209, 213
Rebbe 68, 237, 244, 295, 297, 298, 299, 300, 301, 303
Rebbe, Lubavitcher 68
rebuke 52
red 46, 47, 111, 170, 177, 208, 209, 211, 212, 259, 260, 261, 266, 280, 281, 297, 304
redeem 216, 235
relationship(s) 36, 42, 59, 60, 67, 88, 89, 90, 91, 92, 98, 114, 115, 131, 148, 156, 166, 173, 235, 255, 256, 282, 312, 317
remember 38, 281
revenge 19, 51, 317
riding 41
river 13, 33, 99, 102, 122, 145, 267, 294
rock(s) (also see *tzur*) 63, 104, 105, 220, 288, 309, 310
rodef shalom 181
Rosh Hashanah 29, 137, 138, 139, 141, 167, 171, 237, 238
rumors 51
run 14, 21, 49, 69, 70, 101, 112, 132, 134, 135, 165, 168, 171, 178, 186, 188, 262, 266, 280, 296
runaway 133
running 32, 33, 49, 77, 185, 228, 231, 280, 283
Russian 169

S

Sabbath (also see *Shabbat*) 31, 33, 34, 43, 184, 193, 207, 212

sacrifice(s), sacrificial 142, 235, 239, 275
sad, sadness 39, 64, 112, 118, 128, 139, 143, 144, 146, 158, 161, 162, 163, 211, 214, 227, 230, 241, 243, 260, 262, 273, 293
safe, safety 32, 42, 46, 69, 89, 117, 121, 128, 173, 195, 201, 208, 224, 269
Samuel, book of 257, 284
Schachter-Shalomi, Zalman 42, 86, 172
school 15, 21, 22, 23, 25, 28, 29, 37, 38, 39, 40, 42, 43, 45, 46, 47, 59, 60, 61, 62, 64, 69, 71, 75, 76, 81, 88, 97, 104, 112, 117, 121, 123, 142, 155, 161, 162, 164, 165, 171, 182, 184, 188, 197, 198, 203, 225, 237, 239, 241, 242, 250, 260, 261, 269, 271, 275, 277, 278, 280, 286
seder 125, 148
serpent(s) 264
Shabbat, *Shabbos* (also see Sabbath) 15, 34, 35, 42, 47, 55, 67, 77, 84, 85, 88, 102, 113, 123, 141, 142, 143, 157, 160, 164, 165, 185, 190, 191, 193, 194, 195, 208, 209, 213, 220, 230, 234, 247, 251, 295, 304
shalom 14, 72, 83, 140, 145, 228, 229, 251, 262
shaman 50
shame, shaming 46
Shapira, Kalonymus Kalman 237, 244
share, sharing 22, 36, 59, 77, 127, 132, 146, 147, 150, 155, 158, 166, 179, 193, 220, 224, 230, 234, 245, 246, 247, 264, 296, 310
Shavuot, *Shavuos* 198
Shechinah, *Shekhinah* 72, 80, 93, 114, 132, 136, 179, 181, 208, 209, 211, 213, 214, 216, 234
Shehecheyanu 272
shem 69, 71, 84, 106, 301
Shema 84, 273
Shemot (also see Exodus) 104, 131, 193, 215, 224, 257, 269, 274, 284
Shimon bar Yochai 93
shmirat haguf 205
Shoah 38, 121, 195
shofar 273
shop, shopping 89, 90, 199, 205, 222, 249
shuk 29
sick(ness) 37, 61, 63, 106, 114, 161, 207, 209, 241, 242, 247, 259, 260, 262, 273, 277, 293, 296, 300, 317
siddur 273, 291, 295

sing, singing 40, 53, 54, 55, 56, 58, 59, 69, 71, 85, 125, 163, 209, 230, 237, 240, 265, 272, 273, 275, 297
sin, sinner 245, 264, 312
sister 15, 46, 133, 135, 184, 188, 238, 267
sleep 84, 85, 107, 119, 138, 177, 184, 185, 208, 210, 211, 217, 265, 291, 294
snake(s) 137, 215
song(s) 14, 71, 87, 132, 164, 209, 238, 240, 241, 265, 274
sorcery 216
soul(s) 25, 26, 70, 77, 83, 87, 122, 123, 131, 181, 207, 208, 240, 285, 288, 291, 296, 297, 299, 300, 313
soup 207, 293
soup kitchen 43, 132
spark 178, 181, 299
spell, casting 207, 208
spirit 42, 72, 76, 85, 87, 99, 122, 139, 142, 177, 194, 210, 215, 299
spirit(s) 72, 207, 241, 297, 303, 304
spiritual will 148, 151
sport(s) 190, 194
steal 136
stone 16, 169, 220, 298, 308, 310
stop to help 173, 317
storyteller (also see *maggid*) 20, 31, 35, 81, 217, 237, 252, 301, 313
stranger(s) 96, 121, 125, 129, 131, 144, 155, 156, 173, 212, 221, 223, 225, 231, 250, 284, 285
sukkah, Sukkot 104, 160, 198, 317, 318
sun 29, 33, 45, 49, 70, 83, 101, 108, 119, 134, 170, 183, 190, 191, 199, 217, 249, 250, 308
synagogue, also see shul, congregation 11, 15, 56, 58, 75, 77, 87, 90, 120, 132, 164, 165, 170, 171, 194, 207, 237, 238, 245, 272, 275, 278, 285

T

tablets 308, 309, 311, 312
Talmud 311
tashlich, tashlikh 139, 140, 141
tear, tears 34, 38, 46, 85, 91, 96, 107, 112, 143, 170, 185, 203, 215, 223, 229, 232, 262, 272, 273, 281, 295, 300
tefillin, tephillin 93

Temple 26, 57, 101, 127, 142, 161-163, 198, 208, 219, 235, 257, 271, 274, 275
tennis 277
tent 155, 175, 267, 307, 309, 310
terror, terrorist, terrorism 64, 203
teshuvah 167
thief, thieves 35, 37, 38, 136
tikkun olam 13, 17, 286
Torah 53, 54, 55, 56, 75, 77, 80, 168
treasure 143
truth 67, 95, 99, 114, 117, 121, 147, 178, 212, 281, 282
tzedakah 13, 250, 268
tzelem 178, 179
tzion, tzionut 68
tzur, see Rock 123, 220

U

Ukraine 159
ulpan, ulpanim 16
uncle 117
United Synagogue Youth, USY 14, 171, 268

V

Vayikra (also see Leviticus) 35, 51, 98, 174, 303
village 31, 70, 95, 96, 207, 294
visiting the sick 247
volunteer 14, 23, 132, 175, 198, 317, 321

W

Wall 30, 37, 40, 107, 162, 163, 168, 169, 183, 191, 271, 274
war 57, 65, 117, 120, 184, 190, 237
Warsaw Ghetto 237
water 29, 30, 33, 77, 98, 99, 111, 137, 139, 141, 144, 162, 169, 195, 196, 215, 218, 220, 228, 229, 249, 262, 266, 267, 269, 287, 288, 290, 294, 295
wedding 222, 223, 224, 251
welcome, welcoming 50, 131, 132, 212, 234, 256, 284
wicked 35, 36, 171
widow 222, 224, 225, 319
wilderness 269, 288, 310
wind 33, 49, 69, 71, 137, 145, 228, 231, 289, 298, 299, 300
wine 297, 301, 303, 304, 305

wing(s) 70, 93, 118, 122, 227, 228, 230, 231, 232, 274
wish, wishes, wishing 16, 98, 161, 166, 171, 185, 211, 219, 231, 255, 256, 257, 266, 272, 273, 293, 297, 298
witch(es), witchcraft 207, 208, 209, 215, 303
wizard 303
work(s) 13, 15, 22, 24, 29, 38, 39, 42, 54, 59, 60, 63, 64, 65, 71, 79, 84, 85, 89, 95, 101, 102, 115, 130, 132, 138, 145, 146, 148, 158, 165, 167, 172, 184, 187, 188, 193, 198, 200, 201, 217, 218, 222, 224, 235, 256, 264, 265, 279, 280, 281, 283, 286, 291, 294, 307, 310, 317, 318
World-to-Come (also see *olam ha-ba*) 297, 301

Y

Yiddish 29, 30, 136, 164, 221, 244
Yitro (also see Jethro) 75, 257
Yom Kippur 36, 285, 295
Yonatan 68

Z

Zayde (also see grandfather) 63, 64, 133, 134, 296
Zionism (also see *tzion, tzionut*) 197
Zohar 93, 122, 246

Index | 335

Printed in Great Britain
by Amazon